Happy

&

You

Know

It

Happy
&
You
Know
It

Laura Hankin

BERKLEY | NEW YORK

BERKLEY
An imprint of Penguin Random House LLC
penguinrandomhouse.com

Library of Congress Cataloging-in-Publication Data

Names: Hankin, Laura, author.
Title: Happy & you know it / Laura Hankin.
Other titles: Happy and you know it
Description: First Edition. | New York: Berkley, 2020.
Identifiers: LCCN 2019039595 (print) | LCCN 2019039596 (ebook) |
ISBN 9781984806239 (hardcover) | ISBN 9781984806253 (ebook)
Subjects: LCSH: Female friendship—Fiction.
Classification: LCC PS3608.A71483 H37 2020 (print) |
LCC PS3608.A71483 (ebook) | DDC 813/.6—dc23
LC record available at https://lccn.loc.gov/2019039595
LC ebook record available at https://lccn.loc.gov/2019039596

First Edition: May 2020

Printed in the United States of America
1   3   5   7   9   10   8   6   4   2

Cover art by James Briscoe

To my mother,

who I imagine was kind

to playgroup musicians

Happy

&

You

Know

It

Prologue

New Yorkers are good at turning a blind eye. They ignore the subway ranters, the men who walk with pythons twined around their shoulders, anyone who suggests meeting for dinner in Times Square.

But on one sweltering August afternoon, when the whole city was trapped in a bubble of heat, a woman came running down Madison Avenue in a full-length fur coat, demanding to be noticed. As she sprinted by, encased in a suffocating cocoon of mink, the sweaty customers at the sidewalk café on East Ninety-Fourth Street couldn't help but stare.

Maybe it was, in part, because of her smell—the staleness of the inky black pelt she wore, plus something else, something sickly sweet and stomach turning. Vomit. Dried bits of it crusted the woman's mouth. Little chunks clung to her hair. She didn't look like someone who should have smelled that way. She looked rich.

Maybe it was the sleek stroller she pushed in front of her. It glided along the sidewalk, the baby equivalent of a Porsche, but without a baby inside.

Or maybe it was the pack of women chasing her.

Afterward, when the media was just starting to whip itself into a frenzy about the so-called Poison Playgroup of Park Avenue, one witness would tell reporters that he had known the women were dangerous all along. He had sensed it from the moment he saw them—even before they tipped back their heads and started to scream.

Chapter 1

Claire Martin didn't want to throw herself in front of a bus, exactly. But if a bus happened to mow her down, knocking her instantly out of existence, that wouldn't have been the worst thing in the world.

If she were floating in eternal nothingness, at least she wouldn't have to hear Vagabond's music in every fucking bar in New York City. It happened for the fourth time not long after New Year's Day, as she sat on a stool in some Upper West Side dive, performing her fun new ritual of Drinking to Forget. She'd managed to swallow her way within sight of that sweet, sweet tipping point—the one where all her sharp-edged self-loathing melted into something squishy and Jell-O-like—and just caught the eye of a curly-haired guy nearby when "Idaho Eyes" came over the speakers, as jarring and rage-inducing as the clock radio blaring "I've Got You Babe" in *Groundhog Day.*

She turned away from her new prospect and leaned over the bar. "Hey," she said to the bartender, who held up a finger in her direction and continued his conversation with a middle-aged man a few stools down. Automatically, she drummed her fingers along with that catchy opening beat before she caught herself and closed her hand into a fist. *"Hey!"*

"What?" the bartender asked, glaring.

She squinted at him, trying to make him come fully into focus. He was a big, scowling bear of a man and alarmingly fuzzy around the edges. "Can we skip this song?"

"No," he said.

Claire considered leaving, but the guy with curly hair intrigued her, and she liked Fucking to Forget almost as much as Drinking to Forget. She swallowed, then flashed the bartender what she hoped was a winning smile. "Please? I'd really appreciate it."

Her smile, bright and effective enough to be a form of currency, had worked wonders for her in the past. In the early days of touring with Vagabond, rattling around in a van for which they could barely afford the gas, the guys had joked about it and had sent her into convenience stores to see if she could get them all free snacks for the road. But this bartender remained unmoved. He folded his hairy arms across his chest. "My bar, my playlist."

Claire gritted her teeth as the verse turned into the first chorus. A nearby couple began to dance, shout-singing along, the man looking into the woman's face with pure love. At times like these, Claire thought that maybe God *did* exist, not as some benevolent being or terrifying father, but as the omniscient equivalent of a prank show host. An Ashton Kutcher kind of God. She took another large gulp of her whiskey. "Don't be a dick, man," she said as the bartender turned away. "The customer's always right, right?"

"I'm a customer, and I love this song," said the middle-aged man down at the end of the bar.

"Well, you shouldn't," she said as a wave of nausea rose in her stomach. "They're terrible." She took a couple of shallow, panicky breaths as, over the speakers, Marcus's and Marlena's voices mingled in harmony. Dammit, they sounded good together.

The middle-aged man, apparently some kind of regular at this dive, made a wounded face, his shoulders slumping. The bartender noticed and pulled out his phone, holding it up right in front of Claire to show her the song playing on his Spotify app. His finger hovered over the skip button. Then he deliberately turned the volume up. The sound grew loud enough to suffocate her, to smother her. She lunged forward to grab the phone away from him.

As the bartender ejected her, none too gently, into the stinging January night, she realized that perhaps it was safer to drink alone in her apartment instead.

A month later, Claire's cousin Thea called.

"How's the wallowing going?" Thea asked in her brisk way.

"I don't know if it's fair to call it 'wallowing,'" Claire said. "That sounds so masturbatory. I think your band getting superfamous right after they kick you out is a great reason to become a shut-in."

"Mm-hmm," Thea said.

Over the past couple of years, Claire had spent so much time on the road that all she'd wanted from her home was a place without roommates where she could immediately take off her pants and collapse into bed. What did it matter that her "kitchen" only had room for a mini fridge and a hot plate? She wasn't exactly whipping up five-course meals for herself. Who cared that the bars on her window blocked out most of the natural light or that she'd stuck up all her posters with tape instead of framing them? But now, from underneath her sheets, Claire cast a look around her tiny studio, at the stacks of boxes from Pizza Paradise starting to grow mold, at the piles of discarded beer cans, at the torn-up remains of a note her parents had sent her, reading: *You can always come home. Jesus forgives, and so do we.*

"The wallowing is getting pretty gross," she said.

"Well, then, get up. I got you a job." Even as a child in their tiny Ohio town, Thea had been the one who got shit done. She'd organized all the bored neighborhood kids into teams for kickball. She'd harangued all the grown-ups until they signed up to bring something for the church bake sale. And then, when her parents had discovered she was gay and threatened to kick her out of the house unless she agreed to go to a conversion program, Thea had wasted no time in getting a full scholarship to Harvard and leaving on her own terms.

"A job? What is it?" Claire asked.

"Singing 'Old MacDonald' to the future CEOs of America. Some woman named Whitney Morgan e-mailed the Harvard list, looking for a playgroup musician, so I sang your praises."

Claire bit her lip. "That's really nice of you, Thea, but that's the kind of stuff I was doing five years ago. I don't know if I want—"

"How much money do you have left in your bank account?" Thea asked.

"Um," Claire said. She swung herself out of bed too quickly and, a little dizzy, reached for her computer to pull up her account balance. When she saw what her self-destructive spiral had done to her savings, her mouth went dry. Her rent was already overdue because she'd run out of stamps and hadn't been able to muster the energy to go out and buy more. And once she sent in that check, her bank account would be down to double digits. She cleared her throat. "What's the address?"

"I'll text you the details," Thea said.

"Thanks," Claire mumbled.

"I'm looking out for you, cuz," Thea said, a note of tenderness creeping into her voice. "Can't have you going back to Sacred Life Christian Fellowship. We're the ones that got out."

"Yeah, we are."

"And, Claire? Before you go, please take a shower," Thea said. "I can smell you over the phone."

It was a doorman building, of course, with a limestone facade on the Upper East Side, bordering Central Park. The doorman, a shrunken man in a forest green uniform, peered at Claire as she caught her breath and wiped the sweat off her forehead. She'd forgotten, over the month she'd spent floating around her apartment like a tipsy ghost, just how unpredictable the New York subway system could be, and had ended up having to run part of the way there, the shifting weight of the guitar on her back giving her the gait of an ungainly penguin.

"Penthouse B," she said, and he picked up the phone on his desk to call up. As he announced her to the person on the other end of the line, she checked the time again. Two minutes late. That was early for her, but Rich People Time worked differently from Charmingly Flighty Creative People Time.

He directed her toward an incredibly well-appointed elevator, all mirrored panels and marble accents. As she zoomed to the twentieth floor, she steeled herself. She knew how this would go. When she'd first moved to New York, she'd gotten a part-time job teaching baby music classes for one of those bouncy children's entertainment companies, thinking it could be a fun way to make some cash while she pursued what she *really* wanted to do. Instead, she'd encountered a bunch of bored, rich moms in yoga clothes and diamonds, talking over her and her fellow teachers, alternately ignoring their babies and documenting their every move with their phones. Somehow these women were paying *just* enough attention to complain about various parts of the class to the front desk in excruciating detail afterward. Once, Claire had called a child by the wrong name, and the mother had looked at her like she'd just revealed a "Bin Laden 4Ever" tramp stamp. It was all a perfect recipe for feeling small. For feeling . . . not real.

The long hallway had only two doors, one marked "A" and one marked "B." She pasted on a shit-eating grin and knocked on the latter. Ten seconds later, the door flew open, revealing one of the most beautiful women Claire had ever seen. Claire's first thought was that the woman framed in the doorway would have been right at home in an eighteenth-century painting of European aristocracy. She was the image of a sheltered, prerevolution French princess, complete with alabaster skin, pink cheeks, and swan neck. She wore a cream-colored blouse with a ruffled collar. (Claire usually called tops "shirts," but there was no way around it—this was a *blouse*.) But the most perfect thing about this nearly perfect woman was her hair. It was silken and unnaturally shiny, as if she'd stolen it straight from the mane of a well-groomed show horse.

"Claire?" the woman asked.

"Yup. Hi," Claire said, waving. "I'm sorry I'm a couple minutes late. The trains . . ."

The corners of the woman's plump lips turned down. "We don't put up with tardiness here. You should just go home," she said.

Shit. Claire's breath caught in her throat as the realization knocked into her—she *was* going to have to go home, and not just to her apartment. She'd have to move back to Ohio. A twenty-eight-year-old failure living in her high school bedroom, if her parents hadn't turned it into a home office or something. The people from her church would shake their heads in sympathy, but inside they'd feel that she'd gotten exactly what she deserved for her sins.

Then the woman broke into a laugh—a sunny, bell-like peal that transformed the very air around them. "I'm kidding!" she said, and then registered Claire's expression. "Oh, no, your face! That was mean. I'm so sorry."

"Wait. What?" Claire asked, confused. "I thought—"

"I didn't mean to— I forgot you probably actually have to deal with people like that all the time. It is *totally* fine. We didn't even realize." To Claire's great surprise, she stepped forward and hugged her, her breasts bumping against Claire's collarbone. She smelled faintly of lavender. Claire relaxed, the tiniest bit, into this unexpected intimacy, her first hug in over a month. "We're so excited to meet you. I'm Whitney. Come in, come in!"

In the foyer, Claire kicked off her boots and placed them next to a neat line of heels. Whitney kept up a steady stream of questions— How was her commute? Was she thirsty? Was this temperature okay for her?—as she took Claire's hand in hers and led her to where the apartment opened up into a living room. Everything was white. Well, white with silver and chrome accents, glacierlike, clean. Along one wall, floor-to-ceiling windows revealed the trees in Central Park, skeletal and damp from melting snow. The ceiling was higher than normal, as if the apartment extended up a story and a half, not content to occupy just one floor of a building like everyone else's did.

A couple of women sat on a white leather couch, wineglasses in their hands, while two others stood by a low table, trying to coax a couple of babies to stand up and grab the fruit on it. In the center of the room, a final woman sat on a checkered mat as more babies crawled and lolled around her like ants at a picnic. There they were: Claire's big audience.

"Have you tried putting his favorite toy out of reach?" one of the women by the table was saying to the other. "That might motivate him."

"No, I've just been dangling a big bag of heroin above his head. Can't understand why it doesn't work," said the other, rolling her eyes. "Yes, of course I've tried the toy. He just wails until I hand it back to him."

"Well, that's the problem. You can't hand it back—"

"Claire's here!" Whitney said, breaking the other women out of their conversations. They all turned to Claire, looking her over and chorusing hellos. The force of their collective smiles nearly knocked Claire backward. She'd forgotten what it felt like to have a whole roomful of people *excited* to see her, anticipating that they all were going to have a delightful time together. She grew flushed with pleasure even as her brain fired off a running commentary about how demeaning this whole situation was.

God, these women were glamorous. Claire had always thought that for the first couple of years after having a baby, you looked like a swamp monster, with spit-up smeared in unlikely places and under-eye circles so deep spelunkers could get lost in them. And yet here these women were, on a random Tuesday afternoon, ready to star in a yogurt commercial. They were so *thin* too, no signs of baby bellies remaining, even though none of these kids could have been much older than a year, if that. It was like the babies had lived within them for a while—raucous, all-consuming tenants—and then once they'd moved out, the bodies had been fully renovated (fresh-painted walls, resanded floors, new appliances) to hide any sign of wear and tear. Claire was the one who had almost been a rock star, and yet, comparing herself to these women, she felt unkempt and mundane.

Whitney scooped up a little pink-clad baby from the floor.

"This one's mine," she said, jiggling her in front of Claire. "Meet Hope." Whitney's baby wore golden slippers and what

Claire hoped was a fake-fur shrug over her dress. God, even these babies were glamorous. How many hours of her life had Whitney spent jamming Hope's pudgy body into beautiful clothing that she'd soon outgrow?

"Hey, Hope," Claire said as Hope stared at the ceiling and popped her fist into her mouth. Whitney kissed the top of Hope's head before putting her back down.

To Claire, babies were like seeds. Interesting for what they might grow into but, for the moment, just dry, dull kernels. If she had to stare at a seed all day, she'd go insane. Claire would be a mother now too, for sure, if she had stayed in her hometown, where Sex Ed had consisted only of the warning that girls would be as useless as chewed gum if they "gave their precious gift" to anyone before marriage. Almost all the girls she'd gone to high school with had children. They posted pictures of their mini-mes heading off to preschool, and Claire felt separated from them by so much more than mere distance. She was pretty sure she didn't want children at all. The idea of a tiny person's life depending on her was enough to make her queasy. She already knew herself to be a killing machine. To date, through a lethal combination of neglect and fear, she'd murdered her childhood goldfish (RIP, Princess Leia), six houseplants, various romantic relationships, and her career.

The two standing mothers turned toward Claire. "I'm Gwen," said the one who was full of baby-taming advice. She was blond with eyes like freshly washed blueberries. She pointed to the smaller of the two babies by the table. "And that's Reagan!"

"Oh, cool, like from Shakespeare?" Claire asked.

"Pardon?" Gwen tilted her head to one side, dimples puckering her cheeks. Her voice was ever-so-slightly nasal but not in an unpleasant way.

"You know," Claire said, "how Regan's the name of one of the sisters in *King Lear*?"

"The evil one," said the mom who liked a good heroin joke. She had a faint British accent, and her skin was dark ebony against her lavender blouse. Another blouse! All the women were wearing blouses, and all those blouses had probably cost more than Claire's rent. Maybe she could just give her landlord, a perpetually frowning old Ukrainian man, one of Whitney's extra blouses this month and he'd leave her be.

Gwen's eyes widened, expanding like Violet Beauregarde in the chocolate factory. "Oh! No," she said. "Not after Shakespeare, after Ronald."

Claire tried to smile as if she thought Reagan was a great name for a baby and not a cruel joke (God, how she hoped Reagan grew up to be an Occupy Wall Street–esque progressive), but the snarky mother wasn't buying it.

She gave Claire a knowing look as she extended her hand and said, "Hi, I'm Amara." A cry rose from the bigger baby, and Amara let out a sigh. "That wailing lump would be Charlie." She turned to go get him, but then looked back at Claire, a hint of mischief coming into her eyes. "And I know what you're wondering: Yes, as in Manson."

"Obviously," Claire said, her strained smile breaking wideopen into a real one. Oh, she liked Amara.

"Those two on the couch are Meredith and Ellie," Whitney

said as the women in question waved. "They're busy arranging their babies' marriage to each other."

"My last name is Masters, and Meredith's is Funk," Ellie announced to Claire. She was compact, pixielike, pale.

"So if they hyphenate," Meredith said, "they can be the Funk-Masters!" She smiled a goofy, unrestrained grin, as if she were about to bite into something. She reminded Claire of a giraffe, with long limbs slightly akimbo.

"Hah. Cute," Claire said. Ellie and Meredith smiled at each other, and then immediately recommenced their chatting.

Whitney laughed and rolled her eyes at Claire. "It's a whole thing," she said, then indicated the woman on the play mat. "And last but not least, that's Vicki."

Vicki merely nodded, before lifting a baby up to her chest, uncovering a swollen boob, and starting to breastfeed, her eyes drifting to the ceiling. If any of these mothers had hired a doula and done a home birth in a bathtub, Vicki was the one.

"So that's our playgroup!" Whitney said. "We're excited to see if we're a good fit with you."

"Thank you so much for joining us on such short notice," Gwen said. "We had a bit of an emergency with our previous musician."

"That makes it sound like he died or we ate him alive," Amara said. Her baby was still crying. "Don't terrify the girl. Or, at least, not until after she entertains our babies." She sighed again, picked up a piece of strawberry from a low table, and put it in her baby's mouth.

"Oh, man," Claire said. "Was everything okay?"

"Yes," Whitney said, and the women all shifted, meeting eyes, holding some juicy collective secret. "It was just . . . So Ellie's sister had her bachelorette party, and—what do you know?—our musician moonlighted as a stripper. We're not prudes or anything—you should live your life how you want—but it turned out that once Ellie had told us all about him thrusting in a thong and a firefighter helmet, it was a little awkward sitting through 'Wheels on the Bus.'"

"He did have a great butt, though," Ellie said. Meredith laughed and swatted her on the arm.

"Okay!" Whitney said. "Now that we've totally overwhelmed you, we're going to sit quietly in a circle and listen to you sing. Do you need anything? What can I get you? Food? Water? Wine?" She winked at Claire and pulled a funny face. "We're not like *other* playgroups—we're a *cool* playgroup."

"Oh, no, thanks," Claire said. "I'm okay to get started."

As the mothers gathered their babies onto their laps and looked at her expectantly, she slung her guitar off her back and pulled it out of its case. She'd bought the cheapest one they had at a used-guitar store in the East Village about a year ago, when she and the guys had been home on a break from touring around. She had been Vagabond's secondary vocalist/occasional tambourine shaker/token female eye candy, but she'd started itching for more, so during the breaks in rehearsals or in between shows, when Chuck the bass player and Diego the drummer had gone outside to smoke, she'd asked Marcus, the lead singer/songwriter/guitar player/benevolent dictator, to teach her how to play. He had shown her the basic chords and progressions from songs by the musicians he had grown up loving: Bowie, the Stones, the later and weirder Beatles. Every one she mastered felt like a revelation, a new puzzle piece in the grand jigsaw that was "good" music. (All the guys in Vagabond had picked their instruments right in elementary school while she'd been playing the flute and—she cringed to remember it—the *handbell*. Then in high school, they'd all formed cool garage bands while she'd been the star musician of her megachurch.) She'd imagined eventually playing this guitar onstage, jamming out rapturously with the guys as their fans swayed and screamed.

She looked at the babies around her. Not exactly the audience she'd pictured. Her fingers felt stiff on the guitar strings, so she clenched them and unclenched them, then made a C chord and strummed. *"If you're happy and you know it, clap your hands,"* she sang, and the women smiled and *ooh*ed in recognition, then grasped their babies' little fists and swung them together, singing along.

Wow, these women were enthusiastic. And they certainly loved their kids. As far as Claire could tell, they had all stopped working to stay home with them. They were willing to pay exorbitant amounts of money for some live music to strengthen their children's developing neural pathways (or whatever science said music did for young brains), happy to participate in a sort of ritualized infantalization in the hopes that they were giving their children a good time. Claire widened her eyes and sang, *"If you're happy and you know it, tickle your tummies!"* and all the women dutifully tickled their babies, laughing.

Okay, maybe this wasn't so bad. A bunch of rich women day drinking and gossiping—it was like she'd gotten her own private spin-off of *Real Housewives* to watch, minus the rage and bloodthirst. But more than that, oh, it felt good to *sing* again. Since Vagabond had kicked her out, Claire hadn't even wanted to sing in the shower. Only now was she realizing how much she had missed it, how it was like she had been walking around with only one shoe on and wondering why she felt so off. Claire let herself forget about the banality of the lyrics, allowing the mere act of making music to carry her away. It was a particular skill she'd honed as a teenager at the megachurch that had dominated her town. The first couple of years after she was invited to sing at Sunday services with her worship group, ecstatically performing songs with titles like "His Grace" that she'd written with her friend Lynae, Claire had felt holy onstage. The congregation would cheer and sing along with so much energy and adoration that it drowned out everything else, including the doubts she had at other times. So what if she couldn't wrap her head around a big man in the sky? That had to be a failure of imagination on her part. She liked believing that Pastor Brian knew what was true—especially since he was the one who kept telling her that she had what it took to make it in Nashville.

But then Thea had come out of the closet, and everyone had been so awful to her, and Claire had begun to wonder how a religion that was ostensibly about love and forgiveness could advocate icing out the best person she knew.

After she'd confessed her doubts to Lynae when they were walking home from practice, Lynae, that bitch, had stood up in prayer circle the next night and said, her cow face pious in the basement light, "Let us pray for Claire, who harbors doubts in her heart. Let us pray that she will once again see the light of Christ."

So Pastor Brian had asked Claire to meet with him at the coffee shop off the church lobby, and they'd talked about her doubts. He'd offered explanations and platitudes, and none of it had made any sense to her. And then he'd said, "Claire, if you don't believe, it doesn't seem right for you to be singing in the worship group."

She couldn't lose her music, so she'd spent the rest of high school pretending to be devout, and furtively messaging with Thea on AIM at night, and waiting for the day she too could get out of there. She lived for the moments every Sunday when she could get up onstage and sing and feel like at least *part* of what she was doing was authentic. Sometimes, she'd picture this guy from her high school when she was supposed to be singing about Jesus. She'd write song lyrics to him, telling everyone else that the song was about Him. (If God did, in fact, exist, she was going to hell for sure for pretending that lyrics like *You gave your body / you gave your heart / for me, for me, for me / And I've been touched by you* were about Jesus, and not lustful fantasies about the asshole to whom she'd eventually lost her virginity in a janitor's closet at the mall.)

Nope. She wasn't going back there. She had to keep this playgroup job until she could get some kind of clarity on next steps, even if she felt pathetic doing it. Nearing the end of the playgroup's allotted music time, she gave her all to "The Itsy Bitsy Spider," as if the spider's struggles to climb a waterspout were an Odyssean quest. Then she glanced at Amara, who had finally managed to make her child settle down, at least for a few minutes. Unlike the other mothers, who were twisting their fingers in a climbing-spider motion, Amara's hand was clenched in her lap.

Her face was unfocused and suddenly drawn. Under the force of Claire's gaze, Amara snapped back to attention. But in the second before Amara recovered herself, something unguarded in her eyes flashed out a clear message: Amara couldn't believe she'd ended up here either.

"*And the itsy bitsy spider went up the spout again,*" Claire sang, letting the final chord ring out. "Okay, and looks like that's our time!"

The sweet, kept women all burst into applause.

"Claire," Whitney said, "you have such a lovely voice! Thank you. That was so much fun."

"Do you take requests?" Ellie asked. "Can you do 'Idaho Eyes'?"

"Yes, Ellie!" said Meredith. "I *love* that song."

"Right?" Ellie said.

"Um," Claire said, making sure to keep her face neutral, even as that familiar pit opened up in her stomach. "I don't think I know that one."

"Really?" Ellie said.

"I thought *we* were supposed to be the lame old ladies!" Meredith said as Ellie giggled.

Whitney got up and started refilling everyone's wineglasses. Vicki lay down on the rug, holding her baby above her and humming softly to him, as if the two of them existed in a bubble. Gwen lifted up little Reagan-as-in-Ronald, smelling her diaper and then making a relieved face at the apparent lack of stink in it.

"You have to look it up!" Ellie said. "What's the band, Meredith?"

"Vagabond!"

"Yeah, Vagabond. They're really fun, but also with some substance to them, you know?"

"All right, let's not overdo it. They're fine," said Amara. She got to her feet and looked at Claire. "You sing beautifully."

"Thanks," Claire said, blood rushing to her face.

"Someone watch Charlie for a moment while I go to the bathroom?" Amara asked.

"I'll do it," Gwen said, and Amara disappeared down a hallway.

"They're better than fine," Meredith said to Ellie, loyally.

"Amara is a bit of a music snob," said Whitney, emptying the remainder of the wine bottle into her glass, "because she used to work for one of those late-night entertainment shows with a lot of musicians."

Claire perked up, suddenly cold-blooded, sensing opportunity. As far as demeaning money jobs went, this one was seeming better and better by the minute.

"Well, I had a lot of fun with you all," she said. "Thanks for having me! I'd love to come back. Before I go, could I use your bathroom?"

Whitney pointed her down the hallway, instructing her to use the second door on the right. The hall was lined with glossy family photos of Whitney, Hope, and Whitney's husband, who, to Claire's total lack of surprise, resembled a Ken doll come to life. God, even Whitney's hallway was gorgeous—clean and white, woven rugs placed at appropriate intervals on the hardwood floor. Not a single square inch had been neglected. A flawless apartment for a flawless family.

She walked toward the second door on the right, silently running through possible conversation starters with Amara in her head, imagining a witty exchange in the hall leading to a fast-blossoming mentorship, leading to a few choice introductions to the tastemakers of late night, leading to a thriving music career, leading to all the members of Vagabond (washed-up, Marcus's lustrous hair starting to thin) watching her on TV and ruing the day they'd kicked her out.

But the second door on the right was open, and no one was inside. Claire looked into the bathroom (gleaming, marble) in confusion for a moment. Then she heard a low, muffled sound coming from the slightly ajar door to her left.

(*Curiosity killed the cat,* her mother used to say when a young Claire asked questions about the Sunday School teachings that didn't make sense to her. Her father had burned her dog-eared copy of *Harriet the Spy* in their fireplace one night, saying the heroine wasn't a good role model.)

Claire turned toward the door on the left and peered in. It was a small light gray room that had maybe been a pantry or a storage closet in another life; it was now outfitted with a desk, some shelves holding wicker baskets with looping cursive labels on them, and more succulents in one place than Claire had ever seen outside of a plant store. Whitney didn't seem to have a job, but apparently she was so rich that she could have a home office anyway, probably for keeping track of her social calendar or for crafting.

And now Amara stood at Whitney's desk, her arm stretched into a drawer and biting her lower lip so hard it had turned milk white, breathing quickly through her nose and rooting through the drawer's contents in a sort of frenzy. All her cool, wry self-possession was gone, replaced by guilty desperation.

21

Well, Claire thought, overcome by an all-out-of-proportion un-ease: She'd found the Winona Ryder of the group. She stepped back silently, ready to get the hell out of there and pretend she'd never witnessed . . . whatever that unsettling thing was, and promptly hit the door handle with her elbow like a fucking moron. At the unex-pected noise, Amara whipped her head up and froze, her eyes lock-ing onto Claire's. They stared at each other for a moment, neither of them moving. Then Amara's nostrils flared.

"What the hell are you doing here?" she asked, her voice like an arrow.

"I'm so sorry," Claire said. She slammed the door shut and ran back into the living room, where Whitney stood in the center of the circle of mothers, all nodding their heads.

"Back so soon!" Whitney said.

"Yeah, I just wanted to wash my hands," Claire said.

"Oh, and she's hygienic," Gwen said. "That's important!"

Whitney smiled at Claire. "We talked it over, and we would love for you to be our new playgroup musician. Tuesdays and Thursdays, sing to our babies, bring us tidings of the outside world. What do you say?"

"Yeah, great. For sure," Claire said as Amara reappeared in the doorway of the living room, frowning.

Whitney gave Claire a hug. "Wonderful!" she said.

"Next time, you should bring egg shakers and bubbles," Gwen said. "The babies love those."

Claire went to put her guitar back in its case while the rest of the women resumed an intense conversation about pacifiers and when babies needed to stop using them. As Claire zipped up her case, Amara paused next to her. "Whitney was out of soap in the bathroom," she said in a low voice. "I was looking for more."

"Okay," Claire replied. Amara gave her a look of pure venom.

In the foyer, as Claire put her shoes back on, Whitney pulled a hundred-dollar bill out of her wallet, plus a fifty. "For today," she said.

Claire hadn't ever held a hundred-dollar bill before. Ben Franklin, that rascal, stared up at her. The idea of carrying it around made her nervous, like she should stuff it into her bra or something to keep it extra-safe.

Whitney pursed her lips and then rifled through her wallet again, pushing aside more hundreds before pulling out another twenty. "And here," she said. "A little tip, for your first time. Go get yourself some really good ice cream, or something like that, on me."

It was very kind, Claire thought, and also completely out of touch, like when billionaire presidential candidates are stumped when asked to give the price of milk. Claire bit her lip to keep herself from laughing. "That's really nice of you. Thanks," she said.

"Oh, please. My pleasure," Whitney said, smiling that warm, effervescent smile of hers, the smile of a movie star or of a Pastor Brian. "Can't wait to see you Thursday!"

Chapter 2

Amara spent the last hour of playgroup feeling pure, full-throated rage. Rage at Charlie, who was crying again like he was getting paid by the wail. Rage at freaking Baby Reagan, who, at a good three months younger than Charlie, was the only other baby who had yet to pull up to standing, but whose wide little eyes seemed to be telling Amara, *Any day now, bitch, I'm making moves.* (Amara used to fantasize about winning an Emmy. Now she fantasized about Charlie beating Reagan to the punch.) Rage at Claire the Playgroup Musician, who had seemed so interesting at first and whom Amara now wanted nowhere near them, ever again.

And rage at herself, for what she'd been doing in Whitney's desk. When had she become such a shitty, unrecognizable person?

Amara pulled Charlie onto her lap and tried to bounce him

into silence, as all the women assembled on the couch and chairs for their next activity. Oh, she was rage-filled about that too—playgroup was supposed to be a time for a bunch of shell-shocked mothers to come together and complain about how they were too tired to screw their husbands. But ever since Whitney's Mom Instagram had started gaining traction, Whitney had begun acting like an Activities Director on a Disney cruise. Some theater had offered Whitney free tickets to a puppet show? Of course they'd bundled their babies up and trekked down to midtown. Some fitness instructor wanted them to try a stroller exercise class in Central Park? They were ready to sweat their little butts off! A discounted trial month of all-natural wellness vitamins specially curated for new mothers? Bring them on!

And now they had to sit and listen to a representative from the supplement company do the hard sell. "So," Dr. Clark said, folding one leg over the other and leaning forward in Whitney's armchair. "How did you all like your trial month of True-Mommy?" Dr. Clark was MIT educated and polished—the kind of woman who looked like she ate scientific journals for breakfast and then worked out for two hours afterward to burn off all the calories. She was a mother too, she told them, so she knew first-hand the way that pregnancy could ravage your body, depleting your essential vitamins and minerals so that it felt like you'd never fully get back on your feet. That was why she'd been so enthusiastic about joining the TrueMommy team. The supplements had been a godsend when she was recovering from her own second pregnancy, allowing her to reclaim her power as a woman, as a mother.

Placebo effect, Amara thought. Also, what kind of a stupid, guilt-inducing name was "TrueMommy"? She was already a true fuck-ing mommy all right, according to the men at her former office, who had stared at her like she was from a whole new species when she returned from maternity leave; to her single female friends, who wrote gushing comments on pictures of Charlie online but never asked her to hang out in person anymore; and to the home-less guy on her corner, who hooted, "Hot mama!" whenever she walked by.

And in general, the whole wellness craze was a load of crap. According to the wellness ideology (as far as Amara could tell), people—but mostly women—had the potential to be so much healthier and happier (and thinner) if only they shunned processed sugars and most of Western medicine and got back to all-natural basics, which, not coincidentally, cost a lot of money. If you mas-tered wellness, you could be efficient and centered and smoking hot, for *you!* All you had to do was drink fancy juice, take a lot of yoga classes, and put a five-hundred-dollar jade egg up your va-gina, and then you could start having the orgasms your body was *meant* to have! You'd never disappoint your partner by turning down sex ever again, because you'd be so empowered and ener-getic that you'd want it all the time!

Perhaps there was a crumb of truth to the trend, but Lord, did people go overboard, and these TrueMommy pills were the per-fect example. The trial month came in a beautiful suede box that looked like it belonged on a shelf at Barneys. Inside, the vitamins were separated into four packets, one for each week, all labeled with their own particular focus and cutesy name, like "Week Two:

Good Day Sunshine" (extra Saint-John's-wort to boost a new mother's mood!) and "Week Four: Energizer Honey" (loaded with B_{12}, for mamas who were ready to tackle their tough schedules with renewed vigor). She'd started taking the vitamins at first only because of the heavy discount and because it seemed like a way to bond with the other women. Back at the beginning of the trial month, her husband, Daniel, had noticed Amara popping the amber vitamins as they got ready in the morning, and they'd had a good laugh over the whole industry.

"Just please promise me," Daniel said, rolling his eyes and grinning at her, "that you'll never end up throwing away tons of money on vitamins you're going to pee out anyway."

"Darling. Do I look like Gwyneth Paltrow?" Amara had asked, and he had squinted at her in mock-seriousness and said, "Hmm, not quite."

But now, the other mothers were smiling at Dr. Clark. "My hair is finally looking full again," Ellie said, "so I'm a *big* fan."

"I've had less of an urge to cram Oreos into my mouth every night," Whitney said, laughing. "Although maybe that's not the vitamins' doing."

Gwen pulled out a Moleskine journal. "I had a few questions," she said, flipping to a long list written in her tidy handwriting. "I showed my doctor the ingredients list, of course, but I wanted to double-check some things with you, because obviously you can never be too careful about what you're putting into your body when you've got children to think about."

Oh, Lord. Gwen might not have known much about Shakespeare, but she was the only one of them to have an older child, so

when it came to the practicalities of motherhood, she fancied herself a regular Einstein, quick to "helpfully" let the other mothers
know when they were doing it wrong. She began peppering Dr.
Clark with a list of questions about whether they'd conducted any
clinical trials ("Yes," Dr. Clark said. "Nine out of ten moms have
reported feeling at least moderately more well rested and ener-
getic, but I'm happy to e-mail you the full data if you'd like."),
why the supplements were priced so much higher than the others
on the market ("We're not about the big mass-market crank out,"
Dr. Clark said with the patience of a saint. "We send small-batch,
individualized packets every month because we want to address
each woman's own personal needs. So, if you've been, say, feeling
particularly tired, or are having a postpartum acne breakout, you
just fill out the form to tell us so, and we curate the amount of
Saint-John's-wort or peppermint or what have you in your particular capsules. Obviously, though, if we've got our fantastic doctors working on customized vitamins all the time, we've got to
pay them!"), and more. Would Gwen shut up already so they could
get this over with and Amara could go home?

Amara could sense Whitney, next to her, trying to catch her
attention, hoping to exchange loving eye rolls like they always did
when Gwen started going on the type A train, but after what had
happened in Whitney's office, Amara couldn't look Whitney in
the eye right now. Charlie was *still* crying, so Amara stood up and
began to walk him back and forth across the room.

How were all these other babies so well-behaved? It was almost
enough to make Amara miss Joanna the Lost Playgroup Mom, the
one they didn't talk about anymore. Joanna's son had been the

most difficult of all. Whenever he'd gone off on a screaming tear, Joanna had looked at him with hopelessness in her eyes, and Amara had thought with a guilty relief that at least Charlie wasn't *that* bad. Joanna lived in Jersey now, but sometimes her grim presence still lingered in their playgroup circle, as if she were haunting them all, reminding them of what they could become.

"We're keeping TrueMommy exclusive for now," Dr. Clark was saying, "because we're going back and forth with the FDA to see if they'll give us full approval, which they normally don't do for supplements. But in the meantime, we wanted to reach out personally to mothers who we thought could be really aspirational brand ambassadors for when we go big, which is how we found you all."

That was about all Amara's patience could take. "'Brand ambassadors'?" she said in a withering tone as Charlie's tears soaked through her blouse. "All right, I have a question. Is this a pyramid scheme?"

Dr. Clark looked at her, a brief hint of annoyance flitting across her face before she replaced it with a smile. "No, no! I just meant that we're waiting on doing a full ad campaign until we hear back from the FDA. Once we do, we're hoping to use real moms in our curated rollout of the website and social media—maybe even on TV too."

"So you're saying we'll be Instagram famous?" Ellie asked.

Dr. Clark laughed. "Well, no promises."

"Okay, but for the record," said Meredith, "I want it noted that I'm very okay with my pending celebrity." She and Ellie launched into another of their extended mind-meld cackles.

"So what do you all think?" Dr. Clark asked. "If you want to sign up as a playgroup, we can just deliver all the supplements to Whitney each month and cut out the individual shipping costs!"

Meredith and Ellie were in immediately while Vicki gave a slow, faraway nod.

"I don't know," Amara said, shaking her head. She shouldn't. The fact that she and Daniel were having to get by on one salary instead of the expected two was already causing serious issues. *Just please promise me that you'll never end up throwing away tons of money on vitamins you're going to pee out anyway.* The price tag on the True-Mommy supplements was absolutely mental. If Daniel saw the cost, he'd be livid.

"I suppose I *have* been more well rested," Gwen said. "Even though Reagan is still finicky at night, I feel like I'm getting close to eight hours of sleep."

It was so tempting, though, to believe in a miracle vitamin— something that could make her feel *normal* again so that she could be a good mother to her beautiful, impossible baby, who had come out of her howling like a wolf and had barely stopped howling in the year since then. Something that would give her the energy she needed to be patient with him. And that reliable old placebo effect *had* been helping to make things seem a little more manageable over the last month, today notwithstanding. If what had happened in Whitney's office was any indication, Amara needed all the help she could get.

"I'm in too," Whitney said with a smile, giving a little shimmy of her shoulders and throwing her hands up in the air. "Why not?"

"We're going to become crunchy, all-natural moms, aren't we?" Amara said. "Pretty soon we'll be staunch anti-vaxxers."

"Well, the thing about vaccines is I just don't know if I should trust them," Whitney said. Amara stared at her, and Whitney laughed. "Kidding!"

"Don't even joke about that," Gwen said.

"I'm pretty sure you can take Saint-John's-wort and still believe in science," Whitney said, waving her hand through the air. "So what do you think, Amara?"

She *shouldn't*.

The other women all turned to look at her and her twisting, splotchy baby. The pity in their eyes was what did her in. It was the same charitable look previously reserved for Joanna.

"Oh, fine. Whatever," Amara said. "I'm in too."

Chapter 3

After they'd all said goodbye to Dr. Clark, it was time to take some pictures for Whitney's Instagram.

Whitney hadn't meant to join the legions of InstaMoms. But during those first few months, she'd been alone with Hope so often, and the minutes had stretched like one of those scarves a magician pulled from his mouth—on and on and on, endless. (And yet somehow, whenever she actually *needed* more time for, say, sleeping or leaving the apartment for an appointment, the minutes flew.) At first, she'd taken the pictures to show Grant when he got home from work to keep him updated on what he'd missed out on. She'd nestle against him as he loosened his tie and hold her phone up toward him, scrolling through: Hope's scrunchy face when she'd just woken up from a nap, looking like a scowling WWE wrestler; Hope learning how to smile, so cute it made

Whitney's insides melty. Grant would say, "She's a beauty like her mom," and then ask if she wanted a Barolo or a grenache with dinner.

Then it had been fun to rearrange the setting a little bit, to make sure that Hope was doing tummy time right by a vase of fresh flowers, or to take the photo with a stack of her favorite books in the foreground. Whitney could use up half an hour finding the right light. The photos came out so well that it seemed a shame not to put them on her Instagram. Grant's sisters would want to see. By that point, she'd stopped showing Grant the pictures. Sometimes, she had a vague sense that he thought of her and Hope as trapped in amber while he was at work and that he didn't particularly care to see her evidence to the contrary.

And then that time she'd bought those gorgeous matching Mommy-Infant sundresses from Petit Bateau, she had to document that too, setting up a timer out on the balcony, the trees in Central Park drenched in brilliant hues behind them, captioning the photo, "My baby bestie and I aren't ready to say goodbye to summer!" Initially, she was surprised when people started following and tagging. She was also a tiny bit creeped out. But it felt nice to be seen again. It took off from there.

Mostly, it was a pleasant little hobby. She didn't have a *huge* following—she wasn't about to start going to those seminars on how to "grow your audience," but she used to work in PR, so she had a few tricks up her sleeve. And it was exciting when some matrix somewhere branded her an "influencer," and people started sending her things in exchange for a mention. She'd never fully gotten rid of that grasping part of herself that tingled for free stuff.

The Instagram made her happy for another reason too: Hope was so small and unspoiled, and Whitney had been given the awe-inspiring power to shape her. What if she accidentally molded this darling creature into someone *less* than she had the potential to be? What if Hope grew up less happy, less confident than she could've been with a different mother? Every time Whitney posted a picture of her child's face wrinkled with delight and read the comments about how cute Hope was, she felt that Hope would grow up to be smart and well-adjusted and kind, made up of only the best parts of her parents. According to her social media, Whitney was doing motherhood *right*.

Because there were endless ways to do motherhood wrong. One could be too indulgent or too withholding. One could work too much or stay home too long. One could be far too lackadaisical or far too anxious. Whitney knew the latter very well. At a doctor's appointment a few months ago, she'd expressed what she thought was a perfectly normal amount of anxiety to her ob-gyn, and then he'd tried to press a Xanax prescription on her, as if she were a cliché, some bored suburban mom who couldn't get through the day without a chemical aid. Whitney didn't need Xanax! Not that she would judge someone who *did* need it, someone who was actually suffering from postpartum depression. Someone like Joanna.

Oh, Joanna. Whitney had meant to go visit her at some point, maybe bring her a cake from the neighborhood bakery that Joanna had liked so much. Maybe if a doctor had prescribed Joanna Xanax, she would still be sitting in their circle with her wounded, troublesome boy, and no one would have had to get the police involved.

Whitney batted away thoughts of Joanna and handed the camera to Gwen, who had become the playgroup's go-to photo taker, since she didn't want pictures of her and Reagan posted on a public forum. She'd told them all a horrible story about a cousin of hers who had posted a few snaps of her kids in the bath together on Facebook—all very innocent. A few weeks later, the cousin was contacted by the FBI because those same darling pictures had shown up on a child porn site. They'd all shuddered, and Whitney hadn't taken a photo for her account that day. In retrospect, though, it was a little annoying, this tendency of Gwen's to ruin harmless fun with that holier-than-thou attitude. In truth, Whitney had spent a lot of time lately trying to quit thinking uncharitable thoughts about Gwen. It was absurdly difficult. Since Gwen's Christmas party, Whitney had entertained multiple daydreams in which Gwen had a psychotic break, severed all ties with loved ones, and moved to a hovel in Lithuania.

Whitney shook her head, lifted up Hope, and popped onto the couch next to Amara. The other mothers played with their babies on the floor in front of them, as Gwen took a few uninspired photos.

Amara was trying to calm a fussing Charlie. She'd been pretty cranky herself during Dr. Clark's visit. Whitney didn't blame her for being skeptical. Packaging "wellness" was a white-hot consumer trend, and even for a former publicist like Whitney, it was sometimes hard to separate out the valuable products from the ones expressly designed to prey on the vulnerabilities of young women—or young moms. Perhaps TrueMommy was nothing but a glorified Tupperware party, the latest thing housewives did to pass the time. And Dr. Clark's promise to feature them in an ad campaign was probably a baited hook designed to get them to sign up for more vitamins. But the science seemed convincing enough—even skeptical Gwen had admitted it!—and Whitney was certain she had experienced a much-needed, all-natural burst of energy since she started taking the bespoke vitamins, in their exquisite suede box. Besides, it was fun—something she and her friends could do together rather than something about which she had to feel ashamed. Take that, Xanax!

If you could afford it, sometimes you could let yourself be taken in a little bit to get some peace of mind. And now, she thought with a thrilling glow, she *could* afford it.

"Hey, what's up with you?" Whitney asked, giving Amara a gentle nudge. She tried not to have favorites in playgroup, but still, Amara was the one she wanted to sit next to, the one she'd trusted with things she didn't tell the rest of the women.

"I didn't get to weigh in on Claire," Amara said through her teeth as she smiled for another photo.

"Oh, sorry!" Whitney said. "I guess you were still in the bathroom. She'll be great, though."

"I think we could do better."

"But you said she had a beautiful voice," Whitney said, angling her face up for the camera so that there was no chance Gwen would catch a hint of double chin. Claire would be a much better musician for them than Joey had been. With his boundless confidence and shameless flirting, Joey had introduced a new competitive element to playgroup. Without meaning to, they'd all started jockeying for his attention, little resentments building when Joey

36

spent the whole playgroup teasing Meredith or complimenting Amara, the only one of them who didn't seem to blush under his focus. Whitney was amazed by how stupid they all became, like preteen girls at a school dance. She had been quietly thrilled when Ellie told them about the bachelorette party incident so they'd had an excuse to go back to being the grown-ups they actually were.

Yes, Claire would be better, with her coppery hair and her slightly skittish manner. She seemed sweet. Whitney wanted to pet her, to protect her.

(Later, Whitney would realize how blind she'd been. Claire would change things between the playgroup women more than Joey ever could have.)

"I liked her a lot," she said. "And everyone else was in favor."

"Well, you still should have asked me," Amara said.

"Okay, *someone's* got a bug up her butt today," Whitney said, and immediately felt guilty for snapping.

"Yup," Amara said, stone-faced. "There's a large praying mantis burrowing its way into my ass."

They looked at each other for a moment, then burst into laughter, right as Gwen took a final picture.

When everyone else left and Whitney looked through the pictures later, that was the magic one. They all glowed, Whitney and Amara especially. "#Wellness and wine with my favorite mamas at playgroup is the best #selfcare," Whitney typed quickly, adding in a few more hashtags and posting the photo and caption online. Then she gathered Hope up in her arms and settled with her on the couch. Hope was toddling about, but she still couldn't walk more than a few feet without flopping back down, and Whitney was grateful for that. "Not yet, rug rat," Whitney said, rubbing her nose against her baby's cheek, and Hope let out a contented sigh, relaxing against her mother's chest. Soon she fell asleep. Whitney didn't. Whitney had been having a hard time sleeping lately.

She could put Hope into her crib and close the door for some private time, but no, the baby was too sweet to move. So she rested her head back on one of the throw pillows and looked up at the ceiling, then out the windows. "Hellooo," she whispered, her voice arcing up toward the light fixture above. Not even in her wildest dreams had she imagined that she'd live in all this space.

When Whitney was a little girl, she had hated her house. It was the smallest one on the block, and in between the deep red brick of the Kellys' on one side and the gray stone of the Silvermans' on the other, the beige siding of the McNabs' looked hopelessly plain.

But once a year, Whitney loved where she lived. On December first, her father would go to the shed out back as dusk started to roll in and return with his arms full of lights. He'd set up a ladder and ask Whitney to hold the bottom, and she would stand there like a proper sentinel, making sure he didn't fall off while he strung and hammered. An hour later, their house would be a glowing galaxy, threaded with little colored stars. The Kellys only put up one string of white lights. The Silvermans were Jewish, so they didn't put up anything.

As the years went on, the galaxy expanded. Her mother would roll her eyes, but then her mother rolled her eyes at pretty much everything her father did. Her father, egged on by Whitney's evident delight, bought a life-sized inflatable Santa who swayed in the wind like he was overcome with Christmas spirit. The next year, a Rudolph joined him. ("How about putting that money toward the weekend in the Poconos you're always promising me?" Whitney heard her mother hiss at her father one night.) The year Mrs. Hollinger started leading the church choir, her father suddenly got much more interested in religion and added a glowing plastic nativity scene in one corner of the yard. The Virgin Mary's face was so soft and sweet, like Mrs. Hollinger's. For a time, Whitney's regular games of pretending that she was Christine Daaé from *The Phantom of the Opera* or a beautiful maiden whisked away to a better life by a lovestruck prince gave way to a new hobby, in which Whitney looked at Mary's expression and then tried to replicate it in the mirror in her room, pretending a scarf-wrapped teddy bear was the Baby Jesus. She'd look down at the bear, her eyelashes fluttering, and try to turn the love from her eyes into something solid that could be felt by the recipient like a warm blanket. She was very pretty in those moments, she could see whenever she snuck a glance back up at the mirror, and she imagined the assembled shepherds and wisemen looking at her and her teddy bear Jesus baby in awe, all of them wanting to protect her, to marry her, to possess her. (She did not yet understand that being a mother generally made a woman less desirable, not more.)

The year Whitney turned thirteen was a confusing one, in which she became suddenly, achingly aware of everything that was wrong with her. Her boobs were too small, and then they were too big, causing older men to show her a new kind of attention.

She was too quiet, except when she was too loud. She was too fat. (She was never too thin.) But when December first rolled around, her father added a motion-activated inflatable snow globe that played a tinkling version of "Holly Jolly Christmas" when people walked by, and things were simple again. She and her father pretended to be ninjas and tried to sneak up the front porch steps without setting off the snow globe, but no matter how slowly they moved, it started vibrating with its merry tune, causing them to abandon their ninja pretense and dance around, shout-singing along.

A week later, Whitney got a ride home from choir practice with Alicia, who went to the private prep school a ten-minute drive from Whitney's public junior high. Alicia was the unofficial leader of the alto section, the one who could keep up the difficult harmonies without trying. During snack time, as the other kids wolfed down Doritos, Alicia took out a Ziploc bag of celery sticks and ate them carefully. She always reapplied her pink lip gloss in the bathroom after they'd finished singing, before reentering the world.

"That's so gorgeous," Whitney had said one time when they'd been the only two in the bathroom.

"That's cause it's not Bonne Bell or some drugstore crap," Alicia had replied, wiping the excess gloss from the corners of her mouth with a finger. "My mom and I bought it at Lord and Taylor."

Whitney desperately coveted Alicia's friendship.

Whitney was waiting at the bus stop, stamping her feet on the ground to keep warm, when a Volvo pulled up and Alicia leaned her head out the passenger-side window. When Alicia offered her a ride, Whitney did her best to act casual.

At the wheel, Alicia's mom looked sleek and young—but not too young. She wore a long-sleeved casual dress and no earrings. (Whitney's mother always wore earrings, sparkly ones that made her earlobes droop and her lined face seem duller.) And she chatted about how their family would be vacationing in Aspen over the holidays in a voice free of the Pennsylvania roundness that so squarely marked Whitney and her parents as belonging to this particular corner of the earth. In her head, Whitney practiced repeating what Alicia's mother said, exactly as she said it, in a voice that could fit anywhere.

"It's just down the block," Whitney said as they turned onto her street.

"Mom, look!" Alicia said, nudging her and pointing toward Whitney's house.

"Uh-oh," Alicia's mom said. "*Someone* on your block goes overboard on the holiday spirit, huh?" She and Alicia exchanged glances, laughing.

"It's so trashy," Alicia said.

"Honey, don't say that!" Alicia's mom said. She paused and then smirked. "'Gaudy' would be better." They laughed again. Whitney managed a weak smile.

"So which one's yours, honey?" Alicia's mom asked.

Whitney, mute, pointed toward the Silvermans' gray stone, and Alicia's mom pulled over.

"Anytime you need a ride, you just let Alicia know, all right? That bus is"—she shot Alicia a grimace—"not pleasant."

"Yeah, and maybe you can come over next week or something!" Alicia said.

"Thanks," Whitney said. "That would be awesome." She got out of the car and stood on the curb as Alicia rolled down her window. "Bye!"

"Oh," Alicia's mom said. "I'll wait till you get inside. I swear, I dropped off a friend of Alicia's brother's once. He went all the way to the front door and waved at me so I drove away, and then that sneaky little sociopath turned right around and went to the park to smoke pot. You remember that, Alicia? The mom was so mad at me! So now I always watch the kids go inside."

"Okay," Whitney said, and turned around, her legs shaking. She pulled her coat tighter and thought quickly. She would tell the Silvermans that she'd forgotten her key and that her parents hadn't answered the door when she'd knocked. Could she come in and call her parents to see if they were home? Maybe her parents *weren't* home yet. Her mom didn't get back from her job as a dental hygienist until seven, and she never knew what her father's construction schedule would be. The Silvermans were nice enough. They wouldn't turn her away. She mounted the first step to their porch, gripping the railing. Four more steps to go.

And then her own front door opened. "Whitney, I thought that was you!" her father said. "What are you doing over there?" He laughed. "Did you get lost?"

She closed her eyes for a moment, like an ostrich sticking its head in the sand. Perhaps it was possible to temporarily erase oneself from the face of the earth, if only one was desperate enough. Shame spread over her like nausea in the winter cold.

"Are you okay, chicky?" her father asked. He clomped down their porch stairs and headed her way, and the snow globe began to play as he passed, its cheap music box tune poisoning the air. He held a bowl of cereal in his hand. Suddenly, to the soundtrack of "Holly Jolly Christmas," in the light of a thousand tacky Christmas bulbs, Whitney saw her father as if for the first time, down to the half a Cheerio stuck in his beard. (All those days he spent at the kitchen table, telling her he was "on vacation" from his construction job—those had never been vacation after all. *I should leave your worthless ass*, her tired, dumpy mother hissed at him, when she thought Whitney wasn't around, while her father shot back, *Good luck finding another man who will want you*.) And she saw herself too, what she would be if she didn't fight it—a cheap plastic Mary stored in the shed after a month on display.

"Whitney?" Alicia said, poking her head back out the window.

"Oh," her father said. "Is this your friend? Hi!" He walked over to the car. "I'm Whitney's dad. Thanks for driving her home."

Alicia shot Whitney a confused look and then giggled as understanding settled over her. Her mother gave her a quick pinch on the arm and then leaned over her daughter toward the open window. "Our pleasure." Then she looked at Whitney with something like pity. "Merry Christmas," she said before throwing the car back into drive.

Two nights later, Whitney snuck outside at one A.M. with a nail she'd taken from the drawer of her father's odds and ends in the kitchen. As the Christmas carol jingled, she jammed the nail hard into the side of the snow globe. The material was firmer than she'd expected—less like a balloon and more like a grapefruit rind. She gave the nail a twist. When she pulled it out, air whooshed with it. She stood and watched the snow globe deflate, the folds of the material covering the speaker until only a weak hint of melody remained.

Grant came home an hour later with his usual noise, dropping his briefcase and waking up Hope, who began to mewl, suddenly cranky.

"My girls!" he said. "Busy bees, I see."

"Hey, honey!" Whitney said. He was so handsome, her husband. He leaned in to kiss her, and she tried not to flinch. She closed her eyes and rearranged his features into another man's face. That helped somewhat.

She pushed herself off the couch to get started on dinner and glanced at her phone to see a larger-than-normal number of notifications. Some account focused on all-natural health had shared the playgroup photo from today, and an influx of new followers was sharing and commenting, her feed a sea of "gorgeous" and "jealous" and "inspiration."

She'd worked so hard. She'd gotten a scholarship to Harvard, where she'd become her own Henry Higgins and banished her accent for good. She'd learned the exact right amount of makeup to put on to make it look like she was barely wearing any at all. She'd made herself love the briny taste of oysters as they wiggled down her throat so that no one would know that she was an interloper in this moneyed world. She'd captivated Grant (although his father had insisted they get a prenup). She'd given birth to their child, the most wonderful baby on Earth. She had enough money to slip Claire the Playgroup Musician an extra twenty dollars like it was nothing. (Claire was clearly struggling. Her boots were that kind you get from a cheap stall in midtown, the soles nearly flopping off.)

Whitney had gotten what she wanted. And she was about to drive a nail into it.

Chapter 4

Okay, Claire was getting back on the horse. Operation Re-enter the World and Prove All the Assholes Wrong was a go. After a few more ego-boosting playgroup sessions, in which the women fawned over her voice (well, except for Amara scowling at her in the corner), she scheduled an audition with a band that was looking to add a female singer. She didn't normally spend a lot of time looking in the mirror, but she fussed over herself that morning, switching her part from left to right and then back again. She did lip trills in the shower. The subway car she got on happened to be totally empty, not because of piss or vomit or anything like that, but just through some thrilling confluence of timing, location, and luck. Claire took it as a good omen and walked from pole to pole, belting out "Killing Me Softly," as the train rattled downtown.

She got to the studio fifteen minutes early for her appointment time and sat down to wait. A few other girls milled around, staring at a gray door from which muffled bursts of music emanated. They were all younger than her—fresh out of college and trying way too hard (one girl had put on so much eyeliner that she looked like Jack Sparrow). Claire wondered if any of them had her tour experience, if any of them had given their all both to small bars sparsely populated with mean drunks and to crowds of a thousand people enthusiastically clapping along. Had any of them rolled up their sleeves and changed a tire on the side of a Florida highway in the midst of a designated-driver shift one night while the rest of the band had been too high to do anything but stare? Did any of them know that particular magic that happened when you and a bunch of unwashed dudes had been trying and trying to finish a song and then, in one inspired moment, the perfect lyrics fell from your lips? Did any of them know what it was like to have that strange, enchanted life and screw it all up?

She shook her head, the memories tainted for her now, and glanced down at a stack of magazines on the coffee table next to her chair. Her gaze skidded across *New York* and landed on the newest issue of *Rolling Stone*. Goddammit.

There, on the *Rolling Stone* cover, under the headline "The Unexpected Conquerors," stood Marcus and Marlena, entwined in an embrace. The photo was striking, vivid. Marcus wore suspenders, gray pants, and a partially undone white button-up. Marlena, her hair wild, her lips bright red and slightly parted, wore skintight, high-waisted black pants and nothing else. Marcus had his eyes locked on Marlena, but she'd turned her head toward the camera so that she stared straight at Claire, a frank, unabashed look on her face.

Claire knew that she should leave the magazine, that she should stand up and move to the other side of the room, but a sick, masochistic curiosity overtook her. Would they mention her? Or would they just pretend she had never existed? She opened the magazine, flipped to the cover story, and started to read.

For years, the members of Vagabond toiled away, not unhappily, in indie rock purgatory. They had fans numbering in the tens of thousands, a record deal with a small label, a handful of sponsorships. Most of the time, they made enough money to pay their rent. They were set for a long, solid career of quietly doing what they loved. And then they found Marlena Rodriguez.

As a ringing in her ears grew louder and louder, Claire skimmed from the writer's description of Marlena's vocals (*she whirls between seductress, she-demon, and naif*) to the story of Marlena and Marcus's fast-blooming romance (*Jones-White told Rodriguez that he realized he was in love with her at the "Idaho Eyes" music video shoot, right before the director called "Action" on the last take, and when you watch it, you can sense a tremulous intensity in their interactions*). Her eyes flicked past the desultory mentions of Chuck and Diego.

Then, a few paragraphs in, she found it.

And if some of the original fans accuse the band of selling out, of trading in a certain rawness (not to mention a completely different female singer) for something more polished and poppy, the band doesn't seem

*to mind. Jones-White declines to comment when I ask him about why
the band moved away from their old singer and sound, except to say,
"She was fine, but Marlena is fire."*

Claire stared at the page until her vision blurred, the words tat-
tooing themselves on her brain. Then the door to the studio
opened, and a young woman came strutting out, a self-satisfied
smirk on her face, the guys in the audition room watching her go.
One of them followed her to the door, looking at a list in his hand.
"Claire Martin?" he asked.

A great lump rose in Claire's throat, and she ducked her head
down, pretending to be engrossed in the magazine, as the man
repeated her name, looking around the waiting room for some
response, the other auditionees shrugging their shoulders.

"Oookay," he said, "no Claire Martin, then." He looked back
down at the list. "Anna Lee?" The Jack Sparrow eyeliner girl popped
up from her seat with a nervous wave—a link in an infinite chain of
younger, shinier girls always popping up like in Whac-A-Mole—
and followed him inside.

Claire practically ran to playgroup after that, biting back tears and
anger at herself and at Vagabond. She craved the uncomplicated
chatter of the mothers, their confidence that singing songs to their
children was just about the most important thing anyone could do.
She was running a little early, but she didn't mind, and she dashed
into the elevator. Amara, evidently running a little late, was already
in there, with Charlie and his stroller in tow.

"Hey!" Claire said, pasting on a smile. Amara gave her a silent nod in return and stared at the floor numbers spinning by. God, she was intimidating, all the planes of her face taut, her bones sharper than ever in these close quarters. But also, it couldn't hurt to try to get back into her good graces. Maybe they could just laugh off the whole Claire-walking-in-on-Amara-stealing-from-Whitney thing.

"So Whitney mentioned you used to work for a late-night show," Claire said, attempting a light and friendly tone. "That's really cool!"

"Yeah. Thanks," Amara said.

"She said you did something with musicians? Booking music?" Claire asked.

Slowly, Amara swiveled her head to look at Claire straight on. "What, you have an EP or something?" she asked, her voice turning drier than Claire had ever heard it. "You're looking for the perfect connection to get discovered, and you think I could be useful to you?"

"Um, I—" Claire stammered.

A vein began to pulse in Amara's throat. "Look. You might think you have some kind of leverage over me, but you don't," she said. "I told you, I was looking for soap. If, for some crazy reason, you decide to tell Whitney otherwise, I don't think there's any chance in hell she'll believe you."

"Wow," Claire said, a laugh of disbelief escaping from her like a bark. She suddenly felt like she was sliding all the way down to the end of her rope. "'Leverage'? Okay. That's not what I was implying at all. I'm here to sing to your babies and make some money so that

I don't have to go live in my parents' basement, not to get involved in whatever shit is going on between you all. I'm not going to mess things up for you. So please don't mess things up for me."

Amara stared at Claire for a moment as the elevator slowed, reaching its destination. "Fine," Amara said, as the *ding* sounded and the doors opened on the penthouse floor.

Claire followed as Amara wheeled her stroller down the hallway to the line of all the other strollers. Those strollers all looked like cars at a luxury dealership, probably with the latest NASA technology installed. In comparison, Amara's stroller looked like . . . well, a regular stroller. *Yup, definitely money issues,* Claire thought as she walked past Amara and knocked on Whitney's door.

Whitney greeted Claire with her usual hug, then stepped back and gave her a searching look. "Is everything okay? Can I get you something? Water? Wine?"

"Oh, no, thank you. I'm all set," Claire said, but Whitney raised an eyebrow.

"I hope you aren't just saying that to be professional. I'm going to keep asking, every playgroup, until you let me shower you in refreshments."

"Then I'll take that wine today," Claire said.

"Yes, Claire!" Whitney said, leading her into the living room and opening up a bottle of chardonnay. "Welcome to the party."

"I wouldn't put the oils on the baby's skin," Gwen was saying to Meredith, "if you haven't talked to your doctor about it."

"Claire," Ellie called. "Come over here! We're testing out essential oils that someone sent Whitney for free, because her Instagram is blowing up. She got like two thousand new followers this week!" Ellie squinted at the labels on the bottles in front of her. "Now, are you feeling anxious, tired, or nauseous?"

"Is there an option for all of the above?" Claire asked as she unzipped her guitar.

"Oh, no, what's wrong?" Whitney asked, handing Claire a wineglass and furrowing her brow in concern.

"Nothing," Claire said. "Just a bad audition."

"Well, if they don't take you, they're missing out," Whitney said.

"Hear, hear," Meredith said, then scooted her baby close to Claire. "Lexington, go give Claire a cuddle."

The little girl laid her head against Claire's shoulder and then began thwacking at her guitar. Ellie scooted her baby, Mason, over too, and then Hope toddled over, joining in on the hugging/ thwacking. Claire couldn't help but laugh at the baby invasion. "Help!" she said. "I'm drowning in cuteness."

"Claire, what's your Instagram handle?" Whitney asked, typing something on her phone. She held up the screen in front of Claire, showing a photo she had just taken of the moment and posted on her feed. In the picture, Claire's eyes were crinkled in happiness for the first time in a long time. "You look adorable."

"Um, I actually got rid of my social media," Claire said. One night a couple of months ago, she'd gone down a Vagabond rabbit hole and found herself researching how to make a troll account so that she could write mean, anonymous messages to Marlena. Catching herself, she'd decided then and there to delete all the apps. That way she could also avoid the occasional well-meaning messages from loyal fans who wanted to know what had happened to her and the less-well-meaning messages from people in her hometown telling her that in times of crisis, they turned to Jesus for comfort. "I just found myself wasting too much time on it."

"That's smart," Gwen said, nodding.

"You've got better willpower than I have!" Whitney said.

"I'm making you a concoction of peppermint, lemongrass, and lavender," Ellie announced. "It might taste weird, but it'll be good for you."

The mothers looked at Claire as if they had discovered the special secret of her worth, and sure, she thought the lives they led were ridiculous and she knew she was just their employee, but still. Claire was at the eye of a hurricane, a new peace and calm coming over her as the women whirled around, that terrible *Rolling Stone* cover blowing away in the wind. Not even Amara in the corner could ruin it. The mothers were mothering her, and she fucking loved it.

Chapter 5

When Whitney came back into the living room after waving goodbye to a slightly tipsy Claire, the other mothers were filling out their TrueMommy surveys for the next month's batch of vitamins, deep in conversation about their husbands.

"That's just what Christopher was saying the other night," Gwen said.

"Ugh, can you please get him to convince John?" Ellie said, then let out a dramatic sigh. "It is a *tragedy* that we've never managed to get all the playgroup husbands in the same room."

Meredith clapped her hands together. "We should plan a big group dinner for all of us! Right, Whitney?"

"That's a nice idea," Whitney said, refilling Ellie's wineglass. "I could do some restaurant research." She startled, as if remembering something. "Oh, Gwen, didn't you say you had something to show us after music?"

It wasn't the first time someone had brought up getting together with all the husbands. Each time it happened, Whitney would nod at the idea enthusiastically and volunteer to plan. But she would never look into restaurants. All of them together in the same room—it was the worst idea in the world.

Whitney shouldn't have gotten so excited about her thirtieth birthday dinner, back in November. That was the problem: She'd set it up to fail from the start. In her expectation of the night, she and Grant had a meal full of sparkling conversation and long, loving looks, and at the end of it, he made a heartfelt speech about how lucky he was to have found her, and they went home and had amazing sex, and it was like the beginning of their relationship all over again.

In reality, they spent most of the meal discussing their upcoming Christmas vacation with Grant's extended family, a conversation full of logistics and fraught, familiar arguments. They both drank more than usual, and then their taxi hit horrible traffic on the way home, so by the time Whitney came out of the bathroom in the scarlet slip Grant always liked so much, he had already fallen asleep.

Well, they'd have the rest of the weekend to make up for it. On Saturday morning, she woke to glorious sun, one of those crisp November days made all the more beautiful by the knowledge that winter could be descending at any moment. After attending to Hope, she crawled back into bed. "Sweetie," she said, nuzzling against Grant's shoulder. "Let's go to the farmers market."

He groaned, letting out a gust of morning breath, and pulled the pillow over his head. "It's early."

Whitney persisted. "It'll be fun! We can get some fresh veggies and cook a nice dinner."

"Why don't you and Hope go?" he said without opening his eyes. "You guys will have a better time without me slowing you down."

"We'd never have a better time without you," she said, slipping her arm around him. His muscles tensed under her touch.

"I need a little break."

She poked him playfully. Sometimes she felt like a parody of herself. "Come on, lazy bones."

"Maybe you've forgotten," he snapped, "but people who work all week like to *relax* on the weekends."

So she bundled Hope into her winter coat, and they set off without Grant.

Whitney hadn't been one of those women who dreaded turning thirty, who viewed it as some sort of terrifying deadline. Anyway, she'd gotten her life together in plenty of time, meeting Grant at twenty-four, giving birth to Hope at twenty-nine. But as she pushed her daughter down the avenue, toward the farmers market, an unsettling ache came over her. In her quest to build the perfect family, had she rushed things, using up all of her allotted excitement and adventure too quickly, leaving the rest of her life to rehashing the same arguments over and over again? No. She was being silly. Motherhood was a new kind of adventure, and she and Grant had plenty of excitement left to enjoy. They were just in a bit of a rut right now because they were so tired all the time. But that would pass.

She wandered from booth to booth, pushing Hope's stroller past the stand selling homemade bread and stopping to look at the farm-fresh eggs. She glanced over at a baby babbling nearby, smiling at her distractedly before recognizing her as Reagan.

"Oh, hey, you!" Whitney said, leaning down and holding out her hand for Reagan to grab onto. She looked up, expecting to see Gwen at the helm of Reagan's stroller, but an unfamiliar man stood there instead.

"Hello," he said, raising an eyebrow.

"Hi," she said, drawing back from Reagan. "Sorry. I promise I'm not one of those creepy women who touches random babies without asking!"

"It happens all the time," he said. "Having such a beautiful baby—it's a blessing and a curse."

Whitney laughed. "I'm Whitney, from Gwen's playgroup."

"Oh, of course, the famous Whitney!" he said, then knelt down by her stroller, smiling. "And this must be Hope." When he straightened back up, he stuck out his hand for a shake. "I'm Christopher." As they shook, Whitney took him in. Gwen's husband had a bump in his nose, like he'd broken it and decided not to fix it, hair that curled down toward his chin, and stubble on his face. He looked around the market in an engaged and open way, different from the other bored, clean-cut men accompanying their wives. When he'd smiled down at his daughter, it had been with a pure, beautiful adoration.

Whitney blinked. "Is Gwen around?"

"No. On Saturdays, she takes Rosie to her dance class, and I bring Reagan here." Good for them, Whitney thought, dividing up parenting duties like that. She'd like to discuss something similar with Grant, when they had another child. "What about your husband?" Christopher asked, as if he'd read her mind. "Is he here? The playgroup spouses need to do some bonding too!"

"Oh, he's at home, recuperating from last night," she said, and then added, offhand, "We went out to celebrate my birthday."

"Hey," Christopher said, his face breaking into a crinkly smile. "Happy birthday!"

"Thanks," she said. "A big one. Thirty!"

"Whoa," he said. "A big one, indeed!" He glanced around, his eyes landing on a nearby sign advertising hot apple cider. "Here, let me buy you a cup of birthday cider."

"Oh, please, you don't have to."

"Reagan," he said, bending down toward his baby in her stroller, "what do *you* think about us buying our nice friend some cider?" Reagan gurgled, and Christopher nodded very seriously at her before turning back to Whitney, saying in a confidential sort of tone, "Well, the boss has spoken, and she says I *do* have to. I'm afraid if you don't accept, she'll think you're very rude."

Whitney laughed, and Christopher ordered them each a steaming cup. They sat on a nearby bench to drink, parking their strollers beside them. "How are you feeling about the big three-oh?" Christopher asked.

"Oh, it's really just another birthday," she said.

"Yes and no," he said, looking at her like he cared what she thought.

"Well," she said, and hesitated. "It does make you do a certain accounting of the choices you've made throughout your twenties."

"It definitely does," he said. "And how do yours add up?"

"Oh, they add up wonderfully. But . . . well, where I grew up, twenty-nine was late to have a baby, and that's not so much the case in New York."

"Mm," Christopher said, blowing on his cider, steam rising into the air around him. "In terms of New York parenting, you're practically a baby yourself."

"Exactly. I'm the youngest one in the playgroup, and sometimes when I listen to the other women talk about the adventures they had—Ellie went off for a year and taught English in South Korea; Amara partied with all kinds of celebrities—I think maybe I should've taken some more time to wander." She shrugged. "I don't know. It's silly."

"I don't think it's silly," Christopher said, pulling out a bag of cut-up strawberries and handing one to Reagan. "Although it was the opposite for me. I turned thirty, looked around at all the adventuring I'd done, and realized I hadn't built anything solid. But hey, then two weeks later, I met Gwen."

"So two weeks from now, I'll probably pick up and move to Japan," Whitney said.

"Exactly." He laughed a nice, easy laugh that lifted the cloud she'd been walking around under all morning. "Just wait till you see forty looming on the horizon. It gets even weirder."

They kept chatting as they drank their ciders, the other market-goers whirling around them, until Whitney's phone dinged with a message from Grant asking where she was.

"Oh, we have to go!" Whitney said, standing. Somehow, nearly an hour had gone by.

"We do too. Great talking with you," Christopher said. "Hey, maybe we'll see you again next Saturday. We come here every week around this time."

"Yeah, maybe. That would be nice," Whitney said. "Tell Gwen I say hi." She waved as he and Reagan disappeared into the crowd. Then she put her hands into her coat pocket, her fingers suddenly freezing.

The next week, when Grant wanted to stay home to watch a game, she ran into Christopher again. "Fancy seeing you here!" she said, and they moved through the market together, trying samples of olive oil and jam, laughing over a particularly bulbous onion that Christopher pulled out of the pile. At the stand selling homemade bread, the elderly man ringing up Whitney's purchases threw in a free packet of sugar cookies. "For the beautiful family," he said, winking at her and Christopher.

"Oh, we're . . . ," Whitney began, but Christopher just smiled and thanked the man.

As they turned away from the stall, Christopher whispered, "We can't turn down free cookies!" So they brought those over to the same bench they'd sat on the week before and ate them slowly, talking until the last crumb was gone.

Whitney pointed to a sign. "Next Saturday's the last market of the season."

"That's too bad," Christopher said. "It's been nice, having fresh produce."

The next week, Whitney woke to sleet and slush. She stared out the window at the unforgiving weather, an out-of-proportion disappointment blooming in her chest. She had just really wanted some cage-free eggs, she told herself.

She'd almost believed it too, until Gwen's Christmas party.

Chapter 6

Baby Reagan was a pretentious little show-off as far as Amara was concerned.

"Look!" Gwen said to them all, taking Reagan's sippy cup out of her pudgy hands and putting it on top of the low table in Whitney's living room. All the women sitting together on the floor, filling out their vitamin forms, turned their heads to watch as Reagan squinted and grunted, then swung her arms up to the tabletop. Amara willed Reagan to give up and be a tiny, immobile slug a while longer—Lord, she was a monster, rooting for a baby to fail—but Reagan pushed and wobbled to her feet as most of the other mothers squealed, clapping their hands, while Vicki gave her slow, faraway nod of approval.

And just like that, Charlie became the last child in playgroup who still hadn't stood up on his own. The slowest of the babies.

Enough already, she thought as Gwen beamed at her daughter. Reagan wasn't the second coming of Christ. She wasn't even that cute. Whitney's hand crept over to Amara's on the rug and gave it a quick, tight squeeze.

Amara let her hand linger in the warmth of Whitney's for a moment, then untangled herself. "We've got to head to Charlie's pediatrician appointment," she said, grateful for the excuse to leave. God, this was breastfeeding all over again.

Sometimes, Amara wished she could lop off her tits and toss them in a dumpster. All her adult life, they'd been causing her trouble. She'd gotten a reduction a few years ago, because when she'd hurried through the hallways at work, the unwieldy buggers threatened to put someone's eye out, and if she'd had one more conversation with a coworker in which she caught him staring, she would have punched him straight in the nose. At the time, her doctor had failed to mention that it could come back to bite her.

Breastfeeding was supposed to be natural. A cow could get a calf to suckle at her teat, and yet Amara, who had a degree from a well-regarded university and had handled some of the most famous celebrities in the world, couldn't get Charlie to latch onto her nipple. Fucking babies. The most narcissistic rock star on the planet was no match for the average six-month-old.

It wasn't like one of those articles on the mom-centric websites: "How My Battle to Breastfeed Taught Me Who I Really Am" or some similar nonsense. The women who wrote those stories would recall how they'd tried and tried until, after some magical words of wisdom from a kindly lactation consultant or a few deep, centering breaths, they'd navigated their babies to the perfect spot and their little angels latched on and stayed on, moonlight from the window draping across mother and child. Only then, in a blinding flash of insight, would the author realize the depth of strength and selflessness that had always existed inside of her. There was always a happy ending, a moment at which a woman knew she was a good mother.

All of that was the exact opposite of Amara's experience.

She eventually attained a basic competence in breastfeeding her son, but it was never easy or mindless or satisfying. Meanwhile, her breasts were perpetually heavy and raw; she'd dealt with multiple rounds of mastitis; her nipples chafed at her shirts, and sometimes they leaked; and she pumped all the time, but never a consistent enough amount to provide real nourishment for Charlie. So her boy was a de facto formula baby, which apparently meant she didn't love him enough because, as people were so fond of re-minding her, breast was best! (But she *did* love him, despite it all, with a steady ache. She'd journeyed through the terrifying, alien wonders of pregnancy and discovered a new sun, even if some-times she wished she could leave Charlie on a church doorstep and take off for South America.)

All the other mothers in playgroup were juicy and bountiful. Especially Vicki. Vicki's boob was a goddamn fire hose. If Vicki whipped her boob out to breastfeed on a park bench, all the babies in the vicinity probably whooshed out of their strollers, desperate for a taste of that liquid gold. Vicki would never stop breastfeed-ing, and her son would grow up with a hearty Oedipus complex. Amara pictured little Jonah in the schoolyard telling the assorted boys, "If you love Mountain Dew, you've gotta try my mother's milk!" At his wedding, he'd clink Vicki's boob against his bride's champagne glass before taking a suckle.

The playgroup women had listened to Amara's woes and suggested all sorts of tricks, like eating a lot of oatmeal or trying a different brand of breast pump. ("You ever notice," Joanna had said as she and Amara took the elevator after one such playgroup, "how people can say they're trying to help you while making you feel worse than before?") Eventually Amara had just stopped talking about it and given up.

But she couldn't just give up on Charlie's motor development.

Sitting in Dr. Katz's waiting room an hour later, in between rocking Charlie's stroller back and forth with her foot and texting the office address to Daniel *again* (he was running late, some meeting at work had gone over), she pulled *The Foolproof Guide to a Happy, Healthy Baby* out of her bag. She read this book the way twelve-year-olds pored over Harry Potter novels, hunting for clues, rereading, and annotating late into the night. She hadn't yet written erotic fan fiction about the two doctors who had coauthored the thing, but hey, given the direction in which her mental health was heading, maybe that was on the horizon. She flipped to the developmental checklist page, which was covered with her own notes. She'd checked woefully few of the boxes. She went over the list of things she wanted to ask Dr. Katz, and her heart raced at the thought of what his answers might be.

"Well, Charlie's still underweight!" Dr. Katz said to Amara and Daniel. This doctor was far too cheerful about everything. Amara's parents had not emigrated from Nigeria to London and worked their asses off to give her every opportunity—even sending her to college in the US, for fuck's sake!—just for Amara's kid to go on a hunger strike.

Daniel was bouncing Charlie on his lap, still out of breath from running the twenty blocks from midtown. His glasses had gone askew in the process, giving him a faintly ridiculous, lopsided look even as he nodded seriously at their pediatrician. "Okay, so what can we do to fix that?" he asked.

Dr. Katz looked at their chart. "His intestinal and kidney tests have all been fine, so it's probably a matter of giving him a higher-calorie diet throughout the day and keeping an eye on it."

"What about standing up?" Amara asked. "He can put weight on his legs when I hold him, but he doesn't pull himself up."

"Uh-oh!" Dr. Katz said, smiling.

"'Uh-oh'?" Amara asked. "What does that mean?"

"It's probably nothing to worry about," he said, patting Charlie's head. "Some babies are just a little slower than others. It doesn't mean anything."

"But what if it does?"

"Well, then we'll know in a few months!" he said, giving out a kindly chuckle like he was Santa Claus distributing toys. (*Here, child, you get a toy train, and you get a Hatchimal, and YOU, little Charlie, get uncertainty about whether or not you're developing normally! Ho ho ho!*)

"Wow. That's very helpful," she said. She had an urge to slap some gravitas into him, so, instead, she concentrated on the wall behind Dr. Katz's head, which was painted with a jungle scene. In the middle of it, a cartoon monkey clutched a vine, grinning. Rather creepy-looking, actually.

"I think," Daniel said, "we're just feeling a little overwhelmed right now."

"Look," Dr. Katz said, "it seems like your son is what we call, in fancy scientific jargon, a difficult baby. But that doesn't necessarily last. How's he sleeping?"

Amara and Daniel looked at each other. "We're having trouble getting him on a consistent schedule," she said, "because *someone* goes into his room when he wakes up in the middle of the night to cuddle him, when he's supposed to be crying it out."

"I wait!" Daniel said to her, then turned to Dr. Katz. "I only go in when it really seems like he's not going to stop. And it works. He goes right back to sleep."

"It undermines the whole thing," Amara said.

"Well," Daniel said, throwing his hands up in the air, "I'm sorry that I want to comfort our son."

Dr. Katz chuckled again. "Sounds like this is an issue you two should discuss with a different kind of doctor."

Later, in the hallway, navigating Charlie's unwieldy stroller through the door that Daniel was holding open, Amara said, "I want to change pediatricians."

"What?" Daniel asked.

"He's too flippant," she said as they headed toward the elevator. "I don't know if he's even taking any of our concerns seriously. And I hate his smug face."

Daniel sighed. "He's taking us seriously, Mari. I think he's just seen it all before, so he knows getting worked up over things isn't helpful."

"So now you think I'm getting too worked up?" she snapped. He gave her a look, and she deflated. She leaned against him, her voice catching. "I'm sorry. I just feel like I'm trying everything, and I'm failing at it all."

"Hey," he said, wrapping his arms around her right there in that sterile hallway, Charlie cooing to himself in the stroller beside them. "You're not failing."

"What if there's something seriously wrong with him?"

"Then we'll give him away," he said, his face gentle and somber. She smiled in spite of herself and pushed him. "No," he said. "Then we'll have a different kind of life than we planned. But we'll love him with everything we've got and rely on each other, and we'll make it work."

"You're right," she said, looking at him straight on. When had he gotten such deep bags under his eyes, and all that gray hair at his temples? "I love you. Let's just go home, order something totally unhealthy, and put an idiotic show on." She tugged on his tie. "Maybe we'll even be able to get him to sleep so we can have a little time to ourselves." She straightened back up and pressed the elevator button.

He grimaced. "I have to go back to the office."

"What? Now? But it's already after five."

"It was the only way I could get out for this appointment."

"Dammit," she said, pressing her fingers to her temple. "It would be *really* nice if just this once, you could tell them to go screw themselves."

"I can't do that."

"Looks like it's me and Charlie, alone again. Cool."

"It's not like I wanted to be the only breadwinner," Daniel snapped, right as the elevator doors dinged open.

The car was packed with people, with just enough space at the front for the two of them. But Charlie's stroller would never fit. "You go," she said to Daniel. "You have to get back to the office."

"Mari . . ."

"Go."

So he went.

She had to let two more carfuls of people go by before she was able to shove herself and Charlie in there. Having a baby in New York City was an insane thing to do, much like skydiving or cutting off one's ear. But she'd gone ahead and done it anyway.

Amara was *this close* to getting promoted to showrunner when Daniel went and put a fucking bun in her oven. To be fair, it wasn't entirely his fault. They only used condoms, even after five years together, because Amara didn't like putting extra hormones in her body—she was perfectly balanced the way she was, thank you very much, and didn't need to go back to the girl she'd been when she went on the pill her senior year of secondary school, crying on the tube every morning for no reason she could name— and when she'd tried an IUD her first year in New York, she'd suffered through a month of bleeding and cramps and then it had slipped without her realizing, meaning she'd had to take a very unpleasant trip to Planned Parenthood. She wasn't going to suffer through more horrible side effects just so her boyfriend (turned fiancé turned husband) could feel extra mind-blowingly amazing, when he already got to feel pretty damn good. Luckily Daniel wasn't one of those guys who whined about that sort of thing. She couldn't have married a guy who did.

Their condom broke the night before a gigantic presentation at work. She was one of the producers at *Staying Up with Nick Tannenbaum*, and she'd been developing a new segment for the show in which Nick would have a rap-battle debate about current events with the celebrity guest. She was always pushing for more substance, especially with the state of the world as it was. Nick, an affable Canadian, got nervous about handling controversial issues, but he *loved* goofing around and freestyle rapping with the crew backstage, so she thought he just might go for it. She'd written up a script about abolishing the electoral college (when she'd come over from England for university, she'd been dumbfounded by the institution—how was this the "great American democracy" she'd heard so much about?—but she tried to be evenhanded in the writing), and convinced the show's bandleader, Kenny, to do one side while she incessantly practiced the other. She knew Nick would get a kick out of that too, if she managed to do it well. He always tried to get her to join in on the freestyling backstage when she was running around making sure a million other things were going the way they were supposed to. "Amara could probably kick all of our asses," he'd say. (She wasn't sure if he was saying that because she was black or if it was a joke because she was so no-nonsense or if he actually meant it.) "I'd destroy you. You'd go home crying to your mummies," she'd always say while double-checking that the space cadet of an intern had put the cue cards in the proper order.

After the condom broke, Daniel had offered to run out to the pharmacy for Plan B, but she wouldn't have been able to do the presentation the way she wanted to with that hormone circus going on inside her body.

The next afternoon, with the staff gathered around in Nick's office, she'd ducked out, telling everyone she had to use the bathroom, and reentered in a Missy Elliott–style tracksuit as one of the band members began to beat box. "This is a rap battle, bitches," she yelled. Nick made a face like a kid entering a candy store. "The issue? The motherfucking electoral college!" She paused. "Obviously we can't say 'motherfucking' on air." Then she'd launched into it.

After the presentation went so well (she'd nailed it; she was a queen; Nick was totally on board), she *had* to go out for celebratory drinks with the guys, and by the time she woke up hungover the next morning and popped the little pill into her mouth, lo and behold, Charlie had already laid claim to her uterus.

She couldn't be a woman who'd had two abortions. She was thirty-two and married, for Christ's sake, to a wonderful guy who'd been aching to be a father since, probably, the moment he'd popped out of his own mother. (He even told dad jokes and wore flannel pajama pants and developed strange, passionate interests in hobbies like watercolors and woodworking that flamed out after six months or so. Prime dad material.) Besides, when she let herself think about it, she liked the idea of a mini Amara-Daniel hybrid waiting for her at the door, hurtling into her when she came home from work, before she'd even had time to set down her purse. Of the three of them snuggling in bed on Sunday mornings, bleary and content, the little nugget watching idiotic cartoons while Amara and Daniel passed the *New York Times* back and forth. She was going to lean the fuck in and master that mythical beast known as Having It All.

She told Nick when she was four months along, and he pounded his desk in congratulations, offering her some of the Scotch he kept in his desk for "special occasions" (which seemed to happen every day; Amara was worried he was a bit of an alcoholic) before remembering that she wasn't supposed to drink. By this point, "Rapping the Issues" clips had gone viral a couple of times, most notably the debate on universal health care in which the celebrity guest, a dainty, young Oscar-nominated actress, threw down like none other.

Nick arranged for Amara to stop coming into the office two weeks before her due date and then to take a full month off when the baby was born before she dove right back in. It was not the ideal time to go away. Their showrunner would be leaving soon to move to LA, and Nick was going to try to take on the position himself. He had no idea the amount of work that went on behind the scenes while he goofed around, so the experiment would probably end in a matter of weeks, and he'd promote one of the producers. Her coworkers were all dividing up her work while she was gone, with Robby taking on her primary duties. Robby was a pompous skid mark of a man, with a beard that badly needed a trim and a beer belly that he carried around like a policeman's badge—proof that he was Chief of the Fun Times Bureau. He never turned down a swig of Nick's Scotch.

So she'd simply have to work her ass off. She came back after her brief maternity leave, her reservoirs of patience near empty, exhausted but ready to go. Nick *oohed* and *aahhhed* over the pictures of wrinkled-up Charlie and told her she should feel free to duck out early if she needed to. At one point, when she tried to talk to Robby about a scheduling issue with a guest, he laughed and said, "Hey, relax! Put your feet up, Mama. You just did the hardest work anyone *can* do." But she couldn't relax. She was a woman, she was black, and now she was a mother. She had to be twice as good—no, *three* times as good—as everyone else.

Near the end of a staff meeting a few days after she'd made her return, Nick brought up "Rapping the Issues." A former boy-band singer who'd struck out on his own was coming in soon, and he wanted to do the segment.

"I was thinking immigration," Amara said. She'd written up a draft for it over the past two nights, in between Charlie's crying, and it had real potential. Now she tried to fluff her shirt out away from her chest without being obvious. She suspected that one of her boobs had started leaking, but she couldn't tell for sure. *Shit*, it hurt, but she wasn't about to hit pause for everyone so she could go pump, especially since the women's bathroom was on a whole different floor. Lord, this meeting was dragging on forever, clear proof that Nick did not know how to run things properly. This would never happen when (*If*, she reminded herself. *Don't get cocky*) she was showrunner.

"Cool, cool," Nick said.

"Oh, man," Robby interrupted, leaning back in his chair. *Just a little farther*, Amara thought, *and you'll tip over*. "You know what would be awesome? If we did it about hoverboards."

"What?" Amara asked. She snuck a peek down at her shirt, which had sprouted a dark stain. She was leaking all right. She tried to cover it with her arm but accidentally knocked that arm into her breast, sending a shock wave of pain through her body.

Robby smirked. "*Nick* knows what I'm talking about, right?" Nick gave that sheepish, adorable laugh of his (it had spawned a thousand GIFs when he unleashed it on the show) while Robby leaned forward, grinning at Amara. "We got one sent to the office while you were gone, and we all got drunk and tried to ride it. Nick totally face-planted in the middle of the hallway."

"Right," Amara said. "But hoverboards aren't an *issue*."

"There's an issue about whether or not they're safe," said Robby. "'Cause they keep exploding. And there's an issue about whether or not they're totally lame. Which they are. We could even do the whole thing with the two of them *on* hoverboards, and it would be hilarious."

"Yeah," Nick said. "Hoverboards! I think that would be fun. We should do it. Robby, do you want to take first pass?"

"Are you fucking kidding me?" Amara said.

"Whoa." Nick looked at her in surprise. The other writers at the table suddenly started concentrating on their sandwiches like grass-fed roast beef was the goddamn *Mona Lisa*. "What?"

"Number one, that's my segment."

"It's just this one time," Nick said. "It'll be fun. And it's so much work to produce. Maybe it's safer if Robby takes the lead, since things are so crazy for you at home right now."

"Things at home are fine. And number two, this is the dumbest idea I've ever heard. It doesn't make any sense to do it about fucking hoverboards."

"I don't get what the problem is," Nick said, his face starting to turn red in annoyance. "I think it sounds fun."

"Oh, I'm sorry. You think it could be *fun*? You hadn't said." Tears began to gather behind Amara's eyes, but she'd never cried at work, and she wasn't about to start now. She pushed her chair back and stood up, as the lily-white writers (all of them men, most of them young) stared at her like she was an exotic animal liable to hurt someone at any moment. The slightest, smarmiest smile played across Robby's face, and she knew she was about to do exactly what he wanted, but she couldn't stop herself. "I need to go pump because my tits feel like they're going to explode. Or perhaps I should stay here, and they'll just shoot out milk like fireworks. That's *fun*, right?"

She went to the bathroom and then boxed up her stuff. They weren't going to fire her—then who would the writers go to when they needed to ask if a joke was racist or just *edgy*?—but she wasn't going to work under fucking Robby. She told everyone she wanted to try out the stay-at-home-mom thing for a couple of years, because she was lucky enough to be able to afford it. She told herself maybe she'd like it.

She made it another month before she started biting off her fingernails with boredom, and a week after that before she found herself tearing a pillow apart with her bare hands because she was so angry at Charlie, who always either had tears coming out his eyes or shit coming out his bottom. Daniel helped when he could, but he'd taken a promotion he hadn't wanted to make up for the loss of her salary, which meant much longer hours at the office. She tried reaching out to contacts at other shows, but nobody seemed to be interested in hiring new mothers. (Or word had spread that she was crazy for how she'd left *Staying Up,* and no one wanted to work with her. She suspected that might play a part too.)

She was never alone. She was so lonely.

Amara and Charlie were sitting in a neighborhood coffee shop one Wednesday morning, one of those expensively shabby-chic places with a shelf along one wall displaying a vase of dried wild-flowers and a rusted washboard. The barista monitoring the play-list was a big fan of watered-down bluegrass. Although the design aesthetic was "old-fashioned hardship," a cup of coffee cost five dollars. Amara wouldn't have chosen it at any other point in her life, but right now, it wasn't her apartment, so it was heaven.

She was eating a croissant with one hand and rocking Charlie's stroller back and forth with the other, in the hopes that the motion would keep him from wailing. No such luck. A guy in his early twenties, sipping a cappuccino and reading a battered copy of *Jude the Obscure,* shot them a dirty look. *Get a job,* Amara thought, and tried to glare back, but it bothered her. You could plan to go to a coffee shop because you wanted to spend one measly half hour sitting someplace outside your apartment, you could take a whole morning getting your baby ready and talking to him in soothing tones, and you could navigate the stroller down the streets, spend your money, find your table, and unload, your aching body collapsing onto the chair. But if, right as the first bite of flaky pastry began to melt in your mouth, your baby decided to start crying, suddenly you were an inconsiderate asshole and a terrible mother to boot, and you'd better leave right away.

Amara took Charlie out of the stroller and held him against her chest, trying to soothe him. Charlie let out a particularly piercing wail, and Mr. Jude the Obscure snapped his book shut. "Seriously?" he said, filled with righteous indignation before looking around the coffee shop as if seeking to rally the legions of people whose lives Amara was ruining. "I mean, come on."

Most of the other people in the coffee shop had headphones on and didn't look up, but a beautiful woman by the counter met the guy's eyes and smiled. She had a stroller of her own, but the baby inside was a sleeping cherub who probably changed her own diapers.

Buoyed by outside confirmation, America's Number One Intellectual looked back at Amara, smug. Well, it was useless to stay here now. So nice to know that the state of the sisterhood was strong. Amara started to buckle Charlie back into his stroller, hating everyone and everything. The other mother made her way toward a table, but then she stopped, right in front of the reading guy.

"Someday when you've got a screaming infant," the other mother said in a low voice, that lovely smile still upon her face, "I hope the people you encounter are understanding." Amara paused in her buckling. Charlie, miraculously, paused in his screaming. The other mother's eyes burned a bright, big hole into the reading guy. "And I hope you are so, so grateful that not everyone is a dickhead like you."

The guy's mouth snapped open, then shut again. He swallowed. Then he stuffed his book into his bag, stood up, and marched out. The door to the shop banged shut behind him, rattling the front window. The other mother turned and looked at Amara, a flush creeping up her face.

"I'm sorry," she said. "That was too much."

Amara let out a cackle. "No, it wasn't," she said. "*Please* come sit with me. I'm Amara."

"I'm Whitney," the woman said, sitting down as Charlie's cries began to fade. Up close, she exhibited some of the markers of new motherhood after all—the darker skin underneath her eyes, a section of hair that had escaped the taming influence of the blowdryer. Perhaps her baby *wasn't* a perfect angel. "God, remember when you could go to a coffee shop like it was nothing?"

"Mmm," Amara said. "You could stay as long as you wanted."

"You could sit and *think*."

"Well, only eighteen years to go, and then we'll be able to do it again. What's eighteen years?" Amara said.

Whitney laughed, tilting her head back, a warm, wonderful sound, and the two of them kept chatting, giddy to find a fellow traveler in the same uncharted land, swapping stories about motherhood, trading recommendations about playpens and pediatricians.

"And do you like your ob-gyn?" Amara asked.

Whitney's face tightened. Amara had clearly hit upon a sore subject. "I think I want to switch. I just came from an appointment"—she hesitated, then lowered her voice—"where he tried to push a bunch of *Xanax* on me."

"Really?"

"I don't think he was even listening to me! It was so practiced, like he does it for every mother that comes in, just hands them some free pills and a prescription instead of actually having a conversation." Whitney indicated her bag, outraged. "I'm just going to throw them out."

"You could sell them on the black market, make some cash," Amara joked. "Or you never know if you might have a long flight sometime, and it'll be handy to have them lying around."

"Good point," Whitney said, then rolled her eyes. "I'll shove them in a desk drawer or something, let them gather dust." She paused. "Sorry. Strange day. Would you mind . . . maybe not telling people about the whole Xanax thing?"

"Ah," Amara said. "Unfortunately, I've already hired a skywriter."

Whitney let out that wonderful laugh of hers again. Then she propped her chin on her hand and leaned toward Amara. "Not to come on too strong," she said, "but I'm starting a playgroup of new mothers in the neighborhood. Our first meeting is next Tuesday. You should come."

So Amara joined the playgroup. And then her life *really* went down the shitter.

Everything in playgroup was expensive. You had to pay for the music and those fucking diamond-encrusted vitamins and bring good wine every once in a while, because even though Whitney was unbelievably generous—God, she even surprised them at Christmas by presenting them with a package for a group wellness retreat in the spring!—it would have been rude to enjoy her hospitality every time without making a single contribution of your own. Then there was the problem of spending hours with a bunch of gold medalists in the field of competitive mothering. None of the women was overt about it, but Amara had a highly cultivated bullshit meter. She knew when other women were judging her and trying to outdo one another.

Still, imagining going back to the stay-at-home life she'd had *before* that coffee shop meeting with Whitney made her stomach roil with dread. Dread about what the other women would say (or *not* say) about her if she disappeared. Dread about what she might do if left to her own devices. (Would she also end up in the hospital for a spell, like Joanna? Would Whitney once again collect money from the other women to send flowers?) So if she wanted to stay in the club—and Lord help her, she did—she would have to dig a little deeper into her private emergency bank account.

Chapter 7

When Whitney opened her door for Claire on Tuesday, Whitney's smile was so tight that Claire thought she might pull a muscle in her cheek.

"Hi," Whitney said. "A little heads-up: My husband is home today with a horrible cold, but he still has to get work done, the poor guy, so we're trying to be as quiet as a bunch of crying babies and chatty women can be."

"Damn," Claire said. "My whole set list today was heavy metal, but I'll see what I can do."

Whitney gave a real smile then, although it evaporated back into a painted-on grin by the time they made their way into the living room. Gwen and Amara were both fussing over Amara's baby, trying to make him stop crying. (No dice. That kid had a set of pipes on him.) On the couch, Meredith was pouring a generous amount of wine into Ellie's glass while Ellie rolled her eyes at something. Vicki sat by the window, staring out at the trees. (Did Vicki talk? Perhaps she was a land-loving, bargain-striking mermaid who'd never managed to get her voice back from the sea witch.)

"Look who's here," Whitney said in a cheerful whisper. As Claire took her guitar out of its case, the other mothers said their hellos and began to gather on the rug. Amara gave her a curt nod. Meredith whispered something to Ellie, and Ellie cackled, her laugh echoing around the room. Whitney stiffened. "Sorry, Ellie. Could you be a little quieter? Grant's trying to work."

"Oops," Ellie said. "Sorry."

"Let's do some nice, mellow music today, huh?" Claire said.

"Yeah, that sounds fun!" Gwen said, trying to hold little Reagan on her lap. Reagan, normally so well-behaved, was extra wriggly today, as if, even though she couldn't control her own bowels, she too could sense the tension in the air.

Claire began to play "Twinkle, Twinkle, Little Star." There was a reason it was a classic. As the simple melody took hold, the babies slowly began to settle. Whitney caught her eye and gave her a grateful smile.

And then a door next to the bookshelf opened, revealing the man whom Claire had seen in Whitney's family photos. He was dressed smartly from the waist up, in a powder blue button-down shirt, but he wore gray sweatpants. He still looked like a Ken doll, albeit one with a runny, inflamed nose and, Claire guessed from the strain on his face, a pounding headache. The open door behind him showed an office in a state of disarray at odds with the cleanliness of the living room, with a large flat monitor on a desk, stacks of papers, and a few coffee mugs scattered around. Oh, he *definitely* worked in finance. Claire was willing to bet that, if she tried to talk to him about his work, she'd soon want to bludgeon herself to death with his computer monitor to escape the conversation.

He moved over to Whitney and stood behind her, putting a hand on her shoulder. "Hey, honey," Whitney whispered, reaching up to cover his hand with her own. The diamond on her finger caught the light from the fixture above. He nodded his head along to the beat as Claire played the rest of the song. Maybe it would have happened with the presence of any interloper, or maybe it was his maleness, but the group's attention trickled to him, heads turning to catch the reactions of this unexpected judge towering above them.

When Claire hit the final chord, he untangled his hand from Whitney's and clapped. "That was adorable," he said. "How's playgroup going, ladies?"

"Oh, it's good," said Gwen. "Thanks so much for having us. We love coming here."

"We're sorry you're sick, Grant!" Ellie said, pouting her lips out.

He shook his head. "These head colds. They really get you. Otherwise, believe me, I'd never wear sweatpants in front of such special guests." Even in the grip of a cold, he was a prep school Adonis, clean-cut and polite. If a man like this approached Claire in a bar, she'd assume he was about to ask for directions. Grant was not the sort of guy to hit on mere mortals.

"Want to join us for a bit?" Whitney asked.

Grant shook his head. "There's nothing I'd love more, but I've got a video conference coming up soon."

"That's too bad," Gwen said.

"So," Grant said, "the thing is, the music." He looked at Claire, holding up a conciliatory hand. "It sounds great, you've got a great voice, and hey, who doesn't love 'Twinkle, Twinkle'? But it's coming straight through that door."

"Well, how long is the call?" Whitney asked. "We can hold off on music for a little while, if Claire doesn't mind." She turned to Claire. "We'd pay you extra for your time, of course."

Under that plastic Ken-doll veneer, Grant's jaw tightened. "I don't think that's a good idea. You never know how long these things are going to go."

"Ah," Whitney said, pursing her lips, her cheekbones nearly slicing through her skin. She blinked. Grant looked down at the Rolex on his wrist and frowned at the time he saw there.

Claire glanced around the circle. Meredith, Ellie, and Gwen wore blandly sympathetic looks on their faces. Amara had no such shield, and for a second, she and Claire locked eyes. (Vicki was sticking her finger into her son's mouth and staring at him as he gnawed on it.)

Then Whitney clapped her hands. "Oh, I know!" she said. "What if we had music on the balcony? We've got such a lovely view of the park, and lots of comfy chairs."

"It's freezing," Amara said.

"I can try playing softer," Claire said.

"Maybe we should just call it off for today," Meredith said, glancing at Ellie.

"Yeah, maybe," Ellie said. In the ensuing silence, they all looked at Whitney.

"Oh," she said. She was still smiling, her eyes bright, but in her lap, one of her hands was squeezing the other, digging nails into skin. "Well—"

"Hey," Grant said, holding out his arms triumphantly, "I've got a great idea. Gwen's apartment!"

"What?" Whitney asked.

"We went there for the Christmas party, right? It's just a couple blocks away, and it's got plenty of space. Win, win!" He turned to Gwen. "That is, if you don't mind."

"I . . . ," Gwen said. "Well, sure. That could be fun."

"There you go!" Grant said as if he had just thrown a life raft into the water.

"Ooh," Meredith and Ellie said in unison, reaching out to grab hold.

"Field trip!" Whitney said, but in her lap, her fingernails kept digging.

So the process of packing and buckling began. Claire had never realized that it was all so complicated, that two blocks could feel like two miles, that there were a million new accessories with which one began to travel in order to keep a tiny human contented and alive. She zipped her guitar back into its case as the women stuffed their babies into coats with varying degrees of ease. (Reagan lay there good-naturedly. Charlie twisted and wriggled while Amara tried to cocoon him.) As Grant disappeared back into his office, Whitney followed him in.

Meredith and Ellie made eyes at each other and scooted their baby prep over nearer to the office door, pretending to be fascinated by zippers. Whitney's voice was too soft to travel, but some of Grant's words floated into the living room easily enough, a snatch of *Is this really such a big deal?* here, a snippet of *Just a playgroup* there.

Back in Claire's hometown, the church drummed it into the girls at Sunday school that they were special, meant to be cherished, but that ultimately, husbands were the boss. Apparently you could get a degree from Harvard and a fancy New York apartment, and still, some things would stay the same.

After a couple of minutes, Whitney came marching back out, spots of pink burning high on her cheeks. "Well," she said, "shall we?"

They all gathered in the foyer. Meredith and Ellie were nearest the door, but they weren't turning the handle. "Oh," Meredith said, "I think we're forgetting the goody bags."

Whitney stared at her for a moment, then smiled. "Of course! Be right back." When she reappeared, she handed each of the mothers a little cream-colored bag made from thick, buttery card stock and tied with wide black ribbon handles. Claire inwardly rolled her eyes.

Then the great caravan procession made its way out into the world. Only some of the women could fit in the elevator at a time with their strollers, so they went in shifts: Meredith, Ellie, and Vicki going down first to wait in the lobby, Gwen and Whitney next. As Amara wheeled her stroller forward to join them, her baby threw his sippy cup out onto the floor. "Go ahead," she said to Claire, bending down to pick it up. "I'll get the next one."

Amara's fingers were just closing around the cup when Charlie hurled a Ziploc bag of rice cereal out the other side of the stroller. When it hit the floor, it exploded, bits of cereal pinging everywhere like confetti. "Oh, fantastic," Amara said.

Some reflex stopped Claire short as the elevator doors closed on Gwen and Whitney. She reached down to gather the pieces of puffed rice from the floor.

"You don't have to—" Amara said.

"It's fine," Claire said.

They swept the pieces off the tile and into their palms in silence. Amara moved quickly, spurts of breath coming out her nose. Then she brushed the cereal into a pocket of her diaper bag, holding it open for Claire and pushing the elevator button with her other elbow.

"Thank you," Amara said.

"No problem."

The elevator arrived, its doors sliding open in one smooth, nearly noiseless motion. As they began their descent, their reflections in all the mirrored panels made the elevator seem full for being so quiet. Then, staring straight ahead, Amara spoke.

"So that was weird, right? I'm not insane?"

Claire glanced at her. "Yeah," she said. "Really weird."

"Like we'd all time-traveled back to the nineteen fifties. I've never felt less like a feminist in my life."

Claire bit her lip. "How many men does it take to screw up a playgroup?"

Amara gave a rueful laugh. "One, apparently."

———

Gwen lived in a brownstone. Not an apartment in a brownstone. Not a brownstone where someone else lived in the basement. Gwen lived in the whole thing.

Some of the women had been there once before for Gwen's Christmas party, but Meredith and Ellie had already bought double-date tickets to *Hamilton* before Gwen's invitations went out. To them, Gwen's place was entirely new, and they cooed over all four stories of it.

"This is *so* beautiful," Meredith said.

"We should have playgroup here more often!" Ellie said.

"Oh, really? Thank you," Gwen said with the blushing alertness of an understudy thrust into the spotlight. "Now, let me see what I can rustle up for snacks. And we *are* a shoeless household."

Where Whitney's apartment was sleek and modern, all clean white lines, Gwen's was classic and old-fashioned, with dark patterned wallpaper, Oriental rugs, and a chandelier hanging from the living room ceiling. A gleaming piano sat against one wall, and there was even a real fireplace with a basket of wood next to it. Signs of an older child marked the house—a scooter tilting against a wall in the entryway, a pair of gossamer pink fairy wings discarded on the cushioned window seat. Claire longed for everyone else to disappear so that she could pour herself a glass of whiskey (this would be the kind of house with an *excellent* liquor collection—she just knew it), climb onto that window seat, and stay there, listening to the sounds of traffic and passersby and staring out at the street as the sun dipped low in the sky. Did Gwen ever do that? Probably not. Gwen didn't seem like the kind of woman who wanted to just sit and think for hours. Window seats were wasted on the wrong people.

"John keeps trying to convince me that we should move to a brownstone," Ellie was saying. "I *need* a doorman. But if any place was going to change my mind . . ."

Whitney stood in the center of the room, and though she smiled and looked around with everyone else, her arms were folded across her chest like a teenager on the sidelines of a dance. *The hostess becomes the hosted,* an old-time narrator voice intoned in Claire's head, and for a brief moment, she looked for Amara, wanting to say it to her, before shaking herself out of the impulse.

"Look at these family photos!" Ellie squealed, peering at the mantle as Vicki, bouncing her baby against her chest, went wandering out of sight.

"Oh, my God, Gwen, you were a little angel," Meredith said as Gwen reentered the room with a heaping plate of glistening cherries and a bottle of wine.

Claire bent forward to look at the photo Meredith was pointing at—Gwen, probably around age five, with a head full of golden curls and a smile splitting her chubby face wide open. She stood on a lawn with two glamorous adults—her parents, no doubt—and a boy a couple of years older than her, with similarly fair features, his eyes wide as if he'd been startled by the camera flash.

"Is that your brother?" Claire asked, and Gwen nodded. "What does he do?"

Gwen bit her lip, hesitating. "He's . . . he's between things at the moment. He hasn't been well lately."

"Oh. I'm sorry," Claire said, and Gwen gave her a small, sad smile.

"Stop!" Ellie shrieked, looking at a different picture. "Wait. This is Christopher? Gwen, your husband is a fox!"

"Um, yes, please!" Meredith said, fanning her face.

Claire leaned toward the picture in question, propped up next to a couple of framed photos of the children—Gwen in a wedding dress, a man in a tuxedo with his arm slung around her. Yup, "fox" was accurate. He wasn't conventionally handsome—no Ken doll for Gwen. Somehow that made him more attractive. He had curling, glinting hair that fell over his forehead, a prominent nose, big, wild eyebrows. Nothing about him was pretty. He was probably amazing in bed.

Hey, good for Gwen.

"If I'd known you all were coming over, I'd have gotten some more appropriate snacks. Just keep the cherries away from the babies," Gwen was saying as she passed around the gorgeous plate of fruit. "Because of the pits."

"You should definitely take a picture for your Insta here, Whitney," Meredith said.

"No, no," Whitney said. "I don't want to put a picture of Gwen's house online if she doesn't feel comfortable with photos."

"Oh, gosh," Gwen said. "Well, as long as you don't put my address in the caption, I suppose it's fine. Maybe by the piano? Unless it's too dark over there."

Amara appeared at Claire's side. "Gwen's cousin put a picture of her kid online, and it got used on a child porn site," she explained in a low voice as they watched the other women gather around the piano bench. Whitney sat down with Hope in her lap.

"Yikes," Claire said back. In the sudden, blinding flash of the camera, Whitney pressed Hope's tiny fists against the piano keys and smiled.

Chapter 8

Hot with embarrassment and shame, Whitney blinked a few times. Where was Amara? Over in a corner whispering with Claire, of all people. Whitney took some deep breaths, trying to will herself into a kind of meditation, to be at peace, even as Ellie and Meredith crowded around the photo that Gwen had just taken and declared it to be beautiful.

Whitney wanted to be generous and kind. She wanted to be the woman on her Instagram—her best self, whose most confessional transgressions were *Today I got a little grumpy with Hope* or *Sometimes I wish I could sleep for a million years!* She wanted to focus on her daughter and not worry about whether or not the rest of the playgroup women were making soft, snide remarks to one another about her marriage. She wanted to slap the self-satisfied smirk off of Gwen's face and then get the hell out of her brownstone, back to where she was less likely to make decisions that could completely upend the careful curation of her life.

She'd told herself, after Gwen's Christmas party, that she was never going to come back here. Arrogant, self-involved Grant had no idea what he'd done.

Gwen's Christmas party had been the first nonparenting-related social event that Whitney had attended since Hope's birth. She and Grant hired a teenage girl who lived on the fifth floor of their building and paid her an exorbitant amount to sit in front of their TV while Hope slept, even though the girl's allowance was probably more than Whitney's mother had earned as a dental hygienist. (But there was a bonus. The girl came with reinforcements: her parents a mere elevator ride away if Hope wouldn't stop crying and the girl panicked.)

Whitney loved Christmas in New York. Perhaps *real* New Yorkers grew to resent the decorated department store windows drawing Midwesterners like moths, but her trashy-tourist heart loved them and always would. She pictured taking Hope downtown to see them when she was a little older and could appreciate them, both of them gaping in delight at the animatronics display, then wending their way over to the Bryant Park holiday market, taking bites of warm Nutella-filled crepes, watching the ice-skaters in the shadow of the Christmas tree.

She'd been so excited for the party, even asking Grant if he would watch Hope one weekend afternoon so that she could go out and buy a new dress. The first experience of shopping for a pretty outfit post-baby was a dispiriting one. Her body translated into new, nonstretchy clothes in all sorts of unflattering ways, the dressing room mirrors specially designed to highlight her stretch marks and lumps, as well as the fine lines just starting to make their way across her forehead. She'd always disdained those women with too-taut faces—she'd prefer to age gracefully!—but then she'd actually started aging. Now, as she looked at herself, she wondered if it was possible to find an understated plastic surgeon, someone who could help her maintain herself with an infinitely subtle hand.

Finally, though, she found a red dress, with an Empire waist that camouflaged the fact that her stomach still pooched out in a way she hated (she *wanted* to lose that final bit of weight, but leaving the house to exercise took energy she couldn't seem to muster) and a low lace bodice that emphasized the one part of her body that she actually liked better now.

She took her time getting ready for the Christmas party, even though putting Hope down took longer than anticipated. She wanted to make Grant's eyes light up when he saw her all dressed up again, the way they had prepregnancy, when they'd spun from the latest new downtown restaurants to weekend getaways and back again. Perhaps tonight could be a kind of reset for them—a chance to feel romantic after so many months of changing poopy diapers, after the disappointing birthday dinner, after the recent sleep-schedule debacle when he'd snapped at her that Hope was *fine* and she should stop staring at the video baby monitor.

But when Whitney made her grand entrance from the bathroom, Grant just glanced at her. "We finally ready to go?" he asked, clearly annoyed that he'd had to entertain the babysitter all by himself. He didn't say anything at all about the new dress.

She'd realized, soon after meeting him, that Grant could be a jerk. But there were benefits to being with someone who didn't make nice all the time. He was a jerk to people on her behalf so that she never had to be, so that she could be the one to smile at the waiter who had messed up her order while Grant instilled the fear of God in him. She could relax in their beautiful apartment, for which he'd done all the tough negotiating.

And, most important, he wasn't a jerk to *her*. He treated her like she was a precious thing, like she had proven herself worthy of more from him. Back before he'd proposed, she'd worried that things might change when she introduced him to her parents, and so she'd held off as long as possible, still making excuses months after she'd met his family over dinner at Jean-Georges. ("Our treat, of course," Grant's father had said, putting down his card like the thousand-dollar meal was nothing.) When Whitney had finally taken Grant to her childhood home, they'd suffered through an awkward dinner during which her mom served oversalted meat loaf and her dad reeked of stale beer. She'd turned to Grant in the car afterward, expecting a new hint of disgust in his eyes. But instead, he stroked her face. "Whitney, you are a marvel," he said, and she saw that her humble beginnings had only made her *more* precious to him, like she was a pearl that someone had accidentally dropped in a ditch, and Grant could help her reach the place where she truly belonged. She'd thought things would stay like that forever.

Recently, though, she hadn't been feeling much like a precious thing anymore.

The party was in full swing by the time they arrived. Gwen hadn't told them that she lived in a brownstone when she'd invited the playgroup (which was still reeling from the departure of Joanna, the members all reminding themselves that they were six now, not seven), and Whitney tried hard not to gape. Her guilty pleasure was looking at houses. In another life, she would have ended up a Realtor in the suburbs.

Gwen's living room was like all the best Christmas movies come to life, a far cry from the gaudiness of Whitney's own childhood front yard. A Douglas fir scraped the ceiling, decorated with glowing colored orbs, along with an assortment of old-fashioned ornaments in painted wood, silver, and gold. The table was laid with hors d'oeuvres (baked Brie with jam conquering the air, but she wouldn't eat it, no), and at a bar cart in the corner, a hired bartender poured Scotch for the men and champagne for the women.

Gwen came over to greet them with a smile on her face, a little red from the alcohol, tugging Christopher by the hand. "You made it!" she exclaimed, giving Whitney a brief hug. The physical intimacy surprised Whitney—Gwen was not particularly tactile, which was how Whitney could tell that she was drunk. "And you've met Christopher, right?" she asked, even as her gaze swept away from Whitney, scanning the party to make sure that everything was in place. Gwen was too uptight to be a natural hostess.

"Yes, my farmers market buddy!" Christopher said in a casual, friendly tone, reaching out to shake Whitney's hand. But as he took her in, the look that came over his face was not so casual. *He* had noticed her dress.

A little girl with wet hair came running out, weaving among the guests, hurling herself against Christopher's legs, trailed by a nanny with a look of horror on her face. "Rosie!" Gwen said. "What are you doing still up? You're going to be so tired tomorrow!"

"It's too dark!" Rosie wailed. The nanny began making apologies to Christopher, but he waved them off and knelt down to look his daughter in the eyes.

"Sounds like you need a story that lights your mind up nice and bright even when you close your eyes, huh?" Christopher asked her. Beside Whitney, Grant stifled a snort and took a big swig of his Scotch, but Whitney watched, riveted, as the little girl gave her father a solemn nod.

"I've got this," Christopher said to Gwen, then turned to Whitney and Grant. "Excuse me. I have a very important story to tell." He swung his daughter up to his shoulders and carried her off toward the stairs, the nanny following behind.

Whitney had been looking forward to talking with Amara and her husband, Daniel, a slightly nerdy man with a kind face and glasses, but they were already on their way out. "One drink and I'm exhausted, apparently," Amara said to Gwen, who hugged Amara goodbye before rushing off to greet some new arrivals.

Amara leaned in close to Whitney, Scotch on her breath. "Don't tell Gwen," Amara said as Daniel grinned and ran his fingers down her arm, "but we're leaving to go do something *really* wild." She and Daniel shared a conspiratorial look. "We're going to walk around in the dark, just the two of us."

"You crazy kids," Whitney said.

"You know it," Daniel said. "Maybe we'll even stop off at a

late-night diner, if we get too cold. Who can say where the night will take us?"

"Endless possibilities," Amara said, laughing. "As long as we get home by eleven P.M., because that's when our babysitter has to leave."

Whitney watched them go. When she turned back, Grant had started talking with some men he recognized from the hedge fund world. Whitney turned to one of them.

"What do you do?" she asked. He went on a monologue about mutual funds while she made pleasant, smiling exclamations. When he finished, he stared at her, waiting for her to ask him another question about himself. She was good at parties, good at talking to strangers and turning on the smile that made them feel endlessly fascinating. But the rigors of taking care of a baby had temporarily depleted her desire to make small talk. So she excused herself and plucked a champagne flute off a tray. Then she headed to the stairs, telling herself that she wanted to go exploring.

In college, Whitney had gone to open houses on the weekend. She scoured the paper for listings in the nice neighborhoods of Boston. Then she'd put on her most sophisticated outfit and some high heels and take the T to Beacon Hill's tree-lined streets. If anyone asked, she'd pretend she was a wealthy twentysomething, looking for a place for her and her fiancé to start a family. It was best when the houses were still totally furnished so she could see what wealth looked like to take notes for her own future. She wanted that house's kitchen, with its six-burner stove top, and *that* house's mantle, with the family photos arranged with just the right amount of clutter.

And sometimes, even after she and Grant had gotten married, long after she'd acquired the enormous apartment, she'd go to open houses when he had to work on the weekends. She never told Grant. There was something . . . not classy about it. After all, people like him who were born rich didn't need to go marvel at other people's homes. But her interest wasn't just covetousness— she loved to see the limitless ways that people made themselves a home. It was a reminder, coming upon her like a flash, that every- one had an inner life, one they attempted to translate into their own corner of the world.

Gwen's house was particularly exciting to look at—a grand, old, nostalgic place like something out of Edith Wharton, with dark carpets and wallpaper. Whitney passed a few others who had sought refuge from the main hub of the party and peered into one room on the second floor, a library lit only by a lamp on the desk. *Well,* she thought, *the door was open.* She stepped inside. It smelled just like she'd hoped it would—leathery, mixed with that particu- lar old book scent. A dark wood, wall-mounted ladder lay against one shelf, and she walked over to it, running her fingers over its smooth slats and then over the books on the shelf. Strange to imagine rigid Gwen's inner life coming out like this. Maybe she'd been one of those little girls obsessed with *Beauty and the Beast.* Or maybe this was all Christopher.

"See anything worth reading?" he said from the doorway, as if she'd summoned him into being there.

"Oh!" she said, startling. "You caught me. I'm being a snoop. I'm sorry."

"No need to apologize," he said, stepping into the room with her, the door swinging closed behind him. "Frankly, I'm disappointed with anyone who *doesn't* want to go snooping around this old place."

She smiled and finished the champagne in her glass. It buzzed and pinged around inside her. "What happened in the bedtime story?"

"The usual. Princess meets prince. They invent a bunch of robots to fight the invading dinosaurs. Rosie's a fan of genre mash-ups."

"She seems like a wonderful kid."

"She really is," he said, his face softening.

"Well," she said, self-conscious about being in a room alone with a man besides Grant, suddenly aware that Christopher looked very different in a suit from the way he did in a winter coat. "I should probably—"

"You need a refill," he said, gesturing to her glass. He pressed a button on the side of one of the bookshelves, and a row of books slid aside, like something out of a 1920s speakeasy, to reveal a shelf of bottles and glasses. He frowned at them. "Hmm. No champagne. Scotch or gin?" He caught her staring at the hiding place and held his hands up in the air. "Not my doing."

"Gwen's?" Whitney asked, incredulous. "And gin, please."

"Her father's. Gwen grew up here. She likes to keep things how they were." He poured a stream of gin into her champagne glass, the glug of it into her flute so much more immediate than the faint sounds of the party below them, and said in an offhand way, "It's like living in a museum."

"So does that make you a tourist or an exhibit?" she asked. He looked at her, cocking an eyebrow, as her stomach dropped. Every so often, to her own horror, her tongue sprinted ahead of her brain, hurtling over pleasantries and all the other barriers she'd erected, exposing the ill-mannered little girl within. She blushed. "I am so sorry. That was inappropriate." She indicated her glass and tried to make a self-deprecating face. "My tolerance seems pretty weak lately." He didn't answer, just put the cap back on the gin and put it away, sliding the cabinet closed as the silence grew oppressive. Conversation had always come so easily when they were sitting in the open air, the bustle of people around them distracting from what lay underneath. "You're not having anything?" she asked.

"I don't drink," he said.

"Oh." Against the almost indiscernible hum of Christmas carols from downstairs, a grandfather clock in the corner began to chime the hour. "That's a lovely clock. An antique?"

He sat on the edge of the desk. "You want to know if I'm an alcoholic, but you're too polite to ask."

"No," she said. "That's not—"

"Don't worry." He smiled a sly grin, like he was fully taking her in. "I won't tell anyone your secret."

"What?" she asked, folding her arms across her chest. "My secret?"

"That you're not as nice as you pretend to be."

"First of all," she said, "that's incredibly presumptuous. Second, are you an alcoholic?"

He laughed. Then he shook his head and pointed to the odd

bent of his nose. "*This* happened in my early twenties, when I was drunk, and it seemed like a good idea to climb a rotting tree." She winced. "After that, I decided that I wanted to be aware of my decisions. So now, if I climb a tree, I haven't wiped away any inhibitions beforehand. I don't have any excuses to fall back on afterward. I own what I do. I'm in control."

She *did* feel like she was in a museum, but not during the bright, good-for-you daytime. Like she was trespassing after-hours, and everything was shadowy, suffused with a sense of exciting menace. "But being in control *all* the time is no fun," she said.

"I'm not in control all the time," he said. "I have children."

"Right." She laughed. "Nothing like a baby to show you how powerless you really are. Maybe what I mean, then, is getting carried away. Don't you ever miss that?"

"No," he said, leaning back, the glow of the lamp casting his face into shadow. "I'd argue that thoroughly weighing an action makes choosing to take it even more rewarding."

Gooseflesh prickled the backs of Whitney's arms. "So, screw spontaneity? Hurray for pros-and-cons lists?"

"I'm not saying there's no room for spontaneity. But, for example," he said, standing up from the desk, "say I were to kiss you right now."

"Oh," she said, unsurprised and dismayed and tingling all at once.

"A hypothetical," he said, taking a step toward her. "I wouldn't be doing it because all the alcohol in my body gave me a momentary, ill-considered impulse or because whiskey made me want to touch someone, and you were the closest person around." He was inches away from her now, nearer with each word, the smell of him heady around her. "I would kiss you," he said, "because I think that you are interesting and sharp and very, very beautiful in that dress and because I don't think anyone has kissed you well in months. Because I—clearheaded and totally alert—want to and *have* wanted to since I met you. And that would make the kiss so much better than if I had just, as you say, gotten carried away."

"I'm still not convinced," she said, breathless.

"I'll prove it to you then," he said, and closed that final distance between their lips.

It wasn't that she forgot she was a mother. (Was such a thing even possible?) But as he backed her into the shelf, pressing her up against book spines, his hands in her hair and on her neck, she forgot the necessary skills of motherhood: the self-sacrifice, the pushing away of one's own needs. She was *all* need now. The rush of real desire came to her again. Over the past couple of years with Grant, sex had grown into a habit. And then, once Hope had been born, it had turned into a duty. She never particularly *wanted* to have it anymore. Breastfeeding had sucked out all the moisture in her body, and she had a hard time getting wet enough for sex not to sting a little bit at best and actively hurt at worst. But when she turned down Grant enough nights in a row, she saw herself turning into one of those cold shrew wives who always "had a headache" and made their husbands wait all year for a birthday blow job. For the good of her marriage, she just sucked it up and faked her pleasure.

Now, though, she was practically dripping, as a pant of anticipation escaped from her mouth. And the triumph of unexpectedly *being* desired came back too with the catch of Christopher's breath as he hardened against her.

But when he ran his hand up underneath her dress, his fingers inching toward that raw, wet place where she wanted him, remorse rose up in her, and she pushed him away, slapping his face once, hard, and then wiping her hand against her lips.

"Stop that," she said. "We aren't doing this." She rushed past him before he could say anything, afraid of dooming herself if she looked back. She wanted to cry from the shock of it. She clattered back downstairs to Grant's side, back to the role of compliant, pleasant wife.

But she hadn't stopped thinking about him. She'd started seeing Christopher's face when she'd closed her eyes with Grant (or, as she'd regained more and more energy, by herself during the day when Hope was down for a nap, sometimes multiple times in an afternoon, a voraciousness she hadn't felt since her first adolescent discovery of masturbation). She liked imagining that he thought about her too in similar moments. *A crush,* she'd told herself. *People get crushes. The important thing is not to act on them.*

She was going to forget about him, she told herself now, as she sat in his brownstone and breathed his air.

Chapter 9

Gwen ran the final uphill stretch of her route in Central Park, pushing Reagan in a stroller in front of her, as a twenty-three-year-old woman in a bright pink T-shirt shouted encouragement at her and the rest of the playgroup mothers. "Yes, mommies!" the twenty-three-year-old screeched. "Empower yourselves! You can do *anything*! No one is stronger than a strong woman!"

Whitney had gotten an invitation for a trial exercise class through her Instagram, which was adding followers so quickly that it made Gwen a little nervous, and had invited them all along. Gwen gritted her teeth and pushed herself as Whitney's Lululemon-encased bottom worked away in front of her. She felt an urge to laugh. The mothers had tried taking a different stroller exercise class once before, back when they'd first formed the playgroup, and it had been a disaster, far too intense for their aching bodies.

But this time, as they slowed down for a few final minutes of cooldown yoga, they all exchanged grins, flushed with pride as well as with exertion. They were Amazons, Wonder Women, whose bodies could go through hell and then bounce back better than before. The instructor came around and gave them all high fives as they caught their breath. "Amazing job, mommies," she said. "I'm going to have to go harder on you all next class."

They headed for the park's exit together, breathing in the first hints of spring in the air, pausing to wait for Amara, who was lagging behind to tend to a wailing Charlie. He had not been the biggest fan of whirling through the park with a bunch of sweaty women, voicing his displeasure at frequent intervals.

"Not bad, team! Remember the last time we took a class like this?" Whitney asked.

"Oh, my God," Meredith said. "Ellie vomited!"

"Hey!" Ellie said. "I think I'd eaten some bad shrimp earlier that day. At least I didn't just quit five minutes in like Amara and sit on a bench." Ellie put on her best approximation of Amara's accent. "'Leave me here to die. Tell Daniel I love him.'" The woman all laughed.

"And Joanna—" Gwen said. She cut herself off as the laughter faded, the women all replaying the scene in their minds. Joanna had simply started weeping as they'd run up their first big hill, a gasping, full-body cry, and when Whitney had stopped to comfort her, Joanna had pushed away her embrace. Then Joanna had grabbed her stroller and walked out of the park without saying goodbye. (*Yikes, I'm embarrassed,* she'd e-mailed them all that night with some blushing emojis. *Guess I'd better start hitting the gym more often!* Joanna had been very good at writing e-mails that made it seem like everything was fine.)

Now a couple of other moms approached. One of them, her face as beet red as the juice she had pulled out of her stroller, tapped Whitney on the shoulder. "You guys were incredible," she said. "I think I've seen your Instagram!"

"Whitney, right?" said the second mother. "Tell me your secrets!"

Whitney laughed. "Thank you so much," she said, glowing with pride.

"Seriously," the first mother continued, "you guys are so inspirational, and your babies are always so perfect and happy."

"Well, except . . . ," said the second mother, indicating her head in Amara's direction and grimacing, then looking back at the playgroup with a conspiratorial grin.

"'Well, except' what?" Whitney asked, her voice sweet, her eye contact with the second mother unwavering.

"Oh . . . I—nothing," the second mother said.

"Strange," Whitney said. "Because it *seemed* like you were about to trash our friend's baby. But that couldn't be it, because surely there's no possible world in which you imagined we'd be okay with that, right?"

Whitney looked around at the other playgroup moms for confirmation, and although Gwen had been privy to a Meredith-Ellie conversation or two in which they'd bitched about Charlie's ability to ruin a perfectly peaceful afternoon and how *surely* there was a way for Amara to keep him a little more under control, now they folded their arms and glared at the other women. "*Very* strange," they said in unison while Vicki and Gwen nodded. The first mother turned even redder than before in secondhand embarrassment, and the second mother wilted.

Amara came up to join the group, having calmed Charlie to the occasional whimper. "Thanks for waiting!" she said. "Shall we?"

"Let's," Whitney said, and waved at the other mothers. "Anyways, thanks for following the account! That's very sweet."

"And by the way," Gwen said to the second one as everyone else began to go, "your baby is getting way too big for that stroller. It's a wonder she didn't fall out."

After the playgroup had all parted ways, Gwen bounded up the stairs of her brownstone, Reagan in her arms. Gwen lived her life in an extremely regimented manner, but sometimes, when she was in a whimsical mood, she'd greet the portraits of her parents in the front hallway as if they were flesh and blood, leaning forward to kiss them on their oil-paint cheeks like she was a little girl again. She did so today. After a series of rough patches, everything had been going so well lately, thanks in large part, however improbably, to TrueMommy. She moved to pour herself a gin and tonic as a reward, then stopped herself. She had to pick up Rosie from school in forty-five minutes. And she didn't *need* the drink. She wasn't her father.

Gwen was six years old the first time she tasted gin. For Labor Day, her family had gone up to the Connecticut house, a mansion stretched like a beached whale along the shore in Westport. Her grandfather had bought the house in 1948 after he made his first million. Past generations of the family had been well-off enough—respected if nominal members of New York society, with a *Mayflower* relative to boot—but it was Gwen's grandfather who had gotten into real estate development and blasted them all to the stratosphere.

Gwen's father had grown up in the Connecticut house, the youngest of three and the only sibling to survive into adulthood. (His brother, Martin, died falling through the ice on a frozen pond at age nine, and his sister, Alice, hanged herself in her bedroom at seventeen as, downstairs, her parents argued about lobotomies.) Sometimes, on cold, windy nights, in certain rooms—the aforementioned bedroom, although it had been covered in heart-patterned wallpaper and turned into a playroom after a suitable period of mourning, or the wood-paneled library, where little Martin used to spin the creaky old globe and point out places he'd someday explore— you could feel the ghosts of the house come upon you, a chill rising on the back of your neck. Perhaps because of that, her grandparents had retired to Palm Beach, leaving Gwen's father as the house's owner, although Gwen's family lived primarily in New York.

Still, in the summer, the Connecticut house had been merry and golden. Gwen's mother would bring the children to stay in the country for a full two months while Gwen's father came in from Manhattan on the weekends or sometimes more frequently. Gwen's grandparents would fly up for a few weeks to join them. When they were sitting on the lawn, an acre of rolling green with steps leading down to the sea, as the sun caressed the tops of their heads, it was hard to believe that anything bad had ever happened, or could ever happen, there.

On Labor Day, guests came to eat fresh shellfish and drink

spritzers on the grass, as the birds chirped above and the sea purred below. The crowd was made up of fifteen or so people—relatives, some old friends of her grandparents, and a couple of friends of her parents. The couple brought a baby, upon whom Gwen doted, and a terrible nine-year-old son, who decided to educate Gwen and her brother, Teddy, in the story of their aunt Alice, bugging out his eyes while imitating Alice's final, twisting moments.

"I don't believe you," Gwen had cried. She hoped that maybe Teddy, age seven, would punch him, but Teddy didn't do those sorts of things. (He was so *sensitive*, she heard adults sigh sometimes.) So she grabbed her brother's hand and pulled him off to find their parents.

Their mother was standing at the food table, dishing potato salad onto a plate for her brother, Gwen's uncle Steve. (Her mother never seemed to fill up her own plate at these sorts of gatherings. "Aren't you hungry?" Gwen had asked her once, and Gwen's mother had said, "Oh, no, darling! I'm saving my calories for special treats." Gwen's mother was *full* of knowledge on how to save calories. The first three bites of any sweet were the best, so there was no need to have anything more. You should chew each mouthful of a meal twenty-five times before allowing yourself to take another.) Uncle Steve had come to the Labor Day gathering with his arm around the waist of a new lady, not Gwen's funny, loud aunt Jill, but a petite woman who stared at everyone with wide, scared eyes. Uncle Steve was a few beers in and correspondingly loose-lipped. "Jill had really let herself go," he was saying to Gwen's mother as she served him up some string beans. "You saw it happen. You understand."

"Mmm," Gwen's mother said. "It's a shame."

(Years later, as Gwen watched Joanna's deterioration over the course of her time in playgroup, the phrase "let herself go" kept ringing in her ears.)

"We hadn't been intimate in so long—" Uncle Steve began as Gwen tugged at her mother's sleeve, and Gwen's mother startled.

"Oh, darlings!" she said. "What's the matter?"

"We're having some grown-up talk," Uncle Steve said. "Run along now."

Gwen's mother pursed her lips, then smoothed Gwen's hair. "Do you need me, or could you talk to Daddy instead?"

So Teddy and Gwen went to find their father. They knew exactly where he would be—at the bar.

Alcohol was her father's most-cherished hobby. Her young, devoted mother was always an eager passenger on the drinking train for as long as she could manage to ride it—the "special treats" for which she saved her calories tended to be glasses of champagne— but her father was the engine that propelled it along. He was a solid man in his mid-forties who had played football in prep school, yet when he was crushing ice, shaving orange peels into delicate garnishes, and pouring out the perfect amount of whiskey into a glass, he became somehow lighter, almost a dancer.

While he had a sizable liquor cabinet in their town house in New York, the Connecticut house was where he truly indulged. He had hired men to block off a rectangular part of the basement and turn it into a wine cellar, complete with temperature control to keep the air cool. Beside the kitchen, in an area that had once been the breakfast nook, he had installed a wall of burnished, glass-fronted cabinets that held a collection of bottles. Gwen liked to put her nose to the glass, studying how the liquids changed in the shifting light, from sparkling gold to deep, deep brown. Near the cabinets, there was a freestanding mahogany bar, about four feet long, with little wells in it for ice buckets and the like.

Her father stood there in a light purple polo shirt, considering an empty glass, and the sight of him filled Gwen with the sort of relief that finally allowed her to burst into the tears she'd been biting back.

"Daddy," she said, the words spilling out as Teddy stood beside her, his eyes also welling up like deep blue lakes. "Daddy, Peter was telling us about Aunt Alice, and . . . and . . . it can't be true—it *can't*, can it? That it happened like that, in the playroom?"

Her father's lips tightened, and he shook his head. Then he put the glass down on the bar, knelt down, and opened his arms for them to run into. "I wouldn't trust Peter," he said into her hair, holding them tight. "He's a little weasel." He drew back and contorted his handsome face into a silly, rodentlike mask. Gwen managed a smile.

Teddy wiped his nose with his hand. "But what if she's a ghost?" he said. "And she haunts the house and comes to suck out our souls?"

"I don't happen to believe in ghosts," their father said. "However, if Alice *were* a ghost, she would be a nice, fun one. She'd bring you cookies from the kitchen as a gift in the middle of the night and help you play pranks on your mother and me. All right?" He straightened up and looked at his two sniffling children. "So, no more tears, eh?"

"I'll try," Gwen whimpered as two more teardrops slid down Teddy's cheek.

Her father glanced around the room to make sure they were alone. "Brave children," he whispered, "can get a very special treat."

Brother and sister looked at each other and swallowed their tears. "We're brave," Gwen said.

Their father appraised them and nodded. "So you are," he said. "Now, don't tell your mother." He took two small glasses from a cabinet and filled them with ice cubes. Then he pulled a bottle of a clear liquid off the shelf. There was a drawing of a man all in red on the front of the bottle. Gwen thought he looked noble, like a character from one of the princess movies she liked so much.

"Guess what this man is called," her father said, pointing at the picture.

"What?" she asked.

"A beefeater! Isn't that funny?" He splashed the smallest amount of liquid into each glass, barely enough to cover their dimpled bases, and handed one to each child. Then he poured a heftier splash into his own glass and held it out. Teddy stayed back, but Gwen stepped up. "Cheers," their father said, clinking with her. She took a sip, expecting the liquid to taste like water. The bitter bite of it made her recoil. Her father laughed at her body's shudder, at her prune face. "Sourpuss!" he said. So she took another sip, masking her disgust, forcing the rest of it down. It made a fiery trail into her stomach. Little sparkles lit up her limbs.

"Hold on now. Leave some for the grown-ups," her father said, and whisked the glass out of her reach. Encouraged by Gwen's example, Teddy took a sip and gave a similar shudder. Gwen put her arm around him. (Once, she'd overheard her father, five drinks deep, tell her mother that Teddy reminded him of Alice. "No," her mother had said. "No, it's just a phase. He'll grow out of it." It wasn't that Gwen *tried* to eavesdrop. She knew it was wrong, and she wanted to be a good girl. But at the Connecticut house, the grown-ups always got extra-chatty at a certain point in the night, and it was hard not to listen.)

"Our special secret, remember?" their father said, putting a finger to his lips and winking. His woodsy scent, his fresh-combed hair, that contagious smile—how she loved him, the P. T. Barnum of her childhood. Gwen was flying, and then she and Teddy went tumbling, chasing, out through the hallway and onto the lawn, where her grandparents and their guests sipped at fizzy drinks in the golden late-afternoon light, where nothing bad had ever happened or could ever happen. They sprinted past stupid weasel Peter, and Gwen knew Teddy wouldn't punch him, so she did it herself, slamming her small fist against his cheekbone, watching his mouth open in surprise and pain, and then running on, faster, until she collided with an older man with a kindly, handsome face, one of her grandfather's friends who picked her up when she fell backward on the grass (how *green* it smelled, how it prickled the backs of her legs).

"Are you all right, little lady?" he'd asked, and she'd nodded before running off again. Later, her grandfather had taken her by the shoulders, the veins standing up in his hands, and said, "That man used to be the president of the United States, Gwen girl. Go apologize like a nice little lady."

Her whole childhood seemed to take place in that golden afternoon light, where everything felt safe and warm, where she never doubted for a moment that her mother and father loved her, where her mother made her elaborate breakfasts in the morning and taught her piano in the afternoons (never yelling, always encouraging) and read her L. M. Montgomery books before bed, where they all took trips to Istanbul and Paris, and sunned at Caribbean resorts, and her parents drank and laughed and drank some more.

And she wanted nothing more than to give her own children a golden childhood too, where she cooked breakfast and taught piano and read them *Anne of Green Gables*, where they could gather with their grandparents on the lawn and know that they were loved.

Twenty years later, at the Connecticut house, her father poured himself a few drinks. (Was it three or four or five? She wanted to imagine him drinking each one, to sit with him in her mind, as if maybe she could pull his hand away and change things somehow.) She assumed her mother drank too, although perhaps not, given that she'd been trying to cut back her caloric intake even further, telling Gwen about a new fad diet each time they spoke on the phone. (Her obsession was sad. Gwen never wanted to be one of those women.) It was mid-January, a couple of days after a snowfall, and some of the back roads still hadn't been entirely plowed. Gwen's mother and father got into their car and headed toward a friend's house. Gwen's father always drove, just like he always managed the investments and always hired the handymen.

Five miles from their destination, the car hit a patch of black ice, spun out of control, and careened into a tree. Gwen's father died on impact. Gwen's mother died a couple of hours later in the hospital while Gwen was at a party, her phone on silent in her purse.

Could one really consider oneself an orphan at age twenty-six? Gwen didn't think so, and yet she hurt as if some childhood innocence had been yanked away. Her mother would never help her plan her wedding. Her father would never walk her down the aisle. She was alone in the world except for Teddy, and Teddy was not doing well.

It turned out, when she went through the family's finances with a lawyer, that they were less solid than she'd always thought, a result of some bad investments on her father's part, a frittering away of resources that they'd all assumed were endless. She arranged to sell the Connecticut house. The ghost of Aunt Alice would have to bring midnight cookies to some other children, not Gwen's.

A few months later, wounded, aching, she met Christopher at a wedding of a mutual friend. He laughed easily and danced with all the grandmothers. He reminded her of her father: that same charm, that same sweetness, that same lust for what the world had to offer. There was one difference, though—he didn't drink. She didn't realize at the time that he might have other vices. She only saw the golden life she could have with him. She reached out and took it.

Chapter 10

The great thing about having sex with strangers, Claire thought drunkenly as a guy she'd met earlier that night bent her over the cheap Ikea desk in her apartment, bills and junk mail falling to the floor around them, was that it was an excellent ego boost.

The bad thing about having sex with strangers, Claire thought the next day as she stared down at the toilet bowl in Whitney's bathroom, where a clear deflated balloon floated in the yellow, was that you had to deal with the consequences all by yourself.

She flushed the toilet, holding the handle down an extra few seconds, and splashed water on her face, hoping to disguise the red in her eyes. What a dumb ass she was. She'd been ten minutes late today, because she was so hungover, and she'd had to get a random guy out of her apartment even though he seemed insistent on making her an omelet, as if knowing how to cook eggs made him a feminist hero. She had choked out some gravelly songs for the babies, hoping that none of the mothers had noticed the rattle in her voice, waiting for the moment she could head home and go back to sleep. And now this disaster. She hadn't realized it had come off last night. She hated that something could live inside her body for twelve hours without her knowledge. She hated that more strange things were living inside her body still.

Amara was in the hallway waiting for the bathroom, using the moments of privacy to swipe at some game on her phone, when Claire came out of it.

"Sorry. Here," Claire said, holding open the door, but her voice caught on the last word.

Amara looked up, her eyebrows furrowing. "What's wrong?" she said.

"Nothing." Claire shook her head.

"All right," Amara said, stepping forward, one foot into the bathroom, before turning back around. "What's wrong?"

"I peed out a condom," Claire said automatically, all in one breath. She put her hand to her mouth, her eyes beginning to smart again. "Shit. Forget I said that. I was kidding. Everything's fine."

Amara stared at her for a moment, then nodded once briskly. "I'll be down in the lobby in ten minutes. Wait for me."

"What?" Claire asked.

"Perhaps I'm incorrect, but from every impression I've ever gotten from you, I assume you don't want to be a mother right now."

"Well, yeah—"

"So I'll meet you in the lobby in ten minutes."

"Really, I don't need—"

"It's nicer to have company for this sort of thing," Amara said. She stepped farther into the bathroom and began to shut the door, catching it at the last second before it closed. She leaned her head against the doorframe. "Besides, Gwen and Whitney have started planning Reagan's birthday party, and I'm bored out of my mind."

So twenty minutes later, Claire walked through the rows of toothpaste and shampoo to the counter in the back of a CVS as a Katy Perry song pulsed through the air, Amara pushing her stroller beside her. The guy behind the counter was even younger than Claire (when did she get older than people with real responsibilities?), and briefly, she imagined the version of her life where she'd majored in something besides music and then straightaway slid behind a counter and into a world of benefits and nine-to-five schedules and stifling yawns behind a hand when she thought no one was around, like the pharmacist was currently doing.

"Hey," she said, stepping forward, as Amara lingered by the rack of trashy romantic paperbacks, smirking at a cover of a shirtless man next to a motorcycle.

The pharmacist startled and hastened to close his jaw. "Sorry," he said. "What can I do for you?"

"I need Plan B," she said, staring straight at him. The only other time she'd needed it, after an ill-advised night celebrating her eighteenth birthday with a boy who could have convinced her to do anything short of murder (he had *promised* her he was going to pull out, and then he hadn't), the two of them had driven two towns over so they wouldn't be recognized. While he waited in the car, she had stared down at the counter at the pharmacy while she'd asked, and then when she'd looked back up, she'd seen the accusation *Slut* all over the pharmacist's face, clear as if he'd tattooed it on. At least this guy's bovine face remained placid. And, Claire thought, Amara had been right. It was nicer not to have to do it alone.

"Sure," he said, and pushed himself off his seat to poke around in the back. He moved sloth slow. The Katy Perry song ended, and a new song began piping through the speakers. Claire's lungs constricted. As Marlena's yowling vocals began, Claire counted down very slowly from ten in her head, an incantation to bring cow-faced sloth-speed man back. Instead, Amara wheeled her stroller over to her side as an elderly man thumped his way down the aisle and got in line behind them.

"This is the song Ellie and Meredith love so much," Amara said, pointing into the air. "The 'Idaho Eyes' one."

"Oh," Claire said. "Oh, okay." Amara gave her a weird look as the pharmacist returned, walking in time to the beat of the music.

He plunked the box of Plan B down on the counter. "Do you want a bag?"

"Yeah," Claire said.

The corners of his thick mouth drooped down in disapproval. "Are you sure? We're encouraging our customers to be environmentally conscious."

"The ozone is disappearing!" the old man behind them piped up.

"Give her a fucking bag, please," Amara said.

The pharmacist and the old man exchanged glances and shook

their heads as the pharmacist slid the package into a plastic bag and tapped at his register. As he tapped, he bobbed his head to the song, humming along with the chorus. If she could get out of here before the bridge started, she'd be fine. "That'll be forty-nine ninety-five," he said.

"Do you know if insurance covers this at all?" Claire asked, trying not to look at Amara as the song's second verse began. The members of the new-and-improved Vagabond were probably partying in thousand-dollar-a-night hotel suites nowadays, and she was haggling over the price of birth control.

"Hmm," he said, screwing up his face in concentration. After a minute, he said, "I'm not sure. I could ask my boss."

"Okay, yeah, that would be good," Claire said.

"He's not in today," the pharmacist said. "And I'm not in tomorrow. Could you wait until the day after?"

"I— What? No," she said. Well, too late—there was the bridge of the song, Marlena's voice soaring on those familiar words. "That's not how Plan B works."

"Oh, really?" the pharmacist said.

"Good Lord," Amara said. She pulled her credit card out of her wallet and plunked it down on the counter. "Here, just use this."

Outside the pharmacy, they lingered in the afternoon's gray light, Claire's body turned in the direction of Central Park, Amara angled as if ready to head the other way.

"I'll pay you back," Claire said as Amara waved a hand dismissively. "Well, thanks. You really didn't have to do . . . any of that."

"I know," said Amara. "But the other option was going back to my apartment and staring at Charlie for hours, so in a way, perhaps you did me a favor."

"Then you're welcome," Claire said. A cold drizzle started up around them. Claire hugged her jacket closer. In the street, a taxi swerved in front of a car, setting off a symphony of honking. The pedestrians around them began to walk faster in anticipation of the drizzle becoming something worse while a man appeared from out of nowhere and set up on the corner, hawking ten-dollar umbrellas.

"You'd better go take that," Amara said, nodding at the bag in Claire's hand as she pulled a tarplike piece of clear plastic over the open part of Charlie's stroller.

"Yeah," Claire said. "Hey, thanks again. It was really nice—"

"Yes, yes, I know. I'm amazing," Amara said. "I'll see you next playgroup."

Claire laughed. "Okay. Bye." She bent down toward the clear plastic and waggled her fingers. "Bye, Charlie. Nice hanging out with you."

In response, Charlie shook his head no, then scrunched up his face and let out a wail, twisting away. Amara shut her eyes for a moment and gave her head a small shake.

"Sorry," she said. "He really is a good baby. He just doesn't like to show it very much."

"You know," Claire said, "I admire him. He's got spirit."

A smile began to curve on Amara's face, shyer than anything Claire had seen from her before. "You think so?" she asked.

Claire thought about the playgroups she'd been to, the looks some of the other mothers shot Amara when Charlie wouldn't stop crying, the way he was clearly the least well-behaved of all the babies. People probably didn't compliment Amara on her child very often. What a terrible feeling that must be. "Oh, yeah," she said. "He doesn't give a fuck. All the most interesting people are that way. He's going to grow up to do great things. Or become a serial killer. One of the two."

"Thanks ever so much," Amara said, rolling her eyes. "That last part truly is a comfort."

The rain started coming down more heavily, anointing them, getting into Claire's eyes so that she had to blink the drops away. "Oh, boy, this is going to be a fun trip home. Bye for real now," Claire said, and turned to go.

"Claire," Amara said. Claire turned back. "Do . . . do you have someone to make you tea and all that after you've taken the pill?"

"Um," Claire said.

"Because you could come back to mine. I'm close, and my husband won't be home for a while." Amara paused, pursing her lips. "God. Despite how it sounds, I swear I'm not trying to seduce you."

Fifteen minutes later, Claire lay on Amara's brown leather couch as levonorgestrel invaded her ovaries, decimating any unwanted invaders. Pow! Pow! Not fertilizing any eggs today, you devils!

She stretched out, her body already heavy and unsettled, and looked at her surroundings. Amara's apartment was small. Well, no, it could've eaten Claire's apartment for breakfast and still been hungry, but Claire's trips to Whitney's and Gwen's had skewed her expectations. Their apartments (or brownstones) held a sense of mystery—they could very well contain secret passageways or maid's quarters or a staircase to the roof. The entirety of Amara's apartment announced itself immediately. The three doors leading off the living room must have been a bathroom and two bed-rooms. The kitchen was only cordoned off by a half wall, so the noises floated straight into the living room—Amara bustling around, the teakettle emitting its high-pitched whistle. And while Whitney's and Gwen's homes were both decorated in one unified aesthetic (sleek for Whitney, classic for Gwen), Amara's home was more the product of a relatively well-off, busy couple who had bought whatever nice furniture caught their fancy at the time and plunked it down wherever it fit.

Well, and then there were a couple of luxury items—a small crystal bowl on a shelf that must have cost a fortune and didn't even have anything in it, a cashmere blanket on the couch with a tag from Saks Fifth Avenue that was the softest thing Claire had ever touched. Had Amara stolen those too, just gone into Saks and slipped them into her purse with that same frenzied desperation that Claire had seen on her face that day in Whitney's office? Claire shook her head, not wanting to think about that right now.

On the floor, Charlie crawled around, grabbing at anything that wasn't nailed down or baby-proofed—a well-worn, dog-eared baby book on the low coffee table (*The Foolproof Guide to a Happy, Healthy Baby*), a set of keys. He settled on Amara's large purse and stuck one of its handles into his mouth, gnawing on it like it was an ear of corn.

"All right, as promised, one cup of tea," Amara said, coming out of the kitchen and setting a steaming mug down on the coffee table. Claire sat up and wrapped her hand around it gratefully.

Tired of his gnawing, Charlie reached into Amara's purse and began scooping its contents onto the ground. The first to hit the floor was a pretty little bag, like the ones Whitney had given out the other week. "Oh, yeah, what's this whole goody bag thing about?" Claire asked as Charlie held the bag upside down and shook everything inside it out.

Amara picked up Charlie, stopping his destruction, and he kicked and wriggled in her arms as Claire plucked the goody bag from the floor, running her fingers over its pretty pattern of embossed golden leaves. "Oh, you know," Amara said as she carried Charlie to one of those bouncy freestanding baby seats, like an inner tube with no water. "Silly wellness things that people send Whitney because of her Instagram. She goes all out and makes us these little party favor bags of them. I think she has too much time on her hands." She slid Charlie in, and he began to jump, pounding at the garish neon piano key buttons in front of him until they released their tinny music. Amara returned to the floor in front of the couch, where Charlie had dumped everything, sat down, and began to gather it all back up with a sigh. "Let's see," she said, holding up a bar of soap in the air like a presenter on the Home Shopping Network. "Today, we've got special, toxin-free soap to make sure your baby's skin is soft as margarine." She picked up a small suede box, delicate and expensive-looking enough to house an engagement ring inside, with a tag reading *TrueMommy* in a clean Avenir font. "Organic mommy vitamins to make your hair shiny and give you the energy to go on. And finally," she said, waving a postcard in the air, "a coupon for fifteen percent off a Mommy-and-me yoga class that I will never go to."

"Man," Claire said, holding out her hand to take the goodies and put them back into the bag. "Whitney gets a lot of free shit. I should start a fancy Instagram."

"Right? The whole thing is kind of insane, but people love her, apparently. The Internet goes wild for beautiful young moms who make all the regular moms feel hopeful. Whitney is an achievable unicorn to them, like if they just drink enough kale smoothies and meditate for ten minutes a day, they'll wake up in her perfect life," Amara said, handing over the objects and then tensing up as though she was worried Claire was going to break the special soap she was stuffing back into the bag.

"I'll have to get her autograph at the next playgroup," Claire said, squinting at the fancy *TrueMommy* description: *A comprehensive supplement & metabolic optimizer for new moms*. "Well, that's a complicated way to say 'these pills will make you skinny.'"

"All right, they do a little bit more than that. Or at least they'd better. I'm paying enough for them."

"What?" Claire laughed. "Do they increase your sex drive and boost your IQ by fifty points too?" What a load of BS. Sure, she'd like to believe that eating activated charcoal could turn her into Heidi Klum, but at the end of the day, she was always going to be herself, unfortunately. She'd bet her left boob that TrueMommy was up-charging these moms like crazy, that these vitamins contained two dollars' worth of herbs but retailed for two hundred dollars.

Amara opened her mouth as if to argue, an unsettled look on her face. Then she bit her lip and got to her feet. "Well, to each their own. Shall I put on some music?"

Claire nodded, so Amara walked over to her phone and began scrolling through it. The bergamot scent of Claire's tea wafted up toward her, and she blew on the liquid, then took a small sip, lying back as the warmth coursed through her body and settled in her stomach. She closed her eyes. Then those familiar, hateful chords began pulsing out of a speaker. Claire startled and sat up. Amara leaned against the wall, watching her with catlike stillness.

"Um," Claire said. "Hmm, maybe we could listen to some jazz instead. Better for a rainy day."

"Don't you want to further your pop-culture awareness?" Amara asked, raising an eyebrow. "Meredith and Ellie would probably cream their pants if you played this in playgroup."

"I'd rather not make Meredith and Ellie cream their pants," Claire said as Marlena and Marcus began to harmonize:

> You'll take those Idaho eyes back to where they belong
> And I'll come too
> I don't belong anywhere except next to you.

"Anyway," Claire said, "I think I get the gist." Over in his baby jumper, Charlie pounded his fake piano keys again, and the metallic notes from that mixed with the lush sounds of the song. Claire's head began to throb.

"Why are you so weird about this song?" Amara asked, laughing.

"Because it's my band!" Claire snapped. Amara reached out and paused the music, and they sat in silence except for a fading sound from Charlie's contraption.

"*Was* my band," Claire said, looking down into the mug of tea before her, unused to saying it aloud. "They kicked me out because they found someone better, and then they got famous, and here I am."

Vagabond had been in the home stretch of a three-week tour when Claire's boyfriend, Quinton, called to tell her that he might have cancer.

She answered the phone flushed with excitement, fresh off having played through "Idaho Eyes" for the very first time in rehearsal, a spidey sense telling her that this new song was the best thing they'd ever done. Her first thought, when she heard the way Quinton said, "Hello," was that he had called to break up with her, and she felt a pang of sadness, because Quinton was so *normal* compared to all the charming, aimless artists she'd dated in the past. Quinton, who had gone to law school, got eight hours of sleep a night so that he'd be well rested for his job at city hall. He talked about art and politics with aplomb. He was training for a half marathon. Claire had a nice time with Quinton, and meanwhile, every time she turned around, another person she knew was getting engaged. She and Quinton had gone on a double date with Thea and her wife, Amy, and Quinton and Thea had traded law school stories.

When he left to go to the bathroom, Thea had said to Claire, "You should marry this guy." Since Claire barely spoke to her parents anymore and didn't much trust their opinions anyway, Thea was the most valuable family approval she could get.

But on the phone, what Quinton had to say was far worse than a breakup. Quinton had a strange rash that wouldn't go away. Quinton had a low platelet count. Quinton had gone to a doctor who told him that they couldn't know anything definitively until the tests came back, but that it *might* be leukemia.

"I know we've only been together for five months. So if it's cancer," he said, a wobble creeping into his voice, "you don't have to stay with me."

"What?" she asked, overcome with worry for him. "No, I wouldn't . . . I wouldn't do that. Of course I'll stay with you."

He let out a breath of relief. "I love you, Claire," he said for the first time.

"I love you too," she said, unsure how much she actually meant it and how much she knew it was what he needed to hear.

Over the rest of the night, as she and the Vagabond boys played for a couple hundred people in Pittsburgh and then went out to a bar to celebrate, a new kind of panic sunk in. What had she just committed to? Would being there for Quinton mean having to quit the band? She took a shot and then another. Marcus stuck by her side that night. Sometimes, after shows, he'd disappear with a pretty fan. Other times, if no fan caught his eye, he'd "accidentally" brush his hand against Claire's breast, then look at her to see how she reacted. (If she was being honest, she'd always carried a torch for him, but it was better to keep things professional, not to get into Fleetwood Mac territory.) She took some more shots, and this time, when Marcus put his hands on her hips, she didn't pull away or feign ignorance. And when he followed her into the bathroom and kissed her, she kissed him back until she felt the bile rising up in her throat and had to pull away to vomit. If she hadn't gotten sick, she didn't know how far she would have gone with him.

The next morning, she woke up resolute (and extremely hungover). They still had one more show left on the tour, in Philadelphia the next night, but she couldn't do it. She was going to surprise Quinton and take him to a bed-and-breakfast in the Hudson Valley, a distraction while he waited for his test results to come back.

"You guys can survive without me for one night," she said, attempting to be casual and jokey, avoiding Marcus's angry eyes. "I believe in you."

"But it's Union Transfer," Marcus said. "This show is fucking important."

"Hey," Diego said, "I bet my cousin, Marlena, could step in and sing whatever harmonies we need. She lives right outside of Philly, and she's a big fan, so she knows all the songs and totally gets our vibe." Claire had felt such relief, even kissed Diego on the cheek in gratitude, as Marcus reluctantly agreed.

So Claire and Quinton had hopped on a Metro-North train and hiked among the changing late-autumn leaves, holding hands, Quinton smiling stoically at all of Claire's frantic jokes.

On Saturday night, as Vagabond was preparing to take the stage in Philly, Claire and Quinton wandered, tipsy, down the streets of the little Hudson Valley town, which people said was the place where hip Brooklynites moved when they got tired of city living and wanted to have a family. Claire looked at Quinton. Maybe that wouldn't be too bad a life.

Music wafted out the door of a local bar, and they went into the noise, pushing through a crowd and ordering sour beers. On a small stage, a band of older men, nearing retirement age, or maybe just retired, played rockabilly tunes. Outfitted in bright suit jackets and funny, music-themed ties, they were talented guys, putting their all into it, wailing away, and Quinton held out his hand and pulled her close to dance. Around them, middle-aged couples twisted and waved their arms. She leaned against Quinton's strong chest. It couldn't be cancer. Or, if it was, they were catching it early enough that everything would be fine.

The beer coated her tongue as one song ended and another began, a Chuck Berry cover. The thirty or so people in the bar's low light danced as if they hadn't gotten a chance to move much lately, eager but with a certain stiffness. Quinton fit right in—he was always a little stiff when he danced. He didn't have a natural sense of rhythm, but he tried. It was endearing, usually.

Somewhere in the third song, Claire's feeling about the whole scene shifted. She couldn't say why. Nothing in particular happened. A sadness just overcame her. How many of these men onstage had thought they would lead exceptional lives, had been convinced they'd be the next Paul Simon? And how many of them now looked forward all week (or all month? How often did they get together?) to this one blip of playing other people's music for a tipsy crowd, this one chance to time-travel back to the false promise of their youth?

She wanted to do something astonishing with her life. The potential to be astonishing with Vagabond hovered, just out of reach. But she could blink and end up a regular here. Around her, people laughed and smiled, but it was like she'd gotten a particular form of X-ray vision she couldn't turn off, and now all she saw was an undercurrent of regret beneath it all. Her limbs tightened up. She drained her beer. Then she tugged on Quinton's hand and asked if they could go.

Quinton didn't understand when she tried to describe it to him on their walk back to the B and B. "I thought it was fun," he said.

"No, it wasn't *bad*. I'm not saying that. They were good musicians, and that's what made it even sadder," she said, stumbling over her imperfect words.

"Maybe this is what they want for themselves," he said, so she let it be.

Surely there was a way for her to be there for Quinton, if he needed her, and to get back to Vagabond as soon as possible. And when she *did* get back to Vagabond, she needed to stand up for herself more. She needed to show up to practice with song lyrics or even full songs rather than just hoping that Marcus would ask for her help. She wanted to be more than just the token female eye candy.

And then on Sunday morning, when Quinton was in the shower, Claire stretched out in their two-hundred-dollar-a-night room with its rose-patterned wallpaper, pulled up a video from the Vagabond show on Facebook, and realized how much she'd fucked herself over. Marlena strutted around the stage, gorgeous, her voice a weird, thrilling yowl. Marlena was curvy where Claire was flat, with dark, striking features while Claire looked like a spare member of the Weasley family. Marlena and Marcus sang into the same microphone for "Idaho Eyes"—how could they have debuted "Idaho Eyes" without her?—their lips almost touching, their bodies moving in perfect rhythm, and the sexual chemistry was so strong, it even turned Claire on a little before she closed out of the video in disgust.

Marcus and the others moved fast, sitting her down for the talk just a few days later. She'd been heartbroken and wildly angry, and spent a lot of time reading articles about Pete Best, the first drummer for the Beatles, who the others kicked out when they were right on the cusp of success. Pete Best, at least, had had the comfort of rumors that the other guys had been jealous, that he'd been the most good-looking one, attracting the most ardent fan attention, and so Paul and John and George had traded him in for goofy-looking Ringo, who was safer. Claire knew that the Vagabond guys had traded up in every way.

All those times she'd spitefully mailed her parents clippings of Vagabond reviews or interviews, wanting to show them that they had been wrong for trying to hold her back, came swimming into her mind, filling her with a hot, sinking shame. Her entire grandiose view of herself as a special talent had come tumbling down, a pyramid crumbling into dust. She'd paraded from Ohio to New York like an emperor but—surprise!—she hadn't been wearing any clothes. The story didn't talk about the emperor afterward, did it? How he felt when everyone realized that he'd been duped, that his expensive new suit was no suit at all? She wanted to know what had gone through the emperor's head, how he'd dealt with it. Did he sleep with any lady who would still have him? Did he drink himself to sleep each night? The story didn't respect him enough to say.

But the *really* bad feelings had kicked in when the "Idaho Eyes" music video went viral, and suddenly, Vagabond was everywhere, from the radio to the home page of Pitchfork to *Saturday Night Live*. Claire tried to hate-watch their *SNL* performance, but it just made her feel horrible because Marlena *was* better than she would have been, and if it were any other band, she would've been a fan.

Quinton didn't even have cancer. It had been fucking bedbugs all along causing the rash—the same bedbugs Claire woke up to find in her own apartment a couple of weeks after Vagabond kicked her out. Quinton had helped her stuff all her shoes and books into bags and sat with her while she did all her laundry on the hottest setting, and she knew that she would never be able to stop blaming him, even though he hadn't done anything wrong. So in short order, she had gone from having a career she loved, a boyfriend she liked, and a certain sense of self-respect to having jack shit.

Excellent, Claire thought, as her eyes welled up. She was breaking down in front of Amara for the second time that day. She hadn't meant to tell her *everything* like that. Not even Thea knew about the Marcus kiss. "Please, don't spread this around to the other moms," Claire said. "It's been nice being around people who don't just see me as the girl who wasn't good enough to stay in the band, you know?"

"Of course I won't," Amara said, an unfamiliar look of sympathy on her face. She shook her head. "That's rubbish. The way they treated you was rubbish. But if it makes you feel any better, they're nothing special anyway. The only really interesting part of that song is the bridge."

Claire let out something halfway between a laugh and a sob. "I wrote the bridge," she said. She'd never asked for an official songwriting credit—she'd done only that one part, and only because Marcus had come into rehearsal completely stumped, soliciting ideas, and there'd been a free-form brainstorming session in which everyone had tried things, and hers ended up being the lines that worked best. And then they were all celebrating the completion of the song, and she hadn't wanted to be a bitch and ruin the moment by demanding credit.

"So what are you going to do?" Amara asked.

"Well, obviously, the dream is to show them that I'm doing just fine. I've been on the lookout for bands that need singers, but I keep freaking out at the prospect of actually auditioning for them." She rolled her eyes. "Maybe I should just find a rich guy who's into artistic types and have his babies."

"I'm sorry," Amara said, sitting down next to her on the couch. "You wrote the only good part of the number one song in the country, and you're going to give up? Don't be an idiot. Why are you trying to just be the girl in someone else's band?" She paused and gave Claire that appraising look she was so good at, the one that left no room for secrets. "Play me something. Not a kids' song. Not a cover. Something of yours."

"Oh," Claire said, shifting uncomfortably. "I think I've embarrassed myself in front of you enough for one day."

"What, you need me to share my hidden shames?" Amara asked. "How about this: I'm freaking out that my baby still isn't standing, my husband and I haven't had sex in two months, and—" She stopped short.

"And?" Claire asked, an image coming unbidden into her mind—Amara with her hand in Whitney's desk drawer, desperation all over her face.

But Amara just shrugged. "And I tried to go back to work and fucked it all up."

"Do you want to talk about it?" Claire asked.

"No. What I *want* is for you to play me a song. So are you going to or not?"

Amara was sitting up ramrod straight, a wry twist to her mouth, drumming her fingers on her knee, and Claire knew how the movie version of this moment went—she picked up her guitar and sang something beautiful and revealing and *true* (while the camera slowly zoomed in on her face), and Amara loved it and called up all her entertainment-industry contacts right then and there. But Claire didn't have a song to play. She'd written snatches of lyrics back in the good Vagabond days and helped Marcus refine his ideas, but she had nothing full to call her own. She'd sat around pitying herself, only to be wildly unprepared when opportunity arose. "I can't yet," she said. "But can I let you know when I'm ready?"

The wry twist disappeared from Amara's mouth. "Yes," she said. "But, and I mean this in the nicest way possible, don't wait forever to get your shit together, all right? Life only gives you so many chances."

Chapter 11

It was important to engage in a little self-care when you were a mother, Whitney told herself, as she handed Hope to the moon-faced Hunter College student she'd hired to babysit. "I'll only be a couple of hours. I'm just going to do a few errands and get a massage," she said, and bent down to put her heels on. But in unfamiliar arms, Hope reached out a dimpled hand to her mother and her face began to crumple.

"Ma! Ma!" Hope cried.

Was there any worse sound than your child wailing your name? A wave of guilt crashed over Whitney. "Oh, no," she said, her arms automatically reaching to take Hope back.

"We'll be fine!" the babysitter said, cheerful as a flight attendant during turbulence, so Whitney let her arms drop back down to her sides, where they hung, restless.

"You've got the emergency numbers—"

"Yes."

"And you know she might be allergic to nuts, so we just steer clear of them—"

"Right."

"And you're certified in baby CPR."

"I am," the girl said. "Don't worry. Just go! Enjoy your 'me' time!"

In the taxi, Whitney's feet began to sweat. She pushed her shoes half off so that they dangled on her toes, trying to air out while avoiding the dusty floor of the cab. She took off one heel entirely, pretending to examine it, and gave it a discreet sniff, as the driver answered her questions about how long he'd been in the United States (nineteen years), what his children were studying (medicine for the girl; the boy couldn't decide yet). The lining of the shoe smelled sour and old, an unshakable record of every time she'd perspired.

She told the driver to drop her off in front of a shoe store. Despite having only a few minutes before her appointment (and when your baby was in the service of a babysitter, every moment counted), she tried on a pair of nude heels in a size seven. The fabric was cool against her skin, exuding that contagious new shoe smell, so she bought the heels, throwing her old shoes in her purse. Then she walked the remaining block to the Windom Hotel and Spa on East Forty-Seventh Street and Second Avenue, breaking the shoes in, feeling where a blister would form on her heel but not yet, not today.

The hotel had recently undergone a renovation, opening what

online buzz said was one of the best spas in that area, even if not too many people knew about it yet. She pushed her way around the revolving door and into the calm, hushed lobby. Reception desk to the left, spa entrance to the right. She looked at the suite number on her phone and took the elevator straight up.

On the eighth floor, she walked to room 811, her heels leaving little impressions on the hallway carpet. She hesitated before knocking. It wasn't too late to turn around, to keep all of this relegated to a fantasy, to greet Grant when he came home from work that night with a clear conscience. To let him turn to her in the darkness after Hope had fallen asleep and try for a few long minutes to get her off efficiently, like she was a piece of furniture he was trying to assemble and the damn instructions weren't clear. To tell him again that it wasn't going to happen for her that night and that he shouldn't worry. To let him jerk back and forth above her while both of them kept their eyes closed, him thinking about who knows what, her thinking about the man inside room 811.

She knocked on the door. When Christopher answered, he looked at her as if she were already naked. "I didn't know if you'd come," he said, a smile curling on his face. The room behind him was beautiful without being extravagant. The duvet had a crease in it where he'd sat to wait.

"I didn't either." Her voice came out girlish, small somehow. She wondered if Hope had stopped calling after her.

After that playgroup when Grant had been so rigid and embarrassing, when she'd posted that picture of herself and Hope at Gwen's piano, Whitney got a direct message: *I see you made a visit to the museum today.* It was signed *—An Exhibit.* Her heart skipped around in her chest. Some resolve inside of her crumbled. She answered back.

"I shouldn't be here," she said now to Christopher, and he reached out, looping his finger around the belt on her waist.

"Whit. Let's not do this part," he said. "Where we have to convince each other. We already know."

So she nodded, stepped forward, and followed Christopher inside.

Chapter 12

Over the weekend, Claire sat down to write something beautiful and revealing and true. She turned off her phone and put it in the bathroom. She looked at herself in the mirror. "Stop being a waste of space," she told her reflection. She lit a fucking candle.

And then she sprawled on the floor with her guitar on her lap. She was going to contemplate life, digging Grand Canyon deep into her soul. Something came to her as she stared at the sputtering candle, an idea about embers in December (a spark in them yet, despite their regret), and she spent a half hour setting it to music before realizing that it was sentimental bullshit. Also, embers couldn't feel regret. She couldn't anthropomorphize embers. She didn't work for Pixar.

Then she tried something about Quinton. Maybe there was a moment in that relationship, an instant when she had felt very deeply that she loved him. That one late night at his apartment, after they'd had sex, when they'd gone to the kitchen to look for a midnight snack, and barelegged and giddy, they'd danced around eating peanut butter in the light from the refrigerator. She sang a makeshift chorus. She pictured Amara listening to it, scorn curling around her lips. Claire had an urge to smash her guitar into a thousand tiny wood shards and to exile herself to Antarctica. Forget digging canyon deep. It was more like jabbing a shovel into concrete over and over again. What a terrible feeling it was, to sift through your heart and guts and soul and to come up short.

This was exactly how she'd felt in the beginning of Vagabond. She and Marcus had met teaching music classes together, at that bouncy, corporate children's entertainment company she'd worked at when she first moved to New York. Their voices blended well, and they made each other laugh by improvising banter that wasn't in the class script. So when he'd asked her to join the new band he was starting, she'd come into their first practice bursting with song ideas, snatches of lyrics and melodies. But he had dismissed them all, saying, "Okay, Jesus Girl. Did you ever listen to anything besides Christian rock?"

She laid her head back onto her mattress and reached for her computer, balancing it on her stomach, ready to numb out on the always available drug of the Internet and temporarily forget how disappointed she was in herself. (Even though, like alcohol, using the Internet to forget your troubles often left you feeling terribly hungover and worse than before.) After a quick scan of Twitter and *New York* magazine, she remembered Whitney's social media and pulled it up.

Holy shit, she had almost fifty thousand followers on Twitter and nearly twice that on Instagram. Whitney had always been so modest about it, Claire hadn't realized she'd reached *that* level of social media fame. Scrolling through, though, she could see why it was taking off. First of all, no surprise, Whitney photographed extremely well. She was stunning in real life, of course, but maybe even more luminous in the camera's eye. And second, the photos she chose were pure visual candy, showing a world in which families only ever delighted in one another, the playgroup was a team of beautiful women who took care of themselves and their friends in equal measure, and Whitney and Hope made a perfect mother-daughter pair whether they were riding a carousel, drinking smoothies, or doing Mommy-and-me yoga poses, the photo captions inevitably sprinkled with "wellness" or "self-care." Whitney modeled a new kind of motherhood in which a woman could be gorgeous and empowered and selfless at the same time, all without breaking a sweat.

Claire Gchatted the link to Thea, who had made it clear that she expected regular updates on all the playgroup gossip, and went back to the Instagram, stopping at a picture of Whitney tickling Hope on her lap. God, had her own mother ever looked at her like that, with such pure love? Given the way they'd fallen out with each other over Thea when Claire was in high school, and the awkwardness of their dutiful, twice-monthly phone calls now, Claire doubted it.

Her Gchat beeped with a message from Thea. *Oh, shit,* she wrote. *Whitney Morgan is Whitney McNab? We took an art history class together my sophomore year.*

Those maiden names will get ya, Claire wrote back as she continued to click through, reading the comments on the picture Whitney had taken of her with her guitar, surrounded by the babies. People loved it! What was this weird, positive, rainbow-sparkle corner of the Internet where the comments section was just people saying how beautiful you were instead of trolls calling you a cunt?

I'm sure she doesn't know who I am, Thea wrote. *Obviously I had a crush on her. Also obviously I never spoke to her.*

Claire smiled at that, and then at Whitney's most recent picture, of Whitney sprawled on the floor on her stomach, laughing, while Hope propped herself up on Whitney's back. *DIY alert!* Whitney had written in the caption. *Pro tip: If a little, lovable tyrant demands all of your time and you haven't been able to get a massage in ages, trick the tiny dictator into becoming your masseuse. Sure, her technique may not be perfect, but I'd still highly recommend.* The comments for that one were filled with LOLs and laughing emojis.

This is propaganda, Thea wrote. *Now I want a baby.*

Bahaha, Claire wrote back, and kept on clicking.

A picture of all the playgroup women, accompanied by a sentimental caption—*These women are my rocks. Parenting can be exhausting, and there's no calling in sick. But my playgroup ladies always show up, and thank goodness for that*—had prompted a slew of comments calling them "inspirational."

It was all a little silly, Claire thought, not to mention privileged up the wazoo. The "self-care" Whitney touted wasn't available to people like Claire, who couldn't shell out thousands of dollars to relax, who had to make themselves feel better in more makeshift ways that often backfired. (A fancy spa day never left you with a condom floating inside your body, for example.)

But also, maybe these women *were* inspirational. They didn't decide they felt like bad mothers and give up on parenting to numb out online. They didn't mope around in self-pity. They showed up. Oh, God, Claire thought with a mix of surprise and dismay, she really liked them all. They had invited her in and somehow become the highlight of her week, something entirely different from the other gigs (occasional catering, a part-time job at a clothing store) that she'd been picking up recently. They brought . . . color back into her life.

She put the computer aside, as their faces swam in her mind, looking at her with that maternal warmth and encouragement they gave so well.

Then she got up and tried to write something else.

Claire came to Tuesday's playgroup on a mission to get to Amara. But when she arrived, the moms were all preoccupied by a juice cleanse they were doing together, a weird, cranky energy pervading the room. Instead of sipping on wine and nibbling fruit and dark chocolate like normal, they clutched little bottles full of dark green liquid, taking delicate swallows.

When they explained that they'd ingested nothing but this specialty juice for two days straight (Each day's mixture had a *ton* of nutrients! They started in the mornings with purified water, cayenne, agave, and lemon, moved on to cold-pressed kale and cucumber, and ended the day with raw cashew milk!), Claire made the mistake of calling it a diet, and they all laughed too brightly and shook their heads, almost in unison. "It's a *cleanse*," Meredith said.

"Yeah, we're just getting rid of the toxins you build up by living in the world," said Ellie. "Resetting and starting out the week with a clean, healthy slate."

"Honestly, it feels amazing," Whitney said.

Amara rolled her eyes. "Really incredible."

Could a person get addicted to wellness like cocaine and have to keep doing more and more to get the same high? Pretty soon the moms would be injecting collagen straight into one another's asses and insisting that they'd never felt better.

Claire went to pull her guitar out of its case and caught Amara's eye, but then Ellie decided to show off her new scarf, a shimmery scarlet thing that fluttered like a leaf in the wind, and the moms all gathered to *ooh* and *ahh*.

"It's Hermès," Ellie said. "Thank you, wife bonus!"

Amara blanched. "'Wife bonus'? Oh, please, God, no. Ellie, you're not John's employee."

"I'm not?" Ellie widened her eyes, then waved her hand through the air, her tone turning snippy. "*Obviously* I know that. But I work as hard as he does for no salary, so I think it's a nice gesture if he wants to reward me for everything I've done by setting aside some money reserved especially for me."

"Are you listening to yourself?" Amara asked.

"Okay, let's not—" Whitney started.

"Nobody here thinks this is horribly unfeminist and retrograde?" Amara asked, looking around. Meredith shook her head, and Vicki popped out a boob to breastfeed.

"Every marriage has to decide what's best for it," Gwen said.

"Okay! How about we do music now?" Whitney said.

Then, when music was over and Claire beelined toward Amara, who was jiggling Charlie in a corner as he twisted and grunted, Gwen intercepted her.

"Claire, I have an important question to ask you." Gwen clasped her hands in front of her as if in prayer, her eyes wide with anticipation. Claire half expected her to get down on one knee. "I think it would be so good for the babies to have a fun, educational activity at Reagan's birthday party. Will you come perform?"

"Oh!" Whitney said. "Say yes, Claire!"

"You can meet all the daddies, and we could pay you three hundred dollars," Gwen added.

"Yeah, sure! I'm in," Claire said.

Gwen clapped her hands. "Oh, good. Christopher will be so pleased," she said, and then turned to Whitney with some thoughts about the planning of it all.

Finally, though, Claire reached Amara. "Hey, I'm ready," she said in a low voice, her hands shaking a little bit at her sides. "To sing you something I wrote."

Amara glanced up, Charlie wriggling in her arms. "What?" she asked. Her voice was tight with frustration.

"Like you said last time we hung out? If you're free after playgroup today, I could come over again."

"I'm not," Amara said, brusque. "I have to take Charlie to get his shots, and it's like he already knows it." She looked at her child. "You're a real picnic—you know that?" He twisted and clamped his mouth down on her shoulder. "Hey! No biting."

"Got it," Claire said.

"Oh, my God," Whitney said, looking down at her phone. "Oh, my God!"

"What? Is everything okay?" Gwen asked, worry etching itself on her face.

"Listen to this," Whitney said, and began to read an e-mail aloud. "'Hey, Whitney! Moms of Insta here. We wanted to reach out because we're in the process of making a gorgeous coffee-table book, due to be published this fall. We're giving some of our favorite InstaMoms a two-page spread each, a combination of some of their own photos and a professional photo shoot we do. We *love* your pics. Your family is so cute, and your playgroup is great too. We love that you have a dedicated professional musician—so good for the babies' development! Want to be part of the book?'"

Ellie and Meredith shrieked and grabbed Whitney's hands, and they all danced around, their energy suddenly back to normal levels. "Congratulations, Whitney," Gwen said, while Vicki gave a faraway smile.

"Guys, if *I* do it, you're all doing it too," Whitney said. "They said they loved the playgroup. I'm asking them if you can all be part of the photo shoot."

"Whitney, you are my hero," Ellie said.

"You don't have to do that," Amara said. "Really."

"Too bad, I want to. *And* they mentioned the music!" Whitney said, turning her blinding smile on Claire. "So, musician, we're bringing you along too!"

In the face of Whitney's generosity, her sparkling eyes, and her certainty that Claire would love to get all dolled up and documented for posterity as someone whose greatest talent involved singing "Wheels on the Bus," Claire hesitated. If Vagabond, or anyone who knew her story, saw her like that, they'd probably never stop smirking. But why in the world would anyone from her past buy a coffee-table book about Instagram moms? She swallowed, catching Amara's eye briefly. "Thanks, Whitney," she said. "That's really nice of you."

She packed up efficiently as Ellie, Meredith, and Whitney went off into a reverie, imagining what the shoot would be like, what kinds of food catering would bring, and, Ellie wondered, if they'd be able to get hair extensions and false eyelashes. As Claire turned to go, Amara came up behind her.

"Hey, wait," Amara said. "Are you free tomorrow night? I know where you can sing for me."

Chapter 13

The next night, Amara pulled on a leather jacket she hadn't worn since the early days of her pregnancy, and looked at herself in the mirror. Not bad. You wouldn't necessarily know, from seeing her on the street, that she'd popped a baby out of her vagina. No mom jeans and minivans for her. (But even if she kept wearing leather jackets and exuding a certain intimidating cool, she knew that someday, Charlie would be mortified by her mere existence. Or rather, she hoped he would be, even as she dreaded it, because that would mean that he was normal.) She paused, then grabbed a tube of bright red lipstick and carefully applied it. Not bad at all.

When she came out into the living room, Daniel did a double take. "Wait. Who are you going out with? Do I need to be jealous?" he asked.

"Don't be jealous. I'm just going to an orgy," she said, and he smiled, cracking open a beer and sitting down on the floor next to Charlie. "No, I told you, with Claire from playgroup."

"Is she the brownstone woman, the coffee shop savior, or a different one?" he asked, lifting Charlie to standing, his hands on his waist, and then taking his hands away. Charlie remained standing for a second as Daniel and Amara watched, their breath in their throats, and then he plopped back down to the floor, letting out a grunt.

"A different one," Amara said. "Oh, Lord, I totally forgot to tell you. Speaking of playgroup, listen to this nonsense. Ellie's husband gives her a *wife* bonus. That's probably the most patriarchal bullshit that a bull ever shat, right?"

"A wife bonus?" Daniel asked. "Like she's his employee?" Amara nodded. "Woof. Not to get all high-horsey, but I'm glad we don't have a marriage where I give you money based on how well you've met my needs, or whatever it is."

"That's probably the most romantic thing you've ever said," Amara said. "I'd kiss you if I hadn't just put on lipstick." She blew him a kiss instead, and he pretended to catch it in the air. "What sort of adventures are you two going to get up to?"

"We're going to drink beer and do some father-son bonding over sports." Daniel turned on the television, where a basketball game was in progress. "You gonna play this someday, little dude? I bet you'll be able to jump higher than all those other guys."

"Don't keep the TV on all night, okay?" Amara asked. "It's not good for him to have too much screen time, especially not before trying to put him to sleep."

"I know, I know. Just a little while longer. Things were pretty stressful at work today," Daniel said, tickling Charlie's stomach. "Besides, it's a special occasion. Daddy's babysitting!"

"Nope," Amara said. "Speaking of patriarchal bullshit, never say that again. You can't babysit your own son. He literally exists because of your sperm. I manage to keep him entertained all day without a screen. You can do it for the hour before bedtime."

"Jesus, Mari," Daniel said. He turned off the TV. He could pout, but they were *not* going to have one of those partnerships where Amara made Charlie do his homework and Daniel took him to the zoo.

"Love you, boys," she said, and ducked out the door.

She saw Claire from a distance as she approached the bar, that red hair a beacon in the evening light. Claire leaned against the brick wall in her cheap, worn jeans as if she hadn't a care in the world, although she ruined the illusion somewhat by fidgeting with the zipper on her guitar case. The nervous movement touched Amara, made her want to stroke Claire's hair and comfort her. When she'd first fallen in love with Daniel, she'd found herself having to suppress an urge, when talking with other people—longtime friends, coworkers, anyone with whom she felt a closeness—to kiss them. Not that she was suddenly attracted to them (she didn't *really* want to kiss anyone but Daniel), but out of a sort of habit, as if her body was so deeply in love that it was incapable of turning off its loving behaviors. Now that same sort of thing kept bubbling up, but with mothering. She shook her head and tapped Claire on the shoulder.

"Oh, hey!" Claire said.

"Let's go in and put your name on the list, shall we?" Amara asked.

An older coworker had told Amara about this place when she was just starting out in television production, working in an office in the Village. They'd go sometimes to watch the open-mic nights. It was always a fascinating grab bag of performers—bright-eyed kids who'd just moved from Long Island and who could carry a tune well enough but were never going to make it; old-timer folk musicians who didn't give a shit anymore and would sit up onstage far longer than their allotted slot, singing a million verses of the same song (invariably about the environment or the government or both). Occasionally, though, a musician made you sit up and take notice. She'd seen a couple of performers there who she'd gone on to book when she was handling that sort of thing.

Claire and Amara got whiskey gingers and sat at a table near the stage, while a young man who consistently sang *just under* the right pitch played a song about a one-night stand that he couldn't get out of his mind.

"Sort of a creepy song, huh?" Amara said. "Sounds like this girl should get a restraining order."

"Yeah." Claire drained her drink and gave a weak smile. "Sorry," she said, drumming her fingers on the table. "Just having the smallest of panic attacks over here."

Perhaps bringing Claire there had been a terrible idea, a spur-of-the-moment inspiration when Charlie had been twisting around so annoyingly in her arms yesterday and Whitney's announcement about the coffee-table book had made her feel like the only thing anyone would ever see her as again was a mother, when all she had wanted was to go back to her carefree, childless life, and this place had popped into her juice-cleanse-addled head.

"Hey," Amara said. "There's no way that you can be worse than Mr. 'I'll Never Forget the Smell of Your Hair.'"

"We'll see about that."

"Nobody here really cares how you are except me," she said, taking Claire by the shoulders and looking her straight in her hazel eyes as the emcee called Claire's name. "And even I don't care that much." Claire laughed. "So go get 'em."

Claire slid in between tables and made her way to the stage, settling herself on the stool. She bumped against the microphone when she leaned forward to greet the crowd and had to catch the stand as it swayed. She gave off the nervous vibe of a girl unused to being onstage all by herself, and at their tables, people seemed to resign themselves to the prospect of another underwhelming performer, half paying attention and half continuing on with their conversations. Amara dug her nails into the palm of her hand as Claire took a deep breath and began to strum and sing.

Oh, thank the Lord, it wasn't awful. Actually, Amara thought, as the song went on, it was rather interesting. Clearly a first draft of something, as if Claire were the human figure right behind Fiona Apple in the evolutionary chart. But there was potential. A sort of righteous rage. And she had some creative lyrics in there— a bit about how some "hot shit" person (clearly a member of her old band) was a "*piece* of hot shit"; some strange religious imagery that she managed to twist in unexpected ways. It wasn't a song you'd ever hear on the radio, but maybe that was a good thing. Of course her voice was lovely too, and as she relaxed into the song, she radiated more and more of a refreshing openness, as opposed to other musicians, who withdrew into themselves when they played. At their tables, some in the audience kept talking, but others perked up and actually listened. When Claire finished, she gave a sheepish smile to the crowd, then sought out Amara's eyes and shrugged her shoulders. Amara clapped, loudly, as Claire wended her way back to the table and sank down into her chair.

"I did it," Claire said. "It's over, and I did not die."

"I liked it," Amara said.

"Thanks. You don't have to—I swear I'm not fishing for compliments. But you know that thing Ira Glass says about taste? How when you're starting out doing a creative thing, your taste is so far beyond your abilities, so you know what you're doing isn't great but you can't yet do any better? That's kind of how I feel right now. I had all those years with Vagabond, but it feels completely different to write and make something all on your own."

"I can see that," Amara said. She leaned forward. "So, tell you what. When you get to a place where your taste radar is going, 'Hey, I'm pretty damn good at this,' let me know. A buddy of mine is the bandleader at *Staying Up with Nick Tannenbaum*, and sometimes he needs people to write these little commercial jingles they do on the show. Could be a good connection. When you're ready, I'll introduce you."

"Really?" Claire asked. "That would be amazing."

"Yeah, yeah," Amara said, and finished her drink. "Well, we did it."

A lanky guy came over to their table, focused on Claire. "Hey," he said to her, "I dug your performance."

"Thanks!" Claire said.

"You used to play with Vagabond, didn't you?" he asked. "I

156

remember, I saw you guys like a year and a half ago at Bowery Electric. I brag about it all the time to my friends now—you know, 'I saw them before they were famous, when it was only a twenty-dollar cover and eighty people in the audience!'"

"Oh," Claire said, deflating. "Um, yeah. That was me."

"Why'd you leave the band?" he asked, a revolting curiosity all over his face.

"You know," Claire said. "Wanted to try something new."

"You sure picked the wrong time to get out, huh?" he said, laughing.

Claire's eyes flickered to Amara, and an understanding passed between them. Together, they turned and stared at the guy, silent, heads cocked to the side as if he were speaking a foreign language until he cleared his throat and scurried away, muttering something about how he had to go meet a friend.

"Lord, people can be idiots sometimes," Amara said.

"Yup," Claire replied, and they sat in silence for a second.

"Well," Amara said, "shall we do some shots?"

"So give me all the playgroup gossip," Claire said after they'd taken their second shot and chased it with a beer. The open mic had ended, and the place had reverted to regular bar bustle. "Who's on the verge of a nervous breakdown? Who's having an affair? Who hates who?"

"Well, sometimes I wish Ellie would shut the fuck up," Amara said.

Claire laughed so violently and suddenly that beer burst out the side of her mouth. "I could see that," she said as she wiped it off the table with her napkin.

"And what else? I'm convinced Vicki is a hard-core pothead."

"Okay," Claire said, slamming her palm down on the table. "I've been wondering something. Does she speak?"

"Occasionally," Amara said, smiling. "I think she's just got a lot of beautiful things going on inside her own head. Either that, or her mind is a David Lynch–style horror trip. She's the richest one of us all, even though you'd never know it. Her father was the CEO of some massive oil company. Honestly, besides Whitney, I don't know if I would've become friends with any of them on my own, but now it's a bit like we're all war buddies. Perhaps I wouldn't be immediate best friends with, say, Meredith if I met her at a party, but we've all been in the trenches of new mother-hood together, so we're bonded for life." She stopped and took a swig of her beer. "Well, sometimes it's that, and sometimes we're fighting one another, all in our own individual armies, to conquer the territory of Best Mother of All. Gwen and Whitney are the favorites to win that war though. I'm just trying not to go the way of Joanna."

"Joanna?" Claire asked, raising an eyebrow.

"Oh, Lord," Amara said, then sighed, bracing herself for the explanation. "She used to be in playgroup with us. And then she had a nervous breakdown in the grocery store, of all places. She just lay down in the aisle, her kid screaming in the cart beside her, and wouldn't get up even when other customers tried to help her." Amara swallowed, Joanna's hopeless face swimming in her mind. "Then her kid, upset and flailing about, knocked some cans off the shelf next to him and cut himself on the edge of one. So he was bleeding—I mean, not that badly, not like he was *hemorrhaging*, but still, bleeding—and Joanna just kept lying there on the ground, not doing anything."

"Holy shit," Claire said, her mouth open in shock.

"Yeah. Eventually, the people at the grocery store called the police to bring her home and to make sure the kid was okay, which, thank God, he was." Amara shook her head. "We'd known that something wasn't right, that she wasn't happy, but we'd had no idea it was that bad."

"So what happened to her?" Claire asked.

"Oh, the most predictable thing in the world. Her husband dumped her in a mental hospital for a stint and started dating a twenty-five-year-old who teaches Barre classes. So now she and her baby are living out in Jersey. Not the nice part, either."

"Wait," Claire said. "How have I been hanging out with you all for over two months now, and this is the first I'm hearing about her?"

"I know," Amara said. "We never talk about her! Like she's a bogeyman."

"Bloody Mary. If you say her name three times into a bathroom mirror, she'll come back and murder you all."

"Or, worse, infect us with her bad mothering, with her bad life," Amara said. "I feel so sad for her child—if she'd stayed married and stayed here in New York, that boy would have gone to fantastic schools, had all the opportunities, lived a charmed life. Instead, Joanna's fighting for child support and desperately trying to prove she's stable enough to hang on to custody of him. And he was already a difficult kid, even without all this. Oh, I can't think about it anymore." She shook her head. "What about you? Give me your gossip. Do you think we're terrible rich ladies who should go back to work? Who do *you* hate?"

"None of you! I've actually . . . I've really appreciated how warm you all have been to me, treating me like a real person and not just the hired help," Claire said. "I wasn't necessarily expecting it, but I really liked you all, almost immediately. Well, except there's this *one* mom who totally scared the shit out of me for the first few weeks there."

"Ah, yes," Amara said. "Sorry about that."

"Everything's . . . okay, right?" Claire asked.

"Yeah," Amara said. Claire hesitated, like she wanted to ask something further—something about what Amara had been doing in Whitney's office that day, something Amara did not want to talk about with anyone. So Amara put down her beer and scanned the room. "Hypothetical: one person, in this bar right now. You get to go home with him. Or her?"

"Mmm, him. Tried the her once, and it was fine, but probably more of a 'fuck you' to my megachurch than anything else."

"You're a megachurch baby? We are absolutely circling back to *that*," Amara said as Claire squinted, scanning the bar and concentrating hard.

"Oh, him," Claire said, then pointed at a bearded man standing at the bar with a bespectacled friend. He happened to look over as she pointed. "Shit!" Claire said, and she and Amara collapsed into laughter. "I'm pretty smooth. What about you? Or am I not allowed to ask that, since you're married?"

"Oh, Daniel and I decided a long time ago to acknowledge that, even though we plan on spending the rest of our lives together, we're still going to find other people sexy. Looking is fine. Touching is not. Unless it's Idris Elba for me, or Charlize Theron for him. Those, we're allowed." She looked around. "Ah, I don't know. Beardo's friend is attractive enough, I suppose." Claire nodded in agreement. "Now no more drinks for me, or I will be *very* unhappy at playgroup tomorrow. I'm going to close out."

Claire pulled some cash out of her wallet, but Amara waved it away and walked to the bar. The list of drinks was far longer than she'd expected, so she gave the bartender her Visa debit card, the one that went to her own private checking account. When she and Daniel had gotten married, they'd merged almost all of their finances. But she'd kept this account, because it was the smart thing to do. *Always have a little money of your own,* her parents had told her. *You never know what life will hand you.*

Someone jostled her as she waited for the bartender to come back with her receipt. "Watch it, jackass!" she said, a pang rising up in her at how long it had been since she'd had the pleasure of yelling at a jerk at a bar. That was one of the strangest things about motherhood. You could love your baby to pieces, be thankful every day for his ten tiny toes and his piercing wail and his all-consuming existence, and yet still mourn the life you'd had before. And somehow it wasn't cool to say that, to treat the birth of a baby as the death of something else. You had to be all joy, all gratitude. But she missed Sundays alone in her apartment, listening to music. She missed cherishing a cup of coffee, sipping it slowly all the way down to its dregs. She missed going out like this with a friend, letting the night take her where it wanted. All this had disappeared, and she'd never gotten the chance to properly grieve.

The bartender reappeared, a frown on his face, holding her card in the air. "I'm sorry," he said, "but it's not working. I think it might be maxed out?"

Fuck. *Fuck.* It was the stupid TrueMommy. She had used this card sparingly in the past, when she felt a little embarrassed about, for example, how much she had spent on the leather jacket she was currently wearing. She always put a bit of her salary into the account too, so it was fine. But now that she was unemployed, more and more purchases made her a little embarrassed, and shelling out a thousand dollars a month for specialty vitamins hadn't helped the matter at all. Lord, she was an idiot.

Okay, she'd just have to stop taking the TrueMommy supplements while she figured something out. No big deal. Except so many days she barely felt like she was holding herself together as it was. And the vitamins, crazy as it sounded, did make her feel healthier, more energetic, more able to deal with Charlie's moods than before, when she'd been constantly discombobulated. She'd been sucked in by those stupid wellness claims on the label. She'd bought in hook, line, and sinker, and now she couldn't give them up.

So she'd just tell Daniel that they were important to her and ask if they could pay for them out of their joint account. And then her lovely, kind, ever-so-slightly uptight and morally superior husband would hear the price tag and think she was insane. "Are you kidding me?" he'd say. "Mari, you're getting taken for a ride!" With Daniel, *everyone* was getting taken for a ride—his parents when the guys who came to mow their lawn up-charged them, people who shopped at stores where yoga pants cost more than fifty dollars, and sometimes when his latent socialist streak came out, everyone in a capitalist society. She hated when he turned "You're getting taken for a ride" on her, as if *he* always had all the answers.

Fuck fuck, indeed. She handed the bartender the card linked to their joint account instead. "This one should work," she said as another option for what to do about her current financial mess floated into her head. All *that* option would require was a complete and utter refutation of her principles. "And actually, can I get another shot of whiskey?"

She tossed it back quickly, then tried to shake herself out of the funk. Her eyes lit on Claire moving through the bar toward her, gloriously unencumbered. Free. Apparently, Amara wasn't the only one who found Claire glorious as she moved. The bearded man Claire had pointed to before approached them, friend in tow. "We're taking bets," Beardo said. "I think you were pointing at me because you think I'm a movie star in disguise."

"And *I* think it's because you were trying to find the doofiest guy in the bar," Glasses said.

"You're both wrong," Claire said.

"We're witches, and we were looking for our next human sacrifice," Amara said.

"Don't worry," Claire said. "We decided to go with someone else instead."

"You're not leaving, are you?" said Glasses. "Stay for one more, on us."

Amara looked at Claire, who raised an eyebrow. "Oh, all right," Amara said.

The four of them flirted about nothing, the kind of conversation that seemed witty at the time, but wouldn't be memorable in the morning. At some point, the person manning the playlist at the bar switched over to "Shout," and they all began to dance, throwing their arms up in the air, and bending down to the ground. Next came Whitney Houston, "I Wanna Dance with Somebody."

Glasses took Amara's hand and twirled her when the chorus started, catching her around the waist. "You're really beautiful," he yelled in her ear.

In her twenties, she would've grabbed him and kissed him. They would've made out right there in the mass of other bodies, maybe snuck into the bathroom and done more.

But now she disentangled herself. She was playing at living her old life, but she could only glide on its surface for so long. This man's handsome young face was no match for Daniel's, with his wrinkles and his exasperation, even though Amara was having *all* sorts of feelings about Daniel right now. "Thanks," she said. "I'm going home to my husband."

Claire and the bearded man were pressed up against each other, throwing their heads back and singing. Amara tapped her on the shoulder. "Hey, you walking pheromone, I'm heading home. You should stay, though."

"What?" Claire said, pulling away from her dance partner. "No. I came with you. I'll leave with you."

"Oh, come on. Go enjoy yourself. Make that hypothetical into a reality. I'm probably just going home to bed anyway. I'm old."

"Stop that. Just give me a second," Claire said. Claire whispered something to the bearded man and bit down on his earlobe so quickly, Amara thought maybe she'd imagined it. Then she turned and grabbed her jacket. "Okay, let's go."

The sounds of the bar followed them out into the cold spring air. Down the block, they came upon a fresh wall of posters announcing Vagabond's new tour, with the two lead singers staring soulfully into each other's eyes.

"Ugh," Claire said. "It's everywhere."

Amara knew exactly how Claire felt. Even now, every time she saw an ad for *Staying Up Late with Nick Tannenbaum*, she wanted to punch something, hard. A thought struck her, and she rummaged around in her purse, among the receipts and the mints and her organizer. She was pretty sure she had exactly what she needed somewhere in the muck of her bag.

Her fingers closed around a Sharpie. Perfect.

Chapter 14

After this, Claire was going to stop showing up to playgroup hungover. At least this time, she wasn't alone in her nasty headache. She caught Amara's eye during "The Hokey Pokey," and Amara winked, then winced.

"Keep a lookout," Amara had said last night, right before charging up to the bank of Vagabond posters and scribbling all over them with a kind of drunken, demented glee. She drew little devil horns on Marcus and a word bubble coming out of his mouth reading, "I'm an asshole, and my penis smells like mold." Claire had watched first in shock, and then in stitches of laughter, as Amara had kept going, filling poster upon poster with blacked-out teeth and creative, filthy insults.

Sure, it was completely immature. But it was also the first time that Claire had been able to look at something related to Vagabond and laugh about it.

Watching this Upper East Side stay-at-home mom graffiti posters like she was a rebellious teenager had brought on a particular, confusing infatuation. Claire hadn't wanted to say good night. She'd wished she could invite Amara back to her place for an old-fashioned sleepover like in middle school, to stay up all night with her laughing and talking about everything, and okay, sure, maybe practicing kissing. Despite her hangover, Claire had power-walked to playgroup, eager to be in the same room as Amara again.

Perhaps dancing "The Hokey Pokey" had been a little ambitious, movement-wise. Now seemed like a good time to sit down and sing some peaceful, quiet songs. She'd bought some sparkly egg shakers on Gwen's advice ("When my elder daughter, Rosie, was in playgroup, the kids *loved* egg shakers!"), and she pulled one out of her bag as she sat, then shook it above her guitar. She tried to catch Gwen's eye to get a smile of approval, but Gwen was looking a little distracted today, her reserved-but-typically-constant smile just an occasional flicker.

Charlie, that tiny monster, reached out and grabbed at her guitar strings, clamping onto them with his strong fists. "Whoa, bud," she said. "Gentle." She tried to pry his fingers off before he snapped a string, but he was surprisingly strong and persistent. She peeled one of his hands off a lower string only for him to brace himself on her arm, rise up to standing with a gurgle, and grab a higher string. Why wasn't Amara doing anything to stop him? Claire looked toward her for some assistance, but Amara was staring at her baby, her eyes wide and shining.

"Oh. Oh, my God," Amara whispered.

"He did it," Whitney said in a similarly awed tone.

And then Amara was up off the ground, lunging forward, swooping Charlie up into her arms and whirling around the room with him. "You little bastard," she shouted, peppering him with kisses. "You did it! You brilliant, brilliant boy." She looked at all the women and said, half laughing, half crying, "He can pull himself up!"

A sense of rapture overtook the room. Meredith and Ellie reached for each other's hands as Meredith wiped a tear from her eye. Even Vicki paused in her breastfeeding and gave a little hum of approval. It felt like church, church at its best moments, with the Baby Jesus swapped out for the Baby Charlie. They were worshipping something miraculous, something holy.

"I'm going to see if we have any champagne," Whitney said, standing up.

Amara pulled her phone out of her pocket and dialed a number as she bounced Charlie on her hip. Charlie looked around at all the women cooing at him that he was a strong, brave boy, and began to frown, overwhelmed. "Daniel, answer the phone! Ah, you're working!" Amara said. "But he did it, Danny. He stood up! Oh, thank the *Lord*. I love you. Call me back!"

A faint pop sounded from the direction of the kitchen, and moments later, Whitney reappeared, carrying a tray crowded with champagne flutes, which she passed out to all of them, Claire included.

The women all held their glasses out toward one another. "To Charlie," Whitney said. "Soon he's going to be running all over the place, and Amara will be wishing she could go back to the days when he couldn't stand."

"Oh, I don't doubt it," Amara said as all the other women chorused, "To Charlie." The clink of glass rang out, and Claire took a sip. This was the good stuff. She'd never had champagne this nice.

The women all continued to sip and reminisce and see if they could coax Charlie to stand again by holding up those egg shakers. Nobody said anything about Claire leaving, so she just stayed, pulled into their warm, joyful conversation, sitting next to Amara and feeling the happiness and relief radiating from her.

"This is such perfect timing with the retreat coming up," Whitney said to Amara. "Now, when we go, you can just relax and not worry about a thing."

"That's going to be so nice," Amara said, then turned to Claire. "Whitney gave us a group wellness retreat for Christmas."

"Sycamore House!" Ellie cried. "I cannot freaking wait."

"She texts me pictures from their website like every hour," Meredith said.

"Were you ever able to get them to change the size of the package?" Gwen asked Whitney quietly. "You know, after Joanna . . ." Whitney shook her head, a brief grimace contorting her features. Amara nudged her leg against Claire's, as if to say, *See? The bogeyman!*

"We could always invite a husband along," Meredith said.

"No way," Ellie said. "It's their turn to take care of the babies and see how we feel all the time. Although I'm honestly a *little* worried that John might forget Mason at the playground."

"Oh, don't say that," Gwen said, and Ellie raised an eyebrow.

"So now you're going to tell us that handsome Christopher is amazing with kids too?" She waggled her eyebrow up and down in a faux-lascivious way. "Does he have any flaws? I mean, I guess if *he* wanted to come on the wellness retreat . . ."

"Claire!" Whitney said, leaning toward her so intently that Claire startled, convinced that Whitney had realized she'd overstayed her playgroup welcome and was about to kick her out. "*You* should come!"

"What?" Claire said.

"We have this extra spot, and it would be so fun to have you take it," Whitney said, warming to the idea. "It's already all paid for. Consider it a belated Christmas present."

Claire wanted to laugh at the ridiculousness of it. She did *not* belong on some fancy wellness retreat, not with these women. She turned to Amara for confirmation, but Amara looked back at her with excitement.

"You should absolutely come," Amara said.

"I mean," Claire said, "are you sure?"

"You have to come, Claire," Meredith said. "They've got amazing yoga classes, food, these gorgeous hiking trails!"

"The only issue is that they don't allow alcohol," Ellie said. "But it's only, like, one night."

"It would be far more fun than having our stuffy old husbands along," Amara said.

"Um, okay!" Claire said, throwing her hands up in the air. "Thanks!"

Whitney cheered, and poured her more champagne.

"One of us," Ellie chanted. "We'll have you taking True-Mommy and doing cleanses in no time."

A strangled noise escaped from Gwen, and they all looked over right as her face crumpled into sobs. The others exchanged glances, confused, and then Whitney knelt down beside her.

"What is it, Gwen?" she asked, gingerly, as if Gwen were a wounded animal.

"It's nothing," Gwen said, even as her shoulders shook.

"Was it because I called our husbands stuffy and old?" Amara asked. "I didn't mean *your* husband, specifically."

Gwen's pale face had gone splotchy. She bit her lip, hesitating. "I think Christopher's having an affair," she said.

Chapter 15

Whitney's blood got hot, and bile rose in her throat. She was so full of disgust at herself that there was no room for anything else inside her body—no heart, certainly, and no brain either.

"Wait. *What?*" Meredith asked.

"Oh, Gwen," Amara said, sinking down on the other side of her and grabbing her hand. "Fuck him."

"Please, don't say that word around the babies," Gwen said. "But thank you."

"What . . . what makes you think that?" Whitney asked.

Gwen sighed, a rattling sound that traveled the length of her body. "He smells different sometimes," she said. "Too clean. Normally I can smell the office on him. The coffee he's had during the day, all of that. But a few times over the past couple weeks, it's as if he's taken a shower before coming home."

Whitney and Christopher had met three times now, always for an hour during the workday, when Christopher would tell his bosses he was taking a long business lunch and Whitney would tell her babysitter she was getting a spa treatment. The last time, they hadn't even made it to the bed. The moment the door shut behind her, he'd turned her around right up against it, pushing up her skirt and pulling down her underwear and fucking her so hard from behind that she imagined all the women pushing their house-keeping carts down the hallway could see the door rattling. It was the good kind of being used, as if he'd recognized the trash inside her and wanted it anyway.

And despite the fact that Christopher could be rough—that he twisted her hair around his fist and pulled it until her eyes watered—a miracle had occurred. For the first time since Whitney had given birth, sex felt good again. The stinging pain she experienced with Grant inside of her was gone.

"Have you checked his texts?" Ellie asked. "That's how my sister found out that her fiancé was cheating, and thank *God*, she got out of that relationship."

"Yes," Meredith said, nodding. "Check his texts."

"What? Don't check his texts," Amara said. "If he's not cheating on you, that's a horrible invasion of privacy. And if smell is what you're going on, that could be caused by a lot of different things."

"Maybe he's just started a new workout schedule," Whitney said. "Maybe he's showering at the gym?"

"Yeah, it could be that," Amara said. "I wouldn't necessarily jump to worst-case scenario. But if it *is* the worst-case scenario, let us know if you need us to kill him."

"You're probably right," Gwen said. "I'm probably being crazy." She waved her hand through the air as if to clear away the expressions on their faces, the sympathy, but also the barely masked morbid curiosity. "Let's talk about something else." Gwen's eyes lit on Claire, who had folded up into herself like she was trying to disappear, and Gwen startled. "Oh, Claire! I'm sorry. It's not your job to listen to this stuff."

Each time their hour had been up, Christopher would retie his tie while Whitney sat on the bed, watching him. He'd leave first, and she'd wait five minutes. The moment the door closed behind him, leaving her alone in a room that smelled like their sweat, she'd promise herself that she'd never do that again. And then each time he sent her a new message, her heart started clattering against the walls of her chest and she could barely breathe until she'd answered him back.

But now she looked at Gwen's milky, tearstained face and promised herself anew. She meant it this time. Not again.

Her resolve held all through the weekend. She was going to be the world's best wife and mother. She wheeled Hope to Whole Foods on Friday afternoon and bought the most expensive cut of organic, grass-fed steak they had, then cooked it so that it still oozed blood when Grant cut into it on his dinner plate. He looked up at her in appreciation as the red pooled on his plate—they'd long had an affectionate argument going about how rare a steak should be. She smiled at him as she struggled to swallow the meat, cold and raw against her tongue.

On Saturday, she coaxed Grant into a family outing to the Museum of Natural History. They walked like experts through the crowds of tourists. Grant was being especially charming that day, making little jokes about the ancient-animals tableaux, playing with Hope. Occasionally, Whitney noticed harried Midwestern moms, with their overstuffed tote bags, turn to look at the three of them in envy or admiration. She caught Grant's hand in hers and kissed it and graciously gave directions to a family who couldn't figure out how to find the big blue whale. Hope stared at the dinosaurs, and Whitney read her the descriptions from the museum labels. A baby's brain could soak up knowledge like water into a sponge. Maybe, years from now, Hope would be studying for a history test on this topic, and the facts would come easily to her, and she would feel very deeply how smart she was despite growing up in a world that gave girls so many opportunities to feel less than.

That night, after Grant and Hope—both cranky from the outing—had fallen asleep, Whitney posted a picture of the three of them on her Instagram. Then she sat and watched as the comments began to roll in. She'd started receiving the occasional negative comment as her following had grown: *"out-of-touch rich bitch,"* or *"too much time on ur hands lol, go back to work,"* or, worst of all, ones like *"Ur baby's gonna hate u when she's old enough to see u whored out her childhood online."* From trolls, she told herself, or people who were jealous and miserable and needed to take it out on her. She always deleted them immediately, sending the judgments into the ether with a swipe of her finger.

Posts with Grant in them usually did well among her primarily female following. He gave good camera. But now Whitney tensed, suddenly worried that some commenter in a Des Moines basement might have an unexpected flash of insight, steeling herself for a *"bet they haven't had good sex in years"* or a *"trying waaayyyy too hard."*

No, the only comments coming through tonight were the heart-eye emojis, the *"TOO CUTEs,"* the *"#relationshipgoals."* She exhaled, staring at Grant, and then at her own radiant face in the photo. Maybe she really was as openmouthed-smile-happy as she looked.

And then on Monday morning, Christopher sent her a message, and she knew that she wasn't.

Looks like you had a busy weekend, he wrote. *I'd recommend a massage on Wednesday.*

She let the message sit there. Underneath everything she did—the errands she ran, the games of peekaboo she played with Hope—it thrummed and rang in her mind like the telltale heart, the steady beat of *Christopher, Christopher, Christopher.* She felt like a tween mashing her face against a Justin Bieber poster—ridiculous-looking from the outside, but inside, filled with an almost holy, previously unknown longing.

At Tuesday's playgroup, Gwen brought up the subject of preschool, and when Whitney said that she hadn't started looking into any of that yet, Gwen went off on a very earnest monologue about how you *had* to figure it out early, or else all the prime spots would be taken, and if a child didn't get the right preschool spot, it put them at a disadvantage for elementary school, which put them at a disadvantage for high school, which totally screwed them over for college. "I started researching for Reagan weeks ago," she said, and Whitney wanted to strangle her.

As soon as all the women left her apartment, she ran to her computer. *Yes, I think you're right about the massage,* she wrote back. *I need it, badly.*

This time, when Christopher opened the door, he led her to the bed and took his time with her, unbuttoning her dress so slowly that it drove her crazy with anticipation. Thank God, all her residual flab had finally gone away, she thought, as he slipped the dress from her shoulders, over the long, lean muscles in her arms. Once he had her completely naked, he didn't unbutton his own pants. Instead, as light from the window streamed in, he began to kiss his way down her stomach.

Whitney's heart started racing. A month after giving birth, she'd examined her vagina in a handheld mirror and had nearly cried at what she saw. She was disfigured, her delicate Georgia O'Keeffe petals now the swollen, split lips of a hockey player after a brawl.

Grant had never been the most enthusiastic oral-sex giver anyway. On the infrequent occasions he did it, he treated it as a warm-up, a couple of minutes of cursory licking to get her wet enough for the main event. Since Hope's birth, he'd never offered, and she'd never asked. Well, it had never felt that good for her anyway, so it was no great loss. But now Christopher was heading down there, and panic gripped her at what he might see or smell. What if she was sweaty or, God forbid, fishy?

She propped herself up on her elbows. "You don't have to," she said. "Really. Here." She reached down and tried to stroke him through his pants, to redirect the action, but he caught her hand and looked up straight into her eyes. Then, to her total surprise, he laughed.

"Don't be stupid," he said. "I want to." He placed his hand on her chest, right in between her breasts. She looked down at his fingers. He'd taken off his wedding ring before she'd arrived. Something about the gesture made her flush. Was it a courtesy to Gwen or to her? Before she could figure it out, he pushed her back so she lay flat against the mattress.

Above her, the light fixture in the ceiling glowed a warm cream color. No merciful, obscuring darkness to hide the wear and tear on her body. As Christopher studied the most vulnerable part of her, she tightened up. "Hey, relax," he said as he ran a finger along the inside of her thigh. He waited a second. "You're not relaxing."

"I'm afraid I might look like a drooping mess and smell like a rotting fish," she said in a rush of honesty that surprised her.

"Hmm," he said, taking a sniff and then parting her lips and staring straight into her. "No fish smell. And actually, you're the sexiest thing I've ever seen."

"Oh, really?" she said in a teasing tone, despite the fact that, at his words, her legs had started to tremble.

"Yes. Now, stop talking, and let me make you come already."

She let out a breath, fully sinking into the soft sheets beneath her as he began to flick his tongue up and down, so lightly at first that she shivered. As he grew more insistent, she glanced at him, expecting to see his face screwed up like someone performing a mildly distasteful task—a dog walker picking up poop, maybe, or herself when Grant was taking a long time to finish—but Christopher actually looked like he was *enjoying* himself. And not just in a "Well, this is fun enough" way. Like it was turning him on. That was what allowed her to fully let go, to focus on the feeling between her legs as it grew and grew, then narrowed to a radiant pinpoint of pleasure, then rushed through every part of her body.

Oh, God. Sweet Jesus. This kind of orgasm was a revelation. Back in college, during a drunken game of "Would You Rather" with her roommates, someone had asked the classic "Would you rather give up cheese or oral sex?" question, and though she'd said she'd rather give up cheese when she realized that was the cool answer, she hadn't understood the dilemma. Of course cheese was better than oral sex, she'd thought, assuming that everyone else was playing up their love of having a man's face rooting around down there too. They were merely a group of girls in sorority sweatshirts pretending to be women.

Well, now she *was* a woman, and she'd largely given up cheese anyway as her metabolism had slowed, and she was thunderstruck by the realization that College Whitney had given the right answer after all.

Later, after Christopher finished too, they lay tangled together, beautifully spent, catching their breath in the minutes they had left. "What are you thinking about?" he asked her, and because she felt afraid to tell him that Gwen's reproachful face had just swum into her thoughts—they had an unspoken rule that they didn't talk about their spouses or their children in this hotel room—she said the next thing that came into her mind. She told him the story of the snow globe in her yard, all the gory details, even though she'd never told anyone about it before.

When she was done, he looked at her like she was the most interesting woman in the world. "I didn't come from wealth either," he said. "My dad was a middle school science teacher. I can still name every bone in the body."

"No way," she said, laughing, so he kissed her, clavicle to ulna, fibula to sacrum, naming them all as she shook with giggles.

"God, it's like I recognize you," she said. "I wonder if we ever passed each other in New York when we were younger. If we were ever in the same restaurant or if we walked by each other on the street."

"Maybe we sat on opposite ends of the same subway car," he said. "Or you got out of one side of a taxi while I got in the other."

Her life could have been so different if only they had seen each other then, if she'd gotten out of the taxi on his side and held the door for him, and he'd decided not to go to his destination after all, but just to walk with her instead, when they were younger, before they'd married the wrong people. Her throat started to tingle with the onset of tears, and she swallowed them away and kissed him.

The fact that sex with Christopher didn't hurt wasn't the only miracle. The even greater miracle—greater and terrifying and so, so inconvenient—was that she was falling in love.

Chapter 16

A bag of fresh fruit—that was the first thing Claire noticed when she climbed into the twelve-passenger van that Sycamore House had sent to shuttle the women upstate. "Help yourselves," said the driver after he finished putting their luggage in the trunk, carefully laying Claire's black backpack atop a pile of designer suitcases. Claire reached her hand into the paper bag and pulled out a pear, ripe and unblemished.

As they drove up into the Hudson Valley, Whitney made conversation with the driver from the passenger seat. Ellie and Meredith prattled away to each other in the back while, next to them, Gwen listened to an audiobook of a Jhumpa Lahiri novel. Vicki stared longingly out the window as the bustle of the city faded into treetops, as if trying to commune with her baby despite the miles between them. Claire's leg jostled against Amara's, and they smiled at each other.

The past week, Claire had gone over to Amara's apartment after both playgroup sessions, staying and talking until the sky outside started to darken. They didn't mention their extra time together to the rest of the moms, so it had an exciting, illicit frisson, even though all they were doing was playing with Charlie and chopping vegetables for dinner. Amara had regaled Claire with tales of her late-night days, about which celebrities were secretly total pricks and which ones had been far too insistent that she do coke with them. Claire had made Amara laugh with stories of her various dating misadventures. But also, Claire had watched Amara tear up with relief as Charlie pulled himself to standing all over the living room. And Amara had wordlessly poured Claire a large glass of wine when Claire had come back in from the hallway, where she'd gone to endure one of her mother's infrequent passive-aggressive phone check-ins. After ten minutes of questions about why Claire needed to stay in New York if she wasn't in "that band" anymore, a glass of wine and a silent look of understanding from Amara had been exactly what Claire had needed.

Now, as they sat next to each other in the van, Amara rooted around in her handbag. "Hangman?" she asked, pulling out a pencil and a pad of paper.

"Yes, please," Claire said.

An hour and a half later, the driver stopped at a guard booth. "Whitney Morgan, party of 7," he said to the man inside, who checked a list and then waved them through, down a driveway lined with sycamore trees (very on brand, Claire thought). Ahead of them, a mansion came into view—regal, made of gray stone, like something out of *The Great Gatsby*, except for the modernized wings flanking either side of it. In spite of herself, a giddy anticipation overtook Claire, and she grinned at Amara. How weird and wonderful, to be *there*, with those women. It was like she'd pulled off a long con.

They walked into the wood-paneled lobby to check in. The woman behind the desk, an efficient ball of sunshine around Claire's age, handed them all reusable water bottles emblazoned with the Sycamore House logo. "Welcome," she said. "Now, I've got a room key for Victoria Elmsworth, who upgraded to the silent-retreat option?" The rest of the moms looked at one another, confused, as Vicki glided forward to collect a room key, waved goodbye, and disappeared off down a corridor.

"Well," Amara said, "I guess that's the last we'll see of Vicki this weekend."

"The rest of you will be two to a room, so pick your partner, drop off your stuff, and then you can get started on activities! We've got a great Vinyasa class in half an hour."

Ellie charged forward, Meredith in tow, and grabbed their room key. Amara and Claire began to turn to each other right as Gwen reached for Whitney. But though Whitney must have seen Gwen's overture, she turned to Claire as if oblivious, clapping her hands together with a bright smile. "Oh, room with me, Claire," she said. "I've been dying for us to get to know each other better!"

"Uh, sure," Claire said. Well, *this* was an unexpected turn. Now she knew what it felt like to be the kid who got picked first for teams in gym class. She shot an apologetic look at Amara, then followed Whitney down the hall into a room with two double beds, each covered in a fluffy white comforter. A large window ran along one wall, looking out onto the forest.

"Let's change for Vinyasa," Whitney said, unself-consciously pulling off her blouse and swapping it for a formfitting tank top made of some fancy athletic material that wicked away perspiration and probably cured cancer too. Claire dug a pair of sweatpants from Old Navy out of her backpack. Whitney glanced at them, then hesitated. "Would you like to borrow a pair of yoga pants?" she asked. "I brought a few."

"Thanks, but there's no way I wear the same size as you," Claire said. Whitney's legs were those of a ballerina. Claire's legs would have been more at home playing on the US Women's Soccer Team.

"Oh, please, that's the beauty of yoga pants," Whitney said, tossing over a pair of sleek Athleta leggings.

Claire slid and wiggled her way into the pants, which vacuum-sealed her in. Goddammit, they really were good quality. *And* they had pockets? Already, she could tell how deflating it would be, the moment that she walked back into her own apartment after this charmed weekend.

"We're practically *The Sisterhood of the Traveling Pants* right now." Whitney beamed.

Turned out that the magic of the yoga pants extended only so far. They made Claire's ass look amazing ("Where have you been hiding *that?*" Amara asked when Claire walked into the yoga room), but they did not automatically make her into a yogi. As the mothers contorted themselves into a series of unfamiliar poses, bending and breathing deep, Claire got sweatier and sweatier, her hands slipping around on her mat. "Find your own truth in your practice today," the instructor said, reaching out a hand to steady Claire as she wobbled. "For some of you, that means extending your stretch out further. For others, that may mean resting in child's pose." Claire snuck a glance at a woman on a nearby mat sinking back onto her haunches with a sigh, and copied her.

After showering, the women went their separate ways for much of the afternoon, Ellie and Meredith going off to an energy-healing workshop, Gwen deciding to listen to her audiobook by the fireplace ("I don't think I've finished a book in months," she said to them apologetically. "I need this."), Whitney, Amara, and Claire taking a guided walk along the property with one of the nature specialists.

They all met back for a workshop entitled "Visualizing Your Intentions: Dreams into Action." A workshop leader instructed them to gather in a circle. Claire sat down next to Amara and looked around the room. It was very beige.

"You should've seen Meredith in that energy-healing work-shop! She got *fiery*," Ellie was saying to Whitney as the other attendees—a retired couple in matching athleisure, a middle-aged mother and her college-bound daughter—trickled in.

"Oh, I don't know," Meredith said, blushing. "He was just talking about how crystals were the best way to heal childhood trauma and I was like, 'Helloooo. I trained for years in cognitive-behavioral therapy, so I beg to differ.'"

"It was awesome," Ellie said.

The workshop leader clasped his hands and cleared his throat to begin the session. "It's springtime," he said, "the time of revital-ization and new life, time for us to set aside self-doubt, self-sabotage, and our false obligations. *We* are responsible for what we manifest here on planet Earth." Claire and Amara looked at each other, and Amara gave the subtlest of eye rolls. "Let's go around the room and state our intentions, through saying, 'This year I *will* . . .' I'll start. This year I *will* live my truth as a nurturer by adopting a dog."

"Ooh!" said Ellie. "This year, I *will* run a half marathon."

"That's a really good one," Meredith said. "This year I *will* look into going back to work again." She smiled her unrestrained grin and looked around the circle for approval, but Ellie turned to her, knitting her brow.

"What?" Ellie asked.

"*Very* part-time," Meredith said.

"How long have you been thinking about this without telling me?" Ellie asked, hurt in her voice, and Meredith reddened.

"I mean, not that long—"

"Let's remember that we are on a *collective* journey right now and save our personal conversations for later," the workshop leader said as Ellie folded her arms across her chest. "Next member of the circle?"

"Well," Gwen said after a moment of uncomfortable silence, "this year I *will* make more room for romance in my marriage."

Whitney blinked. "Hmm," she said. "This year I *will* be the best mother I can be."

"Oh, yes, of course," Gwen said. "Add that to mine too."

They all turned to Amara, the next one in the circle, who shifted in her seat. "I don't know. I suppose my goal is to stay sane."

"Remember to phrase it as 'This year I *will* . . . ,'" the workshop leader said.

"This year I *will* stay sane," Amara said, her tone exceedingly dry.

On Claire's turn, she cleared her throat and said the only thing she could think of that was both vague and true enough to share in this room full of her employers. "This year I *will* take better care of myself." Whitney flashed her a supportive smile as the circle moved on to the retired couple, so it seemed like she'd done okay.

The workshop leader had them close their eyes and visualize themselves achieving their goals, then handed them each a piece of paper on which they were supposed to write out concrete steps they were going to take. *Only drink 4 nights a week,* Claire wrote slowly, then scratched out the "4" and wrote "5" instead. She shot a look at Amara, who was chewing on her lower lip, her forehead furrowed as if she were troubled by something.

By the time the workshop was over, Claire was starving. The moms and Claire headed toward the dining room in a flock, like migrating birds. Ellie linked her arm in Gwen's and power-walked them down the hallway, chatting loudly with Gwen about her resolution to put the spark back into her marriage. Meredith hung back, fiddling with a strand of her hair.

"You okay?" Claire asked her quietly.

"Yeah, totally!" Meredith said, flashing an unconvincing smile.

"Okay," Claire said.

Meredith took a breath as if to say something, then waved her hand. She walked a few steps before stopping and turning to Claire, agitated. "I didn't mean to drop the work thing on her in front of everyone. I haven't even thought about it that much! It's just that it was at the top of my mind after that energy-healing workshop."

Claire nodded. "Yeah, that makes sense—"

"And it's not like I'd be *deserting* her. It would only be, like, ten hours a week!" They crossed the threshold into the dining room, where Ellie had already settled herself at the table between Whitney and Gwen. Meredith exhaled. "Whatever. I probably won't do it anyway. But she doesn't have to be a jerk about it." She marched to an empty seat on Gwen's other side and promptly began studying her menu.

The young waiter filling water glasses at their table held out Claire's seat for her. *You don't have to do that,* she wanted to whisper to him. *I serve these women, just like you!* But that didn't feel wholly true anymore. So she just thanked him and opened her menu, scanning the options, from fire-roasted eggplant to Chilean sea bass to lamb tagine with quinoa. Each item had a string of numbers listed underneath. She assumed they were prices at first glance, but upon a closer look, she saw that they were actually a list of the calories, the grams of fat, and the amount of sodium in each dish.

Claire leaned over to Amara. "Wait. Where are the prices?"

"Oh, food is included," Amara said back.

"Like, as much as we want?"

Amara nodded. Fuck yes, this place was all-inclusive! And yet it wasn't *called* "all-inclusive"—a term that conjured up sweaty tourists gorging themselves on guacamole at the Club Med buffet, not the delicate plate of marinated raw scallops the waiter laid before Claire as her starting course. Claire stared at the glistening little circles, sprinkled with pomegranate seeds and splashes of olive oil, a plate so beautifully arranged it looked like a work of art. Then she dug on in.

"Gwen, no phones at the table!" Ellie said.

"Sorry," Gwen said, looking up. "I just wanted to check in on the kids."

"Good point," Whitney said, and in a synchronized motion, the moms all pulled out their phones, reading the text messages they found there with various exasperated sighs ("I walked Greg through the grocery list before I left," Meredith said, "and he *still* sent me five questions about olive oil."), typing out *I love you*s with private smiles on their faces, showing one another pictures that husbands had sent over of their children doing adorable things.

"Claire, when are *you* going to have babies?" Ellie asked. Five curious heads leaned forward and stared at Claire as if she were a zoo animal or an emissary from some nation of young, free-spirited aliens.

Claire swallowed her scallop. "I think I'm more of a cool-aunt type." Sure, being around their babies all the time had caused the occasional twinge of longing in her ovaries, but it had also hammered home how much fucking *work* it all was. She still didn't trust herself.

"Oh, you'll change your mind," Gwen said, "when you meet the right person."

"Yeah," Ellie said. "I was really into my single life, back when I was in law school and I dated all these guys who were just disgustingly immature. Like, peeing into bottles they kept beside the couch because they didn't want to get up to go to the bathroom. So I was, like, 'Ugh, no way I can procreate. Men are all children themselves.' But then I met John, and I just *knew*. You just have to find your John." Claire caught a glimpse of Meredith rolling her eyes.

"Stop being so smug," Amara said. "Maybe Claire won't change her mind. Not every woman has to be a breeder to have an interesting life."

"Ooh, look," Whitney said, quickly. "Our main courses are coming!"

That night, back in the room, Claire lay on her bed, wearing the Sycamore House bathrobe she'd found in the closet, with a mug of peppermint tea she'd made from the room's tea-and-coffee supply. "I don't think I've ever been on a more comfortable mattress," she said to Whitney as Ellie's and Meredith's muffled, strained voices floated in from the room next door. "Thank you for bringing me here."

"Of course!" Whitney said, finishing up an aggressive moisturizing routine. "My one complaint is that I wish they had a spa. I haven't gotten a massage in forever. It's amazing how carrying a baby around all the time can ruin your back." She put down her lotion and leaned against the wall, trying to get at a stubborn knot in her shoulder, then jokingly shook her fist up at the heavens. "Damn you, Hope!"

Claire laughed, and Whitney paused, then perched herself next to Claire on the bed, sitting cross-legged, as if they were just two girls at a sleepover, which, in a way, they were. "I do hope we didn't make you feel uncomfortable about having kids at dinner."

"Oh, it's fine," Claire said.

"Okay, good. Because obviously it's not the right choice for everyone. And even if you decide it *is* the right choice for you eventually, you've got so much time. You're, what, twenty-five?"

"Twenty-eight," Claire said.

Whitney reddened. "I'm sorry. I didn't mean to assume! Twenty-eight is still so young—"

"Whitney," Claire said, amused, as next door, Ellie's and Meredith's voices grew less agitated and melted into laughter, all seemingly right in their world again. "It's fine." Seeing Whitney flustered, so defenseless in her silk pajamas and night cream, put Claire at ease. "I just don't know if I'm cut out to be a mom." She rolled her eyes. "I didn't exactly have the best example growing up."

"In what way?" Whitney asked. "You don't have to talk about it if you don't want to."

"I don't mind," Claire said, putting her mug of tea down on the bedside table. "I grew up in this megachurch town, and my mom and I had a fine enough relationship when I was little. But then my cousin Thea, who was basically my mom's second daughter—you e-mailed with her about the playgroup job on the Harvard list; she's a kick-ass lawyer now—she came out. Or I guess she was *forced* out, 'cause her parents walked in on her with a girl."

"I imagine," Whitney said, "that didn't go over well in a mega-church town?"

"Bingo," Claire said, remembering the look on Thea's face when she'd burst into Claire's kitchen that day. Thea was emphatically *not* a crier (even when she'd sprained her wrist bike riding with Claire, she'd simply bitten down hard on her lip and told Claire to bike back home for help), but in the kitchen, she'd been blinking faster and swallowing harder than Claire had ever seen her do before.

"My parents found out I like girls," Thea had said, squaring her shoulders defiantly. "And before you say anything about it being wrong or bad, you should know that I think that's bullshit."

"But . . . but I thought you had a crush on Justin Timberlake," Claire had said, trying to wrap her head around a new truth.

"Claire," Thea had replied. "Come on."

In the warmth of their hotel room, light-years away from that Ohio evening, Claire looked at Whitney. "Her parents were going to kick her out of the house unless she went to one of those 'pray the gay away' camps." Whitney shuddered, and Claire nodded. "Yeah, exactly. And I promised her that she could come live with us. I mean, she was over at our house all the time. My mom loved her, and I was sure my mom would be able to convince my dad. Thea thought my mom would say no because she didn't want her to corrupt me." Claire rolled her eyes. "To turn me gay or some-thing. But Thea was wrong." Whitney leaned forward, as inno-cent and trusting in a mother's love as Claire had been back then. "My mom said no, because she didn't want to look bad in the eyes of the church."

"Oh, no," Whitney said, reachi
holding it, her palm soft and warm.

"Oh, yeah. Thank God, Thea is t.
know and managed to couch-hop her
ously this was way shittier for her than i.
lightbulb moment when I realized how
that if I ever did something that didn't
choose the church over me too. It was m
keep up appearances there than to do r
loved." Claire shrugged. "So, I can't help
had a kid, I'd probably still care more about
up like she screwed me up."

"Oh, Claire," Whitney said, putting he
pulling her into a hug, with such kindness
envied Future Hope for all the times she'd
for comfort. Sure, Whitney could go overbo
but Hope would never have to doubt her mon
disappointment in her own mother was som
she'd come to terms with long ago, but now, in
lump rose in her throat.

"When I look at you, I don't see a screwu
stroking Claire's hair. Then Whitney pulled t
hands on either side of Claire's face, looking her
"I think you have such a huge capacity for love."

"Thank you," Claire said. She kind of want
laughed instead. "Ugh, you're so good at this mo

Whitney laughed too. "I try," she said.

―――――――

cked up their luggage with a new com-
m, exchanging jokes about how Whit-
illow, how Claire had slept curled into
when Whitney went to the bathroom,
ncy tea bags their hotel room had been
d them into her backpack. She had to go
e could take a little bit of this weekend

Chapter 17

Amara wheeled her suitcase into the Sycamore House lobby behind Gwen. When they'd gotten back to their room last night, Amara had steeled herself for an emotional heart-to-heart about Christopher, but Gwen had simply kept listening to her audiobook, teary-eyed, and then gone to bed at nine P.M. Well, it would be nice to get a good night of sleep for once, Amara had thought, switching off her own light. Then she'd lain awake for an hour, thinking about that stupid intentions workshop they'd done and how she'd lied. When that crunchy manifestation leader had made them close their eyes and visualize their goals, she hadn't seen herself staying sane. She'd seen herself getting her financial house in order.

Now, as the other women filed into the lobby, Vicki floating in from God knows where, Gwen pulled out her Sycamore House booklet. "I think we have time to squeeze in one more activity before we head back to the city," she said.

Claire and Whitney walked into the room, laughing. "Like a cute little tennis ball," Whitney was saying. Amara stared at the two of them chumming it up and gritted her teeth. Oh, Lord, was she jealous? She made her way to Claire as Ellie and Gwen began to debate an abs workout versus an acupuncture workshop.

"I need a break from all this healthy shit," she whispered. "Take a walk with me?"

"Yes, please," Claire said, and they snuck out the side door, down some stone steps, and into the trees.

"How was your Whitney time?" Amara asked.

"It was really nice, actually," Claire said.

Amara put her hands on her hips. "Don't let her steal you away from me!"

"I'll try, but it's not easy, being so popular," Claire said, fluffing her hair jokingly.

They traversed the property, passing the budding flowers that the nature specialist had told them all about the day before, the dew on the grass soaking their sneakers. Everything was so *quiet* here—no jackhammers, no honking taxis, no wailing babies. Sort of eerie, actually.

"All right, so," Amara said. Her voice came out oddly formal, and she cleared her throat. "Hypothetically speaking, do you think there's ever a way to do a wife-bonus situation that *isn't* horribly unfeminist and regressive?"

Claire glanced at her sideways. "Hypothetically speaking," she said, her words coming out slow and carefully chosen, "that's a tough one. Is the hypothetical husband putting all the money he earns into a shared bank account that the hypothetical wife can access anytime?"

"Cutting the hypothetical crap, Daniel puts the vast majority of what he earns into a shared bank account, and then a tiny percentage into his own private account, just like what I was doing when I was working. But then I *stopped* working without fully consulting him and ever since then the financial situation has been all kinds of messed up. And there are times when a lady wants to make a purchase without having to justify it in the joint account, you know?"

"Mm," Claire said. "Like all your porn."

"Exactly."

"Why don't you just talk to him about all this?" Claire asked, as they walked past a burbling creek. "He seems like a good, understanding guy, from all you've told me."

Amara sighed. "I know. He is. But all these little financial resentments have built up since I quit my job, and he's always so drained by the time he gets home every night and we get Charlie to bed that he's too exhausted to fuck me, let alone have a serious, thorny, fiscal conversation." She paused. "That's the other problem here. My vagina is growing cobwebs."

"So you guys should have a date night," Claire said.

Amara grimaced. "I'm reluctant to inflict Charlie on unsuspecting babysitters who have no idea what they're getting into." The last time Amara and Daniel had hired someone was for Gwen's Christmas party. When they'd gotten home, the girl had greeted them like she'd been locked in an underground bunker for decades and they'd finally come to set her free.

"I'm not unsuspecting," Claire said as they turned onto the winding driveway, where the Sycamore House van waited to carry them back to their real lives. "I could babysit."

Chapter 18

So at six thirty-two P.M. on the following Friday night, Claire knocked on Amara's apartment door. Amara answered looking frazzled but also stunning, in a sleeveless gold blouse and skintight leather pants, as wails emanated from a distant corner of the apartment.

"Charlie's being an asshole," Amara said. "I am so sorry." Sure enough, when Amara led Claire through the living room and into the small nursery, Charlie was standing up in his crib, holding the slats, his tearstained face so angry, he resembled a miniature Hulk. "I wanted to get him to bed by the time you got here, but, well . . ." She held up her hands in a defeated gesture.

"Hey, bud," Claire said, taking a tentative step toward him. Man, this kid had liquids coming out of him everywhere—eyes, nose, mouth, probably the parts she couldn't see too. Had a hapless babysitter ever drowned in baby fluids before, or would she be the first?

"You are a goddess for doing this," Amara said. "Hopefully he'll wear himself out in a few minutes, and then you can spend the rest of the night watching TV. And seriously, help yourself to whatever. We've got food, drinks, very soft blankets on the couch. Just don't get *too* smashed, I suppose. You've changed a diaper before, right?"

"Yeah, totally," Claire lied.

Amara nodded in relief, then looked at the dinosaur-themed clock on Charlie's wall. "Ah, shit. Daniel's probably almost at the restaurant." She peered at Claire. "Erm, will you be all right?"

"What, why?" Claire asked, trying to relax her face.

"You know, I can absolutely tell Daniel to just come home." Amara bit her lip. "Yeah, I'll tell him to come home. I don't even know that I'm up for a big-deal dinner tonight. It's probably more trouble than it's worth."

"Stop. Amara," Claire said, grabbing her hand. "Don't freak out. Your baby will be fine. I'm already pretty sure I don't want to have kids anyway, so if he screams for the next three hours, it'll just reinforce my life choices. *You* are going to have a nice date with Daniel and rekindle your spark or whatever and be really glad you went. Okay?"

Amara pursed her lips and let out a breath from her nose. "Okay," she said, squeezing Claire's hand. "Thank you, Claire." She kissed the top of Charlie's head, then turned to go, pausing at the doorway. "Hey. I'm glad we're friends."

"Yeah," Claire said, blushing. "I am too."

Amara whooshed out. Immediately, Charlie began wailing even louder, staring at Claire as if she'd kidnapped him.

"Um," she said, then cleared her throat and began to sing. *"A B C D E F G."* No dice. Maybe he needed some bouncing? Babies liked that. She picked him up, and he squirmed in her arms as she continued the song, pacing the room. She'd walked from the subway to Amara's that night with a confident strut. Charlie always seemed to quiet down during music time at playgroup, which meant she'd be able to work some kind of magic trick as his babysitter. *She'd* be able to sing him to sleep no problem. She'd been delusional. She glanced at the dinosaur clock, where smiling T. rexes frolicked with pterodactyls. Ten minutes had gone by, but they'd felt like an hour.

And then Charlie let out the largest, wettest fart she'd ever heard. Immediately, a stench straight out of a nightmare pervaded the room. As she let out a yelp of disgust, Charlie gave a gurgle and then a devilish smile.

"Was that what this was all about, you little jerk?" she asked. "You just had to fart?"

But within seconds, his face collapsed back into tears. Apparently a fart was *not* what it was all about. The stench lingered. She had to go into the diaper zone.

She pulled out her phone and typed *how to change a diaper* into YouTube, clicking on the first video that came up. A plump, smiling woman cuddled her baby, talking into the camera. "I quickly realized," she said, "that diaper time could be *bonding* time. Talk to your baby while you're changing his diaper, maybe even tell him a story, and it can be fun and healthy for both of you." The woman went through a series of easy enough seeming motions to the soundtrack of an Enya song, while her baby stared at her adoringly. Claire closed out of the video and laid Charlie on his changing table.

"Okay," she said to him as he wriggled and knocked a bottle of hand sanitizer off the table. "Let's do this." She unsnapped his onesie and grabbed the sticky tabs on his diaper, then took a deep breath in through her mouth. Moment of truth.

Ugh, she thought when she opened up the diaper. It was *everywhere.* How could Charlie's tiny body even contain this much waste? Had he been saving it up for weeks in anticipation of that night? This was worse than she'd ever imagined a baby could produce, like a sizzling shit tornado had blown through his diaper and decimated everything in its path.

She stared at him in horror, then bent down to grab the hand sanitizer off the floor. She'd be needing it. By the time she popped back up again, a still-wailing Charlie had stuck his fists into his own mess and rolled over, smearing it all over the changing table, the wall, and his onesie as if he fancied himself some experimental artist, like Julianne Moore on the pulleys in *The Big Lebowski.*

"Gah, no!" Claire screamed, bubbles of panic rising up in her stomach, and grabbed onto Charlie before he could paint the rest of the room with his poop. Of course, that meant he simply swiped streaks of it down her arms instead. "Why?" she asked. In response, he grabbed a strand of her hair. "Perfect," she said. "I was thinking of shaving my head anyway."

She pressed her hand onto his chest to hold him steady on the changing table and leaned back as far away from him as she could.

"Calm down, Charlie Craplin," she said, gritting her teeth, wishing for a gas mask and a burning-hot shower. "You've made your point." She studied the scene and tried to remember what she was supposed to do. Rewatching the diaper-changing video would only contaminate her phone. She'd have to do the best she could with what she remembered. "Once upon a time," she said, as she reached for a diaper wipe and began the process of cleaning him off, "there was a little bundle of chaos who decided that he was going to take over the world." God, there were so many crannies in baby skin that could get disgusting. She reached for another diaper wipe with one hand, holding Charlie's tiny, velvety feet in the air with the other. Distractedly, she registered that his dimpled toes really were perfect. "He was ruthless and stinky and okay, yes, kind of cute." His cries began to subside with her story until he was letting out only the smallest of whimpers. Finally, five diaper wipes later, he seemed clean enough, so she bundled the trash away (the onesie appeared beyond repair so she put it in the trash too—*Sorry, Amara,* she thought, hoping it hadn't had sentimental value) and pulled a fresh diaper from the pack.

"So sometimes he won his battles for control," Claire continued as she slid the new diaper on Charlie's body and checked that it was facing the right way. "But sometimes," she said, as she pressed the fastening flaps into their proper positions, "his opponents did okay too."

Charlie let out a little contented sigh and smiled up at her with the purest, sweetest smile she'd ever seen. Dammit, this was how they got you. She shook her head at him—he wasn't going to fool her—slid on a onesie that *wasn't* spotted with poop, then lifted him gingerly and carried him to his crib. He grabbed onto a stuffed lamb, its fur matted from repeated gnawing, and curled up.

While she sang Beatles songs in her most calming manner, she scrubbed off as much of the mess from the wall as she could manage with the cleaning supplies by the changing table, then squirted half a bottle's worth of hand sanitizer onto her fingers. Satisfied, she snuck a glance at Charlie. His eyelids were drawing ever closer together. Claire grabbed the baby monitor, backed out of the room with all the stealth of a Navy SEAL, and then listened at the door for a minute. Oh, thank God. Glorious, glorious silence. She started to slump against the door, then remembered just in time that Charlie had turned her into a biohazard.

Her hands were clean enough, thanks to the hand sanitizer, so, following Amara's admonition to help herself to anything, she power-walked to the kitchen and took a quick slug of high-quality Scotch as a reward for surviving that (literal) shit storm. Then she headed for Amara's bathroom. It was a little weird to use Amara's shower without asking her, but better to do that than to interrupt a romantic date night with the news that she was currently wandering around their apartment covered in shit. So, very carefully, she stripped off her clothes.

The whole bathroom was beautiful, with slate gray walls and clean white tile. In particular, Amara's glass-enclosed shower was a dream. Claire's own showerhead spat out water at irregular intervals and temperatures, but Amara's copper one released a steady warm rain. Claire scrubbed and scrubbed with a bar of some organic soap that smelled like oatmeal, humming a new melody that had been flitting around her head recently, until the water streaming off her came out clear and her shoulders loosened in relaxation. It was like going to a spa. Luxurious. She could have stayed in the shower forever, using up New York City's entire water supply, until the Hudson River (or wherever the city's water came from) became a mere trickle, and the citizens of NYC tarred and feathered her for being an environmental menace.

Reluctantly, she turned off the water, then rolled her head from side to side, her muscles sore from going to a Barre class with the moms after playgroup the day before. The studio had been running a special where, for an extra twenty dollars on top of the forty-five-dollar class fee, women could drop off their babies with some childcare experts in one room and then squat and shake for an hour in the room next door. Whitney had invited Claire along, lending her more fancy workout clothes, plunking down her credit card and waving off Claire's halfhearted offer to pay for herself. So Claire had hoisted her leg up onto a ballet bar and stretched until muscles that she didn't even know she had burned. When they'd all walked out of class together, Claire's body had quivered with exhaustion but also with something else, a kind of rush from being part of their joking, sweaty clan.

Now she stepped out of the shower and checked the baby monitor. Charlie was still sleeping. She had plenty of time before Amara and Daniel were supposed to come home. She toweled off, then ran her fingers over a satin lavender robe hanging on a hook next to the towels.

God, it was soft. She stared at it, a longing blossoming in her chest. It couldn't hurt to try it on, just for a minute.

She shrugged it over her shoulders and belted it around her

waist, then stared at herself in the mirror. She looked sexy, but *classy* sexy, like an old-time movie star in a seduction scene.

"Hello," she purred at her reflection. "Welcome to my penthouse apartment." She pursed her lips and pushed out her breasts, then laughed at herself. Her eyes lit on a shelf of Amara's beauty products, lined up in straight rows like French schoolchildren. Some, like the fancy vitamins, were clearly recommended by the playgroup women. They practically screamed, "EXPENSIVE ALL-NATURAL BULLSHIT." Others, like the cocoa butter, she could safely assume that none of the other playgroup women had tried.

Staring at all the costly-looking products, Claire wondered if Amara had pilfered any of them, if she'd gone into some organic beauty store and slipped a ninety-nine-dollar bottle of hand lotion into her pocket when no one was looking. Then she thought about the Sisyphean life Amara had been leading for the past year—calming Charlie down, changing his diaper, and then doing it all over again, every day, and all without earning any money to fully call her own. No wonder she needed to steal the occasional luxury item to stay sane. If Claire were in that situation, she would probably have to start robbing banks. It no longer mattered to Claire what Amara had been doing in Whitney's office, she realized. She trusted her.

And sure, maybe these women went a little overboard with the wellness routines, but now, with the vast array of Amara's products stretched out in front of her like a mountain range and with the experience of Sycamore House lingering in her mind, Claire started to understand the appeal. She had never really been a fancy-lotion kind of person, but if she were, would her life be any different? Would the world be kinder to her if she spent half an hour every morning applying various creams and makeup? Would she glow like the playgroup women and give off an aura of money that made people want to give her more? (After all, money was like bunnies—once you had a certain amount of hundreds in your wallet, they just kept multiplying. Either people respected you and gave you opportunities that led to more money, or you put it in the stock market, sat back, and watched it give birth over and over again.)

She hadn't taken particularly good care of herself on the road with Vagabond. She'd shoveled down pizza and beer most nights along with the rest of the guys, and bathed a bit less than she should have, and hurriedly slicked on red lipstick for only the important shows. If she'd had the energy to go for a run each morning while the guys slept in, to put an array of products into her hair and onto her skin, maybe Marlena wouldn't have been able to march in and usurp her so easily. Maybe Claire would have fascinated the guys enough, and they would've stayed loyal.

Or maybe nothing would have changed. But in this particular moment, it was tempting to try on a Whitney-and-Amara kind of life, to pretend that she wasn't messy, flawed, exhausted by the world. To imagine that a new and content Claire could rise up from the discarded parts of the old one, that people could be awed by her. *Help yourself to anything,* she thought, and squeezed a pump of "skin-repairing" eucalyptus lotion onto her palm.

She made her way down the line with the growing excitement of a child snooping in her mother's jewelry box. Humming to herself, she put on a drop of hair oil to stop her frizz and rubbed her cheeks with exfoliating cream that smelled like the sea and billed itself as "a facial in a jar."

"Luminous skin? Me?" she said to her reflection. "Oh, you're too sweet. I just woke up like this." She came to the TrueMommy supplements and popped one into her mouth. "Why, yes, I *did* just give birth a day ago," she said. "But of course I'll be on the cover of your fashion magazine. What? No photoshopping necessary? If you say so!"

As the vitamin made its way into her system, she half-expected an instant transformation, like when she went to the gym for half an hour and then checked her stomach for a six-pack. But the same old Claire stared back at her in the mirror. She screwed the cap back onto the supplement jar and kept making her way down the line.

Instant transformations weren't possible, but she *could* take better care of herself. Maybe this silly playing around in Amara's beauty supplies could be the start of a new phase, of becoming a woman instead of some liminal creature still acting like a girl. She just needed some discipline, like the playgroup women had.

Then a thought hit her, and her heart started to race. These TrueMommy things were expensive. Did Amara count them? What if she noticed that she'd come up short at the end of the cycle and realized that Claire had taken one?

No, Amara would probably blame the manufacturer. Or even if she figured out Claire had taken one somehow, she might think it was weird, but she wouldn't *hate* her for it. It was just a fucking vitamin. Claire could buy her a whole bottle of Flintstone Gummies to make up for it. But none of her rationalizations made her heart slow down. It raced even faster, weirdly so, in a way that she'd felt before, although not recently. She put her palm on her chest and felt the kicking pulse. And then Claire's stomach dropped.

She'd done a fair amount of drugs in her day. She had been in a band, after all. Thanks to a series of long, hazy nights with the Vagabond crew, she knew the unpredictable beauty of acid, the drowsy pull of pot, the glorious kick of cocaine. Marcus had managed to get a prescription for Adderall, and sometimes they dug into it on long days when they wanted to be extra-productive with rehearsals.

And this "vitamin" working its way through her system was no all-natural supplement. It was straight-up speed.

Chapter 19

Amara sat at a corner table at Les Trois Cochons and swirled her pinot noir around in her glass. What the fuck was taking Daniel so long? She had sprinted half the way to the upscale French bistro after foisting off Charlie when he was *not* in a state to be left so that she wouldn't be more than a few minutes late for their date night, and now, ten minutes later, she was still sitting here alone while a disdainful, helium-voiced waitress hovered, asking if there was anything she could get her while she waited. Elderly Upper East Side couples cut into their steaks, Édith Piaf played in the background, and the smell of onions wafted out from the kitchen. Amara took a big sip of wine, trying to push away her annoyance. She didn't want the night to be ruined before it even began.

Finally, Daniel raced into the restaurant, his suit jacket over his arm, his expression worried as he scanned the room for her. When he saw her, he waved and began to scoot in between the tightly packed tables to get to her. He stumbled over a middle-aged woman's chair leg and caught himself by bracing himself on her shoulder. "Sorry! Sorry!" he said, pushing his glasses up while the woman frowned at him.

Not exactly the smoothest man in the world, her husband.

He slid into the chair across from her and wiped his forehead. "Oh, yes, I need some of that," he said, plucking the bottle of wine from the center of the table and filling his glass with a hearty pour. "Code-red-level frustrating day today." He threw his hands up in the air. "Sometimes, it becomes crystal clear that the only reason we have a philanthropy department is so that the bosses can make themselves look good while they're screwing over the world. Apparently, I'm a sucker for pushing for meaningful forms of charitable outreach."

"You're not a sucker," Amara said.

The waitress approached, pad and pencil in hand. *"Bonne nuit,"* she said. "Are you ready to place your order yet?"

"I'm sorry," Daniel said. "I haven't even opened the menu."

"Fine," the waitress said, exhaling sharply through her nose. "I will come back." She stalked off toward the rear of the restaurant.

Daniel really looked at Amara for the first time, over the flickering candle on their table. "You're mad," he said. "Because I'm late. I really tried to leave on time, but . . ." He shook his head. "Yet another reason why it was a frustrating day."

"Yes, I'm a little pissy, but I'm going to try not to be," Amara said. "You're here now—that's what matters."

"I'm sorry," Daniel said. "Thank you."

"You know you're still *helping* people," Amara said, resting her hand on his. "You might as well grab as much of the money from Satan's fat wallet as you can and use it for good."

"Yeah, I just have to sell my own soul to do it. After a while, Faustian bargains really get you down."

"Well, we've got a night away from Charlie, so let's try to relax for the moment, all right?" Amara asked.

"Yeah," Daniel said. "Yeah, you're right. I'm going to look at the menu so our waitress doesn't hate us any more than she already does."

"Good idea," Amara said, picking hers back up. "Oh, and at some point after we order, I want to talk with you about something."

"What?" he asked, looking up in concern. "Something bad? Is everything okay with Charlie?"

"Charlie's fine," Amara said. "Nothing too serious, really."

"Okay," Daniel said, and went back to his menu, scanning the list of entrées for a few seconds before snapping it shut. "Well, now I can't concentrate on ordering. Tell me what it is."

She shook her head. "Just a financial question."

"Ah, yes," Daniel joked, "you're going to beg me for a wife bonus, aren't you?"

"Ha-ha," Amara said, and then stared at her menu in silence, an ugly panic taking root in her stomach.

"Wait," Daniel said, leaning forward and staring at her in disbelief. "You're not, right?"

"No!" She paused. "Not exactly."

"Mari, just a week ago you were ripping the concept apart!"

"I know!" she said, a defensive edge to her voice. "But I think I was thrown off by the absurd 'wife bonus' term, rather than what it actually *means*. Because when you really think about it, it's not fair that you're putting aside money for yourself if I can't, when I'm working really hard too. That's all!"

"Hey," he said, rubbing his temples. "I'm not opposed to us reconfiguring what we do with my income so that you feel like it's more fair."

"All right," Amara said. "Thank you."

He nodded, then stared at his menu in silence, biting his lip like he always did when something else was bothering him.

"What?" Amara asked.

"Nothing."

"*What?*"

He snapped his menu shut. "I feel like you're implying that I'm making all these unfair financial decisions that hurt you, when I never wanted it to be this way. I've always wanted us to be equal partners in this. You're the one who made a really big financial decision that affected our family without consulting me at all."

"I know," Amara said quietly.

"Sometimes I hate my job so much, it feels like a hundred paper cuts on my soul. But I would never quit without talking it through with you first."

"I'm sorry," Amara said. "I shouldn't have done that like I did. But unfortunately I can't invent a time machine and go back and change it, so I'm not really sure what to do." She sighed. "If it makes you feel any better, I'm not exactly having a grand old time in my new situation either."

"Of course it doesn't make me feel better, Mari. I want you to be *thrilled* about our life. I just don't . . . I know being a stay-at-home mom isn't always a picnic, but from the outside, it looks like you've got it pretty good, okay? So maybe I'm a little jealous that you get to hang out with Charlie all day. I'd love to do that and have some time to think about how to start my own business and go to fun playgroups."

"Oh," Amara said, her ears getting hot like she'd just rubbed jalapeño juice all over them. "I'm *sorry*. You think that's what being a stay-at-home parent is like? That you just 'hang out' and Charlie takes long naps and you have plenty of brain space to get a new business off the ground? No, no. I never get a break. That beautiful demon we made needs constant attention, plus I'm always worrying that I'm doing something to screw him up for life. Did you know how much conflicting information is out there, once you go down the parenting-advice rabbit hole? 'Oh! Co-sleeping is a nice way to bond!' says one reputable source, while another tells you, 'Oh, co-sleeping means you'll smother your baby in the night, *murderer*.' At my job, at least I could see if something I was doing worked or if it made the show shit. With Charlie, I'm producing a new twenty-four-hour entertainment episode every day, but who the hell knows the consequences of everything I put into it? We probably won't *see* the consequences until ten years from now, and then we'll realize, *Oh fuck! Actually, I should have been teaching him Mandarin!*"

The waitress marched back up to the table. "*Excusez-moi*, what would you like to eat—?"

"We're not ready to order yet, so sorry!" Amara said. The waitress glared and huffed away. "And sure," Amara continued, leaning forward, "I go to playgroup and drink wine, and sometimes it's quite nice, but sometimes I'm freaking out that the other perfect, beautiful moms are judging Charlie for being difficult and judging *me* for not controlling him well enough or for not being rich enough to buy thousand-dollar succulents for all my windowsills, and sometimes I'd love nothing more than to skip it, but if I do, then Charlie won't get the socialization he needs, and he'll never understand how to form healthy friendships or some bullshit like that. And on top of that, I feel like I can't complain or can't be unhappy, because I'm so fucking privileged to get to do all this. *And* my brain feels like it's withering inside my skull." She paused. "*And* sometimes I just want to crawl into an old bog and die."

She and Daniel stared at each other in silence for a moment. Then he let out a long, low breath. "Wow," he said. "I . . . Okay. I was not aware of how strongly you felt."

"I wish we could do a *Freaky Friday*. You'd see it's not a walk in the park. Even though often it does literally involve walking in the park." She bit her lip as her eyes began to tear up. "And I'd probably have a better appreciation for how hard you're working to sustain our situation. Because I know you are working very hard."

Daniel reached across the table and grabbed onto her hand. "So neither one of us is particularly happy right now," he said. "What can we do to fix that?"

"Well, I was looking forward to tonight, for starters," Amara said. "But I think I ruined it now."

"You didn't ruin anything," Daniel said. "We can start over and make it romantic."

"Oh, yeah? How?"

"I can run out and buy you a dozen roses."

Amara cleared her throat. "I could give you a hand job under the table."

Daniel's dark brown eyes lit up, and she laughed. "Oh," he said. "Was that *not* a serious offer? Because it's mean to play with my heart that way!"

Amara looked around the room and lowered her voice. "I think everyone in this restaurant hates us now. The tables are too close together, and that couple over there was definitely listening in on our conversation."

Daniel raised his hand in the air and signaled the waitress, who rolled her eyes and came back, a long, drawn-out *Fiiiiinally* clearly reverberating in her mind. "I'm so sorry," he said. "But could we get the check?"

They drained the bottle of wine and, hand in hand, ran to a dingy diner a few blocks away, one of the last remaining dingy diners in the neighborhood and maybe all of Manhattan. They ordered greasy hamburgers and Greek salads with big blocks of feta cheese, watery lettuce, and slightly too ripe tomatoes. They'd never been good at fancy date nights anyway, Amara thought, as the burger juice ran down Daniel's chin. They'd never even really had a first date.

Amara met Daniel at business school. It had been a momentary life-path mistake that she'd made with heavy encouragement from her parents, and she'd realized within her first month that she was *not* interested. People partied like they were back in college, except with an even greater urgency, because they'd experienced the real world and knew what it was like. More than classes or grades, the important thing at business school was the schmoozing. The university gave its students endless opportunities to get drunk on free alcohol with the underlying understanding that you were supposed to Always! Be! Networking! So even if the person you were talking to was so drunk that he couldn't touch his finger to his nose, he was still sizing you up: Was your uncle's friend's sister in charge of hiring at McKinsey? Did you have a trust fund and a desire to invest in an exciting new venture that would revolutionize the way people sent out their laundry? Amara was happy to use people, sure, but she wanted *some* pure things in her life.

One night, at a particularly raucous event, she sat at the bar, nursing a gin and tonic and planning her escape while a bunch of her classmates stained their button-downs with beer, roaring with laughter. These boys and occasional girls were paragons of good breeding, their pale foreheads glistening with sweat.

"So," the guy sitting a couple of stools away asked, "which one of them do you think will be our generation's Bernie Madoff?"

She turned, surprised. Daniel was one of the quieter, more bookwormy ones in the class who often seemed overwhelmed by the boisterous men around him and who, like Amara, tended to leave these sorts of things early. He'd never spoken to her directly before.

"Hmm," she'd said, cocking her head to the side, swishing a sip of gin in her mouth and studying the crowd. Then she pointed at one of the red-faced men, his arm thrown around a buddy, beer belly beginning to strain his shirt. "Eric."

"Really?" Daniel asked, squinting. "I would've gone with James."

"James is too obviously a shifty ass. To be a successful Madoff, I think you've got to have a good facade. Eric, final answer."

Daniel nodded, serious. "Okay. I can see it. I guess we'll have to check back in with each other in forty years to see if you're right."

"Deal," Amara said, and smiled, signaling the bartender for another drink.

They talked for another two hours that night as, one by one, their other classmates straggled out. He was from Massachusetts, where he'd been one of only two black kids in his grade. He had a bit of a socialist streak and wanted to change the business world from the inside. His father was a local judge, and when Daniel and his two brothers were small, they'd all sit around the dinner table on Sunday nights and air their grievances for the week (for example, Daniel's older brother had punched him but only because Daniel was being annoying) while their father very thoughtfully and seriously adjudicated the disputes. She had never heard anything more charming in her life.

At a certain point, she put down her drink, stood up, and said, "All right, then, let's go."

"What?" he asked.

"Well, do you want to fuck me or what?"

They'd carried on for a week before she decided to drop out of business school and move to New York to see if she could get a job, any job, at one of the late-night shows that had been keeping her sane recently. She wasn't going to stay someplace she hated just because of a fling, even if Daniel *was* extremely kind and funny and pretty damn good in bed to boot.

And she didn't believe in anything as sentimental as fate, but four years later, she ran into him in a coffee shop in the West Village. They were both casually dating other people, but they picked right back up where they'd left off.

As they strolled home from the diner, going out of their way to walk along the Central Park side of Fifth Avenue, Amara draped Daniel's arm over her shoulder. "If you want to quit your job and start your own business, I support you," she said. "Even if it means we have to sell the apartment and move the family to a place where the cost of living is lower, like—I don't know—Cleveland."

He smiled. The spring evening air smelled of budding trees, of damp grass. "I support you too, Mari," he said. "Whether you want to work out some new kind of financial arrangement for staying at home or consider going back to work." At the mention of going back to work, a lot of confusing feelings she couldn't quite identify—panic or excitement?—began swirling around inside of her. He saw them on her face. "Or become a rodeo clown," he added.

"How did you know that rodeo clowning was my secret dream?" she asked.

"I know you," he said, kissing her cheek. "And here's our cross street. Time to head home and release the babysitter?"

It struck her that bringing a kid into a marriage was like getting a huge promotion, but with no raise and still having to do all your old work of being a good partner too. Despite the promise of fairy-tale weddings, marriage *was* work. But she'd gotten very lucky with her coworker.

"First," she said, pointing to a secluded spot in the park, "do you want to sneak into those bushes over there and have a quickie?"

"Yes, please," he said.

In the elevator, zooming back up to their apartment, Daniel picked leaves and other various park detritus out of Amara's hair. "Oh," she said, giddy. "I can't wait for you to meet Claire!" Introducing two people who were both grade A excellent was one of life's great joys.

"Wait," Daniel said, starting to put two and two together. "Claire from playgroup is babysitting tonight?"

"Yeah," she said. "She's not a mom—she's our musician. I have a cool young friend with whom I'm a bit obsessed. Is that weird?"

He laughed as the doors slid open onto their floor. "No weirder than anything else about you."

"She's a delight and you're a delight, and we should all hang out and have fun together," Amara said, pulling out her keys.

"I'm looking forward to it," Daniel said as they swung the door open.

Claire was sitting on their couch, her knee jiggling up and down, staring straight ahead. "Claire! Beautiful, sanity-saving Claire," Amara said, running to her side. "Meet Daniel!"

"Hi, Claire," Daniel said, smiling and holding out his hand for a shake. "I've heard that you are a delight."

"Oh," Claire said as she stood, distracted. "What? No, I'm . . . Hi. Nice to meet you."

"She's a very talented singer and songwriter," Amara said to Daniel, then turned back to Claire. "Thank you *so* much. We had a lovely time. Well, after a bit of a rough start. We had to switch restaurants. Daniel, you should tell her about—" Through her haze of happiness and wine buzz and post-sex endorphins, she noticed that Claire was avoiding her eyes. That wasn't like her. "Oh, no," she said. "Charlie was very difficult, wasn't he?"

"Um," Claire said. "He had a poop explosion, but after that, he was fine. I hope it's okay, I rinsed off in your bathroom."

"Oh, Lord," Amara said. "Of course that's fine. I'm sorry you had to deal with that."

"He's really got a special talent for pooping," Daniel said. "We're not sure which side of the family it comes from." He put his hand up as if to block his mouth from Amara and pointed to her while whispering her name. Claire gave a half laugh that got stuck in her throat.

"Do you want to stay and have a drink?" Amara asked. "Oh, let's all have a drink together!"

"No," Claire said. "I mean, I should let the two of you continue your date night." Amara started to protest, but Claire waved a trembling hand through the air. "My stomach's feeling weird anyway."

"Oh, that's too bad," Amara said as Daniel reached for his wallet and pulled out three twenties. "Well, we'll see you at Reagan's birthday party on Sunday, right?"

"Yeah," Claire said, gathering up all of her stuff.

Amara walked Claire to the door and stared after her as she disappeared into the elevator, an uneasy feeling starting to replace all her prior giddiness.

"She seemed . . . nice," Daniel said, coming up behind her and putting a hand on her shoulder.

"I think Charlie broke her with his poo," Amara said, shutting the door and turning the lock. "She's different than that normally." She shook her head. "Well, you'll get to know each other at the birthday party. The birthday party will be great."

Chapter 20

So *this was how they did it all,* Claire thought as she ran through Central Park in the dark, her body filled with too much unwanted nervous energy for her to stand and wait at a bus stop. *With a little help from hard drugs.* Beyond the aspect of potential child endangerment, Claire didn't mind the speed itself, exactly. What really filled her with an unexpected anger was the fact that they were cheating. All the natural health that Whitney had espoused, all that "wisdom" Amara had fed her—don't wait too long to get your shit together, that whole act—it was a lie. If you were wealthy enough, apparently you could just pop pills to lose weight and give you endless energy, and no one would mind. Quite the opposite, in fact. They'd beg for you to be in their coffee-table books so you could make all the normal women out there feel inferior. Someone like Claire would never be able to glow and awe like them, because there was no possible way to catch up.

God, their poor children. Claire thought of Whitney stroking her hair at Sycamore House while Claire poured out the story of her mother choosing appearances over what was best for her child, pretending to empathize while she was doing the exact same thing. The playgroup women probably all thought Claire was an idiot, laughing at her after she left Whitney's apartment each time for the way that she had fallen for their act. (Because they *had* to know—there was no way you could delude yourself into thinking a pill of that strength was some all-natural vitamin.)

Dammit, she had really, really liked them. Especially Amara. What a head-spinning, soul-annihilating disappointment.

She slowed down and pulled out her phone, dialing Thea's number. The phone rang and rang until a text from Thea popped up. *Not a good time. Let's talk later.* Claire put her phone back in her pocket and jogged on.

Probably a dumb idea to run through the park at night. That was how people got murdered. *Oh, well,* she thought as the color that the playgroup women had recently brought into her life leached out, leaving the world around her bloodless and gray. She ran all the way home, jumping back when the occasional rat scrambled across her path, blisters forming where her fraying Chucks rubbed up against her heels.

It had been a while since she'd really indulged in some good old Drinking to Forget alone in her apartment, but now seemed as good a time as any. She lost all of Saturday to the clanking bottles of whiskey she pulled down from her cabinet.

Sunday morning came in far too bright, the sun insistently flaunting itself against her window like a spray-tanned child in a beauty pageant. The lure of curling herself underneath the covers, only coming out to order a pizza in another hour or two, was strong. But she had to get up. It was Reagan's birthday party.

So maybe the women took speed. She could still take their money. No matter how much she'd deluded herself lately that they were adopting her, that she was their little pet or maybe even a real friend, she was just the hired help. None of them owed her anything except the money they'd promised to pay her, so she might as well go and collect that. Besides, there was the Amara connection for her music too, and she'd be a fool to give that up. Beyond that, screw them all. They could do what they wanted.

She pulled on some clothes and ran a brush through her hair, determined to harden her heart. Hey, she'd passed herself off as a devout Christian for years. She could continue to joke around with the Wellness Goddesses as if she believed that they actually cared about all-natural health.

Gwen's ridiculous brownstone had pink and white balloons tied to the steps out front to mark the party inside. When Claire stepped into the foyer, Gwen's older daughter, Rosie, was half-heartedly taking coats, although what she was *really* doing was wearing a tiara and fairy wings and twirling around the hallway.

"Thanks, Rosie," Claire said as she handed the girl her jacket.

"Call me by my princess name," Rosie said, and then sang out in a warbling voice, "Rosalindaaaaaa!"

Claire smiled, a smile that disappeared as soon as she heard Gwen say her name from the top of the staircase.

Gwen wore a string of pearls and a rose-colored dress with a floral pattern, her hair blown out into perfect loose curls. Very Disney princess meets fifties housewife chic. Very Momstagram-worthy. Very hopped up on speed. On her hip, Gwen bounced Reagan, who wore a gold-edged bib with the words *BIRTHDAY GIRL* emblazoned in pink block letters. Gwen waved at Claire, her blueberry eyes wide in anticipation. "Come on in," she was saying, "and put your guitar down. Let's start the music in twenty minutes so that we can do the cake before the kids get cranky. And in the meantime, help yourself to refreshments and make yourself at home!"

It was a relatively small affair—mostly the playgroup moms and their husbands, plus a few relatives and coworkers and some rambunctious friends of Rosie's, but even though the guest list might have been limited, Gwen and Christopher had gone all out. A professional photographer wandered around, exhorting people to smile. In the corner, a bartender served up a specialty cocktail called the "Reagan Rickey"—Claire took one immediately and thanked God for the gin burning down her throat—underneath an entire archway made of those same pink and white balloons from outside woven together, with a floating silver balloon in the shape of an "R" at the center of the whole thing. Streamers flapped down from the chandelier, and a young woman did face painting by one of the windows, dappling children's cheeks with unicorns and rainbows. (Maybe the face painter was also an aspiring artist who had expected better things from her life by now. Maybe she really wanted to be dappling gigantic canvases to hang on gallery walls.) The coffee table was bursting with presents wrapped beautifully in patterned paper and curling ribbons. Had everyone there gone to a freaking professional gift wrapper? There must have been at least thirty boxes of things little Reagan would soon discard. It was all a whole lot of effort for a party Reagan would never remember.

Claire wandered into the dining room, where the table practically groaned under the weight of all the refreshments it held. How wonderful it would be to be hungry right now, for everything to be normal again, for her to embrace Ellie and Meredith, who were bearing down on her, with uncomplicated joy.

And you're *a lying speed freak,* she thought as Ellie hugged her, then passed her off to Meredith while their much less well-kept husbands looked on. *And so are you.* It was like Claire had run a black light over a beloved room, and now she was seeing all the stains she hadn't noticed before, when she'd been blinded by radiance. Of course they were so thin, Claire thought, as Ellie put a bony arm around her and introduced her to John, who was holding little Mason in his arms. Of course they had time and energy to meticulously plan the perfect outfits for themselves and their babies, she realized as Meredith showed off little Lexington's poofy hair bow, which she'd had to go to five stores to find.

"Did you talk to Whitney?" Ellie asked. "The coffee-table-book shoot is this Thursday, so we'll be meeting there instead of at her apartment. It's so exciting!"

"I agree. I always wanted to marry a model," John said. Ellie shoved him affectionately. John was solid, with a bit of a beer belly, his hair graying—the kind of man who had definitely belonged to a fraternity in college and who probably rhapsodized about his crazy days in Kappa Delta Alpha or whatever with great frequency.

In his arms, little Mason started crying, his face wrinkling up, and John bounced him, but Mason only continued to whimper. "Here, you want Mama, don't you?" John said, passing the baby off to Ellie and turning to the refreshment table, then loading cheeses and meats onto a plate for himself. "So you're the music teacher," he said to Claire. "Maybe you can convince them that worrying about preschool already is crazy!"

"Not according to Gwen!" Ellie said as she attempted to calm Mason to no avail.

"It's true, John," chimed Meredith in support. "I've heard from a bunch of people that it's really important to do your research."

Ellie nodded along and went in for the kill. "We could just send Mason to public school, honey. But I can't imagine your mother would allow *that*."

"Okay, I should go get ready for the music," Claire said.

"We can't wait!" Ellie said.

"Oh, by the way, we're going to get manicures before the photo shoot," Meredith said. "Do you want to come? It'll be our treat!"

"Is this your nice way of telling me my nails are disgusting?" Claire asked, waggling her unadorned fingers and smiling like she meant it, and Meredith giggled. "Excuse me."

As she walked away, she caught sight of Vicki on the window seat, wearing her usual floaty garb, feeding a fussy Jonah. The veins in her exposed breast glowed blue in the daylight from the window. As Claire watched, an unfamiliar woman—probably a coworker of Christopher's, judging by her sleek, boardroom-ready haircut—bustled up to Vicki. "Excuse me," the woman said. "But you're making my husband uncomfortable." Vicki stared up at the woman, her face placid. The woman shot a look back at her husband and then tried again. "Do you have a cover you can use?"

Vicki shook her head and shrugged her shoulders in an apologetic manner, then began to turn away. The woman unwrapped a scarf from her neck. "Here, you're welcome to borrow this," she said, her voice dripping with graciousness. Vicki languidly stretched out her hand for the scarf. As the woman passed it over, Vicki smiled as if in thanks. Then she slid open the window and dropped the scarf onto the sidewalk outside. The woman let out an indignant squeak and rushed away to retrieve it.

Vicki settled back, running her hand over her son's curly hair, her calm expression slipping for a moment as two angry red spots rose on her cheeks. She noticed Claire staring at her and mouthed a hello, and Claire began to mouth one back as Vicki's son resumed his feeding. Then Claire's stomach dropped. Fuck, could speed get into breast milk?

Unable to think about that horrible possibility for a moment longer, she looked away and into the laughing, drinking, glass-clinking crowd, to where Amara stood by the bar with Daniel. Amara lit up in recognition and started waving her over, but Claire pretended not to notice and ducked into the kitchen instead.

It was airy and full of light, thanks to a large window that looked onto the house's tidy backyard. A few guests milled about, getting glasses of water or simply seeking an escape from the rest of the party. She could have used a glass of water herself. Her mouth was as dry from nerves and dread as it had been when Vagabond sat her down for the talk. She headed for the sink. Over at the kitchen island, a man with curling golden hair was sticking candles into a multilayered cake, puffy with frosting, decorated with a ring of strawberries at the base. A group of Rosie's friends ran through, and he gave them all high fives, then teased them about how he was going to eat the entire cake himself.

"No!" they shouted, giggling.

"It's true," he said. "I've already eaten five cakes today, but I need *more!*"

So this was Christopher, she thought, eyeing him with disdain. The breaker of hearts and vows, the suspected ripper of strange women's panties. He was even sexier in person than she'd expected.

"You must be Claire," he said when he spied her, and held out his hand for a shake. "Gwen's been singing your praises for weeks now. We're all really looking forward to the music. I've been warned not to sing along, because my voice makes dead musicians roll over in their graves, but I'll do all the dancing you need." Ugh, and he was charming too, with a strong handshake. He held on to her fingers just a second too long. Yup, he was totally cheating on Gwen. He reminded her of Marcus from Vagabond, actually—that same kind of golden-boy gleam that came from a high success rate of getting women into bed.

"Claire! Hey, you," Whitney said, sweeping into the kitchen in a gorgeous sundress and heels, throwing her arms around Claire. *Speed speed speed speed,* went the voice in Claire's head. "We had a spill out there, so I've been sent on a mission to find paper towels."

"Right over here," Christopher said, indicating the counter behind him. "Whitney, right? Nice to see you again."

"Christopher," she said with the studied coolness of a woman being civil to her close friend's cheating husband. He held out his arms for a hug, and she walked behind the kitchen island to give him a stiff kiss on the cheek, resting a hand on his shoulder to balance herself as she went up on tiptoe.

"I was just telling Claire," he said, "that I can't wait to see what all this playgroup-music fuss is about."

Gwen poked her head in. "There you are, Claire! Ready to get started?"

So Claire set up her guitar and the props Gwen had bought for her to use—a bubble machine, a parachute, sparkly egg shakers, and rainbow-colored scarves—in the middle of the living room while Gwen ushered the older children to spots on the rug and the women gathered with their husbands and babies. Claire strummed a C chord.

"Hey, everyone," she said, mustering all the positive energy she could find. "Who's feeling happy to be here for Reagan's birthday?" The audience *whoo*-ed, some of the adults lifting their children's arms into the air. "Well," Claire continued, and launched into song, *"If you're happy and you know it clap your hands."*

As she sang, her eyes landed on Whitney, leaning over toward her husband, who was holding Hope and moving her little hands in a clapping motion for her. There was Vicki, now bouncing her baby next to her buttoned-up husband, a contrast so stark Claire almost wanted to laugh. And then she locked eyes with Amara.

It was all well and good, in the mustiness of her apartment, to say, *Screw them all!* But as Claire watched them laughing with their babies and their husbands, these women who had made her feel wanted again, a great wave of sadness crashed down upon her anger. Goddammit. She could feel a reckoning coming on.

Chapter 21

In the crowd of people, Whitney stood in between Grant and Christopher. Oh, the thrilling disaster of it all, the nearness of Christopher as he casually settled himself on her left side while Grant reached for her hand on the right. She was racked with guilt and wetter than she'd ever been before.

It had started in the kitchen. She'd known he was in there, so when one of Rosie's little friends had spilled a cup of juice, she'd jumped at the chance to go get paper towels, just to see him, to say hello as if she barely remembered him.

She'd gone behind the kitchen island and, marshaling every ounce of self-control she had, kissed him casually on the cheek. And then he had reached his hand up where the island hid their lower halves and run a finger underneath her dress, slipping it for one heavenly second inside her underwear and into her while he kept talking to Claire and the others in the kitchen.

As everyone else began to slowly migrate into the living room for the music, Whitney made her way to the counter and grabbed some paper towels. "It's a lovely party so far," she said.

"Thanks!" he said as she walked back behind the island, where the path to get by him was quite narrow. "Yes, we're very happy with how it's going."

"Oops, excuse me!" she said as she brushed her ass against the front of his pants, and he stiffened.

She was appalled at herself, of course, at the kind of woman she had turned out to be—an adulteress. A friend betrayer. A liar.

But she also felt a perverse thrill of excitement and maybe even pride at the kind of woman she had turned out to be—someone who had discovered a whole new level of desire and sensuality that she hadn't known existed before. An adventurer giving a big middle finger to all the rules she'd worked so hard to follow. Not just a wife and mother, but an interesting and flawed and full woman.

Now she squeezed her legs tight against each other and focused on Claire, who had launched into "Old MacDonald." That was good. Nothing remotely sexy about Old MacDonald and his farm. Unless Old MacDonald was really more of a middle-aged MacDonald with Christopher's face, and he wanted to take you for a roll in the hay in the barn out back . . .

And then the strangest thing happened with Claire. One minute, she was doing fine—not quite reaching the heights of fun and talent that she showed at playgroup, but maybe she wasn't used to performing for such a big crowd. The next, her performance turned completely unfocused. Her voice broke once and then caught again, like she was about to cry or like she had forgotten how to breathe. She started singing about Old MacDonald having a cow, even though she'd already done that animal.

Whitney stared, concerned. Oh, this was *bad*. What was going on? Had Claire suddenly come down with food poisoning? Had her cat died that morning, and she'd only now been hit by the weight of its loss? (Wait. Did Claire have a cat? Whitney realized with a shock that she cared about Claire very much—that Claire had filled the space that Joanna had left behind, making the playgroup seven again, like they were meant to be—and yet Whitney knew scarcely anything about Claire's day-to-day life.)

Within the span of a minute, fickle Rosie and her friends, the bigger children who had gathered and clapped enthusiastically at first, lost interest and drifted away, climbing on a nearby couch and jumping while Gwen tried to cajole them to keep listening to the music. Next to Whitney, Grant gave a little shake of his head and took a large sip of his drink, while some other adults whom Whitney didn't know exchanged raised eyebrows. Outrage rose up in Whitney on Claire's behalf—these strangers had no idea how talented she was, how sweet. How dare they judge her like this when it was clear that something else was going on?

Whitney tried to catch Claire's eye to give her an encouraging smile, but the one time Claire's glance landed on hers, Claire immediately looked away, her voice catching again. So Whitney sought out Amara's eyes instead, and the two of them shot worried, befuddled looks at each other. Amara gave Whitney a nod.

Action time. They picked up the shakers that Claire had tossed out, shook them enthusiastically, and sang along to the song with gusto. When the other playgroup women realized what was happening, they joined in. Daniel and Christopher did too. Whitney did a shimmy and grabbed Amara's hand to twirl her. The kids jumping on the couch looked over, having second thoughts about their decision to leave.

Claire looked up at them all, saving her, and seemed to make a decision. She finished the song, took a deep breath, and switched on a smile again. There she was, the normal Claire. "Oh, I've got a great surprise. It's parachute time," she said, and unwrapped the large billowing cloth. The older kids came running back, laughing, and the adults lifted the multicolored fabric up and down, up and down.

Chapter 22

When Claire finished her set, having won back the approval of the children and the adults who didn't know her, she set down her guitar in a corner and disappeared out the door to Gwen's back deck. Amara handed Charlie off to Daniel and followed.

She found Claire leaning against the railing, staring into the glorious, sunny May sky. It was sweater weather still, and Amara shivered a bit, having forgotten hers inside. Claire wore nothing over her black V-neck T-shirt, and her arms were prickled with gooseflesh, but she didn't rub them or stamp her feet or shake herself to keep warm. She stood still, as if listening very hard in a private conversation with God.

"What happened back there?" Amara asked. "Are you all right? Or are you having a bit of a breakdown?"

Claire turned around. All the strange tremulousness she'd shown during that off moment in her set was gone. Instead, she seemed lit from within by a sense of purpose that Amara didn't understand, far more mature than ever before. "I know this isn't my place," she said. "And if you guys need to fire me for saying this, that's okay, but I can't sit around while you all dig yourselves into the ground in some misguided quest for perfection. So I'm just going to say it. I think it really sucks that you're taking speed."

"Um. What?" Amara said, Claire's words knocking the breath out of her like a sucker punch.

"You don't need it," Claire continued. "Or maybe right now you feel like you do—I know addiction is a hell of a monster. Like, I don't *think* I'm an alcoholic, but sometimes I feel like I'm going to kill someone if I don't get a drink, so I can only imagine how much harder it would be to stop popping pills all the time. But I'm sure you can do it. You're strong and amazing, and ultimately, you'd be much better off without it, and—"

"Wait," Amara said. "What the fuck are you talking about?"

"You don't have to pretend," Claire said. "I tried your True-Mommy."

"You . . . ," Amara began, having trouble finding the words to continue. A terrible awareness started to dawn inside of her. No. It couldn't be true. But also, of course it was.

"I'm sorry," Claire said. "I know it was a total invasion of privacy, but when I was babysitting, I was playing around and I popped one into my mouth, and almost immediately, my heart started racing."

"Oh, no," Amara said, her legs going weak beneath her. She grabbed the railing and sank down so that she was sitting on the top step leading down to Gwen's yard, a picture-perfect postage stamp with a rosebush and a flagstone path, a homemade bird feeder swamped with sparrows, a little metal slide on one side for the children, and a patio table with a couple of chairs for the adults on the other. Objectively, those things were there in her line of vision, but all she could see was Charlie's little face, staring balefully up at her. "Oh, *shit*. Oh, motherfucking holy bloody hell."

"It's okay," Claire said, sinking down with her and grabbing her hand. "I'm not going to tell anyone."

"Wait. No. Are you sure it was *speed*?" Amara asked, giving Claire's hand the same death grip she'd given Daniel in the delivery room, staring straight into Claire's eyes as if by looking hard enough, she could open up a portal and return them to the proper reality they'd somehow gotten detached from. "Not just a bit of caffeine or something?"

"Um . . . no, I'm pretty sure it was some kind of amphetamine. A relatively low dose, but still," Claire said. "We used to take Adderall on the road sometimes, and this felt exactly the same." She peered at Amara. "Hold on—you didn't know?" Amara shook her head. "Oh, my God. But how could you not know?"

"There were no fucking side effects when they started! They were just normal vitamins!" Amara said, then gasped. "Oh! *That's* why the trial month had the packets separated week by week. Not because they were 'curating' them! Those sociopaths at TrueMommy must've upped the level of the drug in them bit by bit. I will *murder* those snakes. I will chop them up with a pickax and feed them to the subway rats." Was it possible that Charlie had felt her heart racing too fast whenever she'd held him to her breast and tried to comfort him?

That maybe part of the reason he'd been so difficult to calm was because he knew that something was wrong? It sounded mental, but babies could sense things. They could be shaped forever by the smallest mistake. She took a shuddering breath and began to cry. "Oh, forget Joan Crawford. I am the worst mother in the world."

Claire put her arms around Amara, rocking her back and forth right there on the landing as, inside the brownstone, the laughter and chatter of the party guests carried on as normal. "Hey, no, you're not," Claire said. "You didn't know."

"But I did," Amara said. "I mean, not all the way, but I thought maybe— No, I knew. I knew something was weird ever since that day in Whitney's office when you walked in on me."

She hadn't been trying to find soap. Whitney kept her bathroom fully stocked. Claire probably thought she'd been looking for money, jewelry maybe, but that hadn't been it at all. Charlie had been so ornery and difficult that day, crying from the moment he woke up at six A.M. till the moment they left the house to go to Whitney's, that she'd completely forgotten to take her True-Mommy. *Oops,* she'd thought when she'd realized. But then midway through Gwen's lecture on how to get Charlie to pull himself up, the pounding headache had started, and it had taken every ounce of her self-control to keep herself from screaming at Gwen to shut her big judgmental mouth. All throughout music, it had just gotten worse and worse, like a hippopotamus tap-dancing on her brain, even though Claire's voice had been lovely, so warm and honeyed. It wasn't so strange. People got headaches all the time. Her own mother suffered from migraines. Maybe it was a family curse finally coming to claim her.

She'd excused herself to go to the bathroom, thinking maybe she'd find some Tylenol in Whitney's medicine cabinet. But then the door to Whitney's office had been open, and Amara had remembered their first meeting in the coffee shop, when Whitney said that she planned to stash the Xanax that her doctor had given her away in some desk drawer. Why settle for Tylenol when she could have Xanax? The impulse seized her, and suddenly she was tearing through the desk, looking for pills, fingers scrabbling against receipts and gift bag materials. Then that noise from the doorway, Claire staring at her like a scared little deer, and she realized how crazy and out of control she was. She was stealing from her friend, stealing something that her friend was ashamed to even have in the first place, and this outsider had caught her doing it. What a fucking nightmare.

And sure, it was a little odd that this terrible headache happened on the day she forgot her TrueMommy. But if that meant anything beyond sheer coincidence, then everything was so much worse than it already was. So when all of Dr. Clark's science sounded so reasonable, and all the other mothers were so enthusiastic, it was easy to believe that nothing was wrong with TrueMommy besides the price tag. All the times since, when she'd contemplated giving up the vitamins only to feel a sense of dread at the prospect, she'd ignored and explained away those too.

"I just couldn't fucking admit it," she said. "The closest I got was thinking that maybe they had a bit of caffeine in them or something, and that's why I'd gotten a headache. But of course that wasn't it. Of *course*." She pounded her fist against the wood of the deck and then winced as a splinter embedded itself in her knuckle. She deserved it. She deserved to be hunted down by a pitchfork-wielding mob like the monster she was.

"Amara," Claire said as Amara tried to pick the shard of wood out of her skin. "I am so, so sorry." The strains of "Happy Birthday" began to float out from the house behind them.

"Thank you," Amara said, giving up on the splinter removal and standing up. "Well, obviously, I'm going to stop taking them. And we've got to let the others know."

"Now?" Claire said. "I am ready for action. Whatever you need."

"No," Amara said as the song wound down. Inside, they'd be cutting the cake and posing for pictures that Gwen was probably planning on putting into a beautifully designed album and decorating with a bunch of stickers and treasuring forever. "Gwen has been putting all of her energy into planning this party for months now. We can't ruin it. Tonight."

So she wiped her eyes, squeezed Claire's hand one more time, and went back inside. In a corner, Daniel was trying to feed Charlie bites of cake without getting frosting all over the place. He was not succeeding. "Uh-oh," Amara said, and scooped up a smear of frosting from Charlie's cheek. "That's one delicious baby."

"There you are!" Daniel said, putting an arm around her. She nestled into him, put her nose against his neck, and breathed in his comforting aftershave. She wouldn't tell him just yet either. She had to talk to the other mothers first, all those blissfully unaware women bustling around their own children and husbands. In the center of the room, a photographer snapped his fingers over his camera, trying to get Reagan to look his way for a picture. Gwen had put a ridiculous birthday headband on her daughter, with a golden cloth crown at a jaunty angle on the top, and Reagan kept trying to tear it off while Gwen kept putting it back on. Gwen looked up and met Amara's eyes, then wrinkled her forehead in concern. Amara flashed back a smile and gave a thumbs-up.

When they got home and Daniel went to change Charlie's diaper, she typed up a text to them all.

EMERGENCY PLAYGROUP MEETING, it read. *Can you all do tomorrow afternoon? In the meantime, stop taking your TrueMommy.*

Chapter 23

When Claire walked into Whitney's the next day, everything was different.

No welcoming hostess swirled around to offer her water or wine or whatever she wanted. No calming eucalyptus scent wafted through the hallway. Instead, Claire caught a whiff of sweat, stinging and rotten.

Amara answered the door, her under-eye circles like purplish bruises. "Thanks for coming," she said, her voice hollow. "I just told them."

"How the *hell* did this happen?" Ellie shrieked from the living room, setting off a cacophony of baby crying, like car alarms.

"To put it mildly," Amara continued, "things are not going well."

"I brought you guys withdrawal supplies," Claire said, holding up a plastic bag. "Some comfort food and plenty of legal pain-killers."

"You are an angel," Amara said, grabbing a bottle of Tylenol from the top of the bag, spilling two capsules into her hand, and swallowing them with a grim determination, no water needed. "Come on in."

In the living room, the furniture was all the same, everything still white and sleek, but it had gone askew, an upside-down version of what Claire had grown used to. Couch pillows and shoes littered the ground. The plates of carefully selected, healthful snacks that Whitney always set out were nowhere to be seen. Instead, Ellie and Meredith crouched over an open package of Oreos on the floor like vultures over roadkill, crumbs on their faces and speckling the rug around them. Gwen trembled in the corner, her eyes red and on the verge of spilling over with tears. Vicki rocked her baby by the window, calm and distant as always. In the center of it all, Whitney sat ramrod straight on her couch, extremely still and covered with a dull sheen of perspiration, staring inward as if she were willing herself not to vomit or scream.

Some of them had gotten halfway through drying their hair in the morning. Some had never even started at all, their normally shiny hair frizzing and waving. Same with makeup—Claire noticed all sorts of new wrinkles and dark spots that she'd never seen before. They all wore either workout clothes or sweatpants, except Vicki, who was in a cottony sundress, and Whitney, who had clearly *tried* to keep up her put-together look, wearing white cigarette pants and a button-down cerulean blouse. She'd forgotten to fasten a couple of the buttons, though, or they'd come undone and she hadn't noticed.

And all around them were the babies, seeming to sense that something had gone horribly wrong, wailing and sniffling and toddling around, leaving destruction in their wake. Little Lexington pulled herself up on the coffee table and started grabbing at a silver vase with a succulent inside. Claire ran and scooped her up before it all crashed to the ground, returning her to Meredith, who gave her a groggy nod of thanks before plopping Lexington into a nearby jumper, where she couldn't move around.

"Wait. Why is Claire here?" Ellie said, mascara puddling on her cheeks and Oreo dust in between her teeth. "Ugh, don't look at me, Claire! I'm a bloated, ugly monster."

"I invited her. She's the one who figured the whole thing out," Amara said. "She's part of it now. And it's good to have someone here who's actually thinking straight as we try to figure out what the fuck to do about this."

"How did you know, Claire?" Gwen asked. Her voice caught, and she buried her face in her hands. "God, I should have known. I feel like such a fool."

"You're not a fool," Claire said, a little glow of pride rising up in her alongside the tenderness she felt for them all. She put her hand on Gwen's shoulder. She had saved them. If not for her, who knows how long they'd have carried on, oblivious? "I tried one of Amara's, and I guess because I wasn't weaned onto it slowly, it was pretty clear that something was wrong. Are you guys okay?"

"Obviously not!" Ellie snapped.

"Ellie," Amara said, glaring at her before turning to Claire. "But no. Imagine the worst hangover of your life, coupled with the realization that you've actually been drunk for months and ruining everything in your life accordingly."

"Screw this. I'm taking one," Ellie said. She lunged over toward her purse and began to root around for the TrueMommy container inside.

"Ellie, no!" Meredith said, and pulled her hand away from the purse. Ellie snatched her hand back and went back to rooting around until, unexpectedly and out of nowhere, Meredith full-body-tackled her, dragging her down to the ground.

"Stop it!" Ellie shouted as Meredith held her down. "What is wrong with you? Like Claire said—we were weaned *on* slowly, so I'm going to wean myself off slowly!" She managed to shove Meredith off for a second and made her way back to her purse, pulling out the TrueMommy. "My little brother was on Adderall when we were teenagers. That's what you're supposed to do!"

"So, what?" Meredith grabbed that beautiful suede box out of Ellie's hand and held it out of reach as Ellie clawed at her. "How are you planning on doing it slowly? Are you going to pay them for more pills?" Ellie elbowed her in the stomach. "Ow! I'm doing this because I love you."

"Guys!" Amara said, trying to get in between them. "Calm down. Let's all stop acting like insane people and talk this out for a minute." Ellie's flailing arm whacked Amara across the face, and she let out a cry of pain. "Are you fucking *kidding* me?"

Gwen ran over and hovered, her arms flapping useless at her sides like she was a baby bird attempting her first flight out of the nest. "Everyone," she said ineffectually, "we need to sit and have a reasonable conversation. We need to figure out what to do."

"Please, stop," Whitney said from the couch in a low voice. "Please, please, stop." It was the first time she'd spoken in all that mess. Claire, who was in the midst of trying to corral and calm all the fussing babies, looked over at Whitney in surprise, realizing how often, in previous playgroups, Whitney had defused situations with her light, teasing comments, how easily and skillfully she acted as the peacemaker, and how quickly things could escalate when she didn't play her part.

Over by the window, Vicki's son began to cry from all the commotion. Vicki pulled down the collar of her dress to expose her breast and latched him onto it.

"Wait, Vicki," Claire said, approaching her tentatively, remembering what she'd read online the night before when looking up amphetamines and side effects. "I don't know if you should be breastfeeding if it's still in your system."

Vicki looked up with her languid eyes, her fluttery light brown lashes. "But I feel fine," she said.

Claire had never heard Vicki's voice before. It was surprisingly deep and clarion, ringing like a bell at dinnertime. At her unexpected words, everyone stopped what they were doing and turned to stare at her.

She *did* look fine. Just like normal, dreamy, sunflower Vicki always looked as she floated through life. No makeup, but then, Claire had never actually noticed Vicki wearing makeup at all.

"Vicki," Amara said, "did you take your TrueMommy this morning?"

"No," Vicki said.

"Did you take your TrueMommy ever?" Amara asked.

"Hmm, about half the time," Vicki said. "When I thought of it. I think I would've known if there was speed in mine. I've done every drug in the world."

As the other women looked at one another in shock, a slow siren of a wail rose up through Ellie's body. "Are you *kidding* me?" she yelled, collapsing onto a couch. "*Vicki* gets to be totally okay? What kind of random monsters run TrueMommy? Are we being tortured by Satan or something? Is this a psychological experiment designed to break us? Good job, Satan. I'm breaking!" As Ellie began to cry, Meredith sat down next to her and stroked her hair.

"Have you guys been to the website?" Claire asked. "It just says 'Under Construction,' and then lists an e-mail address. And I couldn't find anything else about it on the Internet."

"I know," Amara said. "I looked last night. I couldn't find anything about a Dr. Lauren Clark from MIT either."

"What?" Gwen asked. "But when we started taking it, I looked it up—I did *research*. I always do research! They had a website then with all sorts of testimonials and this nice, clean design. I haven't googled it since February, though, so maybe it was all fake and they just put it up when they were trying to convince us to buy in?"

"We've got to destroy TrueMommy," Amara said. "I want those motherfuckers to wish they'd never been born."

"I agree," Ellie said through her sniffles as she crammed another Oreo into her mouth.

"Whitney," Claire said, clearheaded and ready for action, "you should post something about it on your Instagram. Blow the whole thing wide-open. Because they've got to be taking advantage of other moms too, right?"

"Yes! Whitney, you should," Gwen said, nodding. "You have so many followers. It would definitely get the word out." They all looked at Whitney, who hadn't moved from her strange, inward stillness on the couch.

"Maybe," Whitney said at last, her eyes still unfocused, her hands still clenched in her lap, pressing the nail of her right thumb, hard, into the flesh of her left palm.

"'Maybe'?" Claire asked, bouncing Charlie in her arms.

"What do you mean, 'maybe'?" Amara asked. "This is serious, Whitney."

"I know that," Whitney said, and for the first time on this uncommon day, she looked at them straight on. "So think about the consequences. Yes, I have a lot of followers. And they love me— they love us. But they hate us a little bit too, because we show them the life they want and will probably never have. If we tell them about TrueMommy, that all this perfection we've been selling them is a lie, imagine how gleefully they'll rip us apart. They'll think we knew *exactly* what we were doing. This is what scandals are made of. It'll be goodbye to the coffee-table book, and hello to a whole different kind of fame: the Pill-Popping Playgroup, the Stay-at-Home Junkies."

"Please tell me that this isn't about the fucking *coffee-table book*," Amara hissed, her hands clenching into fists.

"It's not," Whitney said. "It's about the fact that once we go public, we could have people—reporters, tabloids—invading every aspect of our lives. They'll follow us around, sticking cameras into our babies' faces. They'll interview people from our past, asking if they ever could have known we'd turn out like this. They'll try to dig up other unsavory things we may have done. We'll be marked forever as bad mothers. I don't want this to be the first thing that someone sees when they google Hope twenty years from now, but it might be. Our children will get dragged into this."

"Wait," Gwen said, shaking a bit and cradling Reagan in her lap. "No one would call Child Protective Services on us, right? They couldn't— I mean, we didn't *know*."

"Oh, God. We all kind of did, though," Amara said, sinking down onto the floor, her face naked and vulnerable. She reached out to take Charlie from Claire and held him close against her chest. "Right? I mean, none of us has been shouting from the mountaintops that we were taking this supplement. On some level, we knew something was off about it. It was too good to be true— the energy it gave us, the way it was finally *easy* to lose weight. How could we not know?" The other women's eyes grew guilty. Gwen began to silently cry, large droplets streaming down her cheeks as Amara went on. "They'll ask me why I was paying for it out of my private banking account, why I didn't talk about such a big monthly purchase with my husband. They'll ask Whitney why she didn't write long, glowing posts about it online."

The mothers all clutched their children and looked at one another with a growing certainty. Claire sensed a seismic shift, a planet stopping its spin mid-orbit and heading the other way, the *wrong* way.

"Don't post about it, Whitney," Ellie said.

"No," Claire said. "Come on. I think people will think that you're brave for coming forward."

"And I think that *you're* vastly overestimating the generosity of human nature," Amara said.

"Then I could tell people," Claire said. "I could try to spread the word."

"We're your only playgroup. It wouldn't take a genius to figure out how you knew about it. With all due respect, Claire," Whitney said, "this isn't your decision to make. You're not the one who will suffer."

"I could look into filing an anonymous complaint with the Better Business Bureau," Gwen said. "Then at least we'll have done something."

"That's a really good idea, Gwen," Whitney said. "And when TrueMommy contacts me about the next shipment, I can tell them that we know what they're up to and threaten to go public if they don't stop what they're doing. They don't need to know that we don't mean it. Maybe that will be a deterrent."

"So we don't spread the word," Amara said. "But is there some way under the radar that we can figure out what the fuck is going on with these monsters?"

"A private investigator," Gwen said haltingly. She cleared her throat. "It's embarrassing, but I was doing research on them anyway, because of the Christopher . . . thing. I found some guys online who seemed like they might be good. I could hire one of them for both—"

Whitney inhaled sharply. "You want to entrust this information to a stranger from the Internet who *seems like he might be good*?" she asked, her eyes blazing. "You want a private investigator—not exactly known to be the most honorable guys on the planet—poking around in your life, having dirt on you, the kind of dirt that could impact your child's well-being?"

"I–I—" Gwen stuttered, then shook her head.

"The more people who know about this, the greater chance it has of coming out, of destroying everything," Whitney said. She took a deep breath and looked them each in the eye. "No. I vote that we don't tell anyone about this. No friends, no husbands. We keep going about our lives as normally as we can. We help one another get through this, like we've helped one another before. We do our best to move forward. I know we want to destroy TrueMommy—believe me, I'd like nothing more than to burn them to the ground—but we've got to think of our families. Agreed?"

"Agreed," Ellie and Meredith said in unison.

Vicki nodded.

"I . . . I guess so," Gwen said.

They all looked at Amara. "Yeah," she said, and then let out a long, low sigh. "Shit. Yeah."

Whitney fixed her gaze on Claire, and the other mothers followed suit. "Claire," she said, "we need to know that you understand and that you're with us on this."

"I . . . ," Claire said, shifting uncomfortably. "I mean, I'm not going to tell people if you don't want me to."

"We need your word," Whitney said. "No getting drunk with your friends and bringing it up as a fun, crazy anecdote, even with our names removed. You can't ever say anything about this."

"Okay, I won't," Claire said, but the other women looked at one another, unconvinced. She'd marched into the apartment today like a savior, and now she'd become a threat.

"Oh, I know!" Ellie said. "Tell us something incriminating so that we have dirt on you too. Then, if you tell, we tell." Meredith nodded and leaned forward like she always did when juicy gossip came up at playgroup, but this time, she had no hint of excitement on her face, just worry.

"I don't really know if there is anything," Claire said. "I probably drink too much?"

"So do we all," Ellie said. "That doesn't count."

Claire caught Amara's eye, and she knew that Amara was thinking about Vagabond and Marcus and Quinton's cancer scare, about everything that Claire had revealed to her that day in her apartment. Amara swallowed. Then she shook her head.

"Come on," Amara said. "Let's not be ridiculous. We can trust Claire."

"Okay," Whitney said. "Then it's settled."

Chapter 24

Amara and Claire walked out of Whitney's building together in silence. In his stroller, Charlie was quiet, almost contemplative, with his bow lips turned down. Claire felt contemplative too and deeply unnerved. Across the street in Central Park, the daffodils bloomed and shook in the breeze.

"It *is* strange about Vicki," Amara said, and cleared her throat. "That she was the only one still breastfeeding when we started taking TrueMommy and the only one who ended up with placebos."

"What do you mean?" Claire asked.

Amara furrowed her forehead as if staring at a complicated jig-saw. "Well, it seems like the TrueMommy people didn't want to give her something that might get into her breast milk and hurt her baby, right?"

"Yeah," Claire said. She stopped walking and chewed on the sleeve of her hoodie. "Yeah, that's got to be the reason."

Amara's words came more urgently now. "But I don't *think* she breastfed in front of Dr. Clark, so how did TrueMommy know?"

"Holy shit," Claire said as the two women stared at each other. "What are you saying?"

Amara thought for a second and then shook her head, all her energy draining away. "Nothing. I'm being ridiculous. She must have put it on the form." She rubbed her eyes, her face more drawn than Claire had ever seen it. "You could submit a form each month if you wanted to, to tell them what issues you were having so they could specifically 'curate' a vitamin mix for you, which of course they probably never did."

"Yeah, but is Vicki the type to fill out a form? It's *Vicki*." Claire paused. "It's convenient too that the flighty one who forgot to take the pills regularly is the only one who ended up with the placebos."

"Well, Dr. Clark probably realized she was flighty from meeting her. It's hard not to. So let's just forget it." Amara turned to keep walking, but Claire tugged at her shoulder

"Really, though, how *did* TrueMommy know?" Claire asked.

"I don't want to talk about this anymore," Amara said, her voice tightening in frustration. "There's nothing to talk about."

"This might sound a little crazy," Claire said. "But is it possible that someone who knows you guys could be connected somehow? Feeding TrueMommy information or something?"

"You think someone targeted us personally?" Amara asked, her jaw clenching. "Like who?"

"I don't know! Someone who's jealous of you, maybe." Claire gasped. "Like Joanna. From what you told me, she's not exactly the most stable person in the world, and—"

"Claire," Amara said. "Are you a conspiracy theorist? One of those 'nine-eleven was an inside job' people? Do you believe that the government killed JFK and faked the moon landing and that Beyoncé is part of the Illuminati?"

". . . No."

"Well, that's what you sound like right now. Maybe poor, depressed Joanna pushed drugs on us, because she's jealous of our playgroup? You don't even know Joanna. She'd never do something like that. This is clearly a fucked-up scam targeting rich mothers with online presences, and we all fell for it, and that's that."

"*You're* the one who brought up that something seemed fishy—"

"Yeah, and then I realized that I was being nuts! This isn't a game, some fun little mystery to solve. It's my life, and it's really, really bad."

"I know." Claire reached for Amara's hand, but Amara pulled it away. "I'm sorry. It's just, if it *is* targeting other mothers . . . you can't be okay with this secret pact you guys made in there. You're not all starring in *I Know What You Did Last Summer: Mommy Edition*. What about your responsibility to the women out there who are still falling for it?"

"My *responsibility* right now is to my child. I've been failing him for months, and starting now I need to do whatever I can to protect him."

Claire threw up her hands. "I don't understand you sometimes! You're so freaking smart and amazing, but you just give up on things like this, like your job, so you can maintain some kind of status quo—"

"You don't understand," Amara snapped, "because you aren't a mother! All right? You don't understand what it's like to worry every single minute that you're doing something to hurt your child, who is the most precious thing to you in the entire world, and then to realize that while you were reading and rereading your baby books, all along you were actually doing something that none of those books ever mentioned, something that could fucking *ruin* him and his future." She spoke slowly and deliberately, every word like a tiny poison dart. "Don't lecture me about responsibility, Claire. You've never had a real responsibility in your life. Grow up already."

The poison darts hit their marks. Claire cleared her throat. "Wow. Okay," she said.

Amara sighed. "Oh, Lord. I didn't mean that. Obviously, I'm extra irritable right now."

"Classic withdrawal temper," Claire said. "And I didn't mean to lecture you."

"It's fine. I think I just need to get home," Amara said. "I shouldn't have brought this up in the first place. Can you please promise me that you'll leave it alone?" Claire hesitated for a fraction of a second, and Amara's eyes narrowed. She leaned forward.

"Hey, I *vouched* for you back there. I made the decision to trust you because you're my friend and I care for you, and now I need you to prove that I was right to do that. Promise me, Claire."

"Okay," Claire said. "I promise."

Amara stepped back and let out a long breath. "All right, then. Thank you. I'll see you at a playgroup tomorrow." She stopped and shook her head. "No, there's no way I'm making it out of the house for that. I'll see you at the photo shoot Thursday."

"See you then," Claire said.

Chapter 25

Amara tossed and turned the entire night. Awful nightmares flashed through her head, a sequence of dreams in which Charlie died because of her negligence. The blanket in his crib smothered him while she danced and laughed like an idiot alone in the living room. He fell off the balcony at playgroup while she drank a glass of wine inside. He choked on a grape, he stuck his finger in an outlet, he toppled a chest of drawers on top of himself, all while she did nothing, nothing, nothing.

Each time a dream woke her up, she crept out of bed. She moved through the apartment, which was as silent and full of dread as a log cabin in the woods, and went to his nursery. She stood above his crib and watched him breathe, the palpitations of her heart booming out into the peaceful room. As she listened to it beat, she became aware too of her own mortality in a way that she'd never been before. There was so much danger in the outside world, within her own body. An accidental overdose, a car crash, a sudden malfunction of her cells could whisk her away from Charlie in a flash, leaving him wounded for the rest of his life, one of those motherless children who was always searching for something he'd never be able to have.

She normally woke up in the morning when Daniel's alarm went off, but on Tuesday, Daniel had to poke her awake right before he left for work. He handed her a mug of coffee with a fresh swirl of milk disappearing into it. "Someone was restless last night," he said. "You feeling okay?"

She looked up at his kind, concerned face, and a bolt of rage passed through her. Not at Daniel, but at the injustice of it all. Why was there no fucking TrueDaddy? The answer was clear. Because men wouldn't fall for it. Not that they were smarter—Amara firmly believed she could trounce the average man in a battle of wits—but because they weren't primed from birth like women were, told that they could be anything they wanted to be while handicapped at every turn by invisible forces, told that they were *more* than just their looks while also culturally programmed to believe that their value was tied to their desirability. Men aged into silver foxes while women aged into obsolescence. And when you added in children, oh, that was when everything really went to shit. Because even though fathers stamped children with their last names, the world didn't ask as much of them. No one really expected fathers to consider giving up their careers to put their children first, to stop managing a company and start managing a household. Women had to grapple with a choice that men never did while remaining uncomplaining and generous so that they didn't nag their husbands straight into the arms of less complicated lovers. And now moms weren't even allowed to acknowledge how much *work* it all was anymore. Modern women of privilege had to claim that their manic exercise routines were about strength, not a body ideal; that their beauty regimens were all natural, designed for emotional balance and skin health, rather than for looking nubile for as long as possible. No wonder they were easy targets. TrueMommy was the same old patriarchal bullshit dressed up as empowerment, and Amara had fallen for it like a fucking idiot.

Daniel kissed her forehead. "Oh, you're sweaty!"

Despite what all the women had said at playgroup, she should tell him the truth. They were partners, after all. They'd taken vows to support each other for better and for worse, and getting accidentally hooked on Mommy Speed definitely qualified as "worse." Whitney had said "no husbands," but Whitney's husband was pompous, selfish Grant. Daniel was different.

Oh, but he was so fucking *good*. He would take care of her and get her all the help she needed, but he'd also never be content to let her and the other women ride out their shame and recovery in private. He'd hop on the Claire train—The "You've Got a Responsibility" Express—and ride it all over the country, barnstorming and shouting until every mother in the land knew the dangers of TrueMommy.

He put his palm against her face, checking for a fever, looking at her with his furrowed brow and pure love in his face. There was another reason she didn't want to tell him. She'd fallen in love with him for so many reasons, but chief among them was how much he respected her. He trusted her judgment. He came to her with quandaries and asked for her advice. He'd never been one of those men who'd run from her ambition, from her forceful opinions, even though plenty of other guys had. Where past boyfriends had tried to diminish her, Daniel had stood right by her side, holding a microphone to her mouth.

But how could he respect her in the same way after this, after she'd endangered the beautiful little jewel of a boy they'd made together?

She'd been a bad mother. And that, it seemed, was the worst thing a woman could possibly be. A prostitute who moonlighted as a contract killer could be redeemed if she was doing it all so that she could tuck her child into a warm bed every night. But a woman could be charming, immensely intelligent, ambitious, strong, and head-turningly gorgeous, and if she screwed up her parenting, the world deemed her a piece of shit.

Would the thought "Unfit mother, unfit mother" ring in Daniel's head whenever he looked at her? Would something between them be irrevocably broken? She couldn't let that happen.

Maybe, over the course of even the best marriages, you acquired a collection of secrets that you walled off in a little section of your heart where your partner would never be allowed to go. And you did everything you could to keep the walled-off section small, to keep the secrets from slipping out of it and pervading all that was good and open and free in the rest of your heart, and you just made it work.

She put her hand on top of his and smiled up at him. "I think I have a little bug or something," she said. "But I'll be fine."

Chapter 26

On Tuesday, no one wanted to leave the house and come to playgroup, so Whitney canceled it for the first time since it had started. They'd just wait until Thursday, when they had to do the coffee-table-book photography shoot, which they'd agreed not to cancel, because that would be a very clear indication that things were decidedly *not* fine. Without the chatter of the other women, her apartment alternated between stifling and cavernous. Hope was being difficult, tugging Whitney's hair, knocking over everything in sight like a cyclone given human form. And all Whitney wanted was bread, but she didn't keep it in the house.

She took Hope to Central Park, to the little playground not far from their apartment. An ice-cream truck had set up shop in the street nearby, blaring its incessant jingle over and over again, pausing in between repetitions just long enough that each time

Whitney thought maybe it wouldn't start again. But it always did. She bought a cone and nearly swallowed it whole, then ate two street hot dogs. She hadn't eaten processed meats and crappy refined sugar like that in years. The binge turned her stomach to an anchor, weighing her to the park bench as Hope sat on the ground in front of her and pulled grass out by its roots.

Whitney smiled blandly when Hope held up the grass to show her. "Ooh, look at that!" she said as, in her mind, she constructed a gigantic red countdown clock of the hours left until tomorrow afternoon, when she'd go meet Christopher for their weekly hotel date, when at least for an hour she could go be a desirable woman and not a swamp monster.

When she wanted to scream—at family dinner when Hope kept throwing her food on the floor, when she ground up the rest of her TrueMommy pills in the garbage disposal because she wanted so badly to pop them all in her mouth, that night when Grant started kissing her in the dark—she focused on the countdown clock. The hours ticked down slowly, but at least they were ticking.

And then, an hour before her babysitter was supposed to arrive, the stupid girl called her to cancel. That was what ruined everything.

"I am so sorry to mess up your 'me time,' but I've been throwing up all morning," the girl mumbled into the phone. "Probably food poisoning."

Probably hungover, Whitney thought, remembering that the girl had mentioned something last week about being almost finished with her finals. *Unreliable bitch.* "Oh, no!" she said, jiggling Hope against her waist with her free arm as Hope fussed and grabbed at her necklace. "Feel better! Do you have any friends who might be able to come in?"

"Hmm," the girl said. Hope pulled the necklace tight around Whitney's neck, nearly choking her. Whitney wrenched Hope's fist away too roughly, and the chain of the necklace snapped, sending beads to the floor. Hope's face teetered on that jagged edge of Happy Baby Land, beyond which lay Tantrum City. Whitney wanted to take a little trip to Tantrum City herself, to collapse onto the ground and wail about the way that everything was unraveling, but that was not an option right now. So Whitney gave Hope a big smile to keep her in the happy place while the babysitter continued. "I don't think so, but I can text around and let you know."

"That would be *so* great," Whitney said. She hung up the phone, tempted to slam it against her marble countertop until it shattered while screaming every obscenity she knew. But that would scare Hope.

She pulled up Instagram and messaged Christopher, *Last-minute babysitter woes! Any chance we could push till Friday instead?* She picked up the tiny beads and tried to calm Hope while the minutes ticked away and she waited for her phone to make a noise, any noise.

And then her phone dinged, with a message from Christopher. *I already rescheduled my meetings, so I wouldn't be able to get away like this again until next Wednesday. Wait until then? I want you now.*

An ache started between her legs, so much better than the ache that had taken up residence in her head the last couple of days, despite the Advil she'd been swallowing. She wanted him now too.

No, it was more than wanting. It was full-on need. She already had to give up one addiction, but no way in hell was she giving up the other. Not right now. *I'll figure something out,* she wrote. *See you soon.*

Still nothing from the terrible college girl she was never hiring again. Was there a Yelp for babysitters? She would give that bitch such a blistering review her skin would peel back. She wasn't about to plop Hope down with some unvetted stranger from the Internet or some neighbor who might mention to Grant that, wow, Whitney sure had been jonesing for a massage on Wednesday afternoon, and it was a *little* odd.

So even though it was probably a bad idea, she called Claire.

"Hello?" Claire said after the third ring.

"Claire!" Whitney said, struggling to keep her desperation from creeping into her voice. "Quick question. Are you by any chance free to come over and babysit in the next half hour?"

"Oh, sorry. I'm actually on the way to one of my other jobs," she said.

"Ooh, busy busy!" Whitney said, then leaned her forehead against the cool silver surface of her fridge. "And there's no way I could convince you to come here instead?"

"Um . . . ," Claire said.

"It's just—it's so silly, but I've been doing this little Wednesday ritual each week where I take some 'me time' and go get a massage. Helps me maintain my sanity, you know? My regular babysitter just canceled on me last minute, and what with everything that's going on now, I *really* could use the hour of relaxation. I could pay you more than your typical going rate for such a last-minute ask!"

"Sorry. I just really don't want to take the risk of getting fired," Claire said. She hesitated. "But I could probably help out some other time this week if you can reschedule the massage?"

"Okay, maybe!" Whitney said. "Thanks, Claire!" This time when she hung up, she did scream some obscenities, only stopping when Hope began to whimper at the shock of it.

"I'm sorry. I'm sorry, sweet baby," Whitney said, gathering Hope in her arms and bouncing her up and down, humming to her until the whimpering tapered off. She kissed her child on the top of her head and then did the only thing she could think to do.

Chapter 27

Claire didn't want to get fired from her part-time gig behind the counter at a new vintage clothing place in midtown. It paid eighteen dollars an hour and was the easiest job in the world. Hardly anyone ever came in, so she had plenty of time to think about song lyrics and melodies. Plus the owner of the store seemed stuck as far back in the past as all the clothing he curated, so there was no chance of Vagabond ever coming on the store's Joni Mitchell–inspired playlist. But after she hung up the phone with Whitney, alarm bells in her brain went *BING BING BING.*

Whitney had sounded fucking *bizarre*, her voice higher than normal and so falsely cheerful, like she was one second away from bursting into tears. Sure, Claire thought, as she ducked around a group of tourists taking selfies right in the middle of the sidewalk,

Whitney was going through withdrawal. But she'd been going through withdrawal on Monday, and then she'd been far more composed. Composed enough to convince them all to take their TrueMommy secret to the grave. So why was she now falling apart over a stupid massage?

Claire shook her head and kept walking toward the store. She'd never gone through withdrawal—it could very well hit a person differently depending on the day. Something rankled at Claire— something she was forgetting—but she needed to shrug that off and get back to reality. Hey, if Claire was used to getting a weekly massage, she'd probably be desperate for one right now too, after the stress of the last few days.

She stopped short on the sidewalk. A "Wednesday ritual," Whitney had called it on the phone, which implied that she'd been doing it for a while. But a week and a half ago, in their room at Sycamore House, Whitney had said she hadn't gotten a massage in forever. Hadn't she? Claire concentrated, calling up the image of Whitney against the wall of their bedroom, trying to get at the knot in her shoulder.

Still unmoving, Claire pulled out her phone, making the tourists on the street duck around *her* for once. She scrolled through Whitney's Instagram, hunting for something she vaguely remembered, past the mommy-daughter smoothies, past a new photo of them all on the retreat, beaming. Yes, there it was, a month or so back, that "DIY Massage" photo with Hope, its caption also claiming Whitney hadn't gotten a massage in ages. Whitney's Momstagram wasn't gospel—it was possible that she casually misled strangers on the Internet to make her own life seem more interesting. But why would she need to lie to Claire about something so small, unless it was to cover up something much bigger?

Whitney had been so fucking adamant that they needed to forget TrueMommy, to not dig any deeper into it. And Amara had said that she was the one who brought the vitamins into the group in the first place and that she was generally the point of contact, the person who handed the vitamins out in those ridiculous goody bags. While she was handing the women their pills, was she handing TrueMommy something right back? Maybe they sent traffic to her social media, gave her kickbacks of some kind, in exchange for information.

It was a stretch, for sure. And what was she going to do, go stalk Whitney because of some half-formed hunch? Claire had promised Amara to leave it all alone, and she wanted to keep that promise. Then she remembered Amara's face the other day when they were talking about Vicki, how Amara's concentration melted into exhaustion when she decided she was only being paranoid. How satisfying it would be to show Amara some proof that her instincts had been right and that she didn't have to hide something her whole life. Because Amara wasn't a hider. Amara was a shining fucking diamond, and keeping terrible secrets would only diminish her.

A shoulder angel and a shoulder devil screamed opposing directives into Claire's ears, but they had somehow switched body parts and pieces of clothing so they were all jumbled up—one with devil horns and angel wings, another with a harp and a forked tail—and she couldn't tell which one was saying what. All she felt in her gut was that Whitney desperately needed a babysitter—not for a massage but for some other reason she didn't want Claire to know.

Half a block away from the clothing store, she texted her boss there that she'd thrown up on the subway and needed to go lie down. Then she turned around and headed toward the Upper East Side.

Chapter 28

When Whitney knocked on the hotel room door, Christopher opened it with that foxlike grin of his. "Get in here now," he said. Then he registered the stroller by her side, and the grin slipped.

"Surprise!" Whitney said, her heart pounding. "I couldn't find another babysitter, and I was already all set to come, so . . . say hi to Hope!"

Christopher stared at Whitney for a moment, then crouched down by the stroller and dangled his hand in front of her baby. "Hello, Hope. Pleasure to see you again." Hope reached out and grabbed on to one of Christopher's fingers, her face opening in baby joy, and he smiled back at her. "You've got a grip of steel! Are you a superhero in disguise?"

Whitney exhaled. Already, Christopher acted so naturally with

Hope. The perfect dad, ready with a joke or a bedtime story. "More like a super monster," Whitney said, wheeling the stroller forward into the hotel room as Christopher stepped aside. "Wait till you see her walk around." She unbuckled Hope and lifted her out of the stroller, placing her on the room's soft, fibrous rug. "She's like a drunk Godzilla!" She turned to Christopher as he came up behind her, and stroked his stubbly cheek. "Hey, you," she said, rising up on her tiptoes to kiss him, thrilling at the warmth of his mouth. She traced his throat with her finger. "Thanks for being understanding about this."

Hope started toddling toward the Ethernet cable, and Whitney crouched down to the floor, pulling her wriggly baby into her arms. "No way, rug rat!" she said, then looked at Christopher, who was still hanging back. "Come closer," she said, tugging him down next to her. "She may be a super monster, but she doesn't bite. At least not yet. I'm hopeful we'll skip that phase altogether." Hope crawled between the two of them and stopped at Christopher, bracing herself on his lap, rising up to stare at him with preternatural concentration. He waved at her again, and Hope's face opened in that contagious, wide-open smile Whitney loved so much. What a special child she had. In a way, it was exciting that Christopher got to spend that time with her. Her body started to unclench as the big red countdown clock in her mind flashed *00:00*. She rested her head on Christopher's shoulder, running her fingers up and down his leg, and watched her baby laugh. For the first time since Amara's emergency text, she allowed herself to believe that, somehow, everything was going to be okay. This hour would cleanse her. She'd show up for the photo shoot tomorrow restored. And after that, she'd just take it day by day.

"Whitney," Christopher said, stroking her hair.

"Mmm?" she answered, turning her face up to his.

"I think I should go."

Whitney experienced a sudden rush of empathy for Wile E. Coyote, for that horrible, inevitable moment seconds after chasing the Road Runner off a cliff, when he looked down and realized he was running in midair. She'd done a reckless thing, and now she'd have to pedal her feet desperately not to break open against the ground. She gave a little tinkle of a laugh, her mouth gone desert dry.

"Oh, no!" she said, widening her eyes in feigned innocence. "Because of Hope? I know it's not exactly the usual Wednesday, but we can still have a nice time."

"Hope's great," he said. "Extremely cute baby. But when we're together, I want you all to myself." He gave her his sexiest crooked smile. "No distractions."

"Believe me, I don't want any distractions either," she said, kissing his ear lightly. "But you know how it is with children. My babysitter canceled, and I wanted to see you. This was the only way I could make that work."

"I get it. I do," he said. "But it might be better for all involved if we call this one a loss and wait until next week."

Maybe if she'd been feeling more like her normal self, she wouldn't have needed to be with him so desperately. Maybe she could have made a little joke and left right then and there. She could have hired a more reliable babysitter for the next week, and who knows how their story would have turned out? But she wasn't feeling like her normal self at all. "We're already here, though," she said. "And I hang out with Reagan all the time."

"Don't say— That's different. You know that's different."

"I don't understand why you're being so weird about this," she said. "You said you really wanted to see me."

"I did. I do."

"Well, here I am." She raised an eyebrow. "Or did you mean just to have sex? A quickie and you're out?"

"Stop it," he said.

"Here, Hope and I will go," she said, starting to stand up. "And you can just call a prostitute to come on by instead."

"Whitney!" he said, exasperated, digging his fingers into his temples. "Stop acting so obtuse. You know what it is. I feel uncomfortable . . . pretending to be a little family. We already have families." Guilt came over his face at his own reminder, his eyes drifting in the direction of his suit jacket, slung over a chair. He was going to leave.

"I didn't come here to play house," she said, and dug in her bag for the cheap iPad she and Grant had bought as their official baby screen—a small one, locked in an indestructible case, loaded with "educational" videos. She snapped it into the front of Hope's stroller, then pulled up the first playlist she could find. A song began, with hyped-up cartoon barnyard animals dancing a square dance. She lifted Hope from the rug and buckled her into the stroller. "Look, Hope-y. Look at the cows!" The lure of the screen worked its magic. Hope leaned forward and began to point at the moving images. "This will be a treat for her," Whitney said to Christopher, over her shoulder. "She hardly ever gets screen time." She cast her eyes around the room, settling on the bathroom door. "And she can hang out in here."

She wheeled Hope's stroller over. The bathroom was lovely, all gray tile, each soap still packaged in its starched paper, the little amber bottles of shampoo gleaming in the soft light. "Ooh, look at this beautiful bathroom!" she said as she pushed the stroller in. "I'll be right back, sweetie." She tiptoed out as Hope clapped her hands at the animals.

She shut the door and met Christopher's eyes again. He was standing now, his jacket in his hand.

"You think I'm crazy," she said.

"Whitney . . . ," he said, and he didn't deny it.

She burst into tears and slid down against the bathroom door to the rug. "I'm sorry," she said through her sobs. "It's just a really tough time right now, and all I wanted was to come here and be with you, and the babysitter canceled, and now I've made a mess of it all."

He hesitated, looking over at her. Then he sighed, laid his jacket back on the chair, and sat down next to her, gathering her in his arms, holding her while she cried against him. He smelled like coffee, rich and peppery. She probably smelled like sour sweat from lugging Hope's stroller around. Through the bathroom door, the faint sounds of barnyard songs tinkled on. Her tears stained the light blue of his shirt to dark navy. His body was rigid against hers. He held her like she was almost a stranger or an old-maid aunt of his who had gotten too drunk and weepy at Thanksgiving, not like she was a lover he'd once said was the sexiest woman alive.

Screw that. She swallowed away the lump in her throat. "I'm sorry," she said into his chest.

"You don't have to apologize," he said, sighing.

"No," she said, dangling her hand down into his lap and brushing it against him, almost as if it were an accident. "I want to."

Christopher tightened in a different way, a sort of snapping to attention, and she ran her hand up and down his thigh more insistently. "I'm sorry," she said, "that I couldn't wait a whole week more to have you inside of me."

She glanced up at him through her eyelashes, still wet with tears. The look of apprehension on his face was turning into a look she liked a whole lot more.

"I'm sorry I kept thinking about the way your breath changes when you fill me up," she said, walking her fingers up to his belt buckle and undoing it. He grasped her shoulder as she slipped her fingers inside his pants, to where he was hardening, and brought him out. "I'm sorry I wanted to taste you," she breathed, then bent down and ran her tongue over the tip of his penis as lightly as she could. A drop of precum dissolved in her mouth, salty as the ocean. He shivered.

She straightened back up and turned away. "But you're right," she said, making as if she were about to stand. "This was too crazy. I'll go."

He grabbed her around the waist and threw her roughly down onto the ground, holding her wrists above her head. "You fucking tease," he growled in her ear, laughing in a sort of disbelief, and then they were kissing, their tongues tasting like her tears, as he ripped open the buttons on her dress and stripped her black lace underwear from her hips.

Some overeager hotel employee had turned on the central AC too early in the year, and a vent blew cold air over Whitney with a low hum. In comparison, Christopher's mouth was hot against hers, as scalding as the hot coffee he tasted like.

She rubbed herself against him, not letting him inside her just yet. Running her fingers through his curls, she tugged him away from her by his hair, wriggling her hips to a new spot on the rug, just out of reach of where he wanted her. She gripped his face and stared him straight in his hazel eyes, her nose inches away from his bumpy one. "Tell me I was right to come here anyway," she said.

"You were right," he said, panting.

She rolled over so she was on top of him, perching just above his penis. Slowly, she lowered herself down, stopping when she'd only taken the first couple of inches of him into her. Her thighs shook. "Tell me how glad you are."

"I'm so glad," he said, grasping her ass, and pulled her hard against him. She let out a strangled moan. As they bucked, he dug his fingers into her skin. "God, Whitney, you make me feel so good."

She smiled against his shoulder as his breathing started to change, and her whole body tingled in anticipation.

And then, from the bathroom, Hope began to cry.

They both looked at the door, their bodies growing rigid. Probably the playlist had stopped. Whitney couldn't hear the tinkling barnyard song, the helium voices, any longer. She shook her head. "It's fine," she said.

"Are you sure?" Christopher asked.

"Yes. Yes," she said. "Keep going."

He thrust again and again, but Hope's cries were echoing off the tiled wall. This bathroom had the acoustics of Carnegie Hall.

Christopher's face set in determination, as if suddenly the act in which they were engaged wasn't about the pleasure he was feeling but merely about needing to cum. Wanting to get it over with.

He flipped her over and began to drive into her from behind, pulling her hair. The walls of her vagina started stinging, just a little at first and then as if he was opening up a thousand tiny paper cuts to the soundtrack of Hope's wails. It felt like it did with Grant, she realized with a sudden shock, her eyes beginning to water. She gritted her teeth and willed him to get it over with. She didn't need her own pleasure today. They could still salvage things, if only he managed to finish. But instead, he pulled out of her abruptly.

"I can't," he said, trying to catch his breath. "You need to go get her." He stood up and walked over to the window.

"I . . . ," she said, remaining curled on the floor for one moment longer. Then she grabbed her underwear and buttoned up her dress, brushing her sweaty hair out of her face. She rushed into the bathroom, where Hope was pounding on the side of her stroller, the screen dead in front of her. As soon as Hope saw Whitney, she held out her arms, and her wails started tapering into whimpers. "Oh, honey. I'm so sorry," Whitney said, lifting her child out of her stroller and bouncing the wriggling, beautiful weight of her in her arms. "I'm here. I'm right here," she murmured. She thought of the dinosaurs at the Museum of Natural History and wondered if Hope would retain something of this too, of this strange man in this strange hotel room, of the unsettling noises coming from the other side of the door while she'd cried and cried. A deep sense of shame spread through Whitney. "You're okay," she said as Hope's whimpers faded too, then turned to call out into the bedroom, in case Christopher was worried. "She's fine."

She carried Hope back out into the bedroom to show him, but he was gone, the door swinging closed with a bang that started Hope's cries right up again. And suddenly Whitney had gone from lover to mother, like a magic spell over which she'd had no control, the reverse of a fairy tale's happy-ending transformation.

She'd only ever be a mother in his eyes now, and not a very good one at that.

Chapter 29

When she arrived in Whitney's neighborhood, Claire pulled the hood of her gray sweatshirt over her coppery hair and put on her sunglasses. Then she found a bench on the border of Central Park, right across the street from the familiar limestone building, and sat down to wait, watching the entryway, feeling ridiculous.

Just as she was starting to believe she had made a colossal mistake, the doorman ushered Whitney out of the building, holding the door open for her as she pushed Hope in her stroller and flashed him a grateful smile. The man hailed her a taxi, and once it pulled over to the curb, Whitney, the doorman, and the taxi driver began the laborious process of collapsing the stroller, installing a car seat, and buckling Hope into it, Whitney profusely apologizing as the taxi driver stamped his feet with impatience. You couldn't take a baby to a massage! She'd *known* Whitney was lying.

Claire hailed her own cab and slid into the back. "Good afternoon!" the driver said, cheerful, as loud Christian hymns played on the radio. "Where are you going?"

"Just follow that cab, please," Claire said, peering out the window

"You got it, lady," the man said, and glanced at her in the rearview mirror. "I hope you don't mind me asking, but are you a follower of Jesus Christ?"

"Um," Claire said. Whitney's taxi took off, and Claire jabbed her finger toward it. "Oh, go!" Claire's driver swerved into the middle lane to follow.

"I take that as a no," her driver said, chuckling. "But it's never too late to accept Him into your heart."

The most stressful fifteen-minute cab ride of Claire's life followed, during which she was torn between worrying that they were going to lose Whitney's trail and that the driver was going to get them killed by following *too* recklessly, cutting in front of other cars and leaving a cacophony of honks in their wake. All the while, he kept up a steady sermon, offering to drive her to church any Sunday she needed, while she chewed her fingernails down to ragged shells of their former selves and the meter ticked steadily upward. She was on the cusp of something, she felt, as they screeched down Park Avenue and turned east, as the buildings changed from tall brick apartments to office buildings ornamented with glass and steel and the trees in the center of the road blurred together into smears of green. Should she confront Whitney—follow her into wherever she was going and blow the fucking whistle—or just go over to Amara's right after this with the story?

Whitney's taxi pulled over partway down the block on East Forty-seventh Street, and then Whitney began the whole car-seat-stroller process again, in reverse. Claire paid her driver with a quick pang of regret at the chunk that the ride took out of her still-recovering bank account, accepted with a distracted nod of thanks the business card he offered her for his church, and slid out of the cab. She ducked behind a mailbox and watched out of the corner of her eye as Whitney finished buckling Hope into her stroller, straightened her shoulders, and headed into the revolving door of a fancy stone building called . . . the Windom Hotel and Spa.

Fuck. What an *idiot* she was. Amara was right. She might as well type up some pamphlet about how Obama was a lizard person and start proselytizing on the street corner.

Vagabond kicking her out had turned her into the side character of her own life—the fine, forgettable one taking up space before the star attraction came along. Now, to make up for it, she was trying to insert herself where she didn't belong. She'd been so desperate to be the hero of someone else's story that she'd fancied herself a kind of Nancy Drew uncovering a vast conspiracy. Really, though, the only thing she had in common with Nancy Drew was that she was a fucking child. And like Amara had said, she needed to grow up.

It was too late to go back to the clothing store. She could use a drink, a little bit of fuzzy euphoria to block out the image of Amara shaking her head at her. She turned around and faced the intersection, scanning for the nearest bar that would be open at one P.M. on a Wednesday. There, right in between a pharmacy and a SoulCycle, was an Irish pub, beckoning like a siren at sea. Thank goodness for the Irish. She headed straight in, sat on a barstool, and ordered a whiskey soda, pushing her hood back.

The Shame Demons, those terrible, disparaging thoughts about her own self-worth, came to her, and she sat with them for a while as she let the whiskey slide down her throat, acknowledging all the insults they hurled at her. Why did she even care so much about what happened to this playgroup of wealthy, overprivileged women?

Because she was lonely. People were meant to have support groups, but somehow she cycled through communities—through megachurch and Vagabond—and ended up alone. Even Thea, her constant, no-nonsense champion throughout everything, had never called her back after the night Claire ran through Central Park, and when Claire tried calling her *again* to see if they were still on for dinner plans they'd made weeks before, Thea had answered, distracted, that she had to cancel, which was completely unlike her.

Bizarrely, Claire had felt at playgroup that that time could be different, that she'd finally cycled to the right place. She'd let herself imagine that she and Amara would grow closer as they grew older, and take strolls with their canes through Central Park together, and feed the goddamn ducks. God, maybe that was why people had children. Because they wanted someone who *had* to sit with them and feed the ducks, no matter how doddering or uninteresting they got. She wanted to take care of her new friends, but she had no idea how to do it, and so they'd all inevitably slip away too.

Well, if she couldn't have community, at least she could have communion, her own particular type of it, taking another person's body into hers. She did a quick scan of the bar for someone she could fuck. Unfortunately, the people who came to a divey Irish pub to get drunk on a Wednesday at lunchtime weren't exactly the cream of the crop. She pictured herself walking over to the group of slurring retirees in the corner booth, crusty old men in sports jerseys, and pointing to one at random to follow her into the bathroom. She didn't have high standards, but even she could tell that *that* wouldn't make her feel any better.

She took a big swig of her drink and contemplated ordering another. At least nobody ever had to know about this stupid, misguided adventure. She'd show up at the photo shoot tomorrow and try to be the person that Amara believed her to be.

The door to the pub swung open, letting in a businessman on his lunch break who sat down heavily a few stools over from her and greeted the bartender. She'd heard that voice before. When she glanced over, their eyes met. Dammit. Christopher. She could see a similar *Dammit* run through his mind before he quickly rearranged his expression, trading in a stressed-out grimace for his usual charming smile.

"Claire the playgroup girl!" he said. "This is a funny coincidence. What are you doing here?"

"I work nearby," she said.

"I do too."

"So, what'll it be today?" the bartender asked Christopher.

"I'll see a food menu," Christopher said. The bartender raised an eyebrow and handed over a dubious-looking piece of paper with a few lines of text printed on it.

"Ah, yes," Claire said. "I hear they're renowned for their food here."

"Uh-huh," Christopher said. "I come all the way from the office for their"—he squinted at the menu—"hot dogs and tater tots." He shook his head, half laughing. "You caught me." He leaned over to grab the bartender's attention, and Claire waited for him to ask for a beer, but he ordered a club soda instead. Then he turned back to Claire, a rueful look on his face. "Every so often, when I've really been having a *day*, I like to come to a bar and order a club soda as a reminder that I can control myself in at least one aspect of my life, you know?"

"No idea what you're talking about," Claire said. "I'm a well-balanced person, and I never have to come to bars to deal with my self-loathing in the early afternoon."

He smiled and held up his club soda. "To self-loathing, that old friend."

"To self-loathing," Claire said, and drained the rest of her drink.

"Give her another on me," Christopher said to the bartender, and moved over to the stool next to Claire's as the bartender handed her a new glass, covered with beads of condensation.

"Oh, fine," Claire said. "Thanks."

Christopher nodded. They sat in silence for a moment, drinking their respective drinks, as a baseball game played on the TV above the bar. He smelled like coffee and something else, something sharper that Claire couldn't place. Sneaking a sideways glance, Claire noticed a sheen of sweat on Christopher's neck. He caught her eye. "You won't mention this to Gwen, will you?"

"What, that you come to bars to drink club soda?" Claire asked. "Somehow I can't imagine that she'd be too upset about that."

He shook his head and said, in a voice so quiet that the sounds of the bar almost drowned him out, "Yeah." He took another deep swallow of his drink, staring into his glass like he was trying to find salvation there.

"Obviously, I won't tell her about today if you don't want me to," Claire said, placing a gentle hand on his shoulder, the fabric of his suit jacket soft under her palm.

At the unexpected touch, he startled, and then all of the charming, foxy scaffolding around him fell away, laying bare the defeated man beneath. "I'm a screwup," he said. "I fail her, and I fail her, and I fail her. She's the one who keeps everything together. She's the one who has it all figured out."

Claire laughed then, an unstoppable, gasping laugh, and he looked up at her in surprise. "Well, I'm glad to see you're treating my misery with the respect it deserves," he said, raising an eyebrow, and she could see the defeat on his face turning to confused amusement.

"I'm sorry!" Claire said, putting her hand in front of her mouth. "No, it's not—"

"Very kind of you. Have you considered becoming a therapist?"

"I just— I have a feeling Gwen has made some mistakes too, that's all. She might be more forgiving than you think." She shook her head. "Sorry. I didn't mean to be an asshole."

"I forgive you," he said. "And thank you for keeping my secret."

The way he said it suddenly made her feel dirty, as if what she had thought of as a small omission was actually something much bigger.

"You've got it," she said lightly. "I'm turning into a one-woman secret repository right now. Step right up, world. Anybody else got something for the Claire vault?"

"You're funny," he said, still fixing her in his gaze, looking at her as if she had revealed something exciting and strange and he wasn't quite sure what to make of it, like she'd just told him that she could speak five languages or that she'd hiked all the way across the country by herself.

"Yeah, I'm thinking of going into stand-up," she said. "I hear that's a more stable career than music."

"It would be a shame if you stopped singing. I didn't get a chance to tell you at the party," Christopher said. "But you have a beautiful voice."

"Thanks," she said.

He brushed his leg against hers so quickly and lightly that she wasn't sure if it was an accident. But then he did it again. It sent a tingle of desire up the backs of her thighs and a lump of anger into her throat. She swallowed.

"Are you kidding me?" she asked.

"What?" Christopher said, holding his hands up.

"You're really going to hit on me right now?" She stood up, grabbed her bag from the floor, and tossed a ten-dollar bill on the bar for her drink. "What a pathetic excuse for a person you are. No wonder you're in here, self-loathing on your lunch break." His face crumpled into regret, his shoulders sloping forward, and he opened his mouth as if to say something, but she didn't want to hear it. "Get your life together, and go home to Gwen."

As she walked through the door and back into the afternoon light, she finally placed what he smelled like. Sex.

Chapter 30

Claire had expected the photo shoot for the coffee-table book to be legit, but the reality blew her away. On Thursday morning, she showed up at a gray building in SoHo. A freight elevator carried her to a loft with enormous windows, which showed jaw-dropping views of the river on one side and the water towers and rooftops of Manhattan on the other. The walls that weren't covered in windows were exposed brick, painted white. In the middle of the room, a photographer in slouchy pants consulted with Whitney and a statuesque, authoritative-seeming woman who had to be the brains behind the coffee-table book. In a corner, a wardrobe assistant rifled through a clothing rack full of trendy pieces that even Claire, who knew practically nothing about clothes, felt sure were designer. In the background, a playlist of today's pop hits boomed from a Bluetooth speaker.

An assistant greeted her like she was someone important, offering her a choice of organic tea, cold brew coffee with almond milk, or fresh squeezed orange juice. (She took the coffee, black.) "If you need to drop your baby off while you get your hair and makeup done," the assistant said, "we've got some child wranglers over there."

Claire thanked her and made a beeline for the free food. A table in the corner held a collection of trendy branded snacks, most involving chia seeds, dried fruit, and various iterations of kale. Amara stood there, her hair and makeup already done, slumping with exhaustion, scowling down at a quinoa, flaxseed, and almond bar. "God forbid they have bagels or muffins," she said when she saw Claire.

"God forbid," Claire said.

"Look, I wanted to apologize again for the other afternoon," Amara said, looking around and lowering her voice. "It wasn't very kind of me to call you a child or compare you to a nine-eleven truther or any of those things."

"It's okay," Claire said, shifting uncomfortably.

"I care about you," Amara said, "and I really appreciate how supportive and helpful you've been during this shit storm. I know your emotions were running high, and so were mine, but I'd really like to try to forget about . . . everything, and just get back to normal."

"I'd like that too," Claire said, and Amara smiled with relief.

The same assistant from before reappeared to usher Claire over to a makeup chair, where a woman in a black smock stared at her face and then consulted a row of brushes and bottles. Another woman stood behind Claire and combed her fingers through Claire's hair. A thrum of excitement ran down Claire's arms. She used to imagine that when Vagabond made it big, she'd go to photo shoots like this all the time, that she'd get so familiar with sitting in a makeup chair and having people stare at her like she was their canvas that it would bore her. Well, maybe Marcus and Marlena and the rest of that gang were sick to death of it by now, but as the makeup woman opened a palette box filled with more colors than in a box of Crayola crayons, and then leaned in close, her soft breath in Claire's face, Claire felt like she was being turned into a work of art.

In the makeup chair next to her, a high-stakes drama in miniature unfolded, as Meredith begged her makeup artist to try something else to better cover up the outbreak of angry pimples on her chin, and the makeup artist responded that she was doing the best that she possibly could. Claire just closed her eyes and surrendered to the tug on her hair in a straightener, the intimacy of another woman brushing cool liquid foundation onto her cheeks.

When Claire's hair and makeup were finished, the assistant whisked her over to the clothing rack, where a stylist looked her up and down, her eyes sweeping over Claire's black cotton T-shirt and old jeans, the corners of her mouth turning down in disapproval. As a wardrobe assistant whirled around, pulling tiny, fluffy accessories for the babies—a headband with a (real?) mink puff on it, a lacy shrug—Claire's stylist rifled through the rack, pushing aside twill and ruffles, faux-fur jackets and silk dresses, to pull out a pair of indigo skinny jeans that resembled the pair Claire was already wearing, just a million times nicer and more expensive.

While the stylist turned back to look for a shirt, Ellie emerged from behind a curtain marking off a changing area, struggling to zip up a pink dress, grunting in frustration as she looked down at her bloated stomach.

The stylist handed Claire a seafoam green silk top that was far more adventurous than anything Claire would've ever chosen on her own. Then the woman turned to attend to Ellie's emergency. "We can safety-pin it in the back," she said, looking over the pink dress. "We do that all the time for people with more natural bodies."

Claire cocked an eyebrow at the blouse in her hand, doubting that she could pull it off. But when she tugged it over her head and looked at herself in the full-length mirror, she was almost unrecognizable, sleek and glamorous, her flyaways gone, her eyes larger and more luminous than ever before. The particular green of the blouse set off her skin so that it became a glowing ivory. Wearing this blouse (not a shirt!), she belonged with the playgroup women, not as their employee but as their equal. Stick a baby in her arms, and she could have passed for a rich mom, no problem. It was an odd sensation, as if she weren't looking into a regular mirror at all but into a mirror that showed you a possible version of your future self.

"You look very nice, Claire," Gwen said from the side. Gwen, on the other hand, still wore her regular clothes instead of something from the fancy rack, with her hair and makeup done the way she always did them, if maybe a little less impeccably than before they'd all stopped taking their TrueMommy.

"Thanks," Claire said. The memory of Christopher's leg brushing against hers under the bar rippled through her, making her flush.

293

Whitney made her way over to the wardrobe area, her Empire-waisted flower-print dress swirling as she walked. Amara, Meredith, and Vicki trailed behind her. "Ooh, looking beautiful, Claire!" Whitney said, and then turned to the rest of the women, gearing herself up as if she were about to deliver the Bill Pullman speech from *Independence Day*. "I'm so glad that we're here together today, despite everything. They're almost ready to get started. And I know we all may be . . . not feeling our best."

"Understatement of the century," Amara said.

"But I think this is a really good opportunity for us all to just have some fun with our friends and our babies. And, hey," she said, smiling, "worse comes to worst, they can always photoshop the crap out of us."

"Okay, mommies," the statuesque woman in charge of it all called out. "Do your final touch-ups, and then we'll bring the babies in and get going. Thank you for being an inspiration!"

Amara rolled her eyes. "Yes, we are real Oprah Winfreys over here," she said, as the other women adjusted their hair in the full-length mirror.

Meredith noticed Gwen standing off to the side. "Oh, Gwen," she said. "Don't you want to join in?"

"No, no," Gwen said, shrinking back. "I'm just here for moral support."

"It's going in a book, not online," Ellie said. "That's different."

"I still want to err on the side of caution when it comes to protecting Reagan," Gwen said. "Especially now."

"Oh, come on, Gwen," Ellie snapped. "Don't make us feel bad about doing something fun! Pervs don't buy coffee-table books."

"All right," Whitney said. "It's Gwen's decision."

"I'm sorry," Gwen said, her mouth twisting. "I didn't mean to imply that . . . I'm just really not in a state to—"

"None of us is," Ellie said.

"It's not just that." Gwen shook her head, as if she were already mad at herself for what she was about to say. "It's Christopher."

"Oh, no. Do you still think he's having an affair?" Amara asked, and Gwen nodded. Claire's heart began to beat faster.

"Oh, my God! What did he do now?" Meredith asked, holding her hand casually over her chin as if nobody would know that she was trying to hide her acne.

"We don't need to get into it. Not when you all are about to do your nice photo shoot," Gwen said.

"You matter more to us than the photo shoot, obviously," Amara said.

"Tell us," Ellie said.

"Well," Gwen said, "he was rattled about something last night, and when I asked him what was wrong, he pretended it was nothing and started being *overly* nice and courteous."

"Oh, goodness," Whitney said. "I wish Grant would be too nice to me!"

Gwen grimaced. "I know, it sounds so dumb. But he smelled too clean again too. He said it was the gym, but I just can't stop suspecting, and I feel like I'm going insane."

"I was watching him at Reagan's birthday party," Ellie said, "and he seemed super devoted to you and the girls."

Whitney crinkled her brow and put a hand on Gwen's back. "Maybe you should head on home, go take a little rest or something. Or treat yourself a bit—you'll probably feel better if you just get a chance to relax."

"Thanks," Gwen said. "That seems like a good idea. I'm just being silly. I think I'm extra paranoid after everything that's happened recently." She made a face as if she were disgusted with herself. "I'm really sorry, everyone."

"I don't know," Claire said, and everyone turned to stare at her unexpected intrusion. "I mean, maybe if you're having these feelings, you're not wrong. You've got to trust your gut and all that, right?"

"Ladies," an assistant said, bustling up to them, "are you ready to go yet? We are on a schedule and want to make sure you get enough time with the photographer."

"Yes, we'll be there in just a sec!" Whitney said.

"Claire," Gwen said, looking at her in a whole new way, fear creeping into her face, "do you know something?"

"No," Claire said. "No, I guess I just got a weird vibe from him at the party, that's all, so I don't think you need to beat yourself up for being silly."

"Oh, well, yes, of course you shouldn't beat yourself up," Whitney said, and then gestured to where the photographer and the statuesque women were conferring, the photographer looking at her watch. "I'm so sorry to do this, Gwen, but we should probably get to it."

"No, of course. The last thing I want to do is make this photo shoot all about me," Gwen said. "Reagan and I are going to go. I'm such an idiot." As she turned to get Reagan, she flashed Claire a painfully familiar look, one filled with such self-hatred and self-doubt that Claire couldn't stop herself from opening her mouth.

"You're not an idiot," Claire said. "I don't know if he's having an affair exactly, but he hit on me."

Gwen's voice got very soft. "At the birthday party?"

"No," Claire said, and it was too difficult to look Gwen in the eyes so she turned her head to the side, catching Whitney in her vision, as she continued. "I ran into him yesterday at a bar."

"But Christopher doesn't drink," Whitney said, a spasm of pain crossing her face so quickly that by the time everyone else turned away from Claire to look at her, it was gone. But Claire saw it. And then everything else started clicking into place, even as Whitney kept on talking in a casual, concerned tone. "I chatted with him a bit at your Christmas party, Gwen, and he mentioned it. Why would he be at a bar?"

In the kitchen at the birthday party, Whitney had greeted Christopher with such studied coolness. Her hand had lingered on his shoulder a little too long for someone who had sounded so detached.

"Oh, God," Gwen said, putting her head in her hands. "I guess he goes to pick up women. I *knew* something was going on."

"Hey, Whitney," Claire said, buzzing with fury from her chest to her fingertips. "How was your massage yesterday?"

"What?" Whitney said, blinking, her eyelashes extra long from her stint in the makeup chair. "I don't see at all what that has to do with anything. I didn't get one. I couldn't find a sitter." She turned away to lead them all into the center of the room, to where they could sit on a couch and smile as if they hadn't a care in the world. "Now, I'm sorry, Gwen. I know this is the worst time, but we really need to get started—"

"So then why did you go to the Windom?" Claire asked.

Whitney stiffened and then turned back around. "What are you talking about?" Her face whitened with a realization. "Were you *following* me?" Claire folded her arms across her chest and didn't deny it.

"What the fuck?" Amara asked, letting out a dazed laugh. "Why were you following Whitney around?" Claire turned to Amara, hesitating, and Amara's confused laughter turned to wariness. "Please, don't tell me it's because . . ."

Claire held up her hands. "Okay, it's going to sound a little nuts, but after you said that something was off about TrueMommy—"

"Claire!" Amara said, darting a look at the other women.

"Wait. What?" Meredith asked.

"Nothing!" Amara said, then turned back to Claire, her eyes narrowing. "I told you to just let it go. You said you would."

"I meant to, I swear, but then Whitney called me, desperate for a babysitter because she had to get some all-important massage, and she was acting extremely suspicious!"

"I don't care how she was acting. You promised me," Amara said in a kind of disbelief. "After I stood up for you, kept your secrets, in front of everyone."

"Secrets? What secrets?" Ellie asked.

"Never mind!" Claire said to her.

Amara kept looking at Claire, that devastating accusation in her eyes. "I told you why it was important to me, to Charlie, and you *promised*."

"I know," Claire said, thrusting her chin up, defensive, trying to push away her shame. If only Amara would just fucking listen. "But if you'd heard her on that phone call—she did *not* sound normal."

"So what?" Amara asked, her disbelief turning to anger, her voice scornful. "Did you uncover some vast conspiracy?"

"No, but—"

"Of course you didn't. You betrayed my trust for nothing," Amara said. "I cannot fucking believe you. How idiotic, to follow—"

"I'm sorry I can't just ignore my gut when it tells me something's wrong, like *you* did for months," Claire snapped, realizing as soon as the words flew out of her mouth that she'd gone too far. Amara stepped back as if Claire had pushed her. "I . . . I didn't mean—" Claire began. "I'm so sorr—"

"All right, everyone. You want to know Claire's incriminating fact?" Amara asked, her spine straightening, her shoulders thrust back. "That 'Idaho Eyes' band that Ellie and Meredith like so much—Claire used to be in it, but they kicked her out because she wasn't good enough." Ellie's and Meredith's eyes widened, and Claire thought that maybe Amara would stop there, which would have been bad enough, but Amara kept going, in a low, devastating tone powered by fury. "Oh, but the *best* part is that, right before they kicked her to the curb, she hooked up with the lead singer when she thought her boyfriend might have cancer." This time, everyone's eyes widened, and Amara turned back to Claire. "Doesn't feel so great to have people betraying your trust, mucking around with shameful matters you'd prefer to keep private, does it?" she asked, practically spitting with disdain.

Claire felt a wave of nausea rise up in her throat, her eyes start to prickle. "Screw you, Amara," she said.

"Guys," Whitney said, desperation creeping into her voice. "Please, everyone is staring at us."

"Whitney, why were you at the Windom?" Gwen asked quietly.

Whitney swallowed. "Well, I tried to get a massage," she said, her voice light. "But they wouldn't let me do it because I brought Hope along."

"There are plenty of good massage places in the neighborhood," Gwen said, staring at the floor. "Why would you bother to go all the way to midtown?"

"It's supposed to be very good. The reviews online—"

"Yes, I've read the reviews," Gwen said, looking back up straight into Whitney's face. "I was interested in maybe going sometime, because it's right near Christopher's office."

"Is it?" Whitney asked, cocking her head, clenching her fists at her sides, the blithe cheeriness on her face resembling a garish mask, her beauty turned grotesque.

"Whitney," Gwen asked, "are you having an affair with my husband?" The other women in their semicircle grew very still, the suspicion coming upon them like a cloud covering the sun.

"What? No!" Whitney said. "What? I don't understand what is going on. I'm sorry that you're upset and worried, Gwen, but we're here right now for this photo shoot, and everyone is waiting on us—"

"I ran into Christopher at the bar across the street from the Windom, half an hour after I saw Whitney go in," Claire said.

Gwen flinched, then turned her big blueberry eyes back on Whitney. "Whitney?"

Whitney floundered, her mouth gaping open and closing. The force of all the other women's stares hit her too as the other conversation in the loft stopped, the ridiculous pop song on the playlist the only sound besides their shallow, anticipatory breaths. "You're fired," she said to Claire, her eyes bright and frantic. "You're fired from playgroup."

"Oh, Whitney, you selfish, selfish cunt," Amara said heavily. She moved to Gwen's side and put an arm around her shoulder, and Gwen sank into her, beginning to wail. "There *is* no more playgroup."

Chapter 31

There could be no photo shoot after that. The women flinched away from Whitney's touch as she tried to get one of them, any of them, to look at her, and then they left her to explain everything to the baffled coffee-table-book woman while they changed as quickly as they could into their normal clothes and gathered their babies, reaching for Gwen's hand, petting her hair, offering her comforts of various kinds ranging from excessive amounts of alcohol (Meredith and Ellie) to a meditation workshop (Vicki) to a willingness to castrate Christopher (Amara).

Gwen turned them all down. She needed to go home and be with her children, she said, and figure out if her marriage was salvageable. She didn't know if she could be around them for a while—too many confusing, sad things tied up in the playgroup now—but she'd let them know if that changed.

"We're here if you need us," Amara said, then turned to the other women. "I suppose I'll see you all around." Her eyes lingered on Claire, who had just come out of the bathroom bearing a handful of toilet paper. Amara took a breath as if to say something before pressing her lips together and buckling Charlie into his stroller.

Claire approached Gwen, offering her the toilet paper to wipe her eyes. Gwen accepted the gesture, giving an embarrassed sniffle. "Oh, Claire," she said. "You're out of a job, and it's all because you were trying to help me." She straightened her shoulders, the old type A Gwen ready to make some plans despite her heartbreak. "I'm going to find you something new. I bet that somebody I know is looking for an assistant or office manager."

"Gwen, you don't have to worry about that right now," Claire said. "Seriously." She looked newly mature under the day's makeup and hair job, with a new, mature sadness too.

"But I will," Gwen said, touching Claire briefly on the cheek before wheeling Reagan into the elevator alone.

When Gwen came out into the SoHo sunlight, she broke down her stroller, hailed a taxi, and buckled Reagan's car seat in. Then she slid in beside her daughter, wiped her eyes, and gave her driver an address in the West Village.

"Are you all right, ma'am?" her driver asked.

"We'll be fine," she said, then smoothed down her daughter's tufty hair. "Right, Reagan?"

Of course she knew that Regan was the name of the ambitious sister in *King Lear*. She'd been an English major at Dartmouth.

The Hudson River sparkled outside her window as they sped

up the West Side Highway. Gwen allowed herself to exhale, then flipped open a compact mirror to examine her makeup. She hadn't been surprised last month—doing her customary check of Christopher's phone while he was in the shower—to find out that he'd been sleeping with Whitney. Like Christopher, Whitney was a radiant force of charisma, one of the shining ones, and the shining ones always wanted more.

While they were stopped at a stoplight, Gwen put in some eye drops, blinked, and then carefully reapplied her mascara. She cleared her throat and did a lip trill or two to get rid of all the gunk clogging up her vocal cords. The taxi pulled up at a brownstone, one of those idyllic West Village town houses that retailed for at least ten million dollars. Gwen paid her driver, unbuckled Reagan, carried her stroller up the six stone steps, and rang the doorbell.

"Julie!" said the lithe, buoyant woman who answered the door, stepping forward to kiss Gwen on both cheeks, even though Gwen knew from extensive online research that she had been born in Kentucky, not Paris. "We're so glad you could make it today!"

"Oh, I know I'm late," Gwen said, carrying Reagan over the threshold. "This one was being difficult this morning, but we finally got out the door." She followed the hostess into the living room, where a playgroup of twelve women waved and smiled at her. "Hey, ladies! What did I miss?"

It had all begun when Gwen was pregnant with Reagan, when the two most important men in Gwen's life decided to screw up at the exact same time.

First, it had been Teddy, Gwen's brother. Brilliant, difficult Teddy had gotten it into his head that he was going to invent a *better* cure for ADHD, using the resources afforded to him by his faculty position at Boston University. He was having trouble coming up with the funding for it all, and he'd asked Gwen to invest, so she'd given him a hundred thousand dollars. She was used to coming to his rescue. When their parents died, he'd become her responsibility. She'd bailed him out of jail when he'd gotten caught driving so drunk he could barely stand up. She'd paid for him to go to therapy when he'd called her in the middle of the night to tell her that he'd been stockpiling pills and was staring at hundreds of them all spread out in front of him on his bed at that very moment, beckoning. This time, at least, giving him the money would help him build toward something he felt passionate about.

Then, when she'd called him for an update, midway through her pregnancy, he'd told her the truth: that he'd gotten fired because of a harassment charge levied against him by a research assistant who he *swore* had been making eyes at him. Nobody wanted to work with him, he said, or give him the institutional support he needed. And worse, he'd already spent her hundred thousand dollars buying supplies and materials through dubiously legal channels, but he now didn't think he'd be able to use what he'd stockpiled, and so he wouldn't be able to pay her back.

Only a few weeks later, it had been Christopher. She'd innocently walked into the den to ask him a question about signing up for a Lamaze class, and he'd sprung up from his seat at the computer as if she'd stuck him with a flaming-hot iron, clicking out of something on the screen.

She'd offered up a quick prayer that it was porn—even something really dirty: nubile cheerleaders servicing old grandpas or some obscure fetish like Furries, but when she'd pulled up the browser history he hadn't had time to wipe clean, she'd found that it was online poker and that he'd lost a significant chunk of their joint money. He only reminded her of her father more and more as they got older.

"No more gambling ever again," she'd said, and he had promised her, had wept and prostrated himself at her feet. But that man had a self-destructive force inside of him, and it was only a matter of time before it found some other outlet.

For weeks, she felt hopeless. At night, she thought of the Connecticut house, over and over, as she lulled herself to sleep. Instead of counting sheep, she counted its gabled windows, the magnolia blossoms in its backyard. She dreamed about it, the kind of dreams she had trouble shaking herself out of in the morning. If she could only get back there, she could regain something that she'd lost in the years since her parents had died—something that she couldn't find in this brownstone that Christopher had contaminated with his golden lies. She could give her daughters the childhood that she'd had.

One day, eight months pregnant with Reagan, she'd dropped Rosie off at her nursery school. And then, on a whim, she'd bought a Metro-North ticket to Westport, called a taxi from the station, and waddled boldly up to the door of the Connecticut house, her heart ricocheting inside her chest as she waited to see if anyone would answer her knock. The property looked the same as it did in her dreams or maybe even lovelier. The flowers in the garden were budding, lilting in the spring breeze. The salt of the ocean perfumed the air.

An older, shorter man answered the door, frowning up at Gwen, his glasses low on his nose, a half-finished sudoku in his hand. "I grew up here," Gwen said. "And I was wondering if you'd be willing to sell."

She charmed him with her childhood memories of the place and with her enormous belly. He'd been toying with the idea of retiring to Florida anyway. The price he listed wasn't unreasonable. About a million more than she'd have after divorcing Christopher and selling the brownstone, if her rough estimates were correct. (Idiotic of her not to get a prenup, to put Christopher's name on the deed of the house right alongside hers in that rose-colored certitude she'd had when they'd gotten married. Christopher had taken so much from her already, and when she tried to get free of him, he would only end up taking more.) She'd told the man that she would be in touch and started thinking.

The answer came to her, of all places, in the hospital delivery room, when Reagan started pushing her way out into the world. As Gwen grunted and gritted her teeth against the pain, she thought of the sleepless nights she'd had with Rosie, the sleepless nights she'd soon have again, the other exhausted new mothers she'd met in Rosie's infant music class and playgroup who, like Gwen, were barely making it through the day. There seemed to be endless, beleaguered women who were simultaneously overcome with love and dazed by the impossible work of caring for a ravenous little despot. Every one of them was living through a moment of radical personal change when they were no longer the stars of their own lives, when they were shaken by a depth of worry they'd never before experienced. They knew they were supposed to shoulder their transformation uncomplainingly and selflessly, like "good" mothers, while also maintaining the body weight and grooming habits of a Disney Channel ingenue. It made a lot of them a little crazy, and it made some of them a *lot* crazy. Sometimes, a mother couldn't hack it. She gave up and scared the shit out of everyone else. (Because her failure didn't just affect her! When she left, her children were cast out too, denied access to their glittering birthright.) But what if there was a way to give all these overwhelmed women a tiny boost, a bit of the calm and competence they craved?

"Regan," Gwen had whispered when her own ravenous creature was laid in her arms, thinking of *King Lear* and the ways in which the men of the world consistently underestimated the women around them. Christopher heard her and thought of Ronald (a picture of her grandfather and the Gipper hung in their upstairs hallway), and that was what had gone on the birth certificate, extra "a" and all. No surprise. She and Christopher had always *just* missed understanding each other, like cars trying and failing to merge into each other's lanes.

Once she'd had a month or so to recover, she went to see Teddy. He had all this supply, and she knew where he could get demand. But they'd have to be smart about it. The "perfect" mothers of the world would want to say that they'd been duped if the truth ever came out. They'd add a bunch of the in-vogue wellness jargon, some fancy packaging to make it seem legitimate, and jack up the price to ridiculous amounts. Teddy had been resistant, but he owed her. She'd taken care of him her entire life, even though he was older, and now that she had two tiny, precious girls relying on her, it was finally the time for him to step up and be the big brother that she'd always wanted him to be.

Besides, Gwen told Teddy when he still hesitated, they were giving these women a *gift*. Their own mother had spent her life yoked to every fad diet that came along, denying herself and denying herself, always hungry for food she couldn't have. She'd given her limited rations of energy to her drunken husband and her wide-eyed little girl and, most of all, to her troubled son until she had nothing left for herself. TrueMommy would make things easier for women like their mother, keeping their appetites at bay, allowing them to actually have some time for themselves. Those women could afford it.

The most flabbergasting thing about it all was that it had worked.

Gwen played her cards right. She learned how to create appealing design templates, how to cover her tracks, and how to open up a secret bank account. Using a lawyer bound to keep her identity private through attorney-client privilege, she started a shell corporation in Delaware so that the women who paid her could make their checks out to "TrueMommy LLC" in peace. But she also offered incentives for paying in cash, a small "playgroup discount" that allowed all these wealthy women to pat themselves on the back for getting a deal. The vast majority of mothers wanted to believe that they could be thrifty even as they paid out insane amounts, and so most of the money made its way to Gwen in the form of hundred-dollar bills, collected by the cute, discreet college boy she hired to do personal TrueMommy deliveries each month. (The women tended to go gaga over the fact that True-Mommy cared so much about its customers that it sent a boy in uniform to hand-deliver the vitamins! Such service!)

Gwen found midsized Momstagrams of beautiful women who needed validation but who hadn't yet gotten quite enough of it. They always revealed far too much information about their where-abouts in the updates they posted. *Going to sail some boats in Central Park with my little sea captain,* they'd write under a picture of their child in a sailor outfit, and she'd run out to the pond and then very casually sit next to them, striking up a conversation, mentioning with a sad sigh that motherhood could be *so* lonely. Their eyes would light up, and they'd either invite her to the playgroup they already had or resolve to start one with her name first on the list.

She never introduced TrueMommy right away. She would attend a few playgroup meetings first, make sure that nobody involved was a crusading-justice type who would care more about blowing the whistle than about self-preservation if they ever had to face the reality of what was in the pills they were gobbling down. And *then* she'd send the message to the Mom accounts and rehearse the actor from Philly whom she'd hired to play Dr. Lauren Clark, prepping her with all the questions that Gwen would bombard her with during the playgroup meeting, as well as anything else she could think of. In general, she'd only show up at a handful of playgroup meetings every month, just frequently enough to make sure that everything was working out as it was supposed to. She'd avoid having her picture taken or getting too close to anyone. And if things started to go south, she could always pretend to be as dumbfounded as the rest of them and drop the specter of Child Protective Services to keep them all quiet.

The Whitney playgroup had been different, because it was actually in her neighborhood. She did want Reagan to have *one* stable thing so that she'd develop healthily and be able to form lasting relationships. Gwen used her real name in that one, invited them to her house when Christopher mentioned how much he wanted to have a Christmas party and meet some of her mom friends, and acquiesced to get together not only once a week, but twice. She hadn't intended to introduce TrueMommy with these women at all. It was too close to home. And Amara was so outspoken and unfiltered that she might be the kind to tell the truth in a worst-case scenario. But then Gwen had watched how Amara worried about Charlie. Amara's fear that she was failing her son could be a powerful resource. Mothers who felt that they were mothering wrong were a uniquely vulnerable group. What had really cemented the whole thing, though, was the Joanna factor. Joanna had spooked them all, priming them to look for a miracle, a way to ward off contagion. How could Gwen pass up such an irresistible opportunity?

Throughout New York, New Jersey, and Connecticut, Gwen had two hundred fifty mothers hooked. She planned to do it for a little less than a year, which would get through most of Teddy's supply, and put her a hair north of the amount she needed for the house. Then she'd gradually taper off the dose of the drug in each week's shipment before she disappeared. But she'd started keeping a list of mothers who'd taken to TrueMommy like fish in water, who thrived on it so much that she had a feeling they'd seek it out even if they knew the truth about what was in it. She had twenty-nine mothers on that list (she'd *had* a tentative thirty-one, before she'd taken Ellie and Meredith off), and perhaps she could work something out with them. It could be a good source of continued revenue. Help her buy some furnishings for the house, send Rosie to ballet lessons.

She fell into bed every night completely exhausted, but also fulfilled in a strange way, the kind of self-satisfaction that she hadn't experienced for years. Whenever she went to work parties as Christopher's date, everyone's eyes would glaze over when she said she was a stay-at-home mom. It had been exhausting to prove that she was smart, so she'd started playing dumb instead. Now, as she widened her eyes and asked about their jobs, which sounded *so* exciting and *so* tough, some badass bitch inside of her threw her arms open and howled into the wind.

In the beautiful West Village brownstone, as all the women sipped their wine and chatted among themselves, Gwen noticed that one of the other mothers, an exceedingly tan woman named Angie, was scribbling various ailments onto her TrueMommy personal-curation form.

"Oh, right!" Gwen said, scooting over. "I need to do that too. I told them the other week that I'd been feeling a little nauseous, and they upped the peppermint oil in my vitamins. I've been feeling so much better."

"Right? Seriously, thank God for the wellness industry. True-

Mommy and acupuncture are my baseline, but I've just started with these collagen-protein shakes too. The combination is *everything*."

Gwen smiled and lowered her voice. "I believe it. Honestly, though, sometimes I think there's something stronger in these vitamins than just oil of lemongrass."

Angie let out a belly laugh. "Honey, you know what? If there is, sign me up for a double dose."

Gwen filed this away, rounding her list up to an even thirty.

She'd planned and planned and planned. There was always that unexpected element, though, the fly in the ointment. And this particular fly had been, crazily enough, Claire. Claire, who came in sweet and wounded and disheveled and grew on them all slowly like moss. Claire, who had gotten just close enough to all of them that she *cared*, but who felt none of the shame and worry and urge for secrecy that came from having actually taken the TrueMommy herself and having a child to worry about to boot. Gwen hadn't realized that the Claire situation was happening until it was too late. Claire had truly surprised her. That was why Gwen had had to blow the whole playgroup up. For once, Christopher had given her exactly what she needed, coming home last night penitent and pathetic, confessing everything from his time in the Windom with Whitney to his run-in with Claire in the bar in a near-religious rush, like Gwen was his priest instead of his wife, begging her to forgive him yet again. All Gwen had to do after that was go to the photo shoot and push people's buttons accordingly.

It worried her that Claire might take her playgroup-musician skills elsewhere and insinuate herself with more mothers like the righteous little snake she was. Gwen would have to keep an eye on her, see if she could find something else to present like a glittering jewel—something that would take Claire far away from the world of New York playgroups until Gwen could wind down True-Mommy, get a divorce, and take her children to the Connecticut house for good.

Chapter 32

The weekend after the playgroup blowup, Whitney finally went to visit Joanna. She took the train out to Rahway, with a red velvet cake from the bakery by Joanna's old apartment on her lap. She left Hope at home with Grant, who was still blissfully unaware of everything that had transpired. She didn't *think* any of the playgroup women would take it upon themselves to tell him about Christopher, but still she held her breath and tried to decide if she wanted to tell him herself. The weight of everything she'd kept from him hung heavy around her. She'd become a completely different person from the woman he'd danced with at their wedding.

Joanna and her son lived in a brown brick duplex a ten-minute walk from the train station, with a small yard surrounded by a chain-link fence. Joanna, dressed in blue jeans and an oversized sweater, her straight black hair showing a few strands of gray, let

Whitney in warily, accepting the cake with muted thanks rather than the touched surprise Whitney had let herself imagine.

Joanna put water on for coffee and cleared some clutter off the kitchen table. They sat and made small talk while Joanna's child napped in his playpen. The duplex had a nice number of windows, but it didn't get good light, dwarfed by the buildings on either side of it. Joanna had largely left the white walls bare. Still, she'd arranged a few pots of herbs on the windowsill, and Whitney gestured to them with a smile. "I like how you've decorated." If Whitney squinted, it looked like a cozy home, perhaps a little bohemian. Not the sad divorcée's quarters she and the other mothers had imagined and feared.

"How's the playgroup?" Joanna asked.

"Oh," Whitney said. "Well, we actually stopped meeting."

"Ah," Joanna said, and made a clicking noise with her mouth as if she'd managed to put a puzzle together. "So that's why you came to stare at the zoo animal."

"Excuse me?"

"You all had a tiff, and now you're looking for an easy way to feel better about yourself."

"I wanted to check up on how you were doing."

"Six months after the fact," Joanna said.

"I've been meaning to come, but you know how it is with a baby—"

"Or is it that you're worried your husband might leave you for another woman too, and you want to take some notes?" Joanna asked, relentless, harsh.

Over the past forty-eight hours, Whitney had largely been in shock at everything that she'd brought upon herself, numb except for a dull sense of dread. But now she put her head down on the cool wooden table, unable to stop the sobs from overcoming her. "I'm sorry," she choked out.

Joanna sighed and patted Whitney's shoulder a little roughly. Then she pushed back from the table and began to bustle around her kitchen. She cut them each a slice of cake and brought the plates over to the table, along with a box of tissues.

"I guess I just wanted to know," Whitney said when she'd calmed herself enough to be able to speak again, "if it has gotten better. I mean, are you happier now?"

Joanna stared at her for a minute. "Am I happier than I was in the literal moment that I curled up on the floor of the canned beans aisle in Fairway? Of course. Am I happier now than I was when I had a beautiful New York City apartment and a doting husband and my whole future bright ahead of me?" She gave a harsh laugh, nearly a bark. "What do you think?" She toyed with a bite of cake on her fork, pursing her lips. "My advice is to hold on to him if you can."

Chapter 33

Fragmented, the moms threw themselves into summertime.

Amara took Charlie to every outdoor activity for children that she could find, plowing through her exhaustion like it was a cornfield and she was a motherfucking tractor trailer. If there was a craft fair or a kid's festival anywhere in Manhattan, she and Charlie attended it. He was going to be the most well-rounded, well-cared-for baby in the whole damn city. She went to the zoo with him so much, she even got tired of looking at penguins, a thing that had previously seemed unimaginable. (They were penguins, for fuck's sake! How could you get tired of looking at penguins unless you were a heartless, screwed-up person?) She bought *The Foolproof Guide to a Happy, Healthy Toddler* and practically memorized it, the old, familiar anxiety that Charlie wasn't hitting all his check marks coming right back. A creeping strangeness began to grow between her and Daniel every time her shame and rage and despair from the whole TrueMommy incident overwhelmed her and she wanted to tell him exactly what was wrong, but bit her tongue instead. (Which happened approximately twenty million times a day.) It didn't help that when she'd told him about the playgroup's demise thanks to Whitney's affair with Gwen's husband, he'd shaken his head and said, "Yikes, it's scary how you can have no idea what your partner's doing," and then, jokingly, looked into her eyes with a solemn stare and said, "Anything you need to tell me?" She met moms on the playground and chatted with them and then never saw them again. Often, they asked for her number and sent her effusive texts asking her to get together. The texts always made Amara think of Claire (these women used so many more exclamation points than Claire would've, and they made her laugh so much less), so Amara never responded. She was the playground-mom equivalent of a charming Tinder ghoster, getting the women all excited about their connection and then leaving them sad and confused. She wore herself and Charlie out during the day, because if she was exhausted at night, it meant less time trying to hide things from Daniel.

Whitney deleted her social media and went out of town. She found a three-room cottage on the North Fork of Long Island, setting up shop there with Hope for June and July. Grant came out on the weekends to join them, and they talked about buying a place like it for future summers. "It would have to have more bedrooms," he said, "for more children," and she smiled and made a noise that was neither agreement nor dissent. For Whitney, it was a crash course in loneliness. She took Hope for long, aimless walks every day, as seagulls arced above them and waves foamed at her feet. As she put one foot in front of the other, Whitney whispered apologies to her daughter for all of her myriad failings. She concentrated on finding Hope one perfect shell, wanting to make her smile and reach her little hands out in awe. So many things gave Hope awe—the grainy feel of sand beneath her toes, the little hermit crabs scuttling about in tide pools—and Whitney felt that she was rediscovering the world through her daughter's eyes. It was almost magical, even though she didn't deserve magic. After the first week, in which she tried over and over again to apologize to Gwen without getting any responses to her voice mails and e-mails, she turned off her phone and only looked at it when she and Grant needed to coordinate something. She stopped putting on makeup each morning and bought herself some mom jeans. They were really damn comfortable. After days of not talking to other adults, she longed for and dreaded the weekends in equal measure, craving the noise that Grant would bring, uneasy about actually being around him. She learned anew each facet of her daughter's face, counted the fine brown hairs on her head. She dreamed of Christopher at night, but also of the playgroup women, seeing their smiles turn to sneers as they learned the truth about her.

Ellie got a babysitter and went to a Narcotics Anonymous meeting without telling her husband, and Meredith did too. Ellie liked that you got to stand up and talk about how you were feeling for as long as you wanted, and everyone had to listen respectfully to you. She actually thought that the meeting was kind of fun, and Meredith did too. Ellie went to the gym a lot. Meredith went somewhat less often.

Vicki just kept doing her Vicki thing.

And they might have all continued on like that as their children grew and changed except for the fact that, on a sweltering Saturday morning in early August, Amara and Whitney went to the same children's music class.

Chapter 34

Another day, another free event that Amara could take Charlie to. This time it was a trial music class at a new kids' space on Madison and Seventy-Seventh, some just-opened franchise that had flooded the neighborhood with flyers announcing their special music event, where the walls were decorated with suns and hearts, where all the employees spoke in such cheery, high-pitched voices that she was surprised dogs all over the neighborhood weren't howling, and where they were desperately trying to lure parents into signing their kids up for the fall "semester," as if it were a university for toddlers. Amara pictured them giving Charlie a diploma at the end of it all. Perhaps some apple-cheeked three-year-old would be crowned valedictorian, and all the adults would have to come sit and listen while the tot stood on a stage and babbled about trains.

The front desk girl pointed Amara down the hall, directing her to follow the crowd and leave Charlie's stroller outside the door labeled "Theater." Amara took off her shoes as requested and plunked herself down on an ABC rug while a heavily bearded man tuned his guitar and his assistant, a bright-eyed girl who had *clearly* moved to New York to do musical theater, went around demanding high fives from all the babies. Charlie did not want to oblige, twisting away from the girl's eager face, and the girl remained crouched down in front of Amara for far too long, trying to get him to touch her hand, until Amara had to say, "He takes a little while to warm up."

"Oh, no! That hurts my feelings!" the girl said, making a fake pouty face, and moved on to the next kid. Amara looked around in vain for someone with whom she could exchange caustic eye rolls.

The walls here were all painted bright purple, with accents of neon green. Why would anyone do such a thing?

Finally, the guy finished tuning his guitar, and strummed a power chord. "WHO'S READY TO ROCK OUT??" he bellowed, and the crowd of parents around Amara *whoo*-ed like they were at a Foo Fighters concert. The assistant girl stuck out her tongue and waggled it—transforming for a moment into a forgotten member of KISS—and then went back to her show tunes smile, clapping her hands as she and the guitar guy began to sing a shitty hello song about sunshine. *(Oh the sun is out and it's shining bright, like the faces you see on your left and right!)* Amara swayed half-heartedly.

Behind her, the door to the classroom opened—a late arrival.

Amara turned her head briefly, catching a flash of thick, wavy hair, and two long, muscled legs sticking out of some baggy jeans shorts as the mother coaxed in a toddling baby. It wasn't until the newcomer had settled down on her own spot on the alphabet rug that Amara really looked at her and realized it was Whitney. Whitney recognized Amara at the same moment, shock coming over her face.

Well. That was the end of *this* music class. No great loss. If Amara wanted someone to screech at her about sunshine, she could always call Daniel's mother down in Florida. She got to her feet and scooped Charlie up, then strode out the door to the hallway, where she'd left her stroller. She struggled to buckle him in, noting with a strange detachment that her hands were shaking.

As she fastened the final strap, the door opened behind her, and Whitney ran out, Hope in tow. "Amara, wait," she said. Amara angled Charlie's stroller away from her and began to push. "Please, Amara, don't run away!"

"Oh, I'm not running away," Amara hurled back. "I'm just going to get Daniel. I thought perhaps you might like to fuck him too?"

Whitney let out a breath like she'd had the wind knocked out of her, then nodded. "I deserve that," she said, her voice steady and low. The hallway around them smelled like cleaning fluid. Noises of a happy class echoed from the other side of the theater door. Hope settled herself down on the floor and began to pull at the carpet. "Or worse than that. Please, let me explain."

"Is your excuse that you're one of those people who takes Ambien and then goes out and drives a car while still asleep, except instead of driving a car, you were screwing your friend's husband and lying about it to all your other friends?"

"No," Whitney said, biting her lip.

"Then it's probably not good enough."

"I know that. I know nothing I say can ever make it better, okay?" Whitney said, sighing. She looked different. Tanner, and a little wilder. Less coiffed. There were some new lines on her face, or maybe it was just that she wasn't wearing much makeup at all, like she had become the kind of person who casually dabbed her lips with ChapStick instead of searching for the proper, muted shade of lipstick. "I've tried to excuse it to myself a million times by saying that it was because Grant and I were not in a good place or that I had so much pent-up excess energy because of the TrueMommy or that I hadn't felt really desired for so long and Christopher came onto me so strong that I couldn't resist. Or that because I was little White Trash Whitney trying to belong in this rich, perfect world, it was only inevitable that I'd screw it up in the worst and most predictable way that I could. And all of those things are probably true, but also, none of them matters. The truth is just that sometimes you think you're a good person, and then little by little, you justify your way into being a bad one."

"Rewind a second. White Trash Whitney?" Amara asked.

"Oh. Yes. My mother was a dental hygienist and my dad bounced between construction jobs and day drinking at our kitchen table, and they were always fighting about money, and for a while, *that* was my secret shame." She gave a rueful laugh and scooped a piece of paper that Hope had found on the ground out of her hands right before she put it into her mouth. "Seems pretty tame in comparison to what I've got to be ashamed of now."

"Wait," Amara said. "What's wrong with being a dental hygienist?"

"I don't know," Whitney said. "Nothing! Anyway, I don't expect you to ever want to see me again, but before you run out of here, I have to tell you how much I've always admired you, and how sorry I am."

Amara crossed her arms. "Don't apologize to me. Apologize to Gwen."

"I've tried. She won't return any of my calls. But I do have to apologize to you, because I didn't just hurt Gwen. I screwed up playgroup. I screwed it up for us all, right when we all needed one another the most."

"Yeah, well, I don't forgive you," Amara said. Whitney looked down at the ground and nodded. "But I guess I know a little bit about screwing up too."

They stood in silence for a moment, the air heavy with their regret. "How *is* Gwen?" Whitney asked.

"How do you think?" Amara snapped, and then bit her lip. "No, I don't really know, actually. We text every so often to check in about how we're handling all the TrueMommy stuff, and it sounds like she and Christopher are working through things, but she hasn't really wanted to see anyone." She shook her head. "The best part of my day is the moment I wake up, those couple of seconds before I remember everything that happened. It's been really fucking hard the last couple of months, carrying it all around and not being able to talk about it with anybody."

"I know," Whitney said, and reached out to grasp Amara's hand. Amara let her own hand relax into the warmth of Whitney's palm, and they stayed there like that until another late-arriving mother came barreling down the hallway, dragging a little boy by the hand, saying in a not-at-all-nice tone of voice, "Come *on*, Jason, come *on!*"

Poor tardy Jason disappeared after his mother into the Sunshine Den, and a snippet of song trailed out into the hallway after them. Whitney grimaced at the guitar guy's hoarse, grasping voice, the assistant's hollow sunny tone. "Claire was so much better, wasn't she?"

Amara felt a twinge, like she'd stumbled across a letter from an old lover. "Yeah, she was perfect for us, in her own strange way."

"Is it true, what you said at the photo shoot, about her being in that famous band?" Whitney asked, and Amara nodded. "I guess I never really asked her much about her life outside the job. And then I screwed her out of that job. Literally."

"Yeah, in retrospect, telling everybody her private business at the photo shoot was not my finest moment either," Amara said. Again, they looked at each other in silence. "Shit," Amara said. "I've got to go see Claire."

Chapter 35

Claire spent much of June and July out of town, thanks, in a weird twist of fate, to Gwen.

About a week and a half after everything blew up, Gwen called to ask if she could take Claire out for tea. They met at a little café over on First Avenue, and Gwen insisted on paying for Claire's pot of Earl Grey. Reagan napped in the stroller beside their table. Gwen brushed off Claire's tentative attempt to ask if she was doing okay with a brisk shrug of her shoulders. "I'd rather not talk about it. I've been thinking about myself too much lately. I want to help *you*," she said. "You're an important part of our lives, after all. You've been so instrumental in Reagan's development."

"Gwen! Great pun," Claire said.

"Sorry?" Gwen asked.

"'Instrumental'?" Claire said as Gwen tilted her head and furrowed her forehead. "'Cause I'm a musician?"

"Oh, my goodness!" Gwen said, and gave a brief laugh. "But really, what are you thinking of doing now?"

It was strange, Claire thought, to spend time alone with Gwen. She had never done it before for more than a minute or two. Unlike Amara and Whitney, and even Ellie and Meredith at times, Gwen had never sought her out one-on-one for conversation, never developed a special rapport with her, never patted the empty seat next to her as an indication that Claire should sit. Now that they were trapped across a table from each other, Claire found something disconcerting in Gwen's gaze, a hint of off-putting intensity in her smile. It was grief, Claire decided, the grief of a woman who had invested all her energy in raising a perfect family only to have it blow up in her face. There must have been total, obliterating sadness underneath Gwen's surface even as she tried to carry on, and *that* was what was making Claire feel uncomfortable. God, the poor woman. Claire swallowed her tea and tried to relax.

"Well, I was thinking of looking into other playgroups or maybe some early-childhood-education places like Gymboree," she said.

"Claire, I don't mean to overstep here, but I think you can do so much more," Gwen said, pouring a packet of stevia into her own tea, then delicately stirring it in. (Did this café even *have* stevia, or had Gwen brought this all the way from home?) "I know you don't want to sing to children. It's a bit embarrassing for you, isn't it? I looked up your old band, and honestly, I think you're much more talented than they are. You just need the right resources, a patron of sorts. So, here." She pulled her classic Chanel bag up onto her lap, reached in, and took out a check, which she handed to Claire. "I know it's probably not enough to make any real difference."

Claire blinked a few times as she looked at Gwen's neat handwriting, how it spelled out both her name and what must have been an error, an extra zero that Gwen couldn't possibly have intended to add, turning a check meant to be for four hundred dollars into four thousand dollars. "I thought it might help you get away for the summer," Gwen was saying. "Rent out your place here, take yourself on an artist's retreat and write some songs, and then maybe there will be some left over to start recording. At least you won't have to work any day jobs for a while." She pulled out of her purse a paper with pictures of a rental apartment, covered in notes. "I found this well-reviewed rental place online, and they're willing to give special artist rates if you book the whole summer. They're holding it for you for the next twenty-four hours. I think you should take it."

"Gwen," Claire said. "Thank you so much." She was having trouble wrapping her head around this unexpected gift. She wanted it. Oh, God, she wanted it. Her mind flashed to an image of her returning from a triumphant summer away, ready to go with music far superior to anything that Vagabond was doing now (and also, improbably, two inches taller and with bigger boobs). But, maybe because she couldn't quite believe this good fortune was happening to her, something seemed off. "I can't take this. It's too generous."

"Well, it was generous of you to tell me the truth, even though it cost you," Gwen said.

"I . . . ," Claire said, staring down at the check. The strangest thought came into her mind. If she went out of town for so long, she and Amara would never have a chance to make things right between them. She shook her head. *That* crazy idea shouldn't be a consideration.

"Please, Claire," Gwen said, her voice catching. "I just want to make something good happen, after everything bad lately."

"Then, wow," Claire said. "Thank you. This is amazing."

Claire took a bus to Jim Thorpe, Pennsylvania. The rental place Gwen had found for her, a basement apartment in a turquoise-painted house, was a twenty-minute walk from the center of town. She laid down her luggage and her guitar in the bedroom, eyeing the twin bed, which was covered with a thin green-and-pink-flowered quilt. Well, she guessed she wouldn't be having any over-night guests there. Maybe that wasn't a bad thing.

She went into town to get groceries and then stopped in front of a liquor store, ready to buy a few handles to get her through the week. She paused with her hand on the doorknob. Maybe it also wouldn't be a bad thing to try a night totally sober. She could come back tomorrow. Her groceries were pretty heavy anyway.

By nine thirty P.M., she'd realized that she could only get inter-mittent access to the Internet by holding her laptop up above the bed in one particular patch of air, and she was desperate for a drink. She ran to the liquor store as a drizzle of rain turned into a downpour. Her stomach dropped as she approached the darkened windows, as she read the sign on the door announcing that they only stayed open until nine. Fuck, she'd forgotten that places out-side of NYC closed at reasonable times. She wanted to cry. That, or break a store window, vault herself over the broken glass, grab a handle, and make a run for it.

Instead, she pulled out her phone to look up the nearest bar. Then she paused. She'd been so self-righteous with the playgroup women when she couldn't even get through one night alone with-out drinking herself into a stupor? Screw that. She'd go dry for one week, like a mini Lent, just to prove to herself that she could.

The mini Lent week was awful. She alternated between feeling bored out of her mind and far too anxious. But once she'd waited one week, she decided she might as well wait two. And then wait-ing two weeks turned into a month. It turned out that when she wasn't numbing herself with alcohol and the Internet and didn't have any playgroup to take up all her energy, she had nothing to do except channel her feelings into songs. With no distractions from the terrible feelings that came up, she just had to sit with them and then turn them into something else. She was a useless lump for a while, and then she wrote and wrote.

At the end of July, she had a hundred false starts, and five full songs. She played them all through and knew in her bones that, even if she got really lucky with connections and timing, these songs would never make her famous like Vagabond. Her music didn't have that sort of mindless catchiness, that danceability.

But maybe she liked what she had made anyway. Maybe she could be okay with a life in which Vagabond never watched her light up their TV screens as they choked on their own jealousy, a life in which the great wrong they'd done to her was never righted and karma never kicked them in the ass, a life where they had everything and she just had—what was it that the *Rolling Stone* profile of Vagabond had said, with a certain degree of scorn?—a solid career of quietly doing what she loved. Maybe that would be amazing.

But to do that, it would help to have the money she deserved. She thought of Amara, the way she'd said, "You wrote the only good part of the number one song in the country?" Claire had, and it was about time she got some credit. Once the idea came into her mind, she couldn't get it out, so she bought a bus ticket out of Jim Thorpe a month earlier than she'd originally planned. Gwen might be upset at the squandering of her gift, but Claire didn't have to tell her. On a sweltering Saturday morning in August, Claire came back to the city and met up with Thea.

They made the mistake of going to Bethesda Terrace in Central Park, under the incorrect assumption that August in New York City was a nice time to be outside, instead of a time when the trash reeked more than it ever could any other month. (They'd lived in New York for years now and should have known better, but each long winter created a kind of memory wipe. Claire thought she should get a *Memento*-style tattoo to remind herself.) They sat by the lake on a bench, glistening, and fanned themselves. To Claire's slight surprise, Thea wore a loose white shirt and athletic shorts, different from her normal, structured wardrobe.

"So," Claire said, "if I wanted to ask Vagabond for my share of the royalties for helping to write 'Idaho Eyes,' would you be my lawyer?"

"Oh, hell yes, I would," Thea said. "It would be my pleasure.

If they don't cooperate, I will help you sue the pants off of those bastards."

"Thank you," Claire said. "Obviously, I'd want to handle it all quietly, if we could, but I think they would too. And I'd like for us all to be in the same room as little as possible. And I don't need a lot from them, just what's fair."

"We'll start out by asking for a lot, though," Thea said, and Claire could almost hear the whirring inside her brain as she calculated percentages and profits. "I'd want to get this hammered out soon. Because, actually, I have something I want to talk to you about too." She leaned forward and folded her hands on her lap, an unfamiliar note of uncertainty and excitement coming into her voice. "I know I've been hard to reach lately. That's because Amy and I are having a baby. I'm pregnant."

For the briefest moment, Claire felt a pang of sadness at how things would never fully be the same between them again. And then joy came and kicked that pang out the door. "Thea!" Claire screamed, and threw her arms around her.

"You'll be Aunt Claire, of course," Thea said, and then they went off on a spree talking about baby names and how this was the first morning in weeks that Thea hadn't thrown up, and although she didn't want to jinx it, she thought she really might make it through the day vomit-free.

Then Claire's phone buzzed. She glanced at the screen, a thrum starting in her chest as she registered what she was seeing. A message, with Amara's name at the top: *Hey there. Any chance that you're free? Can we meet up and talk?*

"What?" Thea asked. "Is it a man?"

"It's nothing," Claire said.

"That is not the kind of face you make when it's nothing." She plucked Claire's phone away from her, entered the pass code (they'd long known each other's passwords by heart, like neighbors exchanging spare keys in case of emergency), and looked at the screen. "Who's Amara?"

"She's just . . . she was one of the women from the playgroup. The one who was the asshole at first." Claire had kept Thea updated on the early stages of playgroup and about her growing closeness with Amara ("I think I'm a little jealous," Thea had said at one point), but had told her nothing about the destruction of it all.

"Oh, right, I want to meet her," Thea said, and started typing something on the phone.

"What are you doing?"

Thea just shrugged and, when Claire reached out to try to grab her phone back, said, "You're not allowed to grab things from a pregnant woman."

When Claire went ahead and grabbed the phone anyway, she looked down at the screen to a series of new texts.

I'm hanging out at Bethesda Terrace, Thea had written. *Come on by.*

On our way, Amara had written back.

"Are you kidding me?" Claire asked Thea.

"What's the big deal?" Thea asked. "I thought you loved her. It's nice that you made a friend, and I want to meet her so I know whether or not I approve."

"You're such a control freak. Let's go," Claire said, standing up, so Thea shrugged and rose quickly to her feet. Then she paused, steadying herself on the bench.

335

"Hold on," she said. "I may have jinxed it." She walked to the nearest park trash can and braced herself on the edge of it, taking a series of deep breaths.

"Are you doing this on purpose?" Claire asked, and Thea shot her a look of pure fire. "Shit. Do you need a ginger ale?" Thea swallowed and nodded, so Claire ran to a nearby cart, waited in the long line, and paid the ridiculous three dollars for a soda, cracking it open and holding it out to her cousin. Claire watched Thea sip the drink slowly and patted her on the back as her adrenaline pumped. She could just text Amara back and tell her not to come after all, but curiosity was unfurling inside of her.

A few minutes later, the women appeared over the top of the hill, pushing their strollers, Whitney unexpectedly at Amara's side. An invisible fist squeezed Claire's heart in her chest, one quick, sharp pulse—had something bad happened? Or had *she* done something bad that she hadn't even realized, and that was why these two women who by all rights should never have spoken to each other again were bearing down on her now, a hesitant team, here to accuse her of . . . what? Telling on them? But she'd kept her word about that, at least. She hadn't even told Thea. (*Oh, no,* Claire thought with a jolt. Thea would soon be a New York City mom in a pretty high-income bracket too, thanks to her job at a fancy law firm. Would TrueMommy target her? Thea would never fall for it, but then again, Claire wouldn't have expected Amara to fall for it either.)

It didn't seem like Whitney and Amara had come to yell at her, though. They scanned the crowd with a tentative air, looking a little softer, a little sloppier, their faces also glistening in the August heat. They could go fuck themselves, Claire thought while simultaneously yearning to run up and throw her arms around them both and their children too.

"I'll be right back," Claire said to Thea, and walked ten feet forward to meet them.

"Claire," Whitney said while Amara just hit her with that thrilling, piercing look of hers.

"What's going on?" Claire asked, her arms folded across her chest.

"We . . . ," Whitney said.

"We fucked up," Amara said. "Massively. In terms of how we treated you."

"And we wanted to say that we're sorry," Whitney said.

"What, are apology cleanses the newest trend?" Claire asked, identifying something strange and new within herself. For the first time, she felt herself to be an equal with these women. She'd viewed herself as their subordinate plenty of times, but at other moments, she'd actually thought of herself as superior. They'd saddled themselves down with children, giving up their jobs, not seeming to have a passion beyond what they'd brought forth out of their own bodies, and then on top of that, they'd gotten accidentally hooked on drugs, leaving her to mother them. But as Whitney and Amara stood in front of her now, asking for her forgiveness, these glorious, screwed-up, monstrous angels whom she had feared and hated and loved and disdained and worshipped seemed suddenly to be no inherently better than she was, but also no inherently worse. They were just human, through and through, and she was too.

"Is there any way we can make it up to you?" Whitney asked, and Claire knew exactly how they could.

"Tell Thea," Claire said.

"Thea? Your cousin?" Whitney asked.

"Yeah," Claire said, indicating Thea by the trash can, where she seemed to have decided that she didn't need to vomit after all (*had* she been doing it all on purpose, then?), and was now Purell-ing her hands, not at all subtly trying to listen in. Thea waved. "She's going to be a mother soon."

"If you have impending motherhood tips, please," Thea said, smiling and walking over, "I am all ears."

"Thea," Whitney said as they shook hands, "I'm Whitney. We e-mailed a long time ago about the playgroup."

"We also took an art history class together at Harvard," Thea said.

Whitney put her hands to her mouth. "I'm so sorry—"

Thea laughed. "Don't worry about it."

"She's looked out for me, and I want to look out for her. I don't want her getting taken advantage of," Claire said, and Whitney and Amara understood.

"Wait. What?" Thea asked, her smile fading, that brisk get-shit-done expression coming back onto her face. "'Getting taken advantage of'? How?"

Amara and Whitney exchanged a look and then, slowly, nod-ded at each other. "If anyone tries to get you to take these wellness vitamins called TrueMommy," Amara said, "steer clear."

"We heard that they're a big, expensive scam," Whitney said.

"TrueMommy," Thea said. "Got it. Thanks." She picked up her phone and began typing something.

"Thank you," Claire said quietly to Whitney and Amara. "And for what it's worth, I screwed up too."

Amara looked at her, a helpless smile coming over her face, lost for words for the first time in Claire's experience with her. "So . . . ," she said, "how was your summer?" Claire laughed, and Amara joined in. Claire bent down to Charlie's stroller and held up her hand for a high five, and he actually gave her one.

"It was . . . well, you know," Claire said. "Gwen paid for me to go away on an artist's retreat."

"What?" Amara asked, raising an eyebrow. "That's quite generous."

"Sorry, Thea?" Whitney asked as Thea continued to type away on her phone. "I hope you don't mind me asking but, what are you . . . are you typing something about the TrueMommy?"

"Yeah, I know a few other mothers and moms-to-be," Thea said. "I'm warning them too."

"You don't have to . . . ," Whitney began helplessly as Thea pressed *send*.

"Women have to look out for one another," Thea said. "Right?" Her phone began to buzz with responses, which she showed to Claire:

Weird! Never heard of it but thanks, I'll keep an eye out.

Yeah, not surprised. Wellness stuff is generally a crock of shit.

Her phone buzzed a third time, and Thea rolled her eyes. "This is my wife's sister, who lives in Hoboken. She's a total nutter. Her greatest ambition was to be a trophy wife, and she got it. I have a hard time believing she and Amy come from the same gene pool. I suspect the milkman." She laughed, but then bit her lip as she read the response, first to herself, next aloud to the other women:

"Uh don't know where u heard that, but no scam. It's totally amazing. Tell me these ladies are not the hottest healthiest mothers in all of New Jersey!!"

"Oh. Oh, no," Whitney said, putting her head in her hands.

Thea held up the phone, showing them a picture of a bunch of blond women sitting on a rug, babies in front of them. Then she handed the phone to Claire. "Amy's sister is the extremely tan one," she said as the little ellipses that meant Amy's sister was typing appeared at the bottom of the screen. With an electronic whoosh, the message came through as Amara, Whitney, and Claire looked down at the phone.

My playgroup!! Minus Tara, who took the picture. She's got this thing about photos because her cousin's baby's picture was used on some child porn site, which is like OMG but also I'm not going to NOT take pictures of my baby, so can u not make me feel bad about it?

Claire, Amara, and Whitney looked up at one another, the realization hitting them all at the same time.

"Oh, my God," Whitney said.

"Mother*fucker*," Amara said.

Claire handed the phone back to Thea. "I'm so sorry," she said, "but we have to go."

Chapter 36

Gwen sat in a far-back corner of her walk-in closet, going over her plan for the next few weeks. Christopher had his own closet and never came this far into this little room of hers—she'd hung up a bulwark of old clothes from her parents that she couldn't bear to get rid of, and the musty coats and bathrobes acted like a charm to ward him off, smelling as they did of her grief at losing her mother and father and her disappointment in him as a replacement. The one time he *had* barged in on her, she'd simply pulled her father's old sports coat off a hanger and pretended to weep into it, and Christopher had backed out, telling her to take all the time she needed. So now it was a perfect place to store anything she didn't want him to see. She took any extra TrueMommy shipments she had lying around, a leather-bound planner full of her records and notes, and cash that she hadn't yet been able to deposit in her private bank account, and put them in old shoeboxes from Bloomingdale's, then shoved them back onto a very high shelf when she wasn't using them, just in case Rosie came in sometime to explore. The closet, which had been intended as a servants' quarters back when the house was first constructed, was big enough for an armchair and bright with recessed lighting. She found it funny that her closet doubled as her office, an appropriate fit for the kind of double life she was leading.

She'd told Christopher that she needed to be alone and rest for a little while, and he—walking on eggshells around her and trying to be the perfect husband over the past couple of months in the hopes that she was fool enough to give him *another* chance—had promised to keep the girls occupied. As she made notes in her planner, the faint sounds of the rest of her family playing together rose from downstairs. Rosie let out a happy shriek as Christopher roared. Gwen could picture him chasing their laughing little girl around the room as Reagan watched and clapped her hands, babbling, "Dada," her favorite word.

The girls would miss him. She intended to fight for near-full custody once she dropped the divorce bomb on him, and she thought she had a strong case. He had a pattern, after all, and if he couldn't control himself around women and gambling, could he really be trusted to parent these girls as well as she could? He would feel terrible and self-loathing, and she would be just generous enough with her concessions that he'd be grateful and not fight her too hard or dig too deeply into finances. She'd let him visit, and the girls could go stay with him sometimes, but for the most part, they'd live at the Connecticut house with her. Sooner or later, she'd be able to find a new man to be a good father figure for them. She knew what to look for this time—a steady, unremarkable man with a well-paying job who felt grateful to have her. Someone who knew that she was supposed to be out of his league and would work every day to keep her and her girls happy.

She looked at the planner in front of her. She was getting so close now. She circled a date in October when she'd start to wind down the whole thing. She could start the new year fresh, with only a small, loyal group of customers. She smiled. A fresh start sounded wonderful.

Downstairs, the doorbell rang.

Chapter 37

Whitney stood on the steps of Gwen's brownstone behind Amara, Claire, and the rest of the hurriedly contacted playgroup women flanking them, all of them slightly out of breath, their children having been left with various husbands. Whitney trembled like she had a fever as Amara rang the doorbell. "I hope you know," Amara said under her breath, "that if Gwen turns out to be a lying monster, that still doesn't excuse you screwing her husband."

"Oh, believe me, I know," Whitney said.

Then Christopher answered the door, cradling Reagan in one arm. That charming smile she had loved so much beamed straight out at Amara and the mass of women. It faded as he saw Claire and then disappeared completely when he registered Whitney's presence. She felt a stab of pain, like the plunge of a needle into unbroken skin, at the look of revulsion that passed over his face, and then a deeper, more abiding sadness at the death of an old Whitney—a Whitney who thought that the passion of a handsome, wealthy man could save her. That Whitney and her ignorance shriveled into dust as this Whitney looked straight ahead. She had more important things to worry about now. She felt capable of lifting a car with her bare hands. Of murder. Of anything.

"Is Gwen here?" Amara asked Christopher.

He nodded, confused. "She's resting upstairs in the bedroom," he said. "Listen, I don't know what's going on, but I'm not sure if this is a good time. . . ."

"Take the children somewhere else," Whitney said. "Now."

Chapter 38

Gwen heard footsteps coming down the hallway, toward the bedroom door. *Christopher,* she thought with a flash of annoyance, and shoved the planner back into a shoebox, leaving the top askew in her haste. She grabbed the nearest coat of her mother's, an old full-length mink pelt, and thrust it on, burying her face in its sleeve and trying to work up some tears that would scare him away.

But Amara opened the door, with Ellie, Meredith, and Vicki filing in behind her. Oh, God, had they come to take her out for some attempt at a girls' night, some misguided gesture of friendship? The last thing she had the energy for right now was some dinner where they all steadily got plastered while attempting to convince her that she was too good for Christopher. (She'd known that for years now.)

Strange, Claire was there too. Gwen had hoped that, during

her forced isolation, Claire would pickle in alcohol and self-destruct. What a disappointment to see her looking healthier than ever. Gwen gave a sniffle, thinking of excuses to send them away.

"Did we catch you in the middle of something?" Amara asked, her voice a little cold for someone about to spirit her off on a fun adventure.

"Oh, my goodness," Gwen said, struggling to her feet, acutely aware of the shoebox next to her. *Just don't look at it,* she told herself, *and they won't look either.* "I wasn't expecting you all!"

"Surprise," Amara said.

"I feel like I'm crying every time you see me now," she said lightly. "It's just . . . my parents died when I was in my twenties, and I've kept some things of theirs, and I come in here sometimes so it's like I'm with them. Maybe you could give me a moment to collect myself, and then I could make us some coffee downstairs?" She looked up, expecting to see their sympathetic faces, only to notice Whitney standing at the back of the crowd. Her stomach dropped. "What is she doing here?" she asked. She fixed Whitney with her most guilt-inducing stare. "If you've come to apologize, I'm not ready." Whitney looked back, brazen, and Gwen's doubts began to grow.

"Oh, that's not at all close to the reason that we're here," Amara said. And then Ellie and Meredith jumped forward, pushing Gwen down into the armchair, restraining her with their arms, and she knew that, somehow, they'd figured it out. Their palms against her shoulders were firm, and she winced at the pressure.

"You're hurting me!" she said. "What's going on? Why are you doing this?"

"Don't play dumb with us," Amara said. "We know about TrueMommy."

"What about TrueMommy?" she asked, struggling against Ellie and Meredith as her mind whirred. "The speed? I don't understand why you're attacking *me*—"

"So you're, what?" Amara asked. "A fucking TrueMommy shill? A plant they send to manipulate women who consider you a friend?"

Things clicked into place. They thought she was some minion. She could work with that. She could spin that straw into perfect gold. "Oh, God," she said, and let her voice choke up. "You're right. I *was* a plant, but I didn't realize I was a harmful one! I am so, so sorry. I never meant to hurt you all like this. I didn't know—"

"Yeah, right," Ellie said, digging her fingernails into Gwen's shoulder.

"Okay, I knew a little," Gwen yelped. "They asked me if I was interested in working out a deal where I got a commission in exchange for doing my best to keep people enthusiastic about it. I thought it was just an innocent marketing tactic, like any brand might do, like *Whitney* did in all her sponsored posts! Then they kept asking for more and more—to report on anything out of the ordinary, to keep an eye on things. I didn't realize how out of hand it would get."

"You'd screw us over for a commission when an entire playgroup can fit in your closet? What the hell is wrong with you?" Amara asked. "What kind of money-hungry monster are you?"

"And what about the group in Hoboken?" Whitney asked.

So they knew about that too. Gwen fell back on the most

trusted weapon in her arsenal—widening those blueberry eyes of hers. "We don't have any money left," she said haltingly. "Christopher gambled most of it away. I had to do *something* or we'd lose the brownstone and wouldn't be able to provide for our girls. You all have to understand—I needed to protect them." She bit down hard on her tongue and let the shock of it bring tears to her eyes. "I knew there was something fishy about the pills, like we all did, but I didn't know details. I closed my eyes to it all until it was too late, and I am so, so sorry for how I hurt you all and the other groups they sent me to."

The hatred in Amara's face started to soften infinitesimally, the wariness in Whitney's posture loosening. Ellie and Meredith began to release their grips on her as Vicki blinked, having already stayed focused far longer than she was used to. They wanted to believe the best in her and the best in themselves. They wanted to think that no one who had gotten to know them so well could want to cause them harm. She'd make it easy for them to hold on to that illusion.

"It was one of those things where you don't realize how deep in you're getting, and when you finally *do* realize, you're too afraid to tell the truth. I *wanted* to tell you so many times, but I worried they'd find out, that they'd harm me and the girls." She looked at Whitney. "We've all made mistakes, haven't we?" Whitney looked down at the ground. "You have to understand. I've hated myself every day since it started." When she finished, the other women were all silent for a moment.

Then Amara shook her head and let out a heavy sigh. "God, Gwen," she said. "You really fucked up."

Triumph began to glimmer inside Gwen, still nascent, but growing stronger and stronger. "I know that. Please. What do you want me to do?"

"Stay away from us," Amara said. "Tell any other playgroups you've been doing this to what's going on. Let TrueMommy know that we're onto them and they'd better stop."

"I will," she said. "I swear." She put her hand to her mouth. "Oh, God," she said. "Where are Reagan and Rosie? They don't know what's happening, do they?"

"No," Ellie said. "Christopher took them to the park."

"Thank you," Gwen said, and Ellie nodded.

"Let's go," Amara said to the other women, and as they all gave Gwen final glances of disgust or regret or bafflement and then turned to go, Gwen allowed herself to relax just a little bit too much.

"Despite everything, I am sorry about Christopher," Whitney said, turning around unexpectedly, far too close to the shoebox, and because Gwen had thought she was safe, she flinched, making a movement toward the box on instinct as if to grab it out of Whitney's reach. She stopped herself, but it was too late. Whitney had seen it.

Chapter 39

O h," Whitney said, and so Amara turned around right in time to see Whitney lunge forward, scooping a shoebox off the ground a moment quicker than Gwen could get to it. What the hell did Whitney want with Gwen's shoes? This wasn't exactly the time to be raiding her closet. But Whitney reached in and pulled out a clear Tupperware container—large enough to hold half a chicken and filled to the very top with loose TrueMommy caplets. She handed the container to Amara and then grabbed a leather journal and began flipping through. "The notes in here don't seem like someone who was just supposed to keep an eye on things," Whitney said. "There are schedules. Accounting."

"What?" Amara asked as Claire held out her hand for the planner.

Gwen let out a strange, disbelieving laugh. "Oh, come on," she said. "You're going to listen to *Whitney*?" Amara bent her head over the journal while Claire turned the pages slowly, both of them looking at Gwen's cryptic abbreviations in her neat cursive. This wasn't the work of some minion. This was the work of a mastermind. Amara felt the world growing fuzzy around her, Gwen's voice like a mosquito in her ear as she buzzed relentlessly on. "Whitney, who lied to you all for months about sleeping with my husband, who might just as easily have slept with any of yours?"

Amara realized she was hugging the box of TrueMommy and wrenched off the top, spilling a conical mound of the amber pills into her palm. The smooth hill of capsules gleamed and beckoned. All this time, Gwen had been pretending she felt their pain when really she was the source of it.

"Gwen. You are a sociopath," Amara said.

"No," Gwen said. "No. I wanted to *help* you. The pills made your lives easier—"

"Our lives," Amara said, dazed, as rage began to gather and swirl behind her eyes. "You never took them at all, did you?"

Gwen hesitated for just a moment too long. "I did!"

Amara rocketed toward Gwen, a short-fused firecracker set ablaze, shaking her handful of pills in Gwen's face. "I should shove these down your fucking throat, you psycho," she yelled. "You've infected our entire lives!" She hurled the pills at Gwen, who flinched as the capsules bounced off her and scattered on the floor, far too light to hurt the way Amara wanted them to. "Do you understand what you've done to us?" she yelled, ready to slap Gwen, to tear out her heartless heart. Claire stepped forward and put her hand on Amara's shoulder, and suddenly, Amara saw herself as if from above, saw what her own wrathful body had become, and hated it. She stepped back. "Of course you don't understand," Amara said, her voice cracking with exhaustion. "You never even took them."

Gwen looked Amara straight in the eye. Then she gathered up a handful of the pills and, as if in an offering, swallowed them.

Chapter 40

The capsules scraped Gwen's throat as they went down, leaving her raw. She would have to humble herself before the women, do what they wanted her to do, distract them. But Amara simply stepped back, her whole body slumping, and turned into Claire's embrace, beginning to cry. "I don't want to be like her. I don't want to live some double life anymore," Amara said between her racking sobs as Claire stroked her hair. "I don't want to keep this secret from Daniel. I don't want to keep lying."

"But what about everything we said before?" Ellie asked. "About Child Protective Services, and everyone finding out?"

"Gwen was the one who brought up Child Protective Services, wasn't she?" Claire asked, and Meredith furrowed her brow as if trying to remember, then let out a gasp as she confirmed it in her mind.

"Oh, *Gwen*," she said.

"Please," Gwen said, desperate. "Please. Just let me wind it down in secret. I'll stop it all. No one will get hurt. I'll find some way to prove it to you. You can look at the records. I can give you the names of all the women so you can check up on them. I'll give you a cut if you want! Just let me take care of it." Her body started to tingle as it absorbed the drug, her levelheadedness disappearing in a million synaptic bursts. She fought to maintain control. She could wind down the operation and still have her smaller group of women who didn't need the wellness excuse. She could still get the Connecticut house.

"I don't know if we can do that anymore," Amara said.

"If I go down," Gwen said, narrowing her eyes, "you all go down too. Everything comes out." She shot a look at Ellie, who shifted uncomfortably. "Every fault or secret you ever told me in confidence." She lasered in on Whitney, spitting the words at her. "Every sordid detail of the affair. Grant will divorce you so fast your head will spin, and then you'll have nothing." She turned to Amara now. "How will Daniel ever love you in the same way again? And, Claire, you wanted to be one of us so badly, following us around and trying our pills? Well, I'm sure there are magazines out there that would *love* to do an article on your whole story." Even if she had to say goodbye to the Connecticut house, there were other options. One of the shoeboxes she'd taken down earlier, which was on the floor farther back in the dark of the closet, had thousands of dollars in cash from this month's latest deliveries. She had plenty in an offshore account too. She could take the girls and get away, hide out with Teddy for a little while, then go to

355

Mexico. She'd studied Spanish all throughout college, even spent a semester in Barcelona, and it would be good for the girls to be bilingual from an early age. "Maybe your ex-boyfriend with the cancer scare will have some choice quotes."

"I think I'll just have to deal with that," Claire said.

Gwen stuck her finger down her throat and forced herself to vomit all over the carpet.

Chapter 41

Amara understood logically that her former friend–turned–drug kingpin (queenpin?) was coughing up waves of vomit on the floor of a walk-in closet. But her heart kept insisting that it wasn't real, that she'd *actually* stepped through a portal to an alternate universe in which anything could happen. She half expected a parade of talking flamingos to come pedaling by on unicycles. A long string of amber-colored phlegm dangled out of Gwen's mouth, and Amara thought that talking flamingos would be a welcome bit of sanity.

The other women had stepped back as Gwen, still in that ridiculous fur coat, heaved and shuddered and then grew still, multicolored chunks on the rug around her, the particular wretched smell of vomit rising up in the close closet air. Ellie and Meredith put their hands over their mouths and looked away.

LAURA HANKIN

When Gwen looked up at them again, her face was bare, stripped of the sweetness or judgment or embarrassed sadness it so often alternated between.

"Please," Gwen said. "Think of my children."

"What?" Whitney asked.

"You turn me in, you're dooming them to grow up without a mother." Her voice grew so quiet that the other women had to lean in to hear. "I just want to protect them."

The others glanced at one another. Amara couldn't stop a short, sharp laugh from coming out of her mouth.

"We're all so obsessed with protecting our children, aren't we?" Amara said. "That's how we got into this mess in the first place. We want to paint a lovely picture that we hang over their window to block out how the world really works, to give them these perfect lives. And to do that, we think we need to keep ourselves perfect too. But no mother in the history of the world has been able to protect her child forever. The world barges in through the front door eventually. Or sometimes," she said, glaring at Gwen, "you invite it in, because it knows exactly what lies you want to hear." Gwen coughed again, drawing back farther into the closet as if she didn't want them to see what she had become, bracing herself on another shoebox. Amara shook her head. "I wish so badly that I could be the perfect mother for Charlie. But since I'm not, I think I'd rather he know that, when I fucked up big-time, I tried to do the right thing, instead of lying to him that everything is all puppies and rainbows. I have to believe that the people who matter to me will understand that."

She looked at Gwen, who had made Amara feel terrible in ways

358

big and small. "I don't want your children to grow up without a mother, Gwen," she said. "That's why I'm not going full Mama Bear on your ass right now, though I'd dearly love to rip your throat out with my teeth. But you also can't pull 'Motherhood' as a literal 'Get out of Jail Free' card. You're a psycho, and you sold out your own, and you have to pay for that."

The other women shifted around her, and Amara looked them in the eye one by one. "The rest of you can go, if you need to, and try to distance yourself from this as much as possible," she said. "But—I can't believe I'm saying this—I'm calling the police."

Chapter 42

For a moment, no one spoke. Whitney looked at Amara, standing straight and still with her new certainty, and didn't know what to do. Gwen was right. If they all came forward, Grant *would* divorce her. He was used to getting what he wanted, so he wasn't the type to try to work through such a huge betrayal. Even though she'd put so much distance between them, she thought now of losing all the beautiful little routines they'd built up over the years, of never again catching a glimpse of his face when he woke up in the morning (for a moment, with sleep clouding his eyes, she could see the vulnerable little boy he once had been), of knowing that he'd never look at her again like he had that night he met her parents. Whitney didn't want to stop being a marvel, to go from being a precious thing to a ruined woman.

And more than that, if she stepped forward, Hope's lucky life would come crashing down. She didn't want Hope to lose a single opportunity, her chance at the best education, an ounce of her happiness. Oh, God, she realized, she was so desperate not to cede any of Hope's privilege that she'd let other women's children pay the price. Maybe Hope would hate Whitney for failing her, in the same way that Whitney had hated her own parents. Or maybe Whitney could impress upon her daughter the thing that she was only beginning to learn—that women didn't have to be perfect to be worthy.

If she chose to stand with Amara, the entire narrative she'd built up around herself would disappear. She didn't know who she'd be anymore. The problem with precious things was that they weren't supposed to change, and people inevitably did. Blindly, trusting, entirely terrified, she stepped forward. "I'm there with you," she said.

Meredith and Ellie looked at each other, then clasped hands and planted their feet.

"Let's do it," Vicki said.

"Call the police, then," Gwen said in a dull voice. She stood up. "I'm going to wash the vomit off my face before they get here. At least allow me that dignity." Shaking all over, she drew the bulky coat close around her and staggered past them all to the closet door.

"Is she actually going to wash her face?" Ellie asked.

"Of course not," Amara said. "Vicki, dial nine-one-one." They all ran to the bedroom door just in time to see Gwen flying down the stairs, her fur coat flapping open around her to reveal a shoe-box in her hand. "Lord, if I didn't hate her so much, I'd almost admire her persistence."

"Gwen, stop!" Ellie called uselessly while Vicki began explaining the situation to a 911 dispatcher who seemed to have a lot of questions.

"Where does she think she's going?" Whitney asked as Gwen stuffed the shoebox in the lower compartment of the stroller that Christopher had left by the front door in his rush to get Reagan and Rosie away from whatever strange situation was going to happen in his house.

"She's got a lot of speed in her system right now, probably," Claire said. "I don't know if she's making the most rational decisions."

Amara waved her hand. "The police will catch up with her eventually."

"Unless she tries something crazy and gets herself killed," Whitney said.

"Let her run into traffic, for all I care," Amara said as Gwen stuffed her feet into a pair of heels by the door. Gwen pulled the door open and tugged the stroller out after her too hard so that it rolled past her and skidded down the steps. The door slammed behind her, cutting off the view from the others.

"Unless she tries something crazy and gets Reagan killed," Whitney said softly.

"Call Christopher and tell him not to let her take the kids from him," Amara said.

"I don't have his phone number," Whitney said. "We always just wrote to each other through my Instagram."

Amara stared at her for a moment. "I will never understand," she said, and sighed. "Dammit, let's go." Then, as one, the women began to run.

Chapter 43

The women reentered the muggy August air just as Gwen turned the corner at the end of the block, heading toward the playground in the park. Sweat began trickling down Claire's back as they sprinted, Amara huffing away beside her.

The pedestrians around them stopped what they were doing to stare at the chase, their expressions changing almost in slow motion as they struggled to register what was going on. Was some kind of danger approaching? Did they need to run too? Soon enough, though, they dismissed that possibility. One man held up his phone and started to take a video. Claire gave him the finger. "Where's the fire?" someone shouted, laughing.

There was no pretense of perfection now, no hope that the mothers would ever be Momstagram worthy again or that Claire would be able to show Vagabond that she was doing great without them. After all this time striving and striving to get famous, she would get her dream in the worst possible way. This particular moment of public humiliation was just the beginning of a long, brutal slog. She caught Amara's eye and knew she was thinking the same thing.

"Well," Amara said, out of breath. Improbably, that hint of mischief that Claire loved came into her expression. "I suppose we should *really* give them something to talk about." And then Amara threw back her head and howled, her voice crackling with frustration and rage but also with a kind of liberation, a gigantic wordless "fuck you" to the expectations she'd worked so hard to meet.

When Amara stopped for a moment to take a breath, Claire let her own yell fill the silence, her throat arcing up and back. The other playgroup women paused to look at them. Then, one by one, they joined in too, one woman's voice picking up where another's left off to gasp for air so that the sound seemed endless, a pack of wolves tearing down the city pavement, ravenous and wild and not at all inspirational to anyone but one another.

Claire didn't know exactly what would come next. But she felt achingly, thrillingly alive and glad that she'd have these women at her side to weather the storm.

As their screams gathered force and flew down the block, Gwen looked back at them in confusion. She glanced their way for only a second as she stepped into the intersection, but that was long enough. She didn't see the taxicab coming.

Chapter 44

The media coverage afterward was fierce, as Whitney had predicted. The photo of the mangled baby stroller, the cash littering the intersection, was everywhere—websites, newspapers, cable news broadcasts. It was just New York news at first, but before long, it made its way across the country. Smirking TV hosts in LA made jokes about "The Poison Playgroup of Park Avenue." (A ridiculous name, especially since Ellie was the only one of them who actually lived on Park.) One website, geared toward millennial moms, wrote clickbait content about it for weeks on end, their writers churning out article after article with SEO-geared headlines like "Who Is Claire Martin? You Won't Believe What She Did Before the Poison Playgroup."

It all got twisted into something else. The women had been chasing Gwen because they wanted to kill her, shrieking the whole time, tottering in their expensive high heels. They had *pushed* Gwen into the road. The überwealthy could be just as badly behaved, just as governed by base desires, as anyone else.

It was only by the grace of God that Gwen hadn't died, that the stroller had taken most of the impact while she'd merely suffered a badly broken leg. Half a foot forward, and she would've been scattered all over the intersection with her cash. Instead, outfitted with an enormous cast, her body blooming with bruises, she told the police and the press everything she had threatened to reveal.

The reaction arrived in waves. First came the hatred, the searing e-mails calling them all cunts who deserved to die, the strangers on the street who approached them with cutting comments about their terrible parenting and how they'd chosen their waistlines over the health of their children, the people they actually knew who stopped talking to them. Then came a bit of a sympathy backlash as other women reached out privately to say that they'd been tricked by TrueMommy too, and the scope of the scam came to light. That clickbait website ran an article with the headline "The One Important Reason You Should Leave the Poison Playgroup Moms Alone." Finally, and a bit surprisingly, came the offers. A publisher approached Whitney with a tell-all-book deal, but she turned it down. She didn't want to tell all anymore, even though the money would have allowed her to stay in the city instead of heading to Jersey as her divorce was being finalized. (Grant had his pick of the women now that he was unexpectedly single again. Ladies were falling all over themselves to prove to the rich, handsome husband that not all women were as heartless as Whitney.) A producer even pitched them a reality show, claiming that they had the potential to be bigger than the *Real Housewives*. Meredith and Ellie were tempted by that at first, until all the others made it clear that there was no way in hell they'd participate. Still, Ellie and Meredith talked about it in secret for a few days more—maybe the producer would be interested in a "BFF duo conquering the world" type of deal?—until Ellie realized that she was pregnant with Baby #2, and everything became about that.

By the time October rolled around, the frenzy had died down somewhat. When Gwen's and Teddy's trials began, all the cameras would surely come out again, but for now, Amara and Claire could walk down the street in the late afternoon, largely ignored, to pick up Charlie and Reagan at day care.

The women all took turns pitching in with Reagan now. A beleaguered Christopher hadn't wanted them anywhere near him and the girls at first. But after the nanny he'd hired leaked baby photos to the paparazzi, he warily agreed to let the women help out. Now they were determined that Reagan would get six bonus aunts in exchange for one fully present mom. A shit bargain, for sure, but better than nothing. They tried very hard not to judge if, say, Amara gave Reagan too much sugar or if Vicki failed to discipline a tantrum. They didn't always succeed in supporting one another in all their flawed glory, but they were getting better.

As Claire and Amara walked into the neighborhood day care center, Charlie toddled over to Amara, tears streaming down his face, and she swooped him up into her arms. "The second day was a wild success, I see," she said to the teacher, who gave her a patient smile in return.

"Hey, a little better than yesterday," the teacher said. "Progress!"

Progress. Yes, there had been some of that, day by day, with Charlie, and with Daniel. That steamy, terrible August afternoon, she'd given the police a statement and then run all the way home to tell Daniel everything before he could hear about it on the news or from someone else. He'd thought she was joking at first, her kind and trusting husband, and she'd had to convince him that it was true, even as her quick-beating heart threatened to burst out of her chest and zoom around the kitchen because she was so terrified she'd lose him over this.

"Please, don't divorce me," she said when he finally took her word that she was telling the truth and grew still.

"Jesus, Mari," he said. Then he stood up from his seat at the kitchen table and took her in his arms. "I'm not going to divorce you. I love you more than anything." She started to cry with relief and with something else, an almost physical shock from her sudden sense of how lucky she was to have found him. He stroked her hair as she shuddered against his chest, the heat of his skin coming through his T-shirt. "But we're starting marriage counseling, stat."

Now, at the day care, another mother coming to pick up her kid shot Amara and the screaming child in her arms a look of empathy, just like Amara was any other mom with a difficult kid. Then, of course, the woman registered who she was and began to whisper to her friend. "Hi," Amara called over to them. "Lovely weather, isn't it?" The moms turned a little red and nodded.

Claire popped up from the nap-time corner with a sleepy Reagan in her arms. "Okay, let's go," Claire said.

Outside, in the autumn air, they buckled the children into their strollers. Claire still didn't know if she ever wanted kids, but she was getting to be a natural at this whole stroller thing. And now that Reagan was starting to have a personality, Claire enjoyed spending time with her. She made a funny face at Reagan while she adjusted a blanket around her, and Reagan laughed a hiccupy laugh. Then Claire took a deep breath and reached into her bag, pulling out a CD.

Getting proper credit on "Idaho Eyes" had been easier than Claire had anticipated. Canny, publicity-smart Marlena had realized that the whole story was going to come out anyway, so she gave a long interview to *New York* magazine about how she was going to make sure the guys did right by Claire. Women had to have one another's backs, she said, and promptly received a slew of think pieces calling her a feminist hero. While it may have been a PR stunt, it *did* translate into actual cash. Claire wasn't exactly swimming in riches, but she had enough to pay her rent for a little while, look into getting some much-needed therapy, and hire some background musicians to help record a high-quality demo.

"I wanted to give you something," Claire said to Amara, handing her the demo. "I know it feels like years ago that you made this offer, but I finished recording those songs, and I thought, if you liked them, you could pass my information along to that old bandleader you mentioned."

"Excellent! Of course," Amara said.

"Only if you actually like them, though," Claire said. "I'm proud of them, but I don't want you to just feel like you owe me because I saved you from Mommy Speed."

"Oh, right," Amara said dryly. "I'd nearly forgotten about that. Only if I actually like them, then." She put the CD into her bag.

"Thanks," Claire said, and they smiled at each other. "Last day of leisure, huh?"

Amara would go back to work the next day. There had been one benefit to the TrueMommy debacle, at least. When she submitted her résumé to places now, people actually started calling her in for interviews. They wanted to talk to her because she was a curiosity, because they thought they could grill her about all the sordid details, but she managed to twist it to her advantage. "I've been through that," she said in the interview for the show that ended up hiring her, "and now I'm fucking unflappable."

"Lord," Amara said to Claire. "Having it all will be a cakewalk after this."

Claire laughed. And then they turned into the golden afternoon light and took the kids to the park.

Acknowledgments

I will never stop being amazed that so many people devoted their time and energy to bringing *Happy & You Know It* to life. I owe an immense debt of gratitude to those listed below. And if somehow I forgot you, I'm sorry. Come yell at me, and I'll buy you a drink.

My agent, Stefanie Lieberman, who found me when this book was just an idea in my head, and proceeded to change my life. She and Molly Steinblatt saw me through all the false starts, gently steering me away from bad decisions while casually tossing around perfect critiques like, "You're not reckoning quite enough with the patriarchal underpinnings of the wellness industry." Thanks as well to everyone at Janklow & Nesbit, and a special shout-out to Adam Hobbins for his scheduling magic.

My editor, Jen Monroe, who is so kind, so cool, and so good at her job. I treasure her wonderful editorial e-mails and am endlessly grateful for her enthusiasm. This book became much richer, juicier, and, yes, *sexier* under her guidance.

The entire Berkley team, from the copyeditors who caught all my mistakes about sports (I don't know what time of year people watch football!) to the publicity pros who worked so hard to make sure this book landed in as many hands as possible. I feel very lucky that *Happy & You Know It* found a home at such a lovely imprint.

Grandma Lois, who told me that I was always welcome to come write at her Connecticut house. No presidents have relaxed in her backyard, but who needs presidents when she bakes the best blueberry pie I've ever tasted?

Kristine Sullivan, for a certain subplot inspiration.

Early readers/friends who gave me invaluable feedback and the encouragement I needed to keep going: Claire Fallon, Trista Olivas, Dominique Salerno, Alex Ulyett, Hannah Barudin, Melissa Yeo, Rebecca Mohr, and Paavana Kumar. Thank you as well to friends like Sash Bischoff, Kara Scroggins, and Jane Bradley, who were always there to talk me through my anxiety about whether or not this book would ever see the light of day.

Stacy Testa, for her guidance, warmth, and friendship.

Inez Sanchirico and Jamie Kolnick, for letting me ask them all sorts of questions about motherhood, and answering thoughtfully and openly.

Olivia Blaustein, for her enthusiasm and belief that this story deserved to be told in other media as well.

All the mothers whose babies I sang for. Special thanks to the woman who named her baby Cordelia, for whom I accidentally did a solo playgroup one time. She was so cool that it made me wonder what would happen if a playgroup mother and her musician truly became friends. Thanks as well to the other musicians I worked with, who made the job so fun.

My father and brother. Through all the times I doubted myself, I never doubted their love for me. I'm so happy to be on Team Hankin with them.